BROWSING COLLECTION
14-DAY CHECKOUT
No Holds • No Renewals

The
Porcelain
Maker

The Porcelain Maker

Sarah Freethy

ST. MARTIN'S PRESS
NEW YORK

First published in the United States by St. Martin's Press, an imprint of St. Martin's Publishing Group

THE PORCELAIN MAKER. Copyright © 2023 by THE WRITERS' ROOM PUBLISHING LIMITED. All rights reserved. Printed in the United States of America. For information, address St. Martin's Publishing Group, 120 Broadway, New York, NY 10271.

www.stmartins.com

Library of Congress Cataloging-in-Publication Data

Names: Freethy, Sarah, author.
Title: The porcelain maker / Sarah Freethy.
Description: First U.S. edition. | New York: St. Martin's Press, 2023.
Identifiers: LCCN 2023028578 | ISBN 9781250322616 (Canada & international, sold outside the U.S., subject to rights availability) | ISBN 9781250289346 (hardcover) | ISBN 9781250289353 (ebook)
Subjects: LCGFT: Epic fiction. | Novels.
Classification: LCC PR6106.R45466 P67 2023 | DDC 823/.914—dc23/eng/20230626
LC record available at https://lccn.loc.gov/2023028578

Our books may be purchased in bulk for promotional, educational, or business use. Please contact your local bookseller or the Macmillan Corporate and Premium Sales Department at 1-800-221-7945, extension 5442, or by email at MacmillanSpecialMarkets@macmillan.com.

Originally published in Great Britain by Simon & Schuster UK Ltd

First U.S. Edition 2023

2 4 6 8 10 9 7 5 3 1

To Mama Bean and my darling Mouse, 143

BOOK ONE

In a tall cabinet, on a glass shelf, lies a white porcelain rabbit—lifelike, plump and pretty. Fluorescent light is reflected in the sheen of its coat. You can almost imagine pulling it onto your lap to stroke, but there is some tension there. The delicately sculpted ears lie flat, and its sightless milk-white eyes roll back in fear. A pet made of prey.

Underneath, where the soft fur of its belly would be, the porcelain is completely smooth and hides the maker's mark; the word 𝔄𝔩𝔩𝔞𝔠𝔥 is stamped in an angular font that speaks of bierkellers, pine forests and Alpine lodges. Above it, painted in flat black brushstrokes, twin strikes of lightning: ⚡⚡

CHAPTER ONE

Donar, Cincinnati

August 1993

The asphalt of the parking lot outside Forsythe's Bargain Auctions was sticky underfoot and ruptured where fists of bittercress had forced their way through. The sallow sun cast a pall over the low-rise buildings. Thunderheads gathered above and static itched the air.

Clad in cheap aluminum siding and squatting between a dive bar and a Baptist chapel, the auction house itself was nondescript. The chapel and the bar showed few signs of life, but half a dozen cars and pickup trucks were parked outside Forsythe's.

Inside the building's metal shell, the thrum of the air conditioner was constant, though it barely made a dent in the day's heat. The main room was cluttered: a gallery of sun-bleached prints and paintings hung on one wall, along with a rack of firearms, and a tall glass display cabinet, sparsely filled. Rows of folding chairs had been set out in front of a small lectern, though few were occupied. The scent of must seeped up from the faded blue linoleum floor and lingered in the air.

At 10 a.m. sharp a compact woman entered at a brisk trot, a sheaf of papers and a small wooden gavel held to her breast. A halo of stiff pewter hair framed her face, while the broad shoulders of her jacket gave her the silhouette of a linebacker. She placed her load down on the lectern and looked up at the assembly, beaming with pleasure.

"Good morning! How are y'all doing?"

Barely a dozen bored bodies sat slumped in waiting, but the auctioneer seemed to relish her task nonetheless.

"OK folks, I'm going to get you to take a look at the sales sheet so we can get started."

Some made a show of picking up the stapled pages that had been left on their seats, though few had much intention of parting with their money.

The auctioneer began to work her way methodically through the lots on the morning's ticket: a mix of catering equipment and farm machinery, high-tech office supplies and careworn furniture. At times her high-cadence, singsong patter was barely decipherable, but everyone in the room seemed to understand its ebb and flow. Under the strip lights bluebottles made slow circuits around the room and a low growl of thunder threatened in the distance. An oppressive stillness settled in.

The spell was broken by the sudden clamor of the bell on the auction house door. A woman stepped inside, and a wave of sullen heat rolled in behind her. She was in her early fifties; deep brown curls shot through with silver. Obviously an outsider, she appeared almost alien in her elegance.

Evidently self-conscious, she hurried to a row of empty chairs at the back of the room and sat down, picking up the sales sheet from the seat beside her.

The auctioneer began the bidding on an air rifle. After a brief flurry of activity, it went to a man who was sweating profusely, plucking his black T-shirt from the rolls of his belly. Then, in quick succession, a jet ski and a powerboat failed to meet their starting price, too rich for the thin blood of the spectators. Sensing the end of the sale in sight, they started shifting in their seats.

"Alrighty, let's go ahead and take a look at our last lot."

She flourished the grainy black-and-white image of a rather kitsch porcelain rabbit, lying on its haunches.

"Who'll start the bidding for this darling bunny at $20?"

The room was silent; few here had money to spare for such trinkets. The dark-haired woman in the back row picked up the sales sheet and held it in the air. The auctioneer accepted her bid with a slight nod.

"Thank you, ma'am."

Every head in the room turned, surprised that this stranger should show interest in such a peculiar item.

"Do I hear $25? No? Going once for $20 . . . going twice . . ."

She brought the gavel down with a snap.

"It's all yours."

The auctioneer moved on.

"Next up we have this pretty little baa-lamb. Reckon this one has your name on it, Roger!"

She sent a playful wink to a florid-faced farmer in the front row, who chuckled and waved her off.

"I'm going to go ahead and get started at \$15 for this adorable little thing."

Again, the stranger in the back row raised her paper. The auctioneer nodded.

"We're at \$15, do we have \$20— No?" She brought the gavel down again. "You got yourself a pair."

A roll of thunder rumbled overhead and a sudden drum of heavy rain hammered onto the metal roof. The auctioneer moved on, raising her voice over the volley of noise. Over the next fifteen minutes, the dark-haired woman won a further eight porcelain figurines: a Viking, a smiling shepherdess, an ornate candelabra and a bear, looming up on its hind legs. A swallow, a greyhound—wet tongue lolling—a mouse and a rearing stallion. The proportions of each were different, but all were intricately sculpted in lifelike detail.

As she brought down the gavel for the last time, the auctioneer found herself staring at the stranger in their midst. The dark-haired woman was gathering her belongings, tucking her sunglasses into her handbag. She somehow seemed to sense the auctioneer's gaze on her and gave a tight and fleeting smile in return. There was no joy or triumph in it, only determination.

A short while later, Clara Vogel found herself sat outside the cashier's office, waiting to pay for the porcelain figurines she now held on her lap. She was fighting the hollow feeling that always came over her after a long-haul flight. She could already picture herself climbing between the clean, cool sheets of her bed at the airport hotel, but that would have to wait. Here and now, she had a payment to make and a promise to herself to keep.

Inside the cashier's office, the man in the black T-shirt was paying for his air rifle. The auctioneer stacked his dollar bills in a cash box and handed over the gun.

"There you go, Nathan. You be careful now and remember me to your mom."

He took the gun from her and passed Clara in her seat, giving the brim of his weather-beaten cap a brief tug. The auctioneer beckoned to her. "Come on in and take a seat. Won't be a minute; I'm just adding up your bill."

The office was crammed with files, towers of paper that threatened to fall from every surface, an inventory of ephemera. Clara sat down cautiously and observed the older woman pecking at her calculator.

"You have ten items, coming to a total of $258." She looked up at Clara. "Wasn't sure if anyone would buy them, truth be told. On account of their . . . historic nature. If you know what I mean."

"The maker's mark."

The auctioneer's face registered her distaste.

"I don't mean to insinuate anything, obviously."

"It's quite all right, I was aware of their provenance. I know it must seem quite macabre."

Clara's English intonation was unmistakable; the auctioneer clapped a hand to her chest. "Can I just say, I love your accent. Where are you from?"

"I was actually born in Germany, but we moved to England when I was very young. Have you ever been?"

"Oh, bless your heart, no!" The auctioneer shook her head at the novelty of such an idea.

Clara opened her handbag and pulled out an envelope of

traveler's checks. She signed her name and handed them across the table.

"Thank you!" The auctioneer tucked them in the cash box, then thrust out a hand. "I'm Peggy, by the way. Now tell me, are you a collector? Because we have some real tasteful porcelain coming in a few weeks, beautiful vases which I'd be happy to put by . . ."

"I'm not a collector, no." Clara shifted in her seat. "But I wonder . . . might I trouble you for help?"

"You're fine, sweetie; go right ahead."

"Is it possible to get the details of the person selling the figurines?"

The woman's doughy jowls drooped in disappointment. "Oh my, I'm so sorry, but no. I just couldn't, in all good conscience. People around here really value their privacy."

Clara had blithely assumed this part of the transaction would be straightforward. She had rehearsed this conversation in her head but made no plan beyond. Now she felt a hot flush rising on her chest. "It's just, I've come such a terribly long way . . ."

She stopped as she felt involuntary tears wash into her eyes, the sudden force of feeling taking her by surprise.

"I'm so sorry, please excuse me."

"Are you OK, dear? Can I get you a glass of water?"

The auctioneer reached across the table to take her hand.

"You must think me very silly. I'm just a little overtired—I flew in from London last night with the express intention of buying these items."

A faint frown of suspicion flickered across the older woman's face.

"You came all the way from England for some china knickknacks?"

"I've been searching for one piece in particular for quite a time. That's why I came myself, you see. I've spent months trying to track down the Viking. I own one already, but this is the only other copy that I've ever come across."

"But how did you even find out that I was selling them?"

Clara sighed, too tired now to tell anything but the unvarnished truth.

"I have people in several countries on a retainer. They've been keeping an eye out for this make of porcelain in general, and that one piece in particular. A collector based in New York telephoned me as soon as he saw it for sale on your mailing list."

Clara paused and then leaned forward, intently.

"Peggy, can I speak candidly?"

"Of course," she said, her eyes now wide with interest.

"I need to find out who owned the Viking because they might be the only person who can tell me who my father is."

CHAPTER TWO

Weimar, Germany

Summer 1925

A warm balm left by the evening sun was still seeping from the paving stones when Max Ehrlich returned home. The streetlights had been lit and his lean frame cast a long, loping shadow.

Across the wide green lawn of the Park an der Ilm came a crowd of his fellow students, their vivid garb cutting through the darkening canvas of the evening—strokes of mandarin, ochre and scarlet. Max raised a hand to them in greeting, conscious that his formal dinner jacket must seem terribly conventional, better suited to more staid surroundings.

Having left his native Vienna at the age of nineteen, Max considered himself a man of the world already. Born to a family of textile magnates, he could have easily stayed in Austria and worked in the business, but he was determined to forge his own path. It took him to the cobbled streets of Weimar and the Bauhaus, the avant-garde school of art that made iconoclasts of all its students. Max had followed suit, rejecting his own religious upbringing and embracing the liberal and expressive.

Now the Bauhaus was undergoing its own metamorphosis, moving to new premises in the city of Dessau. Max hoped that a department dedicated to the study of architecture might follow and allow him to realize his dreams. Until then, he was determined to make the most of one last Weimar summer.

When he arrived at the broad steps of his stucco-fronted building, he was struck by a barrage of noise. Max felt a momentary flicker of concern: had the party started without him? But it was not yet nine o'clock; far too early for the festivities to have begun in earnest.

He pushed open the heavy front door and stepped into the cool lobby, where two young women were engrossed in conversation, their blunt bobs swinging close together, dark-stained viola lips almost touching. A languid young man leaned against a nearby pillar, his muscular frame clad in a dark-blue coverall, which had been printed with rolling white-capped waves. He was watching the women intently when Max clapped him on the shoulder.

"Evening, Richard. Up to no good?"

The young man jumped. He swept back his mop of thick blond hair, eyeing Max's outfit with distaste.

"Is that what you're wearing?"

"Don't fret. I'll change. How are the preparations?"

"All in hand." Richard's eyes shone as he beckoned Max to follow. "Come on, you have to see the mural."

"I hope you've been treating the place with respect?"

"Only as much as it deserves. Besides, you're moving out

soon, so don't be too precious. This party is long overdue, and you know it."

He glanced back at his friend, suddenly serious.

"How did it go with your parents?"

"They decided to take the train back to Vienna tonight, thank God."

"And?"

"And . . . they agreed." He grinned. "They'll continue to support me, so I can come to Dessau with the rest of you reprobates."

Richard clapped him on the shoulder, "Then why are you looking so doleful, old man? Come on, this is cause for celebration!"

As they entered the apartment they were immediately engulfed by noise. The radio crackled and blared, a swooping clarinet blending with a chorus of excited young voices that filled the suite of high-ceilinged rooms.

The place had been all but emptied of its furniture. A group of young men rolled up a heavy woolen rug, exposing the polished parquet floor beneath. Still others stretched from ladders to the ceiling, where they pinned swathes of parachute silk in parakeet shades, creating the impression of rooms within rooms, their layers overlapping.

Off to one side, the narrow galley kitchen was filled with chattering energy and a sweetly acrid blend of smoke and alcohol. A willowy blonde applied a sweep of kohl in a hand mirror, while her red-haired companion kept up a steady stream of chatter. She stirred a steaming vat of wine, her ruddy face flushed and glowing. The blonde locked eyes with Max and raised a pencil-thin brow at her friend's enthusiasm.

Richard thrust a bottle of beer at him, keen to break her spell.

"Come on, you have to see this."

At the far end of the room a pair of tall French doors opened out onto a formal garden. The warm night air stirred the silk sheets here, parting them for a moment, so Max could just make out the dark edges of a mural, which had been painted on either side. He moved closer to examine it.

Two giant female figures had been daubed on the wall, as if guarding the way out into the garden. They filled the space from floor to ceiling, their thick legs planted firmly in the ground, muscular arms rising overhead, seeming to support the entire weight of the building up above. They looked as if they had been wrought from rough clay: thighs and breasts like slate-gray slabs, the slash of their sex dark and muddy, their faces featureless and unforgiving. The artist's thick brushstrokes had captured their kinetic energy, but something about their appearance unsettled Max. They bore no relation to the classical forms of Greek architecture, who lifted heavy burdens with some grace. Rather these were Amazons, born out of the earth, rising up, their strength brutal and basic.

"Quite arresting, aren't they?"

Max recognized something in Richard's tone, a mixture of arousal and repulsion. He looked up at their dark, impassive faces and laughed.

"I can't decide if they're beautiful or terrifying."

"I think you need to meet their maker." Richard stepped out through the doors.

The communal garden was a labyrinth of flower beds and

formal hedges, enclosed by a high wall that ran around the whole perimeter. A line of brilliant paper lanterns illuminated a path across the lawn, which led to a terrace where chairs and tables had been set out. Hanging like fat-bellied fruits—sunshine through stained glass—each was decorated with a naive face. Their blank eyes and gaping mouths were masks made of elementary forms: earth, air, fire, water.

At the end of this luminous string of pearls a young woman perched on top of a wooden stepladder. She was dabbing a face on the last lantern: half-moon eyes over smiling apple cheeks. Her dark hair, a short, staccato bob, was pulled back and held in place by a red silk handkerchief, and she was dressed in a formless tobacco-brown smock. Richard paused at the foot of the ladder and lit two cigarettes, handing one up. The painter took it without comment and continued with her work.

Max waited a few moments for her to acknowledge his presence, then took it upon himself to break the silence.

"Richard tells me that I have you to thank for the mural."

She did not respond, so he pressed on.

"I'm not sure if my landlord will appreciate the expanse of flesh on display in there, but"—he gestured to the radiant faces swaying in the heat—"these are rather lovely."

The painter turned to face him at last, her large gray eyes serious.

"And useful, I would hope? Unless you want your guests to break their silly ankles."

She started down from the ladder, taking a rag from her pocket and wiping the paint from her brush.

"As for the mural, it is mine, right enough. I must admit

to being rather fond of an expanse of flesh, but perhaps you're not."

A little furrow appeared between her brows. She turned to Richard.

"Is he always such a prude?"

Max began to protest that she had misunderstood, until he caught sight of Richard's grin. The girl's eyes were sparkling with suppressed delight at his obvious discomfort. No longer able to maintain the pretense, she burst into peals of laughter and Max's solemn face relaxed into a dimpled smile of relief.

Richard took his cue. "Bettina Vogel, this is Max Ehrlich, our host. Future Bauhaus architect extraordinaire."

With a pantomime of formality, Max gave a faint bow. "Delighted to meet you."

"So, Herr Ehrlich, you don't approve of my golem?" She raised an eyebrow in mock offense.

"What in God's name is a golem?" asked Richard.

"Ever the vulgarian." She rolled her eyes. "Golem are figures cast from clay. Legend has it that a rabbi made one and brought it to life, so it could protect the Jews in the ghetto from persecution."

She caught Max half smiling at her.

"What—did I get something wrong?"

"Not at all. I just don't think I've ever met a German gentile who had heard the legend of the golem."

Bettina shrugged. "Professor Adler talked about them in a lecture on folklore and they really stuck with me. When Richard told me the theme of your party was the elements, I thought something earthy might be appropriate."

"Entirely so. But I think you might have one thing wrong; I believe golem are always male."

Bettina snorted. "Who decides?"

"Well, it seems fairly self-explanatory to me. They were created for their strength."

"Caryatids are female and they hold up whole buildings; why can't golem be the same?"

Max smiled wryly. "I'm no authority on golem. Or on women, come to that."

He turned to Richard, who was leaning up against the ladder, watching them spar.

"Come on, Richard, back me up."

"You're on your own, old man." He laughed. "Good luck."

Bettina's cheeks were flushed. "The female form is always depicted as servile—little girls shouldering slabs of marble as if they're tea trays. Tell me, why do men get such a thrill from keeping women on their knees?"

Max grinned at her sudden burst of fury and put up his hands in mock defense.

"There's no need to take it personally."

"But why shouldn't I? You're criticizing my work and by extension me."

She drew deeply on the cigarette and stabbed it into the paint-smeared rag, scattering a fistful of embers on the ground.

"You presume males have the monopoly on strength, but it comes in many forms. A woman's power is mutable—the ability to transform and bend, like clay. I have no use for an obdurate male, no matter how strong they think they are."

She spat the words out, her eyes flashing with unexpected fury.

"Shall we save this for a seminar?" Richard interrupted. "I refuse to get drunk with either one of you until you both get changed."

He turned from them and started to walk back toward the party.

"You coming, Max?"

Max tried to catch Bettina's eye, to dampen the heat of her wrath, but she refused to engage. Jaw set hard, she packed away her paints. From inside the building the sound of fresh voices rose above the music, vying for his attention. He hesitated for a moment and then turned from her and made his way back through the garden, excited by the promise of the night ahead.

Max didn't see Bettina again until the early hours of the next morning. By then the apartment was overflowing with sweating bodies, dirty glasses, cigarette smoke and, above it all, a heavy pall of noise. Clamoring voices climbed over each other, and the gramophone and radio engaged in an auditory duel that reverberated through the still night air. Guests spilled outside, eager to escape the smoke and heat. A raucous few raised their voices in song, while others sought out the garden's darker corners to fumble lustily.

In the kitchen, Richard held court, arguing with a couple of intense young men about the eternal place of politics in art, despite the incongruity of their appearance. In keeping with the party's motif of "the Elements," one was wrapped in a papier-mâché representation of a water molecule, while the other had literal feet of clay. Richard still wore his hand-painted boiler suit, but Max had changed from formalwear into his own interpretation of "Air," all clean lines and immaculate simplicity. He wore a well-tailored white shirt and a pair of crisp cotton trousers in a sky-blue twill. Where others found their release in chaos, Max sought perfection through constraint.

He moved about the main room, refilling glasses and doling out cigarettes, before taking command of the gramophone. As Gershwin ascended, he pulled the blond girl with the arcing eyebrows into the center of the room, long fingers entwined in hers, a light hand on the small of her back.

From the garden, a sea of sound began to rise, a wave of clapping and stamping. Curious guests wandered out through the golem-guarded doors, eager to see what fresh diversion the noise might promise, and Max found himself pulled along in their wake.

A crowd was gathered around a bonfire of logs liberated from the wood store. Circling the flames were half a dozen young men, their naked torsos turning amber in the reflection of the fire. Max recognized a few of them, former acolytes of the charismatic Professor Itten. He had left the Bauhaus two years earlier, but his influence could still be felt.

The fire spat plumes into the sky as Max strolled toward it. He had almost drawn level with it when a young woman appeared out of the shadows in front of him and stepped into the circle of light. She wore a floor-length sheath of crimson silk and a sheer black cape embellished with hand-painted rings of fire. He recognized her immediately.

Bettina stood, arms outstretched, like a diver poised to leap, her face emblazoned with a smile. Feeding off some primal energy in the gathering crowd, she shivered, as if bracing for the plunge, then reached up under the cape and shrugged off the narrow straps of her dress, dropping it to the floor. Her naked body was white as porcelain. A raucous cry went up from the ecstatic crowd, their blood quickening to the pulse of stamping feet.

The night breeze speckled Bettina's skin with goose bumps. She basked in the flickering light, which transformed her into something like a high priestess. Max felt a sudden flame of desire surge through him, tempered by a fear that she might fall.

Without warning, the sudden sound of heavy banging started somewhere deep within the building. The noise snatched Max from his reverie. Someone was beating at the door to his apartment. Around the fire a dozen heads turned toward the sound, which resumed with rising urgency. A single word began to ripple through the crowd: *Polizei.*

Lost in the thrill of her own daring, Bettina seemed oblivious to the threat it posed. Max started through the crowd to get to her, pushing people out of the way and leaning down to sweep her dress up as he went. He grabbed her by her naked shoulders and spun her away from him, urgently pushing her on, out of the light and deep into the shadows.

"What on earth are you doing?" she cried, incredulous.

Behind them, from inside the building, he heard the sounds of orders being barked and breaking glass.

"Come on, we have to get you out of here, it's the police. They hate students at the best of times. They love nothing more than teaching us radicals a lesson. If someone tells them there's a naked woman out here, then it's a night behind bars at the least. Gropius is lenient, but you still might be expelled if you get charged with public nudity."

"*Scheiße!*" She scanned the shrubbery. "Can I get out this way?"

"You can, but you might want to put some clothes on first."

Max shoved the slip of silk into her arms. She stumbled in the dark and struggled back into it. She pulled up the straps and he grabbed her hand, drawing her further into the shadows of the high garden wall. He got down on one knee and she laughed, incredulous.

"Are you trying to save my honor by proposing?"

"I'm trying to save your skin." He offered his cradled hands. She grinned and slipped off her shoes. He hoisted her up and she clambered over the wall. Dusting off his hands and knees, Max peered back through the branches shielding his hiding place. He could make out half a dozen officers herding the guests inside. The clamor from the gramophone and radio suddenly stilled, and an ominous silence descended.

Max weighed up what lay ahead for him: the angry neighbors, the accusations and apologies, the strong likelihood of a fine for disturbing the peace and the necessity of clearing up the debris left in the party's wake. He hesitated for a moment, then turned back to the wall and leaped. Grasping the brick capstone, he threw his weight up and over and dropped down into the street, panting heavily. Bettina was leaning against the wall, pulling her shoes back on. She cocked her head to the side, while balancing on one leg.

"I can't help but notice that you seem to have abandoned your guests in their hour of need."

"It does appear that way." He grinned.

The tree line of the Park an der Ilm had started to brighten and, somewhere deep within, a lone blackbird began to sing. Max looked at his wristwatch. It was 4:14 a.m.

"Fräulein Vogel, may I escort you home?"

"You don't think you ought to stay and face the music?"

"I probably should . . . but on reflection, I think a walk through the park might be more appealing. Shall we?"

He offered her his arm, but she grabbed his hand instead and began to run, pulling him after her. The thrill of escape sang through them both as they dashed toward the safety of the trees, checking behind, all the while dreading the shout of discovery that never came.

When they reached a broad grove of silver birch, they slowed to catch their breath. As they wove their way through the trees, Max found himself observing his accomplice: she was graceful, her long limbs slender as a sapling. Her face was framed by swooping brows and a blunt fringe; the promise of a smile carved in the curves of her dark, painted lips.

They strolled into a meadow of tall grass, flushing out a pair of startled rabbits that dashed across a clearing, toward a well-proportioned white cottage with a gray slate roof and trellised walls.

Bettina's pace slowed to an idle. The dawn-wet dew soaked the hem of her red silk dress, turning it to wine; she shivered in the cool air.

"I suppose I ought to thank you for rescuing me."

"I felt more than a little responsible; it was my party, after all. It occurred to me that your parents might not appreciate their daughter getting sent home in disgrace."

"I'm not sure that my family has the capacity for any more disapproval." She flashed him a sardonic grin. "My mother already thinks that studying art at the Bauhaus makes me tantamount to a fallen woman. She hoped I'd be a farmer's wife by now, not frittering away my youth on something she doesn't even want to comprehend. Meanwhile my fascist brother is terrified they're turning me into a radical." She laughed. "Though he's right on that—they have."

"And what about your father?"

"He wouldn't have approved, but he passed away a few years ago."

"I'm so sorry." He frowned.

"Don't be. I might only be here under sufferance, but at least I'm here. And I'll do anything I need to stay."

Behind the birch grove the rays of the climbing sun began to pierce the bright green canopy. Max and Bettina slowed and sat down in a patch of light, side by side, their hands and hips almost touching, each acutely aware of the distance between them. The air above was filled with pollen, motes of powder falling through the trees, suspended in a sunbeam. Max leaned back on his elbows and gestured to the handsome white cottage on the far side of the lawn.

"You see that little garden house? It used to belong to Goethe. There's something about that kind of simplicity that just sings to me, like frozen music. I want to design compositions that consist only of that which is elegant and necessary. Nothing else."

"Sounds like a pretty decent manifesto for an architect."

"So, what's yours?"

"You'll think me terribly naive. Don't laugh, but . . . I truly believe art should serve a purpose beyond beauty. At the very least, I want mine to leave a mark. Or what else are we here for?"

The pollen settled on them both like a dusting of snow.

Bettina leaned over to brush the grains of gold from his face. Her eyes met his, which were almost black in their intensity. He closed the lids briefly at the touch of her fingers on his cheek, then broke into a dimpled smile that lit him from within.

"What else indeed? It seems as good a place as any to begin."

CHAPTER THREE

Over-the-Rhine, Cincinnati

August 1993

As the taxi sped through the rain-soaked streets, Clara watched the buildings flicker past. At least in the city some structures were closer to the high-storied historic buildings of home. Still, the sensation of emptiness returned, coupled with nervous anticipation at what might lie ahead. Nausea welled up as the cab wallowed through potholes, throwing out waves of water that crested the sidewalk.

The driver called out to her, shouting to be heard over the radio.

"What number ya got on Sycamore?"

Clara took out the note Peggy Forsythe had pressed into her hand.

"It's 1046, Bide-A-While Assisted Living."

"Got it."

Clara felt his eyes on her in the rearview mirror. She turned to look out of the window, reluctant to converse. He'd already quizzed her on the origins of her accent and her name, both hazards she feared she must now navigate every time she opened her mouth.

"You got folks from Over-the-Rhine?" he inquired.

"I'm sorry?"

"Over-the-Rhine. That's what your Europeans called this part of town when they moved here. I just figured, with a name like yours—"

She cut him off: "Not that I know of."

She held tight to the box of clinking porcelain and clenched her teeth against another wave of exhaustion. The cloying, sweet stink of the air freshener hanging from the mirror was overpowering. She rolled down the window, inhaling deeply. After a moment she became aware of a different aroma: musky, salty and as familiar as childhood. She breathed it in, filling her senses with a nostalgia for something she couldn't name.

"It's the Play-Doh factory."

She turned and found the driver already smiling at her in the mirror. That was it! She felt her fatigue vanish in the thrill of recognition.

"Gets me every time I come down here," the driver said. "Nothing else quite like it."

On the radio a girl declared with sunshine sweetness that she loved someone's smile. Clara felt her mood lift, by the song, by the sweet-scented air and the eternal buoyancy of this place, which seemed so guileless in its optimism.

The taxi slowed to a stop at the corner of a busy intersection. Bide-A-While filled half a block, behind a broken-down chain-link fence: four floors of brown brick, ribboned with fire escapes. Under the cover of an overhang, a few stooped seniors were sitting at concrete tables playing dominoes, their weathered eyes watching the world go by.

Clara paid the driver and made a dash across the wet concrete, heading into the shelter of the dark building. She walked through a sterile lobby and into a long corridor lined with closed doors. Flickering strip lights illuminated a low, Styrofoam ceiling. There were few indications of life, save for the low burble of a television behind a door marked "Superintendent." Clara took a deep breath and knocked, gently at first and then again with force. A woman in a quilted polyester housecoat opened the door and peered out. Clara sensed they were roughly the same age, though she seemed somehow infinitely older.

"So sorry to disturb you—I'm looking for Miss Williams?"

"You found her. You the one Peggy says bought my statuettes?"

"I am."

The woman stood back and beckoned Clara in. The room was filled with mismatched furniture. There was a TV mounted on a bracket in the corner of the room and two padlocked glass cabinets of prescription drugs. Miss Williams motioned Clara to sit in an ancient armchair covered in transparent vinyl. She lowered herself down next to a sleeping dog of some indeterminate breed. She scooped it up and laid it across her meaty forearm to stroke.

"I wasn't sure she'd have much luck in selling them. They weren't to my taste."

Nor mine, thought Clara.

"I'm not sure if Peggy explained, but I wanted to ask how you came to own them?"

"They were given to me by one of our residents. Mr. Ezra Adler, on the second floor."

Clara's mouth felt dry as sand.

"Is Mr. Adler home today?"

"Lord no, he's dead. Been gone a month now, since. Pneumonia."

The tide of exhaustion returned with full force and she felt herself sag. Miss Williams frowned in consternation.

"Did you know Mr. Adler? Only Peggy didn't say."

Clara shook her head.

"I didn't know him, but I hoped he might help me find my father."

She pressed her temples, trying to dislodge the pressure there. The folly of coming such a vast distance, only to find herself at a dead end.

"One of the figurines was of a Viking. My mother owned one just like it; the only other that I'm aware of. Before she died, she told me that my father made it. I had thought, perhaps naively, that the owner might tell me who he was."

Miss Williams eyed her with suspicion.

"Well, all's I know is Mr. Adler was some kind of sculptor in Europe during the war. Came over here and got a job making models for Play-Doh. He lived upstairs these last ten or so years since he retired."

She fixed Clara with a frown.

"You don't have the same accent. You from Poland, too?"

Clara shook her head and Miss Williams shrugged.

"That's where he said he came from. He used to invite me in for a cup of coffee if I took him up his mail or some new medication. He made it strong! Used to tease me for adding my Sweet'N Low, saying I was sweet enough."

She chuckled and the warmth of it took Clara by surprise.

"I miss him; he was one of the good ones."

A thought occurred to Clara.

"Might I ask, what happened to the rest of his belongings?"

"Still up there. Nothing much of any value, mind. I've got a new tenant due in next week, so I've been packing it all up to go to the Goodwill."

"Would you mind if I went and had a look around? Just to see it for myself. I've come all this way . . ."

Miss Williams regarded Clara sharply, trying to decide if she was worth the time and effort she demanded.

"I can go up by myself; I don't want to be a nuisance."

With another heavy sigh of reluctance, Miss Williams unhooked a large ring of keys from her waistband and rifled through them before removing one.

"It's the second floor, room 21. I would come with you, but my stories are about to start."

"Thank you. It'll only take a minute." She stood to leave. "Did he mention any relatives, back in Poland?"

Miss Williams had already turned toward the screen, lifting her feet onto a stool and increasing the volume.

"None that I know of. Most folk in here don't have anyone, or else they wouldn't be here. They live alone and die that way as well."

Minutes later, Clara stepped from the narrow confines of the single, creaking elevator and went in search of Ezra Adler's room. The sound of a dozen different televisions, all turned up to full volume, bounced off the hard surfaces. Canned laughter blended with gunshots, while a baying talk-show crowd whooped over the snake-oil rhetoric of an evangelist preacher.

Clara passed by door after door, all of them open, their single occupants sitting on La-Z-Boy recliners or on beds with polyester coverlets. Most stared at the screens, while a few just gazed off into the distance, their jaws slack.

The last door was the only one entirely shut. Clara took the key from her pocket, placed it in the lock and turned it with ease. Inside the room was airless, a layer of dust accumulating on every surface. It was sparsely furnished: a small table and two aluminum chairs at the window, a lone wingback arm-chair and a narrow bed, neatly made up with a thin blanket and ancient linens. In the center of the room a pile of boxes showed evidence of Miss Williams' work—cups and bowls and pans were piled up and wrapped in newsprint, alongside an aging kettle and a small *Kaffeepresse*. On a side table sat a neat stack of yellowing pamphlets showing dozens of delighted children playing with absurdly well-crafted creatures in primary colors. Ezra Adler had clearly been quite the Play-Doh artist in his time.

Clara rifled through the contents of the boxes, but there was nothing which spoke of a life before America. She sank down onto the hard single bed and surveyed the relics of the only person who might have been able to tell her more about who her father was. All that remained of Ezra Adler lay within these walls and yet he was unknowable, forever out of reach.

Minutes passed as she sat and watched the dust she'd disturbed swimming in the heat. She knew she ought to go, but could not shake the feeling of inertia. Finally, she gathered enough energy to stand and cross to the small en suite and splash some water on her face. Her eye landed on a pair of framed photographs hanging by the door. There was an ancient sepia-toned portrait of a bearded, broad-shouldered man. He was dandling a baby on his knee, stiff-limbed and doll-like. Beneath it, a stylized group shot from another era. Four smiling figures stood in a light-filled studio, surrounded by works of art, tall urns and statuary.

In the center stood a beautiful young woman, eyes flashing, dark bowed lips half smiling. She wore a formfitting skirt and jacket with wide shoulders and a nipped-in waist. An exquisitely sculpted hat was pinned to her shining hair and she was flanked by three men. Two of them wore loose white coats, the third a sharply tailored three-piece suit and wire-rimmed spectacles.

Clara gazed at the photograph with curiosity and detachment until the unfamiliar began to take form in front of her. In a moment of unsettling clarity, she recognized this vision, this beautiful, vivacious woman, was her own mother.

The youthful Bettina looked the same in all such early photographs. Stylish, magnetic and magnificent, she commanded the camera's attention, but for Clara she remained an enigma. This was a version of her mother she'd only ever seen in two dimensions, black and white. She seemed far removed from the woman Clara had grown up with—every bit as beautiful, but delicate as an eggshell, a faint crackle of fault lines running across the surface like a glaze.

Bettina was like a china doll that had been broken and brought back together—you could not play with it without being aware of its fragility and the potential it held to break again, perhaps this time beyond repair.

With shaking hands, Clara took the picture down from the

wall and turned over the old wooden frame; it was held together by two rusting tacks. She levered it open and lifted the picture from the glass, reading the words written on the back in a fine, spidery hand: *In the studio at Porzellanmanufaktur* Allach, *Dachau with Max, Bettina and Holger 1941.*

Though Bettina had remained entirely silent about the war years, Clara had always known her mother's life in Germany had most surely shaped her. She turned the photograph over, trying to identify which man might be Ezra Adler. The shorter of the two in white had the same stocky frame and barrel chest as the man in the portrait with the baby. She brought the picture closer still; she was fairly certain it was him. Standing there in his white coat, jutting out his chin, holding a porcelain rabbit.

Something about the image snagged her eye. She patted her coat pocket, and pulled out a pair of tortoiseshell reading glasses. She took the photograph toward the light. Underneath their white coats, both men were clearly dressed in the same way. Heavy cotton with broadly striped ticking, instantly recognizable as the uniform worn by prisoners of a Nazi concentration camp.

CHAPTER FOUR

Berlin

Autumn 1932

A thick mist hung over Berlin in the half-light of the November morning. Tramlines squealed and people skittered between the buildings, collars up, their eyes cast down. In the parks and avenues, tall trees shed their leaves, filling the air with the high, sweet scent of rot.

In the attic of the narrow townhouse, Max lay naked, still asleep. His body was contorted, all lengths and angles and ruddy elbows, a Schiele sketch with sheets wrapped around his restless limbs like dockyard ropes. In the seven years since that golden Weimar summer when they first met, Bettina had become as familiar with the contours of his body as her own; his broad shoulders and narrow waist, the curl of his chestnut hair and the full, fruit-soft flesh of his lips.

After their first meeting, they had moved together to the Bauhaus campus in Dessau, their future seeming as bright as the light reflecting off the waters of the Elbe. It illuminated their faces as they worked together, side by side, and was only dimmed a little when the local Nazi upstarts began to make their lives intolerable. They felt angry, fearful even, but they were young and Berlin beckoned, offering escape.

Now, curled up in a chair at the foot of their bed, high above the city, Bettina sketched the familiar form of her lover for the thousandth time. The charcoal stained her fingers as she marked down the arc of his collarbone and the grace of his long-fingered hands. Max was always contained and controlled in his waking life; she always felt compelled to capture his sleeping alter ego, so languorous and unrestrained.

Absorbed by the process, she didn't notice when he started to stir. It wasn't unusual for him to wake and find that he'd been cast in the role of muse, especially in recent months. Bettina always lost herself in work when the world threatened to over-whelm. The haste of their departure from Dessau and their subsequent relocation to Berlin had triggered a streak of pro-ductivity. Her mentor, the Russian painter Wassily Kandinsky, encouraged her forays into expressionism—she had blossomed in the warmth of his attention. Max envied her; his own talent came from craft and application, while hers seemed to flow from a wellspring of creativity.

Max watched her from the comfort of their crumpled sheets, his deep brown eyes hooded. He yawned and stretched, rubbing his face and running his hand through his unruly mop of hair. A grin slowly dimpled his features.

"*Mein kleines Kaninchen* . . . come back to bed, little rabbit."

His voice was thick with sleep, as enticing as the warm bedsheets.

She glanced up and waved him off, intent on capturing the

angle of his arm, but still, the spell was broken. Reluctantly she put down the charcoal and smiled at him, then stood and stretched. Her legs were stiff; she hadn't noticed the numbness creeping in. She laughed at the odd discomfort and rubbed the blood back as she limped over to the little stove.

"I'm getting old."

She picked up the *Kaffeepresse* and poured out two cups, carrying them back to the bed. She lay down beside him, spooning back into his crescent form. Max's hand reached over her hip and under the teal silk of her kimono to touch the warm core of her peach-soft flesh, but she pinned him tight between her thighs.

"Now then, I must get ready, there's still so much to do before tonight. I'm supposed to meet Richard at the gallery in an hour and I'm going to be late as it is."

But despite the urgency of her tone, she made no move to rise. Max's fingers did not continue their voyage of exploration, but neither did they retreat. His hand remained in place, applying pressure that was not yet solid enough to warrant being batted away, but certainly enough to derail her train of thought. She softened, her breathing deep and slow.

"Come then, tell me what you need to do," he whispered into the nape of her neck.

"Don't distract me!"

"I'm not, I'm helping."

She laughed, "So you say. Well, I need to make sure that they've hung the new canvas on the right-hand side as you enter—they'd stuck it in the back, can you imagine? The lighting there is dreadful."

He breathed her in.

"And we need more wine. The last thing I want is for it to be a dry old party, because then what would people say?"

As she spoke, his hands, his model maker's fingers, dexterous enough to create a whole world out of nothing, applied their gentle unrelenting pressure until all anxiety, all thoughts of what she must do and be began to fragment and drift away. So she could sink, her entire being dragged back down, into the depths of her desire where everything else was extinguished.

An hour later, Bettina could still feel the aftereffect of Max's touch sustaining her as she washed and dressed. She dashed around the apartment, gathering up what she needed. Though she knew it drove him to distraction, she somehow scattered her belongings over every surface and no amount of gentle chiding could make her change her ways. She found one stocking easily, but its pair remained resolutely lost until she spied the sheen of it tucked behind a cushion. She pulled it on, rolling the thin film over her knee and fastening it at the thigh, before smoothing down her skirt.

Under the skylight, Max was working on his model of a new autobahn. She worried he might strain his eyes in the thin light; their studio in Dessau had been all white with a large expanse of glass. Part of her still ached for that simplicity, despite the thrill of being in Berlin; there was an abundance of energy here, but stimulation had its price.

"Got everything?" Max asked. He didn't look up, his vision so intently focused on the task in hand, but she didn't for a moment doubt his genuine concern.

"Almost. Have you seen my portfolio?"

He gestured to the sofa. "You left it under there when you came in last night."

"So I did! Aren't you clever to remember."

She knelt on the floor and dragged it out; two panels made from planks of pine and bound together, a rough leather handle pinned at the top, her name in swooping chalk along the side. She placed the sketch she'd started that morning in among other less fully realized ideas of shape and form, each one a different stage in the cycle of abstraction she was working through.

She picked up a soft russet-colored beret and placed it on her dark hair, tilting it just so in the mirror and biting a bruise of color into the bow of her lips.

"You better get going or Richard will give you hell."

Richard, her best friend and champion for going on a decade. He had become her manager in all but name and seemed content to abandon his own artistic ambitions in favor of making deals and new connections. The faith he and Max had in her talents gave her the courage she required.

"He's becoming such a tartar, but I can't complain. He has all the instincts I lack when it comes to showing work."

"Your greatest champion. Well, second greatest . . ."

Bettina walked over to him and leaned her chin into the crook of his neck, draping an arm across his shoulder.

"How goes it?"

"Slowly."

"I envy your precision."

"You're not exactly lacking in it." He smiled.

"No, but I don't have your focus or control; my brain is too messy, and I can't rein it in."

He pulled her down onto his lap, "Your mind was not meant to be tamed, so don't waste your time trying." He held her to him tightly, though both knew it couldn't last.

"What time will the family arrive?"

"Good God, they're not coming here—can you imagine? Better for everyone's sake we keep up that pretense. I've arranged to meet them at the gallery."

Safe in the warmth of Max's embrace, she made no move to leave. In truth, she was apprehensive about their reaction to her work. Her brother made no secret of his disgust for modern art and she knew her mother wouldn't understand it. She felt so far removed from the backwater where they grew up, it was a foreign land to her now.

Max lifted her chin to meet his gaze.

"Now listen here; don't be nervous about tonight. Wassily wouldn't encourage this if he didn't think you ready. You have something to say, and the world is ready to hear it."

"You really think so?"

"I have always known it."

"I honestly cannot fathom how I'm going to summon the energy to smile all evening."

"I imagine Richard will offer you his little vial of plenty."

She raised one perfectly arched eyebrow. "It's just a pick-me-up, you know. Everyone does it."

"And everyone becomes an absolute bore, especially Richard. You must admit that; Berlin has changed him."

"He's still the same old Richard underneath."

She groaned and reluctantly levered herself up out of his grasp.

"Now, wish me luck and wave me off."

"You are your own luck, little rabbit."

She scrunched her nose at him, grinning as she ran down the narrow stairs, taking them two at a time.

Despite her nerves, when the exhibition opened a few hours later, the artist was in her element. Max watched her from across the room: her eyes sparkled and her gestures were expansive, as if trying to fill the space and match the magnitude of the moment. Richard stood beside her, full of paternal pride though he was scarcely a year her senior.

Dozens of chattering spectators had gathered for the show, despite persistent drizzle. An animal scent rose from the press of warm bodies in their wet woolen skirts and suits. The gallery was on the first floor of an abandoned telephone factory on the Birkbuschstraße. Its vast windows had been designed to flood the workers with light as they bent to their labors, but the same benefits applied every bit as much to art and artists.

Fifteen paintings hung on the whitewashed walls, each surrounded by an assertively plain wooden frame. The color and texture of their surfaces invited touch. Max's favorite canvas was almost entirely indigo, as dark as the November night and deep as the river Spree. Half-submerged kites of color seemed to rise to the surface: flashes of sour yellow, paprika red and a pale flesh pink, which he knew to represent Bettina. It took him back to Dessau and the summer nights when they'd escaped the sweltering heat of the studio to swim together naked in the lake.

Everyone agreed the exhibition marked a confident debut. Especially for one so young. Especially a woman. Still, by the time darkness descended, the art itself went largely unobserved, the gathering crowd now more intent on seeing and being seen.

Max drifted toward Bettina and the group surrounding her, but lingered on its edges. Richard was busy making proclamations, ever the elder statesman since he'd made the move to Berlin just one year ahead of them.

"I did wonder if there might be protesters, though so far we seem to have escaped their scrutiny."

Not content with forcing the city council to stop funding the Bauhaus in Dessau, the Nazis were using their growing influence to promote the so-called Struggle for Art. They had decided that almost all modern art was an act of aesthetic violence: a plot by the Jews and communists against the German people. Any number of artists, galleries and exhibitions had been attacked by brown-shirted thugs intent on causing trouble.

"The very idea that some crazed zealot might decide my work is an example of bourgeois Bauhaus decadence." Bettina laughed at the prospect. "I'd consider it a badge of honor!"

She was flushed and giddy, the champagne and attention swirling through her bloodstream. And maybe something else? Max wouldn't be surprised if Richard had prescribed a stronger tonic to quash her nerves. He moved to her side and took her hand, feeling the quiver of nerves she worked hard to conceal.

"Max darling, let me introduce you to Libertas. She published those lithographs I showed you. The ones with the exquisite typography?"

A young woman took his hand. She wore a tailored tuxedo and her cropped hair shone with brilliantine.

"Delighted to meet you."

Her heavy-lidded eyes stared into his intensely for a moment, before returning to Bettina.

"Betti darling, I know they seem ridiculous, but don't dismiss these people lightly. They're ignorant and vicious and they cast themselves as eternal victims. It's a dangerous, combustible mix."

Richard nodded fervently. "They're everywhere now. You two haven't been here long enough to see it, but it's changed. It feels terribly ominous."

Max sighed. "The Nazis forced us to leave Dessau, Richard. They're not just a problem in Berlin."

"Well, the scale of the city magnifies these things, you'll find."

Bettina squeezed Max's hand. She could sense when Richard's all-knowing air began to eat at his nerves.

"Well, at least I seem to have escaped their scrutiny tonight. And now I'm afraid this artist in residence needs to do a tour of the room. Max, keep me company? Do excuse us, Libertas."

Bettina steered him away and whispered, "Don't be cross with Richard; he means well."

"He can afford to. He treats us like his cousins up from the country, but he has no idea what's going on outside Berlin. It's a bad time to be an outsider."

Bettina stopped him with a kiss. Even after seven years they still had the power to soften his tirades. She looked at him in earnest.

"You're right; he's still a boy playing the world-weary radical, but you know he cares for us both, very much."

The soothing power of her touch, her voice, her reason, brought him back to himself.

"Everybody loves you, Bet. Just look at the success you've made of this."

He knew the sacrifice required, the years of mastering her craft. Few women were accorded such an opportunity. She'd earned her place through dedication.

"Well, I just thank God the strike is over; no one would have come at all, if they'd had to cycle in this rain."

Max put his arm through hers. "Come on, let's get another drink and toast to your success."

He started to steer her through the throng when he felt her stiffen. At the entrance to the gallery an elderly woman was shuffling in, desiccated and decades older than the bright young birds that filled the room to bursting. The woman's shoulders were hunched and wrapped in ostentatious widow's weeds. She clung to the arm of a much younger man who appeared overly solicitous, ensuring her slow progress was not impeded by the crowd. He had once been handsome, but it was his stiff brown shirt that made him stand out from the crowd of bohemian Berliners.

"Mama! Albrecht!" Bettina trilled, an edge to her voice that only Max might discern. He had never met either one of them before, but he recognized them instantly from her descriptions. The somber mother looked around her with disdain while her surly son stood by.

Bettina hissed, "Dear God, she's getting so decrepit . . ." It had been three years since Bettina had last made the journey south. She'd gone to see them on her own, concerned they would condemn her for living out of wedlock with any man, let alone an Austrian Jew. Her brother had never hidden his dislike of anyone he considered other, but she still held hope that seeing her happiness at first hand might make them more approving.

"How are you, Mama? How was your journey?"

Albrecht answered on her behalf.

"It was damnably slow, as you might expect. The trains are barely back in working order. We shouldn't have come."

Max observed them both, fascinated by the similarities and differences they represented. The dour, dull mother was a por-tent of what Bettina might look like in older life, if all the light was leeched from her. Her brother Albrecht was the masculin-ized version of her now, his handsome face sharp in contrast to the high curves of her own. Max could sense the familial quick temper just below the surface, but unlike his sister, Albrecht's was ice-cold and ill-concealed.

He became aware that the pair of them were staring at him.

"Albrecht, *Mutti*, this is my good friend Max. He's an archi-tect and has just won a very prestigious prize to design a new autobahn."

"Frau Vogel . . ." Max held out his hand in formal greeting and the older woman limply took it, remaining mute. The brother simply ignored it when proffered and looked around the room, contemptuous.

"In your letter you said this was a gallery."

"It is," Max interjected. "It was a factory, but it's part of the art school now. Professor Kandinsky made it possible for Bettina to show her work here . . . it's an honor but very well deserved. Come on through; you must see the paintings."

He led the way past a press of people, many of whom were openly eyeing the incongruous couple. Max stopped in front of the nearest canvas, a recent painting of a mother and child, their faces scored onto the canvas in a palette of pink and green. Full of pride, he turned back to them, but stopped short when he saw their faces, a bitter posset of confusion and disgust.

Albrecht scowled at Bettina. "I don't understand; what is it all supposed to mean? I thought the idea of attending art school was to teach you how to paint, and give you a trade in something, perhaps ceramics."

It was true that most Bauhaus teachers steered their female students toward more domestic mediums: textiles and ceramics. It was only Kandinsky's encouragement that gave Bettina the license to paint at all.

"I've been very lucky, Albrecht. Professor Kandinsky thinks I show promise."

Frau Vogel, who had been peering at her daughter's pictures in confusion, opened her thin mouth for the first time.

"Oh Bettina, what happened? The things you used to draw looked so . . . real, as if you could reach out and pick them up."

Bettina flushed with shame. She tried to force a smile, but her eyes shone with a panic it pained Max to witness.

"That's not how I work now, Mama. This is about capturing the essence of something, not making an accurate facsimile. We have photography for that."

Albrecht scoffed, "Why must you always be so desperate to be different?"

He turned to his mother. "I told you we shouldn't have come. She's just being her usual contrarian self, trying to shock people for the sake of it." He glared at her. "If I'd known you were wasting my money on this . . . I can hardly call it art. Where's the beauty? It's a damnable mess."

Tension radiated outward from the group and those nearest sensed the tenor, if not the specifics. The ripple spread and Max spied Richard and his coterie start to move in their direction.

"Frau Vogel! How lovely to see you again, but you must be exhausted."

Richard bent over the mother's hands in a show of gallantry.

"So good of you to come. May I offer you something to drink?"

Albrecht responded gruffly, "I'll take a beer."

"Of course. Let's see what we can lay our hands on."

Richard fetched a beer and pressed it into Albrecht's hand.

"Tell me, how are things in Allach?"

"Same as ever."

"And have you seen my wayward brother recently?"

"I haven't. We don't mix in the same circles anymore. I don't have much truck with communist sympathizers."

"So I see." Richard stared hard at Albrecht's brown-shirted uniform. "You didn't tell me your brother had joined the National Socialists, Betti."

"I didn't know." She cast her eyes down.

Albrecht shot his sister a look. "You would, if you ever came home to help on the farm instead of running around Berlin, frittering my money away."

Bettina scanned her brother's face anxiously. "What happened to you, Albrecht? I hoped that you at least might understand."

"I was prepared to support you when I thought you were doing something useful, but no one in their right mind needs this . . ." He gestured around him at her paintings.

"You don't think the workers deserve art just as much as the next man?" Richard interjected.

"They need food in their bellies and pfennigs in their pockets."

Libertas, who had been listening to their exchange, snorted loudly in disgust.

"That's the mistake you people always make. Life isn't just food and pfennigs. Art gives it meaning, design gives form to function. If aesthetics have such little value, why waste your time getting all dressed up and parading around in uniform?"

Richard flashed her a warning look. "Libertas . . ."

"There's just no point in trying to reason with them, Richard. They're all willfully uneducated and vulgar."

Albrecht's face drained of blood. The young woman smiled in triumph as he started toward her, his fist rising, the veins and tendons in his neck a study in tension. Bettina and Frau Vogel moved fast, familiar with his mercurial temper; they grasped his wrists to hold him back and moved together to drive him through the crowd, down the stairs, and out into the night. Richard and Max trailed behind, exchanging wary glances.

"I've been here before," Richard muttered under his breath. "He and my brother used to be friends, back in the day, but he's always had a temper on him. Let me handle it."

Outside, Albrecht was pacing the pavement, his body flooded with adrenaline.

"It's women like that, if you can even call it a woman, that have brought this country to its knees. Disgusting whore!"

He glared at Bettina and jabbed a shaking finger at her chest.

"These are your people—deviants and communists, foreigners and filthy *Juden*."

He shot a dark look at Max. Richard tried to calm him, but Albrecht brushed him off.

"Don't talk to me, traitor. You're just as bad as your brother. A subversive and a radical. Well, he'll get what's coming to him. He told me you'd look after my little sister, but what did you do instead? Introduce her to bourgeois agitators and Semites. *Abschaum* scum, the lot of them."

Bettina was shaking, white-faced and winded. Max put a protective arm around her as Frau Vogel approached Albrecht and started to drip whispered words into his ear. She begged him to come away, to take her back to their night's lodgings near the station, to leave this den of reprobates. Albrecht bridled at his mother's ministrations and turned back to his sister.

"You disgust me. You'll see no more of my money."

"She doesn't need it." Max's voice was hoarse with fury. "I'll look after her."

Albrecht spat on the ground at their feet.

"*Entartete Kunst*; bunch of degenerates."

He stormed into the night. Frau Vogel shuffled off behind him, without a glance at her daughter, hunched against the rain. Bettina stood mute and watched them go.

Determined to revive Bettina's spirits and escape the gossips at the gallery, Richard led the way to a busy nearby nightclub. She held tight to Max's hand as they crossed the monochrome floor and slid into seats at a table laid with crisp white linen. Richard pressed a handful of notes into the palm of the waiter and called for champagne, which arrived moments later, ice cold. Bettina lifted her glass, threw her head back and drained it in one elegant move.

"How are we?" Richard asked.

"I'm declaring myself a free woman."

"I'll drink to that."

"Furthermore, I've decided that you and Max are my chosen and only family now."

"Excellent. Prost?"

"Prost!"

Together, the three raised their glasses. The cacophony of the room allowed them all a moment of respite.

Inside and out, the dazzling lights of Berlin blazed as if this night city was entirely separate from the gray streets of the day—a mirage of neon. Handsome girls and beautiful boys danced and drank until they'd drowned any thought of tomorrow and were left with only now.

The three of them had lost the rest of their party somewhere along the way. Wassily first, then Libertas, followed by close friends and finally the hangers-on. All had drifted into the night, until only the three of them remained. They sat, each lost in thought, bubbles of quietude floating in the raucous flow.

Max watched Bettina, her head resting lightly on Richard's shoulder. He was still their closest friend and seemed utterly at home in Berlin, though it was a world away from Weimar and Dessau. Each had had its moment in their lives, but Berlin was where Richard had finally found himself, his quicksilver appetites easily satiated.

Max was grateful for his protective presence. He'd played

a vital part in Bettina's life since he first met her as a girl in Munich, her prodigious talent evident even then. Richard had taken her under his wing and there she'd sheltered until she'd learned to fly. Max knew that Richard had always loved her, in his idle way, and was content to let him. She needed them both, he reasoned, for no one else in the world cared half so much for her well-being.

"So, what next?" Richard was determined to turn the night to her triumph.

"American cocktails on the Ku'damm!"

He stood and clicked his heels together. He tapped his top pocket to ensure he had the little glass vial of fuel he needed to keep going. "I will return."

A constant stream of dancers moved, as if with one mind, across the floor. Max yawned, almost beaten by the prospect of the hours that lay ahead. Bettina caught his look and grasped his hand, whispering conspiratorially, "You have my blessing to go home."

"I do?"

"You do. If I'm with Richard, then I'm sure we'll make some transitory companions for the night. I rather feel like losing myself, but I'd like someone to keep an eye on me while I do."

"He always does, I'll give him that."

Max watched her as she looked across the crowded room. It was busy, crawling with industry; all the pretty bees gathering their nectar. He hesitated for a moment and then.

"I've been thinking . . . maybe we should run away. What do you say, little rabbit?"

Bettina frowned at him, confused.

"Not tonight," he clarified with haste. "You must stay, have fun—you've earned it. I mean maybe we should leave Berlin . . . The two of us."

He carried on, now warming to his theme: "We could go to Paris, or London, New York. Anywhere! Wassily has spoken about leaving and even Richard joked about moving to Moscow, although I know he doesn't mean it."

"Why now?"

"Because we can; there's nothing to keep us here and . . . I don't like the way that things are going. I know you feel the same."

"I do, but what about your autobahn? You can't abandon that. It's going to make your name, I'm sure of it."

"What's that worth if I can't even make an honest woman of you? Although can you imagine what your brother would say?" He continued in mock horror: "A girl from good, strong German farming stock, wasted on an Austrian Jew."

"That's not funny, Max. You know I'd marry you in a second if we could. I want nothing more than to spend the rest of my life with you."

"I know," he reassured her.

"But this is our home, too. If all of us run away, what's left?" She pressed his hand. "Things have to change soon, I'm sure of it. The pendulum will swing the other way. Every generation thinks they're living through uniquely terrible times."

"Some of them must be right."

"I don't want you throwing it all away just so we can marry. What difference does a ring make? Build your autobahn, make your name, so neither of us need rely on anyone else again. Then let's run away together. Somewhere warm though, promise me?"

"I like the sound of that," he said.

She leaned into him as he put an arm around her. Together they gazed out across the swarm of revellers; all the mindless worker bees, bent to their ceaseless labor in perpetual motion, flying from bloom to blossom, circling each other, making honey, moving on.

CHAPTER FIVE

Cincinnati

August 1993

It was almost 6 p.m. by the time Clara returned to her airport hotel room, but she was in no hurry; she had more than a day to kill before she could catch a connecting flight and start the journey home.

She shut the bedroom door behind her, pulled the chain across the lock and placed the box of porcelain figurines on the writing desk in the corner. Tired decor, pale gray and peach, declared it had been years since anyone had considered the aesthetics of the space. Still, it had everything she needed.

Clara walked to the bed, lay down on the slippery coverlet and levered off her heels, kicking them to the floor. She stared up at the ceiling and made a plan: to order food, shower and eat, all in quick succession, so she might finally succumb to sleep. She still felt numb and knew she would need hours, if not days, to process anything of what she'd learned. She feared that none of it had brought her any closer to the truth.

She forced herself up and lifted the handset of the bedside telephone, pressing the button for room service. She ordered a club sandwich, then headed to the bathroom.

By the time the food arrived she had showered and wrapped a terry-cloth dressing gown around her. Her sandwich sat sweating under a plastic cloche. She devoured it all in seconds, desperate to fill the void.

Finally satiated, she set aside the tray and opened the box of figurines. The first piece at hand was the lamb, loosely wrapped in an old page of the *Cincinnati Enquirer*. It was so long-limbed it looked a little like a fetus; a sterile specimen, floating in formaldehyde.

The second piece she pulled out was the rabbit; she would have adored it as a child, but to her jaded adult eyes it looked far too saccharine and sentimental. She set it to one side and opened the third parcel—finally, the prize. A bare-chested male, five inches high, standing on a rocky plinth, a determined set to his square jaw. This was an image she was already entirely familiar with, based as it was on her mother's most famous work. She had painted it before Clara was even born. Though she'd never laid eyes on the original, she felt as if this figure had been a constant in her life. Reproductions of the piece, known only as *The Viking*, could still be found in junk shops and on the walls of aging inns across Germany. She'd stumbled across his image in incongruous places throughout her life.

Clara realized it was years since she had really stopped to look at him properly: he was a young man in the prime of life, muscular arms, torso and legs all flexed. His expression was inscrutable; he stared out to sea, as if preparing to face a coming storm. His profile was both classically handsome and yet absolutely of its time. Clara did not upend the figure to check the maker's mark beneath. She neither needed nor wanted confirmation of the dual strikes of lightning, that taint of Nazism that had long colored her response to it.

Though she could not recall ever being told directly, Clara had always understood that certain subjects were off-limits with her mother. Uppermost of these, any discussion of her father and the war. Both were somehow related and equally verboten.

Throughout Clara's childhood and adolescence Bettina suffered from depression, a sadness so profound it exerted a gravitational pull on both of them. When it threatened to overwhelm her, Bettina would retreat from the world almost entirely and their German housekeeper Heida would act as surrogate. Heida had traveled with them to England and was fiercely loyal to Bettina, but still she sometimes let things slip.

During one bout when Bettina couldn't find the strength to rise from her bed for days on end, Heida told Clara her mother had once been married to a very bad man; a Nazi named Karl Holz. A dim recollection had surfaced of a man in a uniform, swinging her up to the sky. Heida had whispered to the wide-eyed child that he'd been unspeakably cruel to her mother and it was his fault she still suffered to this day.

Appalled and intrigued, Clara took to listening at closed doors. She overheard her mother telling Heida how hard it was, that her daughter looked so like her father and how at times she could not bear to set eyes on her for fear of seeing him. Clara had tiptoed away then, ashamed and consumed by a secret terror that the bad man must be her father and that was why her mother never spoke of him.

That night she'd awoken crying from a nightmare. Heida came to comfort her and Clara sobbed and hiccupped for almost an hour before reluctantly revealing the cause of her terror through heavy, heaving breaths.

"Hush now, *Liebchen*, don't fret. I promise you, that coward Holz was not your father." A brief grimace twisted Heida's mouth.

"I only thought, because no one ever tells me anything . . ."

"Well, we don't want to cause your mother any pain. She has had more than her share."

Heida turned away as she spoke, her voice somehow thicker.

"She just wants to protect you, Clara. I cannot say more, but know that and rest assured."

Heida seemed so sorrowful that Clara had resolved there and then not to wound her mother, or her beloved surrogate, by pressing them for answers.

Decades later, in the weeks following Bettina's death, Clara had come across a letter from Karl Holz among her mother's effects. Clara wished she could turn to Heida for help deciphering the unfamiliar handwriting, but she had passed away by then.

With dictionary in hand, Clara finally managed to extract some meaning from the letter. While not quite a suicide note, it was clearly a farewell from Holz, alternately beseeching Bettina to forgive him and trying to justify his actions. To Clara's eye it seemed full of maudlin self-pity. He did nothing to disavow his poisonous beliefs, and the presence of the SS sigil on both his letterhead and the collection of porcelain somehow tied them all together, along with the question of her father's identity. She fervently hoped that Heida had been telling her the truth.

In her hotel bed, lulled by the constant drone of planes overhead, Clara placed the figure of the Viking on the bedside table and finally turned out the lamp. She glanced again at the figurine, which seemed to gleam a ghostly blue. She reached out to touch it like a talisman before sinking into grateful sleep.

For hours her consciousness remained deep and dreamless, but eventually the clock inside began to reassert itself, forcing her to start the long swim to the surface. Little fever dreams floated by; she found herself in her mother's apartment in Putney, surrounded by her porcelain collection, a reliquary of secular saints. Her mother was lying there in state, scarcely breathing. Then her bed became a Viking burial ship, waiting for Clara to set it alight and push it out to sea, floating on fire, until it sank them both beneath the waves.

Clara slept on, but the dream of her dying mother refused to fade. She felt caught by the starchy bedsheets, which bound her heels like seaweed and left her floating in an inky darkness, listening, remembering . . .

The key turned in the lock, the tumblers fell, and Clara stepped inside. The air in her mother's apartment was heavy, filled with the warmth of a late spring day.

Outside, the plane trees filtered the sunlight. Within, the smell of rich beeswax polish mixed with Bettina's sea-salt scent. And . . . something else? The faint sting of ammonia. Clara wrinkled her nose and walked over to the window. She pushed it open, letting the sounds of the Heath and the street below wash in.

A grand piano sat beneath the window, a vintage Viennese tapestry thrown across its lacquered back to deaden the sound. Clara straightened it reflexively as she glanced around, taking stock. She hadn't visited in some weeks, but nothing here seemed to have changed.

"Mama?"

She said it quietly. There was no reply. Clara slipped off her shoes and walked down the corridor toward her mother's bedroom. The fabric of this building felt like part of her DNA, but as soon as she crossed the threshold her sense of self began to erode. Unwittingly she reverted to teenage Clara—turbulent, brash, tempestuous.

She stood at the bedroom door and listened for a moment. Hearing nothing, she pushed it open and peered in; Bettina was asleep, her slight body barely visible under heavy blankets. Clara could hear her labored breathing, proof that she was still alive at least. For years her mother had seemed to be retreating from the outside world. Now, near the end, she was content to be contained within her bedroom walls and further still, to the confines of her solid oak sleigh bed.

Clara stepped back into the hall and gently pulled the door to. She tiptoed to the kitchen, where the changes since her last visit were far more obvious. A small platoon of nursing staff had been employed to keep her mother at home and in some comfort. Evidence of their existence littered every surface: by the sink, a lacquered Venetian tray was loaded with pill bottles, medicines and tissues. On the kitchen table, a pile of boxes contained silicone gloves and plastic aprons of a bright turquoise-blue. Flesh-toned rubber tubes spoke of more invasive procedures and all the small indignities that lay in wait at the close of life. Clara skirted around them and filled the heavy-bottomed kettle, placing it on the stove. She lit the flame and waited for it to boil, crossing to the telephone on the wall, lifting the receiver and dialing her own number. It rang and rang. She pictured her house, oddly empty, until eventually the answering machine kicked in. She waited for the tone and spoke quietly.

"Darling, I'm at my mother's. I should be home for supper, but don't wait. There's a steak in the fridge. I'm . . . not sure where you are?" She let the question hang there. "But don't call back; Mama is sleeping and I don't want to wake her. I'll see you tonight. Love you . . ."

She hung up frowning; why hadn't he answered? Her brain provided her with several increasingly alarming scenarios until the whistle of the kettle punctured her self-absorption. She rushed to lift it from the stove and muffle its shriek. She took a teacup from the drainer and poured scalding water over dried peppermint, inhaling its grassy scent. She carried it carefully, pushing open the door to her mother's bedroom, then padded back inside.

The room was sunk in shadow, the windows hung with heavy curtains of a shell-pink damask silk. They dropped and pooled on the parquet floor, submerging the room in dappled shade. It was, as it had always been, elegant and subdued, though peppered with her mother's more eccentric touches: a chartreuse velvet chair; a mercury glass vase of ostrich feathers; a vintage kimono hanging on the wall, patterned with teal peonies against tomato red. There were a few signs of the ephemera of ill health: a wheelchair, ugly, gray and functional, and a stainless-steel bedpan, discreetly tucked away.

Clara sat down lightly on the bed and observed her mother, who slept on, seemingly oblivious. Bettina had always maintained rigid control over her slender body. Her attention to her appearance remained intact long after other mothers seemed to stop caring, but now she looked thin to the point of emaciation.

Clara sipped her tea, relishing the silence as she surveyed the room. She found herself gazing at the wall above the bed, where three recessed alcoves housed her mother's collection of glossy, white porcelain artifacts. Angled spotlights suffused them in a subtle glow, two dozen different objects on display, each one hyper-realistic and highly detailed. They had always seemed so incongruous to Clara, at odds with the rest of her mother's simple tastes and the few pieces of her own work that she chose to display. Bettina hadn't kept any of her "later work," as she described it. Her most famous paintings had all been sold off or donated to various museums across Europe. Clara understood that they had, for a time, given her a certain cachet in the German art world, but that fame had been short-lived. Little wonder—from the reproductions Clara had seen, the work was beautifully executed, but too romantic. That kind of realism had rather had its day.

Before that had come Bettina's expressionist period. Though that era had been brief, the zest of the work reminded Clara of the greats: Kirchner, Kandinsky, Klee, all of whom had been her mother's inspiration. The vibrant colors, the energy of the brushstrokes, the hollow-faced features, often a sickly sort of radiance in neon and limelight—these were the works that Bettina had chosen to hang in her own home. And it was these that Clara loved.

She stood up, quietly crossing to the wall where the white gloss figurines watched over her sleeping mother. There were greyhound dogs and song thrushes, milkmaids and athletes, each one faithfully reproduced, yet strangely bloodless. Clara lifted down the central figure cautiously, a male with tousled locks and a naked torso, muscular legs braced against a rocky outcrop, a sword at his side, a tiny rabbit crouched at his feet and a thick fur cape thrown over his shoulders. She ran a fingertip across his face—noble but impassive.

"Do be careful."

Clara jumped and instinctively gripped the figure to her chest, afraid of dropping it. Bettina, seemingly still half asleep, was looking up at her, silhouetted in the dim light.

"Sorry," she croaked. "I didn't mean to scare you."

Clara put the figurine down on the night table and Bettina slowly turned toward it, wincing with the effort.

"My Viking."

She reached out a delicately boned and birdlike hand to stroke the porcelain. She chuckled. "You remember who made it, of course?" Her voice was as dry as seeds in a husk.

"No, I don't think I do," Clara replied.

"Silly girl, you must—the porcelain maker of Dachau, of course! Meine wahre Liebe. *He made it just for me."*

In recent months her mother's mind had started to drift, the flow of memories floating back downstream, more real to her than anything in the here and now.

"Do you mean Karl?" asked Clara as gently as possible. "I thought he was an art dealer, not an artist."

"Not Karl!" Bettina gave a snort of derision. "God knows, the only artistry he possessed was good taste and a thick wallet. No, Karl gave it to me, but he didn't make it for me."

"Then who did?"

"Clara's father, of course."

In her chest the tide pulled back, like water rushing across shingle. The tick of the grandmother clock on the mantelpiece seemed suddenly, terribly loud; blood beating time, a metronome in her ears.

"Who do you mean?"

"You know very well, Heida. Don't be so obtuse!"

Heida. Her mother's housekeeper, companion and confidante, who had died the year before. Both women still felt her loss keenly.

Bettina shivered. "It's chilly. Are you cold?"

Clara reached down to pull the sheet up. Her mother's cool fingers circled her own and pressed them tight.

"Thank you, dear. You have always been such a solace. I don't know what I would have done without you."

"Mama, it's not Heida, it's me . . . Clara."

Bettina let go of her hand.

"Clara?"

"Yes."

She peered up, her eyes darting and anxious.

"What are you doing here?"

"The day nurse couldn't come; she phoned in sick. Mama, what did you mean, about my father?"

Bettina kept very still.

"Mama, did you hear me?"

"I'm sorry, Liebchen. I have a terrible headache."

There was an edge to her mother's voice, a profound melancholy she could read all too well. Still, Clara pressed on.

"Who was the porcelain maker of Dachau? You said he was my father."

Bettina tried to sit up; Clara could see her arms were shaking with the effort.

"Talk to me, Mama."

She slumped back down and shut her eyes against her daughter's insistent gaze. She turned her head away, lips pressed together in pain.

"Clara, please . . . I can't. I haven't got the strength."

Tears spilled from her, silently dropping on the counterpane. Clara held her breath. After a moment, she patted the paper-thin skin of her mother's hand, which trembled as it gripped the sheet.

"I didn't mean to upset you, Mama. It's all right; rest now. I'll make you some tea."

Clara walked back to the kitchen in a daze. She put the kettle on to boil again and held tight to the marble worktop, clenching her jaw, working it so hard it ached. Eventually the kettle started to whistle, but she found she could not loosen her grip and so the whistle built into a screech and then a scream that filled the room.

Clara was jolted awake by the metallic shriek of a 747 flying low overhead. Sweating and tangled in her sheets, she turned her head and her eyes sought out the dim red digits of the radio alarm clock. It was 2:30 a.m. She lay still for a moment, bathed in a sheen of perspiration, before accepting that real sleep would elude her now; she was too tired to read, too wired to rest. Unwilling to risk a return journey to the mausoleum waiting in her memories, she threw back the covers and went into the bathroom to drink a glass of water.

Now wide awake, Clara walked back to the bed, the light from the bathroom illuminating the ceramic warrior on the nightstand. She picked up the phone and dialed an outside line, long distance, and waited as it rang and then finally connected.

"Lotte, darling?"

"Mum?"

"*Liebchen*, how are you?" The line crackled, phasing in and out.

"I'm fine. It's pretty early."

"Earlier still here."

"Where are you?"

"I'm in Cincinnati."

"Is everything OK? This must be costing you a fortune."

"It's fine. Listen, I'm flying back tomorrow. Can you come and stay this weekend? I could do with your advice."

CHAPTER SIX

Berlin

Summer 1937

Berlin was baking, the air heavy with a shimmering heat that rose from the pavements and pressed in on every side. Buildings were choked with the stale aroma of breath and bodies, of food quick to rot and milk already curdled in the glass.

In the street, tensions simmered and strangers passed too close for comfort. Pedestrians, woozy from the heat, would suddenly veer into the road, like wasps half drunk on rotten fruit. Max rode his bike home along Wilhelmstraße, dodging the tramlines, which threatened to throw him off. The riding was hard enough already; his bike was unbalanced, as he'd tied a dozen rolls of sketches and blueprints to it, to work on back at home. The weight of them altered his center of gravity, but he had reserved the basket in front for a very special cargo. It was an offering so delightful, so exotic, that it must surely guarantee the recipient would be filled with joy.

When he first spotted the banana cart at the side of the

road, he had been stunned to see the jaunty, citrine-yellow jewels hanging, swinging in the sun. They were so startling he'd stopped his bike and laughed out loud. He was hesitant to spend his precious pfennigs on something so frivolous, but found himself digging deep to dredge them up. He'd placed the smiling treasure in the basket for safekeeping and began to cycle home, checking on it, grinning back.

Max had spent the morning drafting designs for Herr Neumann, the senior partner at his new architectural practice. The elderly man was approaching his retirement and had been struggling to keep up with the times. He'd hired Max in desperation but soon came to rely on him. Real innovation and ingenuity were seldom required, but he added a veneer of modernity to their otherwise old-fashioned propositions.

Max still endeavored to look forward, not to waste time on regrets and recriminations, but even he found it hard not to mourn some losses. For a while, he and Bettina had felt like they might conquer the world. Now, just getting by was challenging enough. At the start, the two of them had seemed destined to rise together. Their future held promise, even if their present was sometimes compromised. It was against the law for them to marry, but really, who cared about convention? But gradually, imperceptibly, they'd felt Berlin begin to change. The strictures that governed their lives tightening week on week. Inconvenience turned into impediment, then legal penalties with ever-growing consequences.

All across the city, the past was being torn down to make way for the future. In this new world, architecture was taking center stage, but not for someone with an old-world name. Max couldn't quite pinpoint when the title of Herr Ehrlich became a liability, telling tales on his lineage instead of announcing his talent. The slide was incremental; passed over for promotion here, a failure to renew a contract there, former friends who now forsook him. His once-grand dreams became reduced to redrafting plans for suburban factories and having to feel a measure of gratitude for even that.

Max wasn't the only one so compromised. Bettina had inevitably been tarred with the brush of "degenerate." Work like hers now had a target painted on. They could still scrape by, but the money his parents sent no longer went as far and soon the radio and gramophone had to be sold to help them make ends meet.

Still, even on the darkest days, they had each other. Max had burned on reading the reports of the World Fair in Paris, jealous of his former colleagues, but Bettina had just laughed at all their posturing as "playing sword fights with their *Schwanze* like little boys."

She helped lift his spirits when the pain of his slow fall became too acute, asking, "Why is it that architects love nothing quite so much as building phallic objects? You all want to deflower the heavens, like those Renaissance hill towns in Italy and their thrusting great bell towers!"

For both of them, the discovery that Bettina was at long last pregnant bought some measure of joy and respite. For a time, the brightness of their future seemed to flower again, until her nausea and the stifling heat began to take their toll. She slept poorly and there were constant blue-black shadows underneath her eyes. A catalog of real and imagined anxieties slowly started to take root; what if someone told the authorities they were living together, a German woman and an Austrian Jew? What if their money ran out, what if he was fired, what if she never

sold her work again, what if he was arrested? He always tried
to buoy her up, but there were days he couldn't find the words
to stop her sinking.

To save money, they moved out of their town house attic
and took a few rooms on the top floor of a *Mietskaserne*. These
imposing rows of tenements were home to thousands of Berlin's
working class: small flats piled high and deep, one above the
other. Sounds passed easily between the floors and walls; a slap,
a sigh, small fragments of frustration, bitten back and swallowed
down too many times.

As Max rode his bike through the long shadows they cast,
he thought about the home he hoped to build in better days.
He had begun to sketch out blueprints for their future: a safe
place to raise a family, the realization of his form-and-function
dream. They talked about where they might settle and what
materials he'd use, envisioning the light that would flood in.

When Max finally reached their building on Kottbusser
the sun was still high and he was sweating, his sleeves pushed
up to the elbow. He wheeled his bike through the archway
and into the square courtyard behind the facade, parking it
and pinning all the rolls of blueprint under one arm. It left
his other hand free to hold on to his precious yellow cargo,
perfect and unblemished. Despite the heat, he sprang up the
narrow flight of stairs, eager to share this exotic wonder with
Bettina.

On the far side of the river, Bettina made her way home more
slowly, the heavy pinewood portfolio banging against her leg,
her feet swollen in too-tight shoes. She had spent the morning
taking her work to an up-and-coming gallery. The owner had

vaguely promised to include her in a small group show, but when she got there, she found the offer was rescinded.

"I know of several galleries that have been forced to shut, their owners persecuted and even prosecuted if they exhibit 'degenerate' art."

It didn't help that no strict criteria existed for art to be considered degenerate; the intention of the artist rarely came into it. Jewish painters, liberals, radicals, all were degenerate by default. If you showed the world as it was, in all its messy beauty, then you were a degenerate. If you tried to give voice to a concept or idea, took liberties with color, shape and form, then you were a degenerate.

The gallery owner was profusely apologetic, lamenting the authorities' narrow-minded strictures, although he did not dare defy them.

"I adore your work, Fräulein, but I can't risk the damage to my reputation. Maybe try to tone things down, make something more . . . accessible. It's nothing personal, you understand."

"But I don't," she replied through a gritted smile. "Tell me, how is this degenerate?" She held out a small painting, a burnt-umber moon rising over Berlin, a nightingale in a tree, the branches sharply geometric.

The gallerist had been unbending. "The National Socialists are intent on purging anything they don't approve of and, I'm afraid to say, they don't approve of you. I don't want to waste your time, or give false hope."

Bettina had wandered out of the gallery and walked around aimlessly for a time, her eyes awash with tears. She became quite lost in the process and had just begun to feel an edge of panic when she turned a corner and found herself at the

Thielenbrücke, which spanned the broad Landwehr Canal. Its surface was coated in a filmy sheen and laced with a scum of foam, but it was still a welcome sight. At least she had her bearings now.

The bridge was teeming with people strolling in the afternoon heat. Crowds had gathered on the banks of the canal, idly wandering past the barges, holding hands and eating ices, as if on an excursion. Bettina searched for a shaded spot where she might stop and give her swollen feet a rest. She sat under the bridge at the water's edge and eased off her shoes, examining the spots where they had rubbed red and raw. Despite some reservations about what horrors might be floating there unseen, she lowered her feet and let the milky brown canal water wash over them. The raw spots stung, but at least the cool might prevent further swelling. They already felt like water balloons, weighing down her ankles.

Bettina lifted her feet back out and let them dry on the dusty towpath. On the opposite bank a young couple strolled together, pushing a primrose-yellow pram between them. She watched as they went by, so proud of their progeny. The woman leaned on her husband's arm and bent down into the pram, to touch the baby's cheek. Bettina felt a pang of envy at her seeming ease. In the weeks since she discovered she was pregnant, instead of the joy she had imagined would come naturally, she often felt weighed down by nameless dread.

Their circumstances were not as they might have planned, but still, it was everything they wanted. Determined to lift herself out of her funk, she winced and pulled her shoes back on. She decided to make her way west, where she might catch a tram. It was a luxury she rarely afforded herself these days, but excusable under the circumstances. She'd be home within the hour.

By now the streets were full of workers finished for the day. When she reached a busy intersection, Bettina got drawn into a crowd that had gathered there. The latest edition of *Der Stürmer* had been put out under glass, allowing passersby to stop and read the headlines, which they did by the dozen. She tried to weave her way through them, but got caught up in a shoal of bodies vying for the best position. Even from some distance, the banner headline leaped out at her:

Degenerate Art Exhibition
Opens in Munich

Bettina pushed forward, anxious not to pass now but to get a better view. Eventually she stood before the case and stared down at the photograph on the front page. She recognized the painting it featured immediately: *Drei Klänge* by Kandinsky, one that she'd returned to time and time again in Dessau. Back then she'd been eager to see the vivid colors for herself; the deep, resounding blue, a swollen magenta moon, and bright vermillion, clear as a chiming bell. She had often imagined it, but not like this. The image reproduced here was ugly, the picture grainy and the paper cheap, saturated by the ink. In the photograph she saw the words *"Entartete Kunst"* scrawled on the wall above the painting. Degenerate art—the final accusation her brother had fired at her from the dark. It seemed she could not escape its brand.

The heat and the press of bodies began to overwhelm her. She feared she might faint, feeling her blood sink through her, a constellation of white stars spraying out across her vision. Someone kicked her blistered heel by accident and she heard herself cry out, her leg crumpling beneath her. She fell forward hard, into the glass case, her solar plexus bruised and aching from the blow. The crowd surged forward, crushing her, eager to see how these so-called artists were finally being held to account. Bettina clutched her rounding belly, desperately shielding it. An older woman put out an arm and tried to usher her away, barking at the men who pressed in regardless.

"For pity's sake, give her some air!"

She shoved them back until they reached the shelter of a shaded stoop, where Bettina sank down gratefully, her legs too weak to stand. The woman stayed with her until the worst had passed and the rushing sound that filled her ears retreated. She helped her limp to the tram stop and waited with her there, finally ushering her on board and snarling at a young man till he gave up his seat.

As the tram moved off, Bettina raised a grateful hand of thanks, then closed her eyes and leaned her head against the window. She touched her belly cautiously, feeling where the bruising sat; it was still sore and sullen. She tried to make herself as small and inconspicuous as possible, praying to be home.

When she finally returned, she found the attic empty and felt a stab of trepidation; could Max have been arrested? Had they come for him as she had always feared they might?

And then she saw it.

On the kitchen table lay a sheet torn from a sketchbook, telling her he'd gone to look for her. At the bottom, he'd drawn eyes and brows and a nose: crooked, sweet and child-like. In place of a mouth, he'd left the curvy, bright banana. It was perfection, not a single blemish on its sunny yellow skin. Beneath he'd written "Something to make you smile."

She laughed, then felt the tears start to flow. Held at bay for so many hours, they finally asserted themselves, dropping hot and fast onto the paper. With no one there to witness them, like a summer storm, they passed as quickly as they came.

She drew a deep breath in and decided to take a bath, to wash off the stink of the street and the taint of her own terror. She gathered up her teal and red robe, a threadbare towel, and their last scrap of soap, before beginning her slow descent to the shared bathroom. It was subterranean, the walls a dull green-blue, the color of the sea on an overcast day. Even in the summer heat, it was never dry down here; mildew made its home, creeping into corners and blackening the ceiling like soot. Above the bath hung rows of stockings, dripping like stalactites. Bettina turned on the tap and a gurgle of water trickled forth, slowly filling the tub and drowning out the noise of children playing in the street.

When the level of the water was high enough, she undressed and stepped over the edge. Flinching, she lowered herself in. It rose to hip height, the cool a welcome shock, raising goose bumps on her soft white skin. She slowly let down her legs and leaned back, surveying the landscape of her body: the small swell of her belly, an island, water lapping at its shore.

She drifted off and woke with a start some minutes later. She roused herself enough to reach for the soap and rub it into her scalp as her hair fanned out around her. She sat back up and scrubbed at her feet where they were not too chafed, then under her arms and beneath her breasts, where the glass case of *Der Stürmer* had left a browning welt.

She rested her forehead on her knees, wet hair dripping into the water in rhythm with the stockings. She looked down and something snagged her eye: a thin plume of scarlet hung suspended between her legs, like the tendril of smoke that spirals from a snuffed-out flame.

The world stopped then and dropped away. Bettina sat perfectly still, knowing that to do anything at all would turn this possibility into a fact and from that point on, there would be no return. She stayed there, shivering, until the evening came creeping in and, at last, the water grew too dark to see.

They left the city on a bright day in late August. The two of them took the train through Steglitz and then due south. The tenement houses loomed over them as they passed between their walls. Washing hung in every courtyard and open window, despite the schmutz that spiraled like a vortex in their wake.

While Max read his book, Bettina stared out at the women going about their labors. She watched them hanging the sheets like sailcloths, dozens of children at their feet, running and ducking beneath. Whole worlds passed by and carried on, oblivious. *How odd*, she thought, *that in the midst of grief, normality appears the most abnormal thing of all.*

The rhythm of the train whispered of sleep, but she'd done more than enough of that. She stared down at the fingers of her right hand. They seemed to her to tremor; she wondered if anyone else would notice.

"How are you doing, *Kaninchen*?"

She looked up at his voice; behind the mask of his slight smile, he was a picture of anxiety.

"I'm fine," she said. "Well, almost fine, at least. You don't need to worry."

He returned to his book and she focused her attention back on her hand. The quick was torn at the corner of her thumbnail: a hard, white catch of skin. She picked at it with the rounded nail of her index finger, exposing the deep pink flush of flesh beneath. She felt the press of ever-present tears; there was a reservoir inside her now, so full it threatened to overflow if even one more drop was added. The train rattled on.

Don't think. Don't think. Don't think about it.

She forced her attention back and pulled at the quick, despite the pin-bright stab of pain. A blossom of blood swelled to the surface and she stared at it.

Don't think.

A sudden squeal of the brakes made her look up and she was astonished to see that the high walls of the city had given way to wider vistas. The train had swept them out into the suburbs, from gray and brown to a green so vivid that it sharpened all her senses. She realized it had been months since she'd seen a horizon that wasn't filled with buildings and was relieved to find she still had the capacity to be distracted by the world. She gazed out of the window, rapt and soaking it all in.

When the train finally arrived at Wannsee, the two of them jumped up. She started to retrieve the packages they'd placed above their seats; a loaf of rye bread, a pound of speck wrapped in waxed paper and an apple cake, the sweet scent of it escaping as she lifted it down. Max took everything from her, loading them against his chest before lowering the window and opening the door. He held out his hand and she stepped onto the platform. The air felt crisp and clean. Out here at the edge of the city, she could feel the promise of change.

She squeezed his hand as they walked together in silence to

the entrance. They searched in both directions, hoping Richard had kept true to his word.

"All hail the city mice!"

There he sat, tanned and with an easy smile, behind the wheel of an open-topped Adler Trumpf, a pretty blond girl at his side, waving with excitement.

"Say hello to Imre," he shouted.

She's young, thought Bettina. *And so pleased to see us, she's wagging her tail, like an eager spaniel.* She lifted a hand and waved to them both, putting on her bravest smile and broad-brimmed sun hat.

Richard always had a propensity for speed; a tree-lined avenue on a bright summer's day was an invitation he could not pass up. And though she was loath to admit it, Bettina found the drive exhilarating. As she held on to the door handle, to brace herself against his turns, she felt something in her reawaken—a patch of thaw. She pressed her tongue against it to see if there were raw nerves there and, finding none, she smiled a little to herself.

Imre turned, her fair hair whipping around her face. She called out over the raw noise of the engine.

"It's not far now. We're going straight to the lake. Have you been?"

"Never," Bettina shouted in reply.

"Did you bring a costume?"

She shook her head.

"Doesn't matter, you can borrow one of mine; I brought a spare. Richard said we were about the same size."

She does seem kind, Bettina thought. *Richard's growing up, just like the rest of us.* In the past he had often been coldly pragmatic with his summer conquests, valuing them as much for their real estate as their character.

When they reached the end of the road, he spun the car to a stop, throwing up a fan of dust. A wolfish grin was spread across his face.

"All good?"

Max groaned. "As soon as my internal organs catch up."

"Liquid sustenance, that'll put you right."

Richard jumped out and retrieved a case of beer from the back while Imre lifted out a basket and some blankets. The two of them led the way down to the lake, where a little wooden jetty struck out from the shore.

The sky was clear, save for a low bank of cloud on the horizon. An occasional breeze stirred the water, but otherwise it remained quite still, reflecting back the wide, cerulean sky. Imre laid out the blankets on the jetty and, once they'd settled, began to dole out food on china plates: potato salad, sauerkraut and sausages alongside tiny, hard tomatoes. She fussed over Richard and Max, making sure that they had everything they might require.

Bettina took off her cardigan and leaned back against one of the stays, dangling her legs over the edge. Eyes closed, she turned her face up to the sun, tuning out the chatter and enjoying the feel of heat on her bare shoulders. She took a deep breath in and sighed. A shadow briefly blocked the light; she looked up, shielding her eyes.

"Can I get you something?" Imre stood over her, hesitant.

"A beer would be nice."

Richard prised the cap off one and handed it to Imre. She passed it over and sat down nearby, watching her.

"Richard talks about you all the time. He says you're a brilliant painter."

"Does he now?" She took a swig of the beer and gave the girl a speculative look. "And what about you?"

"Nothing so exciting. I teach kindergarten."

"Sounds exciting enough. But tell me—I'm curious, how can a kindergarten teacher afford to stay out here all summer long?"

Imre gave a nervous laugh, color rising quickly to her cheeks, making Bettina immediately regret her teasing tone.

"Sorry. That was crass of me."

"Not at all. My parents have a house here. I teach because I want to, not because I must, if that makes sense?"

"Perfectly."

Anxious to make amends, Bettina inquired about the promised loan of a costume. Imre brightened immediately and leaped to her feet, beckoning Bettina to follow her. Together they strolled back to the car. Keeping their eyes averted from each other, they crouched down behind it, shrugging off their clothes and pulling on the costumes. They laughed together, nervous but colluding in this shared act of adventure. Bettina turned to Imre, a sudden thrill of daring stirring in her.

"What do you say we give them a surprise?"

She jumped up and made a mad dash across the dust and pebbles. The soles of her feet felt like fire until they hit the jetty where the weathered wood was smooth. She laughed, then shouted as she galloped down the landing, past the watching men, their eyes wide in astonishment. She reached the end and held her breath as she jumped, wrapping her arms around her knees, then dropped deep like a stone, suddenly surrounded by a rush of bubbles that kissed her skin and cradled her. It was cold and dark as night down there, and silent, save for the distant sound of Imre's shout as she jumped, too. Bettina pushed back up toward the sun at the surface, breaking through and breathing in great gulps of air, blinded by the light flashing off the waves.

On the jetty Max watched them both, laughing as they bobbed back up, shivering and shrieking. They shook their wet heads, a great shower of droplets filling the air.

"Well look at that," said Richard. "She's found a friend."

Max leaned back on his elbows. "I'm glad to see it. God knows, she needs to let off steam."

"How's she bearing up?"

"Not well. It's all been fairly awful, truth be told. But I think that this will do her good. We needed to get right out of the city."

"Glad to help." Richard took a deep swig from his bottle and looked at Max. "And how have you been?"

"Worried sick."

"About Betti? Don't be. She can look after herself."

"She's not as tough as you might think."

"But maybe not as fragile as you fear."

They watched her as she climbed back onto the jetty and waved at them, her face aglow. She turned, arms out, preparing to dive back in. A vivid memory came to Max of the night they met, when she'd stood just so, poised for flight before the fire. It had burned into him like a sunspot.

He drained his beer. "I need to ask your advice."

"Much good may it do you."

"I think the time has come for us, for me and Bet, to leave

the country altogether. I know that you're determined to stick it out here and she has always felt the same, but it's become unbearable. When we found out she was pregnant it seemed better to stay, safer somehow. But now . . . well, you see how things are."

Richard paused for a moment, then asked hesitantly, "Have you given any thought to where you'd go? Only it might not be quite as straightforward as you imagine."

"You think that we ought to stay?"

Richard shook his head. "It's not that, it's just . . . I fear you may have left it far too late. It's all but impossible to get the right paperwork and from what I understand most countries in Europe have virtually closed their doors—they say they've filled their quotas. That's the bind—they want to make it intolerable for you to live here, but harder still to leave."

"What about America?"

"There's a belief that refugees would compete for jobs and overburden their resources. You'd need someone there to sponsor you. Besides, the passage costs a fortune. Have you any reserves?"

Max looked downcast. "Money is in short supply right now. I'm earning very little. My parents help when they can. They've been talking about leaving Austria, looking for someone to buy the business and their house, though my father still maintains it might all yet blow over."

"Well, if you can get together enough money for the passage and all the right paperwork, I would think you'd stand a decent chance. You just need to prepare for a long wait. I don't have to tell you, but Germany is not the only country to harbor ill will

against migrants of any stripe and Jewish migrants in particular. That particular brand of poison has no regard for borders."

"I see." Max sunk his fingers into his hair.

"I thought you knew," Richard said. "You both seemed so
determined to stick it out, despite it all."

"I suppose we both naively hoped things might improve, that
the world would come to its senses. I didn't want to believe it
could all get so bad."

Richard sighed deeply. "There's no herd of great white
horses to warn us when we pass the point of no return. Just the
long-drawn-out death of democracy. It seems that people will
swallow anything if you feed it to them piece by piece."

Max gave a shaky laugh. "You take a fairly dim view of
humanity."

"I'm afraid I do. There is no bottom to the well of man's
self-interest. As a species we can only maintain outrage for so
long and then . . . we just grow bored of it, move on and forget
that something ever gave us pause."

At the end of the jetty, the two women climbed out of the
water and lay down to dry themselves in the sun, their faces
turned away, their slick wet heads pressed close together. Pale
necks and shoulders lay exposed, an unmarked canvas, drops of
water marbled on their skin. They whispered conspiratorially
and laughed together. Max was glad to see Bettina in better
spirits, though he had hoped he'd be the one to lift them.

Richard knocked out a cigarette from the paper packet and
offered it to him. Max shook his head.

"What made you decide to stay?"

"It's so much easier for me," said Richard. "I don't attract anything like the scrutiny you do and I can fight back a little, from within; there are some pockets of resistance . . .”

He paused and picked a fleck of tobacco from his tongue. “You remember Libertas, the firebrand—you met her at Betti’s exhibition, years ago? She’s well connected in Berlin. She has friends who might help expedite the visa process for you, at a price.”

“There’s the rub.”

“Indeed. And I’m afraid Betti won’t be much help; her work will simply not sell. The tide has turned against any form of expressionism. Figurative art is the order of the day, we’re told. Heroic and ‘pure,’ all for the greater glory of the Reich . . .”

“She knows. It breaks her heart. Almost as much as losing the baby.”

Richard glanced away; he had no words for their fresh grief. Max rubbed a hand across his mouth.

“So, here we are then. Nothing to be done about it.”

“Don’t give up hope. I’ll see what I can do . . .”

“Thank you.”

“But I can’t promise any miracles.”

Richard reached out and squeezed Max’s shoulder, then stood and stretched, calling out to the two women, “Race you to the pontoon?”

He pulled off his shirt and shoes and then looked back at Max.

“You coming?”

“In a minute.”

Giggling, the women got a head start. Richard ran down the jetty, roaring out a warning of pursuit, and dove in after them.

Max sat in silence, watching as the three of them swam away. A strong breeze chopped up the once-still surface of the lake and raised the gooseflesh on his arms. Bettina reached the pontoon first and clambered out. Though she was quite a way off, he could still hear her shout of joy; she was triumphant. The wind carried it back to him, across the water.

He'd always thought of himself as an anchor to hold her steady, but what use was an anchor in the teeth of a storm? *It might just hold you down,* he thought. *Until you're dashed against the rocks.*

CHAPTER SEVEN

Putney, London

September 1993

As the sun set over Putney Heath its last rays suffused the sitting room in a peachy glow. Waiting for her daughter, Clara looked out on the street below. Since childhood she had enjoyed this view and the feeling of being high above the fray, able to see the bustle of humanity, but still remain removed from it. Her mother often said she'd chosen the white-fronted, Art Deco mansion block because it reminded her of apartment living in her native Germany. As a teenager, Clara had sneered at its concrete curves and resented the cold winds that whipped across the Heath, rattling the metal-framed windows. She'd longed for modernity and couldn't wait to escape.

She'd returned here reluctantly after her divorce, dropped into the foreign land of her new life. It surprised her that it felt like coming home. More than anything, it helped her appreciate how acutely alien London must have seemed to her mother when she'd first arrived.

From a distance, Clara spotted her daughter: long legs striding purposefully, a tangle of dark hair flowing out behind. Although Lotte had never lived at the flat full-time, she'd spent so much of her childhood with her beloved Oma, it was like a second home to her.

On hearing the long-anticipated clamor of the intercom, Clara hurried to buzz her daughter in. She opened the door and waited, until finally her only child appeared, headphones around her neck caught up in the waves of her hair, her cheeks flushed with the exertion of the climb. She had a rucksack slung over one shoulder and wore a large black turtleneck and scarf, which swamped her narrow frame.

"Hey, Mum."

Lotte leaned forward to kiss her while she levered the rucksack off and let it fall heavily to the floor. Clara wrapped her in her arms, as if she was still taller than her daughter, though Lotte had now far outgrown her. She squeezed her hard and wouldn't let her go, ignoring her daughter's gentle pats, which indicated she was ready for release. Eventually Lotte wriggled from her grasp, smiling and sighing.

"Enough!"

"I've missed you, little *Bärchen*."

"It's only been a few weeks," Lotte chided her gently. "But I missed you too."

"So, how's college?"

"Fine. Chaotic. You can imagine."

"I want to hear all about it."

Clara headed for the kitchen, turning back briefly. "Coffee?"

"Please."

She watched as her daughter bent to pick the rucksack up.

She had a ballerina's grace, though she'd barely danced a step, even as a child. So much natural elegance, yet she was always in her head, hardly conscious of her body: just a brain piloting an artist's hand and eye.

Clara began to fill the kettle as Lotte followed her into the kitchen.

"I still can't quite believe it's your final year."

"I know. I'm already knackered."

"Well, you can put your feet up this weekend."

"Did I tell you; I've started working on my statement of intent? Finally decided on the focus for my degree show . . ."

"So? Don't keep me in suspense!"

"It's going to be my response to Oma's paintings."

Clara looked at her in astonishment, then moved to her to wrap her in her arms again.

"Oh, darling, that's fantastic! She would have been so thrilled. Which ones?"

Lotte's brow wrinkled. "Not sure yet. Probably one of the early ones, I think."

"Well, you must have a proper look while you are here, though what I have is hardly representative. She sold a great many when I was young and left so much behind in Germany. You know, we came here with nothing . . ."

". . . nothing but a couple of cardboard suitcases and the clothes on our backs!" intoned Lotte, laughing. "You know, I think you might have mentioned that before."

Clara poured the coffee while Lotte looked around.

"Love the new cabinets."

"Oh, thank you, darling. I must admit I'm very pleased."

Lotte's father had told Clara he wanted a divorce mere months after Bettina's passing. Reeling from those twin blows, she'd moved into her mother's empty apartment as a temporary measure. That had been three years ago.

"It felt like it was time to make it more my own. Put my stamp on it. I might even redecorate the sitting room next."

"Don't you mean 'der Salon'?" Lotte asked, her eyes twinkling at the rather grand title her grandmother had conferred on the room.

"For a farm girl, your *Oma* was full of affectations." Clara smiled. "I'm not sure she would have approved of my changes, though it has been oddly therapeutic. I've been able to say goodbye to her in my own time."

Clara reached down under the counter and brought out a heavy wooden chopping board. "I was planning on making stroganoff, if that meets with your approval?"

Lotte narrowed her eyes. "Mushroom, I presume. Or did you forget that I'm a vegetarian now, Mother?"

"Of course I didn't!" she retorted, although of course she had. The bones of old contentions were never fully laid to rest.

"Mind if I put some music on?"

From the depths of her rucksack Lotte pulled out a wallet of CDs and a well-worn sketchbook.

"Go right ahead, my love."

She left the room and Clara called out after her, "Nothing too depressing, mind!"

It had become their established routine that Lotte put on her music and sketched while Clara cooked.

Moments later a spare riff of percussion echoed through the

flat. Lotte returned and sat back at the marble-topped island to begin her sketching. She was adding meticulous detail to an ink study of a silver birch. From the next room a resonant piano joined the looping drum, and then a pure, impassioned voice sailed in high above it all.

"Who's this?" asked Clara. "I quite like it. Less maudlin than the usual."

Lotte ignored the provocation and handed her mother the case.

"Talk Talk. *Colour of Spring.* It's quite old."

"Not by my standards."

The cover was an intricately detailed painting of butterflies and moths, each one seemingly layered with symbolism and coded meaning.

"Oma would have liked the artwork."

Lotte wrinkled her nose.

"Nah, she liked things messy. That's much too clean for her. I really like it though."

Clara chopped an onion into small even pieces, quickly and methodically. By the time she was Lotte's age she had taught herself to be a proficient cook, defining herself in opposition to her mother, who avoided doing anything so prosaic as cooking.

"While we're on the subject of Oma . . ." Clara began, "I think I may be a little closer to solving the mystery."

She kept an eye on her daughter, to watch how the statement would land. Lotte's head shot up; the puzzle of Clara's paternity was one of the few things she found more engrossing than her sketchbook.

"You found the figurine?"

"I did, by a fairly circuitous route."

"For God's sake, Mother, how did you keep that in so long? Tell me everything!"

Lotte had been instrumental in Clara's decision to start her quest. In the aftermath of her divorce and Bettina's death, facing middle age and menopause alone, Clara found herself adrift. She hadn't worked outside the home in years and had no clear idea of how to fill her days.

Lotte was making plans to start an art foundation course and encouraged her mother to start on something new herself: the search for her father's identity.

For Clara, discovering the letter to Bettina from her husband Karl had only left her with more questions. She began to share them with her daughter, looking for some common ground in the bombed-out battlefield of their family. She told Lotte about the brief conversation she'd had with her dying mother, about the Viking and the unknown man Bettina had referred to as "the porcelain maker of Dachau." It was Lotte who had taken the Viking figurine into college and showed it to the professor of ceramics. Lotte, who had returned with the news that though he didn't know the sculptor, he thought the Viking was a fine example of Allach porcelain made just outside Munich, near the town of Dachau. A factory owned and run by Nazis.

Clara had been shocked to learn of this, and yet acknowledged it all made perfect sense.

"Oma was born just outside Allach, so perhaps this porcelain maker lived nearby, in Dachau town? It could be a neighbor, maybe someone she grew up with."

Newly enthused, Clara had begun to fill her empty days with research trips. She started at Sir John Soane's Museum and moved on to other notable London porcelain collections, speaking to specialists at auction houses and beyond. Some were disturbed by the connection to the Third Reich, but over time she found a small number who agreed to help by keeping those pieces on their radar. They informed her that the Viking was a rarity, but Lotte would not let her be downhearted by the news.

"So that should be your focus next. It was the most important piece to Oma, in any case. Based on her painting, made for her, bought as a gift by Karl Holz. If you can find another one, then surely it must be worth chasing."

Months passed by and Clara all but gave up hope, until the call had finally come to say a small haul of Allach porcelain had been put up for auction in Cincinnati. Among the pieces, at last, a second Viking.

As she stirred the stroganoff, Clara described her American odyssey to Lotte in more detail, from discovering the shabby auction house to the excitement of bidding for the figurines. She told her how she'd stumbled across the photograph of Bettina in Ezra Adler's rooms. She handed it to her daughter, who was immediately enthralled. She pored over the inscription, dissecting all the details.

"This says Porzellanmanufaktur Allach, Dachau . . . I don't think that just means the town of Dachau, Mama."

"I don't either. Look at the uniforms under their white coats," Clara said, grim-faced. "Honestly, Lotte, I don't know where to turn to next. Or even if I should."

After dinner they moved through to the sitting room and both curled up in twin armchairs. Clara poured herself a third glass of wine; she couldn't help but notice her daughter had barely made a dent in her first.

"My choice of music this time," Clara announced, putting on *Harvest Moon*.

Lotte stood up and wandered over to the wide marble mantelpiece, scrutinizing the painting above it: broad and a deep blue-black, with flashes of putty pink, bright red and acid yellow, seeming to float beneath the surface.

"What's this one called?"

Clara frowned, reaching for an answer that she'd known her whole life.

"I think that one is *Mulde Flood*, 1931. They're mostly just places and dates from that period. It was her later paintings that got the more grandiose titles."

Lotte remained there, peering at it intently. Eventually she said, "I find it so incredible that she could paint like this and then just stop so suddenly. I don't think I could do it. I'd be compelled to keep going, even if it was just for me. Did she ever tell you what made her decide to stop?" She moved to sit back down.

Clara shook her head. "No, it is yet another mystery. One of the many subjects I just knew to be off-limits. She was indomitable—a force of nature. Nothing could shift her if she set her mind to something. You are like her in so many ways, though much, much more optimistic, thank goodness."

Clara took hold of her daughter's hand. "She changed when you were born; it was the first time I can honestly remember seeing her truly, wholly happy and content. It meant a lot to her, to get a second chance."

Lotte kissed her mother's hand, then tucked her knees up inside her capacious black sweater. Clara sipped her wine.

"I dreamed of her the other night. It brought back that whole awful time: learning about this, losing her, and then your father leaving . . ." She shuddered. "If only she had lived a little longer, but we didn't get that chance. Instead, I'm left with this strange sense of . . . bewilderment. I was so curiously incurious before we had that conversation. I never really felt like I was missing something, but being given those few clues . . . it made it all feel so unsettling. I don't really know what comes next."

"You keep on digging, surely? The photograph opens up so many more avenues to explore."

"But what lies at the end of them? Look at what we know already. She was married to an objectively terrible man who did something so bad it very nearly destroyed her. He was an avowed Nazi, and now there's this photograph of her with prisoners from a concentration camp. Maybe there's a damn good reason she kept the truth from me so long."

She felt a sudden wave of tiredness and reached for the bottle to pour out the last remnants of the wine.

"What if I found out something truly awful, something I just could not forgive her for? I'm not sure I can face the thought of losing any more."

The following morning, Clara woke to the sound of clattering from the kitchen. Lotte was already awake, making pancakes at the stove for the two of them.

"Morning, Mother. How's your head?" She pushed a bottle of paracetamol toward her. "Coffee coming up."

Clara took Lotte's customary seat, delighted by the reversal in their usual roles.

"So, pancakes first, with lemon and sugar, then what do you say we head out for a walk and find some fresh air? I don't have to get back for a few hours and I can't remember the last time we actually went for a walk on the Heath together."

This wild stretch of land, so close to the city, was overlain with memories for both of them, stacked up like sedimentary layers, waiting to be excavated. Childhood summers with Oma; first tastes of teenage freedom; winter walks in early adulthood. Clara remembered taking Lotte's father there on a summer's night in 1969. They'd spent hours watching the astronauts of Apollo 11 as they stepped out onto the very edge of existence. After the broadcast had finished, the pair of them felt a profound urge to search the night sky for themselves. They'd lain on a blanket under the stars and he'd proposed to her, setting them on their way: to Lotte and a lifetime together. Or so she'd thought.

As Clara stepped out into the autumn morning with their daughter some twenty-four years on, she couldn't help but reflect on it. *I was so careless with my joy back then, imagining that all of life would be made up of such shared adventures.*

She tucked her arm through her daughter's and reached up to stroke her curling hair.

"Oma always loved it here. I'd hoped to take her out the last time I saw her, but she didn't like having to use the wheelchair. If I'd known, I would have tried harder to persuade her. She died so soon after." She sighed. "If only there was some way to know something is final, so you can savor it. I have no memory of the last time I picked you up and carried you. I'd give almost anything to have you be that small, to feel your weight again."

Lotte groaned. "You're so bloody sentimental! You know that, right?"

"I do." She leaned her head on her daughter's shoulder as they walked on.

"She would have liked a little picnic, though." Lotte smiled as she pictured the scene. "A sliver of Sacher torte and a thermos of hot chocolate."

They walked on, listening to the lull of distant traffic overlaid with birdsong. Eventually, Lotte broke the silence.

"I've been thinking about what you said last night . . . that if you carry on, you're afraid of what you'll find?" She stopped and looked at her mother determinedly. "I get it, but I think you're wrong. Not knowing would be worse. That's where you are right now, all these dire possibilities playing on your mind."

Clara looked at her daughter nonplussed. *She's far more mature than I was at her age,* she realized. *This is her now; fully formed.*

Lotte continued. "I loved her too. In lots of ways, she made me who I am. I want to try to understand her, both as my grandmother and as an artist. I think it's all bound up together, don't you?"

Clara squeezed her daughter's arm, nodding gratefully. "I do. I really do."

"You dealt with an awful lot when you were growing up and you went through it on your own. Same since Oma died and Dad left. But you're not alone now—you have me.

"I want to help you, Mum. I can be Watson to your Holmes, Cagney to your Lacey. From here on in, let's both do this together."

The fallen leaves were thick beneath their feet. Over the pond, a lone swallow wheeled against the brilliant blue, its wings spread wide. They stopped and watched it soaring in the still air, diving down to skim the water.

Clara felt tears swim to her eyes, blurring her vision, almost overwhelmed by sentiment again. She held on tight to Lotte's arm. *There will come a day*, she thought, *when it will be our last one here together. Perhaps, on reflection, it might be better not to know it at the time.*

CHAPTER EIGHT

Berlin

Autumn 1937

Berlin woke to a thin haze. The sounds of the city were subdued, and steam rose in patches on the pavement where the sun broke through. Along the softened rooflines, rows of statues gazed down, seemingly benign. Beneath them hung banners of black, white and blood-red, the fabric damp and deadening.

By 9:05 a.m. most of the city was hard at work. Only a few lone stragglers scurried to their posts, past unhurried hausfraus heading to the shops. The news vendors could finally sit back on their single-legged stools, like a line of wading birds. Their headlines heralded Great Britain's erstwhile king and his twice-divorced bride, who were due to tour the city later that same day.

The street was almost silent, save for the trill of starlings, until a gaggle of young men in brown shirts came bowling through. They left a path of aggravation in their wake, jostling a news seller, tilting him on his stool like a plate spinner in the circus and knocking his hat and papers to the ground. A group of matronly women paused to admonish them, then went on their way, chattering like birds.

Das Romanische Café was filled with slanting shadows that slashed across the ground. Chairs and tables were laid in neat, straight lines so their clientele faced out across the street. They squinted up into the hazy sun and drank their *Milchkaffee,* nibbling at warm *Franzbrötchen*, which filled the air with the scent of cinnamon and butter.

Richard sat outside at a corner table, with a prime view across the broad boulevard. He had the paper spread out on the table in front of him, but he kept his eye on the brown-shirted boys as they barreled down the street, on the lookout for another victim. He took a coin from his pocket and flicked it so it rolled into their path, watching them tear after it like a pack of quarreling hyenas. The fastest boy got his foot on it, snatched it up, and took off, pursued by his companions.

Richard saw Max and Bettina approaching from a distance; they made a handsome couple, he in his dark-blue worsted suit and she in her small-brimmed hat and burgundy coat with its velvet collar, her cheeks flushed pink. They crossed Hardenbergstraße together, hands clasped tightly, looking for all the world as if they hadn't a care. Richard stood up as they approached and wrapped his solid arms around Bettina, then gripped Max tightly by the hand.

"By God, it's good to see you both."

"We haven't been here in an age," Bettina said. "I love this place."

A waiter bustled up.

"Hot chocolate, please."

"And another pot of coffee. Thank you."

Richard smiled at her as they sat down. "I always forget your sweet tooth."

"Deprived childhood. Still making up for lost time."

He folded up the paper to make more room at the table. Max took it from him, glancing at the photograph of the Duke and Duchess.

"That explains all the posturing from the Brownshirts. They're out in force today."

"So I saw—better keep your wits about you. Now, tell me, how have you both been?"

"Good." Bettina reached under the table and squeezed Max's hand. "At least, better than when we saw you at Wannsee in the summer. Much, much better, thank you."

"Well, I'm glad our day trip did the trick."

"How's Imre?" Bettina asked. "She promised she'd come up to town."

"She's starting work at a kindergarten in Charlottenburg next month. I'm sure she'd love to see you."

The waiter brought out their drinks and set them on the table. Richard waited till he'd gone and then leaned in, lowering his voice. "So, perhaps we ought to get down to business before this place fills up."

Bettina flashed a worried glance at the nearest table. A bosomy woman sat with a dachshund in her lap, feeding it crumbs of pastry. She caught her looking and turned away tutting, shielding the dog from view.

Richard laughed. "I don't think we need worry about rogue dachshunds just yet. It does serve us all to be a little cautious, though."

He lit a cigarette and drew it in deeply, narrowing his eyes against the smoke and slanting sunlight.

"I've spoken to a few people, well-connected friends, and they agree, it would be better for you to get out of Berlin entirely. You especially, Max. As much as anything, you two have been living together openly for years, which leaves you quite exposed. One of your neighbors could report you any day."

Max sighed. "The writing's on the wall at work, in any case. I have a sense it's only a matter of time before they let me go."

Richard flicked his ash onto the tiled floor. "I'm glad I don't have to convince you."

"If Max can't work, we can't afford to stay here anyway. We're barely making ends meet as it is."

"But where do we go?" Max asked. "You said in Wannsee there aren't all that many options."

"I still maintain it. Ideally you need to go right away: USA, Canada, South Africa . . . But refugees aren't exactly being welcomed in with open arms. And you'd need money for the passage, which I assume is still in short supply?"

Max looked down at the table and gave a slight, embarrassed nod.

Richard continued, "So it seems like our priority is to find you a place of relative safety, where you can work and start to put some money away, apply for visas and find out where will take you in."

He paused to see how his words had hit. Bettina appeared tense and agitated, Max more resigned to it all. Richard turned to him first.

"My brother, Peter, has offered to help. He's found you a job,

Max, and a small house to rent nearby. It's at a porcelain factory owned by the SS, so we'll need to get you a new identity—they won't employ you if they know you're Jewish. Can you get your picture taken?"

Max nodded.

"Good man. It's mostly laboring, I'm afraid. Heavy work."

"I don't mind that," said Max. "As long as we're together."

Richard frowned. "Well, therein lies the problem. It's just not a good idea for the two of you to keep on living in flagrante. But Peter and I came up with a possible solution . . ."

He flicked a nervous glance at Bettina.

"The factory is in the town of Allach, where my brother lives, just west of Munich. Betti's family live nearby . . ."

Bettina stared at him, the color draining from her cheeks. He jumped in, quick to quell her fears. "Now Betti, I know it's far from the perfect solution, but we don't have many options. They're family. They have to take you in and besides, it's only temporary."

"I hate them, Richard. And they hate me. You know that."

"I do."

"Albrecht is a Nazi and an anti-Semite, lest you should forget."

"And I wouldn't suggest it if I could come up with any other practical solution, but at least this way you'll be nearby. Most importantly, you'll both be safe, able to work and able to start saving all the money that you can. That has to take priority."

Max could feel Bettina trembling, but she straightened up and tried to brave it out.

"Of course. I see the sense in it. I don't mean to sound ungrateful."

She laid a hand on Max's arm. "If you can stand to do hard

labor, the least I can do is spend a few months under the same roof as my own flesh and blood, whatever I think of them."

"That's my girl," said Richard. "Well, that's settled then. As I see it, Allach is the best option that you have right now."

Max put out his hand, though he could feel his palms were sweating, and Richard clasped it tightly.

"It's a good plan and we thank you for it."

"Very well. I'll talk to Peter and make all the arrangements. He knows people who can get you a new identity and the relevant papers: an *Österreich Kennkarte* in a false name should do it. You'll need to leave as soon as possible and travel light, so see what you can sell. I'll borrow Imre's car and drive you down myself."

Two weeks later Richard arrived at the tenement on Kottbusser in the Adler Trumpf. Once it was dark, they loaded the car up with two small suitcases, as well as pans and plates, paintings, brushes, their portfolios and bedding. Everything else had been sold or given away in their haste to leave Berlin.

Since the morning at Das Romanische Café, Bettina had felt the spores of suspicion spread through all her interactions with their neighbors. In truth, she had never felt entirely understood by them, but though they did not share her interests, they did exchange some pleasantries each day. She had always felt part of their collective domesticity, but now she just felt anxious when she passed them in the hall, not only the adults, but the children too. She would fret for hours over a frown, worried that spite or boredom or some other petty grievance could be festering unseen. One wrong word could bring disaster to their door.

By the time the day to leave arrived, Bettina had half convinced herself they were all in imminent danger. Stealth would be the safest way to go and so they loaded the car and left without saying goodbye.

Less than an hour into the journey, the fear that had gripped her began to lift and silent tears started slipping down her cheeks. She missed their life already and felt ashamed that she had ever doubted the neighbors.

Richard drove them through the night, wanting to get a good start on a journey that would take a few days. He planned to stop in Dessau on the way, "To see if the old place has changed."

"Goodness only knows, the three of us have . . ." murmured Bettina.

The first hours of the journey were fairly tedious. The suspension was hard and the roads were washed with rain. Only a good stretch on the autobahn provided some relief. Bettina watched with delight as Max, who'd spent months modeling these very roads, truly relished their reality. He leaned out of the window, whooping as Richard put his foot down. Only her cries of anxiety could pull him back inside. His eyes shone for an hour afterward, which made it all worthwhile.

Still, they began to grow road weary after that with only the prospect of a stopover in Dessau to buoy them up. They had planned to revisit some old haunts, but on arrival there, it quickly became apparent that the city they'd left behind had changed. In front of the Town Hall, platoons of Nazi Youth were being drilled, making it almost unrecognizable. The drizzle, and the weight of the intervening years, settled heavily on the three of them, dampening their spirits. To Bettina, it seemed as if their golden summers must have happened somewhere else entirely. Even the modernist buildings looked shabby in the gloom, losing the unorthodox grandeur her youthful eyes once lent them. The following morning, they drove away in silence, all three wishing they had never come.

On the afternoon of the third day, they finally reached Allach, tired and travel sore. Richard drove straight to his brother's house, a tall building on the Munich road, surrounded by houses, factories and farms. It had been years since Bettina had last met Peter Amsel, but he had barely altered. His face was sculpted on the same lines as his younger brother's, though far more serious. He didn't have Richard's easy charm and wit, but they both shared the talent of giving others their full attention. It was apparent that Peter had thrown himself into the task of arranging things for Max, which gave her some relief. As well as finding him work, he had secured a small house and suggested that they walk the route together.

"I can show you the factory—it's on the way."

The plan was for Max to start work in Lindenstraße 8 the following Monday morning. Peter pointed to the white gabled building with its pitch roof, tucked behind a ragged picket fence. A square white chimney towered over it, belching smoke. Outside, in the yard, were trucks and wooden pallets, loaded high with sacks of minerals and coal.

"They produce high-quality porcelain," Peter explained. "Decorative statues, urns and the like. All madly popular with Nazi high command, who collect them. Himmler is obsessed with it, by all accounts, and uses them for propaganda. He owns shares."

Richard said, "See Betti, that's where you've been going

wrong. No more paintings; you should be making porcelain dolls for the Nazis instead."

"It's no joke," replied Peter. "They're planning on opening a second factory down the road at Dachau, at the SS training camp. It's a good thing, too—it means they're in need of laborers to stoke the kilns and shift the raw materials. Plenty of work, so you should be all right here if you keep your head down."

Bettina held tight to Max's hand. She imagined his long craftsman's fingers blistered from shoveling, lifting and carrying, his knuckles cracked and bloody. She made a conscious effort to expel the image from her mind.

Max surveyed the building and his prospects. "Porcelain doesn't sound too bad, all things considered. Takes me back to our ceramic lessons."

Richard gave a hollow laugh. "Albeit on a slightly larger scale."

The four of them moved on in silence, each one lost in thought.

Finally, they reached the house that Peter had rented for Max. When they climbed the stone steps, they found it clean and surprisingly comfortable. It was another huge relief for Bettina, who had been dreading the prospect of leaving Max in some squalid hovel. There were just a few small rooms and the furniture was sparse and plain, but it was functional and cozy: an armchair, a simple table, a little painted bookshelf and a washstand. The wood-paneled walls were weathered and in the corner of the kitchen, a little potbelly stove sat and emanated heat.

"We'll make it just like home," Bettina promised Max, with forced cheer. "And in the evenings, I will come and paint, and you can draw up your blueprints. We've got more to plan for now than ever."

Peter had filled the few cupboards with some basic supplies. The three men perched where they could, drinking beer, while Bettina cooked a stew of chicken and potatoes on the stove. The reality of their coming separation hovered over the proceedings. Bettina tried hard to keep her focus on the few remaining hours they had together, pushing away the thought of the time they would soon be forced to spend apart.

"Do you have that photograph?" Richard asked Max.

He dug into his wallet and presented the small black-and-white portrait, which Richard then carefully glued into place on a set of well-worn papers, the *Österreich Kennkarte*.

"We made some minor alterations and Imre's brother agreed to lend his name—you're Friedrich Marchen now, so mind you stay out of trouble."

"That shouldn't be a problem," said Max. "I don't intend to get into any."

"It often finds one anyway."

When it grew late, Richard and Peter bade them a farewell. Max and Bettina unpacked their bedding and made a nest of eiderdowns, which smelled of home. They crawled beneath them, too sad and weary to do more than fall asleep.

The following morning Richard returned for Bettina.

"You ready?" he inquired.

"Not in the least."

She forced a smile and kissed Max, then hoisted her small suitcase into her hand and walked briskly down the stone steps into the sunlight, which strained to shine between patches of thick fog.

*

On Monday morning, Max woke early and alone. He found that the first frosts had followed them south, so when he stepped out from the little house and exhaled, a wraithlike mist escaped. He was swaddled in a heavy greatcoat, gloves and a warm woolen scarf, although the Allach factory was only a short walk away. By the time he arrived at the gates, his fingers were numb and the tip of his nose was already turning pink.

The prospect of starting work had been filling him with dread, so it was a shock when he entered the building and found an atmosphere of calm creativity imbued with a sense of order. He was shown to the administrator's office and asked to wait. The building was awash with activity and noise: rattling typewriters and ringing telephones, the chatter of industry inside and out. Despite the cold, the heat from the kilns in the basement kept the building temperate, so Max removed his scarf and gloves and waited nervously. Men in dusty overalls walked past carrying clay urns lined up along planks, which they hoisted on their shoulders, somehow holding them perfectly steady, serene as swans cutting through the water.

"Please forgive the chaos."

Max turned at the sound of a low voice to see a man in his late thirties. He was tall, svelte and stiff, dressed in a well-pressed suit with a high collar and a pocket watch tucked neatly away.

"Holger Ostendorff," he said, extending a slender hand. He smiled warmly, wire-framed glasses perched owlishly on an aquiline nose.

"Friedrich Marchen," Max replied. Despite practice saying it out loud, the name he borrowed from Imre's brother still felt foreign to his tongue.

"Glad to have you here, Friedrich. As I say, excuse the chaos.

We're running at capacity and falling short on space. Too much success, if such a thing is possible. Shan't complain, though." His keen eyes twinkled. "Keeps us out of trouble. Now then, let me show you around."

At a brisk pace, Holger led him through the building, explaining the process room by room and the tasks performed by almost every worker. The factory was divided into areas, each of which had a separate character, defined by the tasks that happened there. Some spaces were, by necessity, dusty or dirty, some spattered with a drying sheen of slip and gobs of clay. Others were immaculate, as clean and polished as a surgeon's table, where razor-sharp blades were wielded with the same precision.

On one floor rows of spinning wheels stood and throwers shaped rounded bowls and urns, their strong hands dripping wet, coaxing form from lifeless lumps of clay. On the next, vast vats of glaze glistened, awaiting the bisque that would soon be submerged and spun by practiced hands, skimming the surface with its thin gloss skin.

There was a drafting room where new designs sprang from the mind and onto the page, while in the studio, sculptors carved the naked clay, shaving it into shape and honing all the detail. The final pieces were examined in the inspection room and destroyed if deemed unworthy. The last stop was the packing room, where one old man sat hunched like Rumpelstiltskin, squatting on a mound of straw. He gathered the flawless, finished pieces in his arms, then wrapped them in handfuls of sweet-smelling, golden grass, before stacking them up in wooden barrels.

As they toured the rooms, Max saw it all with an architect's eye, from the gabled roof with its tall, square chimney, to the furnace, hot as hell and choked with soot. Like a dollhouse, the building opened up before him in his mind and all made sense. Each part of the process required precision and artistry in equal measure and everyone understood their role. The procedures were methodical, the construction of each piece both fluid and repetitive, the seeming simplicity of every element belying the skill required.

At the end of their survey, Herr Ostendorff opened a door into a small, blue baize-lined room where examples of the finest Allach porcelain were displayed on open shelves. Throughout the factory there was a sea of noise; the metallic thud of machinery mixed with the grunts of men at work, but as the heavy door swung slowly shut, all external noise diminished, and a sense of quiet reverence settled over Max.

He found himself standing before a tall display case where, for the first time, he was able to closely examine these fabled porcelain figurines at first hand. There were human forms and animal, each wrought in quite exquisite detail. A bust gazed out with unseeing eyes. A pale cavalcade of Lilliputian soldiers filled half a shelf, along with urns and plates and candelabras. The cold china clay was pure white and, in places, as translucent as a petal.

Max had trained in ceramics at the Bauhaus, where simplicity, clean lines and a functional aesthetic were the order of the day. By comparison, the porcelain of Allach seemed almost kitschy and sentimental; far too pretty for his liking, though it was evident Holger cherished each and every piece. He cradled them adoringly, pointing out the finer details.

"Porcelain is such a miraculous substance. The constituent

parts start out so pliable, and yet are made impervious by the end. It simultaneously embodies strength and fragility: resistant to heat, to water, to rust, it has existed for thousands of years, although the precise method of making it eluded Westerners until relatively recently. The final product is pure white, undefiled, but to get there it must pass through a baptism of vitrifying heat. To me, there is no medium quite like it. Porcelain is art and alchemy in equal measure."

As he talked, Holger's eyes shone with such enthusiasm that Max found himself looking again at the figurines that lined the wall. They still seemed pallid and a little pompous, but the older man's excitement changed the lens; he understood the artistry and skill they required.

When they were done, Holger led Max back to his office. It overlooked the main yard and through the window Max could see half a dozen broad-backed men bent almost double as they helped unload a heavy cargo truck. Considering how refined the end product was, Max was struck by the contrast to the raw ingredients required: stacked pallets of kaolin, china clay and petuntse; of silica, quartz and feldspar. There were tons of coal to service the furnace, piled high alongside rotund pitch-pine barrels for slip and glaze and packaging. It was a dirty and demanding business and the process consumed as much human sweat and toil as minerals. Max looked down at his own uncallused palms until he noticed Herr Ostendorff observing him. He shoved both hands back deep inside his pockets.

"Have you done this kind of work before?"

Max shook his head, "Not exactly, but I'm a quick study, rest assured."

"What did you do previously?"

"I trained as an architect, but I learned the basics of ceramics as a student at the Bauhaus."

"Goodness! Really? It seems a shame to waste those skills, but I'm afraid we only have positions for manual labor, at the moment."

"I'm not afraid of hard work," Max said in haste.

"I don't doubt it."

The man's slight smile reassured him.

"Do you have your papers to hand?"

Max pulled out the *Österreich Kennkarte* that Richard had given him, willing his hands to remain steady. Herr Ostendorff took the documents and scrutinized them for a long moment. He put them back down.

"I see you're from Vienna—beautiful city."

He opened a large ledger on the desk in front of him and wrote the date and the name "Friedrich Marchen" in a florid, fluid script. He slid the papers back across the desk to Max, who went to pick them up, but found he had not relinquished his hold.

"Before you go, Friedrich . . . you understand that attention to detail is of the utmost importance in what we do?"

Max nodded and murmured his assent.

"Good. Then I'm sure it's just an oversight that the stamp on these doesn't correspond with the photograph."

Max felt the blood drain from his face. Holger let go of the papers and held up both hands.

"Perhaps it was damaged and needed to be replaced?"

Max nodded stiffly.

"Very good."

Max stuffed the *Kennkarte* back into his pocket.

"Thank you, Herr Ostendorff."

"Please, call me Holger." He smiled with absolute sincerity.

Max bobbed his head and hastened from the room. He made his way out to the yard, where the foreman directed him to join the queue of men behind the truck, where sacks of silica were still being offloaded. When his turn came, he braced himself but still gasped as the weight of it descended, knocking the breath from him and buckling his knees.

When Bettina first asked her mother's permission to return home, Marielein had grudgingly replied that she was welcome, she supposed, as long as she gave her brother the respect he deserved. Bettina had written back with a great show of remorse, explaining that she realized she'd fallen in with the wrong crowd in Berlin. She threw herself on her mother's mercy. How glad she would be, she said, to return to the familiar simplicity of the farm.

Bettina applied herself to fitting in. She was dutiful, helping in the kitchen and listening to Albrecht with his endless tales of woe, imagined slights and petty rivalries. In his eyes, the world was set against him—he worked hard where others failed; he had clarity of vision while everyone else was blind. He seemed to be thwarted at every turn, while others had luck they'd done nothing to deserve. The petty tyrant of her childhood years had grown into an angry, bitter and resentful adult.

Every evening played out in the same way. Albrecht would return home mean-spirited, ready to air the day's grievances at the dinner table—stories of an SS underling who'd gained some recognition that should, by rights, be his. Or the Bolshevik butcher who had swindled him and, in so doing, earned himself a beating. After a meal, Albrecht would set his boots on the table and drink yet more, while both women cleaned up around him. He would turn ever more maudlin as the night wore on, while Marielein stayed silent and kept a watchful eye on him. She monitored his state of inebriation until such a point that she deemed it safe to steer him off to bed, shushing him up the stairs.

Bettina felt the need to remain hypervigilant at all times in case Albrecht decided to turn his ire on her. She found it utterly exhausting and longed to escape to see Max, but feared raising their suspicions. She stayed at the farm for two weeks straight before deciding it was safe enough to venture out. Even then, she dared go only after dark, when the whole house was sleeping. She crept from the back door and pushed her bicycle until she reached the rutted road, before cycling off, with only a small battery lamp to light her way.

Max was often so tired he could do no more than doze while she read to him, or sketched, or stroked his hair. He tried to reassure her that the job itself was not so bad, though he was utterly exhausted by the stamina required. At least, he said, it afforded him the time to think and fully plan the house he'd build for them one day. It was coming into focus in his mind: an open space, clear of anything superfluous, where light and nature could encroach, where she could paint, and their children might play.

He resolved to stay cheerful in the face of all adversity, to work hard for Holger and prove himself indispensable. Bettina loved him for it, though it pained her heart to touch his cracked and toughened palms. The heavy sacks had left their scars already and a carapace of rough skin had formed, his body's bid for self-protection.

"I think I might be turning into a golem," he teased when she rubbed her fingers over the calluses.

She determined to buy him a salve for his hands and materials to sketch with, so he might preserve on paper the home he built for them in his imagination. She told Albrecht and Marielein that she needed to travel to Munich for art supplies and, with some bad grace, Albrecht agreed to take her to the station. He even gave her spending money, for which she thanked him, pocketing it quickly. She and Max could have lived off the amount for weeks in Berlin. Most of it would go toward their escape fund, but she decided she could afford to spend a little on more immediate rewards.

When the day came, she woke to the sound of rain hammering the roof, peppering it like hard nails driven into tin. Albrecht drove her to the station and then left her there, waiting on the platform while the rain fell in sheets. She shivered, holding her umbrella almost parallel to a wall of wind and water. When the train finally arrived, she climbed aboard and shook out her sodden coat. She rubbed at her shoes and stockings with a handkerchief and stared through the steamed-up, rain-washed windows, as the farms and factories flew by.

For weeks she had longed to escape the suffocating confines of her new world. A few short trips into Allach had brought home to her the risk she ran by coming back. So many people knew her and were excited at her reappearance; the prodigal daughter, returning to the fold. It made her ache for anonymity and yearn to lose herself in a city crowd.

As the train clattered through the outskirts of Munich, she thought about how she might spend her day. It had been years since she'd been to the city, despite studying there as a younger woman. She and Richard had forged their early friendship there, jointly plotting their escape to greater things—to Weimar and the Bauhaus. Munich had given them both a taste of freedom, which made them hungry for much more. Now, after she'd spent weeks in the backwater of Allach, the promise of a day in Munich felt like feasting after starvation.

Bettina realized that shopping for Max wouldn't take her long, leaving plenty of time at her own disposal before she needed to return. She would take lunch in a café and then, if she was able, feed her soul by visiting a gallery.

The prospect stirred a recollection; her mind was taken back to that scorching day in Berlin when she had wandered lost and then been jostled by the crowd. She realized that the "Degenerate Art" exhibition that *Der Stürmer* had reported on should still be on, and would be within easy reach of the station.

From her perspective, it promised to be a collection of some of the century's most exciting art, the work of her contemporaries and heroes, many of them Jewish artists, homosexuals or communists; expressionists, cubists, surrealists all. What the Nazis called degenerate she saw only as visionary.

As soon as the train pulled into München Hauptbahnhof she felt the scale of the city reassert itself. No one here cared who she was as she walked under the station clock, just another face in the morass of people passing through.

She headed first to Neuhauserstraße, which was teeming with people, despite the persistent rain. Huddled under their umbrellas, they dashed to and fro between the bright buildings—haberdashers, grocers and bookshops.

Bettina skipped from the shelter of one awning to another, dodging trams as she crossed the street. She stared into every shop window, hungry for the novelty, before finally descending into a narrow basement that she'd frequented since her adolescence. The scent of it always thrilled her: warm wood shavings, pungent paper, glue and acrid turpentine. The ceiling was low and tobacco-stained, piles of canvas stretched on frames leaned against each wall. Boxes filled with brittle sticks of charcoal and the endless possibility of pigments—gouache, ink and oil.

She focused first on Max: a sketchbook, a roll of tracing paper for schematics and a wooden set square. A new protractor and a scale, as well as a fresh box of watercolors and a soft, sable brush. It wasn't much, but it was enough for him to sketch their future out and transport himself away. She knew he would share her delight in the uncracked spine of a brand-new sketchbook.

For herself she picked up a few canvasses in different sizes, a few new oils, a simple sketchbook and a box of charcoal, though she still wasn't sure how to navigate her brother's critical assessment of her art. She left the packages to be wrapped and promised to return for them before the day was out.

When she reemerged onto the rain-washed street, she realized that she had no one else to answer to for the first time in weeks. She found herself walking north, feeling the push and pull of fear and curiosity. Without stopping to second-guess herself, she marched on, past the twin towers of the Frauenkirche, up through the Hofgarten, beside the fountains and formal flower beds, and on and on until she reached the high, hard walls that ran the length of the Galeriestraße.

She could see the banner from the end of the street. The words "*Entartete Kunst*" in jagged lettering. Free entrance, come one, come all. For months she had been trying to parse the meaning of the title: the "Exhibition of Degenerate Art." The thought of it consumed her and now, finally, she was here, standing outside the very building where it was housed. She knew that it was supposed to show how dangerous and disgusting modern art could be. How the "elite," the Jews and communists and intellectuals, had taken over the art world and remade it in their image: ugly and unskilled. She knew in theory it was propaganda, but could not understand how it would work in practice. Surely to anyone with eyes, these pieces would still speak for themselves.

The steel-gray sky sent down more rain, but still she lingered, afraid to cross the threshold. Then finally, she summoned up the courage to step inside. She was met immediately by a wall of noise and heat. A sheen of perspiration sprang to her face and chest. Dozens of people milled around her in the lobby, buffeting her as she slipped off her coat and wrapped it over her arm, like a shield. She moved into the first room cautiously, pressing through the crowd that bottlenecked at the entrance. Most people seemed to have come with one or two companions and they all had a lot to say; there was a constant murmur, like the hum of an engine, as people circled around the space.

The exhibition had been open now for many months, so she had expected to find it quiet and fairly empty. Instead, the gallery was full to bursting. The noise and the crowds stunned her and made her wonder why they'd come. Art as a cautionary tale didn't seem like an alluring prospect, and yet here they were, swarming through the warren of rooms.

As she watched the ebb and flow of the crowd it dawned on her that this was a form of voyeurism. Humans with an appetite for someone else's shame—they flock to gawp at executions, sniff at decay and stand in judgment of one another. These crowds were drawn by the salacious promise of immorality, and it seemed as if it didn't disappoint.

She understood this all objectively, though the reality had quite the opposite effect on her. Filled with prints and paintings that she'd longed to see for years, this was a Mecca for a modernist; images she'd only ever known in reproduction were here in living color. The reality was overwhelming.

If the works had been hung in a clean, calm space, it could have been magnificent. Instead, they had been thrown up on the walls in a haphazard and chaotic manner. Dozens of sculptures, each meant to be seen in isolation, were crammed together, jostling for space. They were made to provoke a primal response from the viewer, but with so many vying for attention all at once, it felt like being buffeted.

In the first room she saw the angular form of *Kruzifixus* by Gies—Christ on the cross, spiky and emaciated—it dominated the low-ceilinged space and made it claustrophobic. In the next room, a canvas by her beloved Wassily was hung at random, next to Klee, Chagall, then Dix and Dada. Many of the paintings and prints had been scribbled on with slurs. They hung unframed, askew; she longed to straighten and rearrange them, in a way that pleased the eye. And then she realized that was the idea: not just to show the work, but to show it here like this. To make its beauty ugly and discordant, like wearing a

hair shirt that itched and pricked and maddened her in increments. These rooms were not curated; this was art as bedlam,
meant to engender feelings of disgust.

At every turn, they pointed up the cost of the collection. She
knew enough about the business of art to see that the prices
had been falsified and inflated, so they could point the finger at
every institute that ever parted with the money of the German
people. Not only has this boil been allowed to fester, it proclaimed, but you paid a pretty pfennig for it, too.

Bettina walked through the center of the three small spaces,
cramped with people and crammed with art. In the first depic-
tions of Christ, in the second Jewish artists, as if the very fact
of their lineage lent all their work nefarious intent. The third
was full of sculpture and surrealism; the body and the brain,
especially the German woman shown as whore or hysteric, or
so the gallery proclaimed.

She moved slowly through the crowd, feeling exposed, as
if the expression on her face might give the game away and
show that she was here for love of art, not loathing. Would
anyone be able to tell the difference? She looked at the faces
around her. Some, like her own, seemed neutral and inscrutable, but many more were laughing openly, or had their lips
curled up in scorn.

She had supposed she might stay here and idle away an hour,
but instead she found she longed to leave. She caught brief
snatches of works she'd always yearned to see. There was *Drei
Klänge* by Kandinsky, in real and vivid color, not the grainy
image on the front page of *Der Stürmer*. She glanced at it as
she went past, not even stopping. The great press of humanity
swept her up and washed her out, depositing her on the street.

She turned her face up to the sky and felt the chill November drizzle. She walked on, numb and dazed. She thought of Stendahl the stonemason and his suffering in Florence; how its surfeit of beauty had induced a kind of vertigo in him. She left untouched by the celestial; this felt more like she'd been possessed, the mocking babble of the mob still ringing in her ears.

She walked in a daze until she found herself on Prinzregentenstraße, dwarfed by the vast, pale columns of the Haus der Deutschen Kunst. She decided to go in and escape the rain, unsure of what she'd find. This was the home of the Reich's official response to degenerate art, but it seemed the prospect of sanctioned Nazi art did not have quite the same draw. Only a handful of people toured its marble halls, even with the dreary weather.

Bettina sat down on the corner of a bench. She found herself in front of *The Four Elements*, a triptych by Ziegler. A fleshy quartet of white-skinned women standing pale against a blue background and a checkerboard floor; Fire, Water, Earth and Air. Four pairs of identical, wide-spaced breasts thrust upward from their chests. Bettina found herself wondering: Had Ziegler only ever seen one woman naked?

When she was young, she used to try to decode paintings, to unlock their secret meanings, like a puzzle. She did it now unconsciously, attempting to decipher the artist's true intentions. What did Ziegler want to say—that all women should be pallid and naked? No. More than that; they must be placid, passive and submissive. Demure, their fire contained and constrained. Fertile as the earth, pure as water, the pastoral idyllic.

It wasn't that it was bad, she thought, it was simply boring—technically adept, and yet still utterly uninspiring. The palette was washed-out and weak, so lacking in imagination that Air held . . . literally nothing. It was flat and bland, unseasoned. She saw in it an absence—not that it should not be done that way, only that it needn't. Mere likeness isn't truth, or even the best way to express it.

After a moment she stood up and walked back the way she'd come, for she had seen enough. The sound of her accelerating footsteps bounced off the marble walls; she realized she hadn't eaten and felt a vacant weakness in her core. She stepped out through the doors and on to the rainswept colonnade, which stretched away in both directions. She sheltered between two great white monoliths and breathed in the damp air, looking up at a mosaic of swastikas that arced across the ceiling, repeating and repeating.

She knew already that the day had somehow changed her, given her a clearer understanding of what they stood against. These people, who so despised all that she loved, who vilified the greatest teacher she had ever known, and looked on loving, gentle Max like nothing more than vermin.

They can't abide the world the way it really is, she thought. *They're scared of it: the ugly, naked truth of it. They'd rather feast their eyes on sugary confections and kick and scream and bend the world to their will. They're petulant, like children—here's what I think you ought to be, not who you are.*

There is no satiating that, she realized. The hollow at the center of it, that gaping, hungry maw. A fear of death and frailty so vast it might consume us all.

Several days passed before Bettina felt she could safely visit Max again. She fixed on the following Friday, guessing

Albrecht would spend the evening in the town tavern with his Schutzstaffel cohorts.

She had been right; he'd returned late and inebriated, struggling to kick off his boots and remain upright. He'd stumbled up the stairs, ricocheting off walls and clattering around his room until, at last, she heard him fall onto the mattress. As soon as the ragged drone of drunken snoring started, she knew the coast was clear.

The sky was cloudless when she slipped from the back door, having tiptoed past the ancient dogs, now only ever alert within their dreams. She fastened her package of supplies to the frame of her bike, then pushed it down the rutted, muddy lane, in case the rattle of the chain should alert them to her absence. The night was viscous as a pot of ink, a crust of frost already crystallizing on the ground. She set off and she didn't see a single soul on her journey, save for a tawny hare who stopped dead and stared when it heard her approach, then bolted as she passed it by, eyes reeling back in terror, its tail a flash of buff.

She arrived at the house in Allach and untied her load, ascending the stone steps, cheeks flushed by the frigid air and physical exertion. She peered through the window and saw Max asleep in the chair. She watched him, reaching out to hold the moment, touching her fingertips to the cold glass. Though he was upright, his body seemed perfectly relaxed; the sleeves of his once-white shirt were rolled up, his trousers and boots covered in a fine film of gray clay dust, his suspenders hanging at his waist. He'd lost some of his softness in these last few weeks and gained a wire frame of ligaments beneath the skin. His hair had grown out, too; it was tousled, falling across his eyes, curled and soft and brown.

She hesitated to wake him, but tapped gently on the glass. He stirred and stiffened, eyes anxious and alert, then saw her through the glass. He crossed to the door in three long strides and gathered her to him. She pressed her cold face deep into his chest, as solid and welcoming as the range when she returned from the fields as a child. She inhaled his warm scent of powdered clay, of bread and salt and ash.

"Aren't you a welcome sight?" he said, kissing the top of her head, his voice muffled by her hair.

He squeezed her to him tightly, then held her back to gaze at her, assessing all the changes. Grinning, she grasped his bicep in return.

"Look at you—my mighty Atlas!"

He flexed for her, a circus strongman. "You like?"

She laughed aloud. "I liked you as you were and I like you now; it's all the same. Shall I put the kettle on?"

"I'll do it. You come on in, get warm."

"Not just yet, for I come bearing gifts. Wait here . . ."

She dashed out to retrieve the brown paper package, which she handed to Max triumphantly.

"Go on, go on—open it."

He took a little bone-handled penknife out of his pocket and slit through the string and paper tape that held it shut. She stood by the fire, warming her frigid fingers.

"Albrecht gave me some spending money, bless his cold, dark, fetid heart."

Inside the package were the sketchbook and art supplies, each item potent with possibility. He exclaimed over them and moved to stand by her.

"How has he been?"

She grimaced but said, "I shan't complain, my love."

"Well, I won't give him my gratitude, but I do thank you." He opened the cover of the brand-new sketchbook and ran his fingers across its clean pages. "I have great plans for this."

"Our dream house?" She smiled. She loved to hear him describing his refinements. "I cannot wait to see."

"It keeps me going, truth be told." He put the sketchbook down and filled two cups with strong black tea from the pot. They sat at the table together, their fingers entwined, as if they must maintain the contact while they could, even just the merest brush of skin on skin. They began to talk, to fill each other in on the minutiae of the days they'd spent apart: the food they'd had, the little things they'd heard or read and stored away to share. For the most part, Bettina let Max unburden himself from the weight of his work.

"It's not that it's hard, it's the monotony that gets to me. If you slip up, you risk injury, so you have to concentrate and that means you can't ever lose yourself entirely. And though it pains me to admit it, I am weaker than the others and they aren't especially forgiving."

Bettina stroked his arm.

"They're not all bad, though," he reassured her. "The artistic director is kind and decent. A lover of the Bauhaus, though he generally keeps that quiet. He has promised to look at my sketches and see if there's any work for me as a draftsman—it would pay more than laboring and I'd be less likely to injure myself irreparably."

He lifted a wooden box stashed under the table and opened it. "I've been pocketing these to show you . . ."

The box was filled with an arbitrary collection of porcelain

pieces, some with cracks, others with fractured features or missing limbs. There was a pretty fawn, its long legs warped and
melted, turned to a glassy puddle underneath. A shepherdess
with half her features blackened. A cherub's arm, the product
of a steam explosion, which looked like a marble relic that
should be resting on a velvet pillow.

Bettina picked up a little whippet, the underside discolored
by a crackled glaze. "Poor thing."

Max mimicked its hangdog expression, making her laugh.

"My God, they're terribly sentimental!"

"Aren't they?" he agreed. "They're meticulously crafted,
there's no doubt of that, but so often the subjects are just sterile
and insipid."

"Are they all like this?"

"Pretty much. A very few are painted, but most are plain
white porcelain. There are plates and busts, all manner of figurines. The craftsmanship is so skilled, but there's something
about them that is . . . gelid. Soulless, even."

Bettina nodded. "Like all the art the fascists seem to favor.
When I was in Munich, I went to see the exhibition of so-
called Great German Art, and it's just the same; everything's
so utterly cloying."

"So absurd, it almost becomes surreal."

Bettina grinned. "I thought exactly that!"

A tension she hadn't been aware of began to dissipate. That
sense of reconnection took a while, but always returned.

"Funny you should bring this up, but I've actually spent the
last few days thinking how I can help us make money so we
can pay our way out of this bloody mess before it breaks you."

She stopped, afraid in case he thought her silly.

"Go on," he encouraged.

"Well, don't laugh, but what would you say if I told you I've decided to try my hand at being a Great German Artist!"

He looked bemused and so she rushed on, trying to explain herself.

"Madness on the face of it, I know, but wait, there's method to it. Wassily used to praise me for my figurative work. He always said you need your foundations to be strong before you can truly embrace abstraction. It was so often the starting point for me, but what if it was an end instead?"

"Go on."

Max leaned back in his chair, listening attentively. She continued: "We've established that this regime wants their art to be classically beautiful and utterly banal; well, I can do that. In fact, I know I can do more. I can certainly do better than half the charlatans filling the walls of the Haus der Deutschen Kunst with their puerile nonsense. I can paint their pretty puppies and monumental heroes; landscapes, seascapes, you name it. I could do it all, and so much better, in my sleep!"

"A poacher turned gamekeeper, you mean?"

"Exactly so! Or maybe an expressionist wolf in representational sheep's clothing."

"But to what end?"

"To sell, of course. I can't even give my recent work away, but I'm certain there's a decent market for romantic realism. I still know people in the Munich art world; my old tutors might help. Perhaps I can reinvent myself." Her eyes shone. "I've felt so dreadfully impotent watching you sacrifice yourself, but if I could sell some work too, imagine the months we might save. If we got lucky, got a visa, we might be able to afford to buy our passage overseas. To escape to anywhere that will have us."

"And what about your family?"

"They can go and hang as far as I'm concerned. I don't plan on telling them. But what of yours?"

"I heard from my mother last week. She is desperately trying to persuade Father to sell up and leave Vienna, but it's not an easy task. He's afraid to lose it all and have to start again. He doesn't want to abandon his life's work and I can't say I blame him, but I fear for them, Bet. I really do."

"Perhaps if we go, it will encourage them to come and join us? I will paint night and day to make as much as I can, as quickly as is possible. Oh, what do you think, Max; is it utter madness?"

He reached out and gripped her hand.

"I think it's brilliant—subversive even."

"Isn't it? I do think Wassily would approve."

"But can you bear to do it?"

"Of course! I'll feel so much better if I can only do my part." She clasped his hand, her gray eyes glittering in the low light. "So, what do you say, Max Ehrlich . . . be my muse once more?"

"Always. With great pleasure."

He laughed, then saw the expectation on her face. "What . . . now?"

"Why not?"

She jumped up, sparking with energy as she set out a canvas from the package. She stood him in front of her and stripped him naked to the waist, moving his limbs into place and positioning his head.

"You're a mythological hero, staring out to sea, about to face down a raging storm!"

She started sketching straight away, with an intensity she hadn't felt in months. He was always her favorite subject, his long, loose limbs and the sharp lines of his face. As she drew, the slogans scrawled on the gallery walls kept coming unbidden to her mind. Here he was, the "revelation of the Jewish racial soul," less than nothing to them and more than anything to her.

She worked fast and realized she couldn't entirely keep her nature from her hand. She felt compelled to be expressionist, to capture his essence and his frailties, the imperfections that made him even more beautiful to her. She decided she would allow herself just this one last time. The painting would be the inverse of her usual approach, expressionist first, then representational. The man, before the mythic.

Hours passed as she worked with ferocity. Eventually, she stood back and saw before her the man she loved—flawed and perfectly imperfect, both real and imagined. And there, at his heel, she sketched herself in rabbit form with eight quick strokes; she crouched beside him, facing the storm together.

Still lost in a meditative state, he came to her side and laid his arm loosely across her shoulders. She turned into him and ran her fingers down his spine, like charcoal on canvas, marking her intention. Her thumb traced the unfamiliar cord of muscle there, and a shiver passed between them, electric, like a charge. Both were now wide awake again, their blood alive and humming in their veins. Wordlessly they moved to the stairs and stumbled for the bed, where they fell together in haste, half dressed. Their mouths met and merged, melting in a white heat that should, by rights, have burned them both entirely. Skin glazed; their fingers fused.

Afterward, they lay against the sheets, their skin cooling. Bettina's shoulders ached and she longed to sleep, but knew that she must rise. She had to be back at the farm long before the sun came up, and with it her mother and a fractious Albrecht, doubtless nursing quite a hangover. She thought about the canvas drying downstairs, found the prospect of painting over it unbearable. But however hard, she knew she'd do it anyway. She'd sacrifice it all for him.

CHAPTER NINE

London

October 1993

Autumn settled quickly over London and the Heath was soon carpeted by a leathery mulch of fallen leaves in cinnamon and russet. The whole city reverberated in the aftershock of bombs on both sides of the Irish Sea and Clara found herself walking as much as she could, reluctant to be corralled into busy, public spaces.

While her daughter dug into the art history books in her college library, Clara drifted in and out of antiquarian booksellers on Charing Cross Road. She pored over microfiche in the British Library, searching out articles on military antiquities and the arts in Nazi Germany, trying to find anything on Porzellanmanufaktur Allach, Dachau, though she seemed to come up empty every time.

On one rainy afternoon Clara and Lotte examined everything Bettina had left behind: the larger, framed paintings, some watercolors, four small oils on hardboard and a half-dozen sketchbooks. There was little else that survived from her German days: some frayed and tattered architectural schematics and a few old books, densely annotated in the margins.

Lotte chose to focus on the picture in the sitting room: *Mulde Flood*, 1931. She discovered Bettina had painted it in Dessau, the second of the Bauhaus schools she studied at. She had been twenty-five years old at the time. Both women worked together to create a timeline of Bettina's life up to that point: born in Allach, Germany, on January 23, 1906, the youngest child of Marielein and Kurt Vogel. Bettina began art school in Munich at the age of seventeen, then moved on to the Bauhaus, first in Weimar, then in Dessau and finally, Berlin. Lotte spent hours in the college library and even found a few brief footnotes on her *Oma* in a heavy publication on the life and work of Wassily Kandinsky.

While Lotte's focus was on art, Clara decided to concentrate on the provenance of both the porcelain and the photograph. On one lone foray to the Imperial War Museum, she spent hours reading through harrowing testimonies from prisoners of the Dachau concentration camp. She became so overcome, she sought out the quiet of the ladies toilets to blow her nose and recompose herself. She got talking to a woman there, who noticed her distress, and Clara found herself spilling out the whole story. The woman listened sympathetically and handed her a pack of tissues. She introduced herself as Catherine—a librarian at the museum. She was, she said, entirely familiar with that sense of impotent despair.

"I'd be more worried about anyone who didn't find it overwhelming."

Catherine asked if she'd ever visited the Wiener Holocaust

Library in central London—a friend of hers worked there as an archivist. Jacob Cohen had been sifting through records on the Holocaust for the best part of a decade.

"If anyone can find a trace of the men in your photograph, or of this porcelain factory, then I'd put my money on Jacob."

Clara explained she didn't want to presume on anybody's kindness. She had so little to go on and no way of knowing how any of it connected, but Catherine insisted on taking her number and all the details that she had so far.

"We can but try. If there is something to be found, then he's the man to look for it."

Two weeks later, Clara rode her bike through the streets of Marylebone and chained it to the railings outside No. 4 Devonshire Street, home of the Wiener Library. Jacob Cohen had telephoned the day before and asked if she could meet him there at 4 p.m. The afternoon was bright and clear, so she chose to ride, passing by tall Edwardian terraces, through long shadows and over fallen leaves. She felt excitement and a little trepidation; he must have found something, surely, or why else would he ask to meet?

She walked up the steps and pressed the intercom button. The receptionist told her to come to the first floor and buzzed her in.

Inside, the entrance hall was tired, with worn linoleum underfoot and wooden cupboards crammed with files of cuttings. The ticking of a lone grandfather clock filled the quiet space. Clara stepped into the old-fashioned lift and stood as it rattled upward.

The Reading Room was busier than she'd imagined; she had expected quiet solemnity, but this was curiously energetic. At the inquiry desk a young woman was simultaneously speaking

on the telephone while handing a stack of pamphlets to a student. The walls of the room were shelved from floor to stuccoed
ceiling, lined with what looked to be thousands of books. Every
space had been utilized; even the fireplace had a card catalog set
in. A handful of people were sitting at tables, reading through
paperwork and taking notes, their German-English dictio-
naries close at hand. A librarian scurried up a ladder with great
assurance.

Clara felt a hand on her arm and turned to see a wiry man
with short silver hair and a manila folder clutched tightly to his
chest. There was a brief moment of awkwardness; then they
both began to speak at once.

Jacob demurred, "No, please, do go ahead." His English
flawless but with a slight, soft German accent.

"I just really wanted to say thank you for agreeing to help me."

"Think nothing of it."

He led her to the far end of the room, where they might sit
and talk quietly, undisturbed. Clara gazed around, astonished
by the sheer weight of paper contained within.

"We suffer from a chronic shortage of space," Jacob explained.
"Perhaps not so surprising, given that we hold almost a million
items relating to the Shoah and the war."

He caught her questioning look.

"English-speaking countries tend to use the word Holocaust,
from the Greek, for sacrifice by fire, but Shoah is the Hebrew
term. It means 'catastrophe.' "

"I had no idea this library even existed."

"We celebrate our sixtieth anniversary this year, though it
is an annually occurring miracle that we can pay the bills." He

gave a rueful grin. "Now, to your inquiry. Did you bring the photograph with you?"

She took it from her handbag.

"Catherine sent a fax, but I couldn't make out the detail."

He flipped it over and read the inscription.

"Porzellanmanufaktur Allach, Dachau 1941 . . ."

Clara pointed to Bettina at the center of the photograph. "That's my mother. She grew up on the outskirts of the town of Allach."

"Well, there was indeed a porcelain factory in Allach, built in 1935, but I don't think this photograph was taken there."

Jacob opened up the slim folder.

"The Allach factory was founded by three artists, all members of the SS. Their stated aim was to manufacture porcelain 'to the glory of the party' that could rival Meissen. Not surprising then that the SS acquired an interest early on and eventually took over the entire operation."

He pulled out a second photograph, which showed Adolf Hitler bent over a collection of baroque figurines, his face lit up in rapt delight. Close by stood a man with glasses, receding hair and a weak chin.

"Heinrich Himmler, leader of the SS and an early investor in Allach porcelain," Jacob explained. "He understood the cultural impact artifacts could have; he wanted to use art to create a mythology about German national identity. The porcelain factory was a means to that end. Some items might cement new traditions, like porcelain lanterns for the solstice, while others would celebrate the expansion of the Reich. After the Anschluss with Austria, for example, Himmler vowed that Allach would set 'a million porcelain soldiers on the march' and place them into every home."

"And did they?" asked Clara.

"They did indeed. A gift of Allach porcelain became the highest honor for the party faithful. German citizens bought them too; it was a way to show loyalty, particularly once the war was underway."

Jacob continued, "The brand was so successful, they expanded operations and built a second, larger factory in the grounds of the SS training camp at Dachau. But the war began to pose a problem: too many skilled workers were being sent off to the front. They had to find a new source of labor."

Another photograph, one she recognized from her forays at the Imperial War Museum. It was an aerial in black-and-white, taken from a military plane. Below were dozens upon dozens of buildings, like the neat lines of a factory farm.

"*Konzentrationslager,* or KZ, Dachau was Germany's first concentration camp, built in 1933. It was a testing ground of sorts; Himmler trialed many inhumane forms of treatment here, including the practice of using prisoners as forced labor. During the course of the war over 14 million people were pressed into service in the *Arbeitslager*—the labor camps."

Clara hesitated to interrupt, but felt a desperate need to know. "So, you think this photograph of my mother was taken at Dachau concentration camp?"

"KZ Dachau spawned nearly 100 subcamps, many of them *Arbeitslager*. They specialized in armaments, engines and other types of heavy manufacturing." He tapped the photograph. "I'm certain this is one of them. Porzellanmanufaktur Allach was built at Dachau in the SS training grounds, close enough to bring prisoners in from the main camp. As time went on, the premises expanded and they built on-site accommodation for the laborers, converting contaminated stable blocks into barracks."

Clara frowned. "I knew that BMW used prisoners to build their engines, but I had no idea of the scale of it."

"You're not alone in that. For myself, I think the labor camps legitimized the whole process for the public. They gave it a veneer of predetermination, which made it easier to ignore. When you blame a portion of society for all ills and then press those individuals into servitude, you create a permission structure for the entire process: their next step was then to take these people they had declared subhuman—the *Untermensch*—and attempt to eradicate them all entirely."

In the warmth and safety of a London library, Clara felt far removed from such a chilling reality, and yet she understood they were surrounded by it. On every shelf and alcove, in the anodyne, dry details, in words on paper; black and white. These walls contained the lives and deaths of millions of people, perhaps even her own father. Clara felt a shiver run through her. *What was my mother doing there?* She knew that was one question Jacob couldn't answer.

"Were you able to find out anything about Ezra Adler and the other men in the photograph—Max and Holger?"

"I think the tall figure in the tailored suit might be Holger Ostendorff, one of Allach's artistic directors. Which makes Ezra Adler this man here, on the far left, at least according to the inscription . . ."

She looked more closely at the two men standing at Bettina's side. Ezra Adler was heavy-browed and stocky. The man beside him, who by a process of elimination must be Max, was broad-shouldered and athletic. Both had shorn heads and clay dust on their hands. They wore white coats: sculptor's smocks with pencils in their pockets, but still clearly visible underneath, the striped ticking uniform of the Dachau concentration camp.

Jacob took out a sheet of slippery fax paper, printed with another grainy image. The central figure in the photograph was recognizably Ezra Adler, in younger, more contented days.

"It seems like Herr Adler was a very accomplished man, a professor of art history in Krakow. One of over 180 academics from across Poland who were deported to Germany in 1939. I have been speaking to a contact at the Jagiellonian University and they very kindly sent this copy of his faculty portrait from 1935."

There was a formality about the man's pose: he looked the very picture of an intellectual.

"After the invasion, occupying German forces were intent on destroying any sense of Polish national identity. Cultural dissidents, such as Herr Professor, were dispatched to the camps in haste. He was sent along with his wife, Zofia, and their daughters"—he referred to his notes—"two-year-old Amelie and Hanna, aged three months."

Clara scoured the portrait of Professor Adler for a clue about the man. He seemed to possess a certain joviality: strong laughter lines around the eyes. She remembered the other photograph on the wall in his apartment. He had been bouncing a doll-like child on his knee. Could that have been Amelie or Hanna? It seemed entirely possible. She pictured this family gathered around him like ghosts. If Ezra Adler was her father, then perhaps Hanna and Amelie could be her sisters. She'd been so intent on her paternity; it had never occurred that she might have more extended family somewhere out there in the world.

"Do you know what happened to them?"

"Only that the entire family were sent to the camp at Sachsenhausen, just outside Berlin. They arrived there together in 1940."

"And after that?" asked Clara.

"There are several documents relating to Professor Adler's transfer less than a year later. The authorities at Porzellanmanufaktur Allach put out a call to the other camps, seeking prisoners who might have the requisite skills the factory needed. He would have been given no choice, forced to leave Zofia, Amelie and Hanna behind. I'm afraid there are no further records of the three of them after that."

Clara tried to picture Lotte at the age of two: sticky cheeks and stocky legs, still clumsy and stumbling, parroting everything she saw and heard. What would have become of her if she'd been taken from her home and dropped into the very depths of hell?

"Ezra Adler was liberated from Dachau in 1945, on the same day as Hitler took his own life in a bunker in Berlin. Herr Professor emigrated to America not long after, but you already know that part of the story."

He looked at his watch. "The library shuts soon, but I can tell you a little more about these subcamps, if you have time?"

"Thank you, I'd like that." She laughed though she didn't think it funny. "Sorry; the word 'like' hardly fits the bill."

"I am never more aware of the deficiencies of language than when dealing with this subject," said Jacob. "I should state at the outset that even with all these resources on hand, I am by no means a specialist, but I can give you an overview, in general terms."

Clara nodded.

"So, though initially built for some 6,000 prisoners, the subcamps ended up with more than 22,000 inmates at various points: Jewish prisoners, homosexuals, dissidents. There were twenty-three different nationalities represented, including the Roma and Sinti, and later many Russian soldiers."

He handed her a long list of figures relating to the different categories and nationalities of prisoners. Clara stared at it all uncomprehendingly: unimaginable suffering converted to the language of the ledger.

"This was a labor camp, but as you might imagine, even highly skilled workers were still seen as entirely disposable. The Comité International de Dachau notes there were two gallows on site: one fixed and one mobile. Seen in that light, as I think it should be, the purpose of Porzellanmanufaktur Allach was never just to produce porcelain—it was there to indoctrinate the masses and it was part of a concerted effort to brutalize the occupants."

He placed the sheets back in the manila folder. Clara rubbed her temples to ward off the headache she felt building.

"Perhaps we should leave it there for now. I have given you a lot to digest."

Clara sighed.

"I'm trying to work out what I do next—what my part in all this might be, or if there even is one. What right have I to presume I deserve any answers?"

"In the aftermath so many survivors of the Shoah wanted to live the rest of the life they had and to forget. Who can blame them? But it means that we, their children and grandchildren, must do the difficult work of finding out their histories, of keeping that alive. It is essential, I would argue. If we fail to understand and share this learning, then we're dooming future generations to repeat the same mistakes."

"I suppose that's why I'm here. For the sake of my daughter, as much as me."

She shook his hand.

"Thank you, Jacob. I'm absolutely certain I would not have been able to find my way through any of this on my own. My German is far too rusty, for one thing."

"I'm glad to be of help." He paused. "My maternal grandfather died at Mauthausen and I promised my mother I'd work to keep his memory alive. This is more than a job for me; I consider it my duty, my *achrayut*."

Outside the frigid air was now a deep and sonorous blue.

"So what will you do next?" asked Jacob.

Clara laughed a little shakily. "I've been asking myself the same thing. I think, perhaps, I need to go and see it for myself."

Jacob nodded.

"I understand that impulse. The main camp at Dachau is open to visitors and the archivists there might be able to help you to continue on your quest, but I'm afraid Porzellanmanufaktur Allach itself no longer exists. It has, for all intents and purposes, been wiped from the face of the earth."

CHAPTER TEN

Allach

Winter 1937

The snow had been falling steadily over the town of Allach for a week. A crisp cover of white redefining the landscape and softening its edges, deadening the sounds. This stifled world seemed to amplify the senses: the soft gray sky was overbright and the crunch of footsteps on the snow crust disproportionately loud.

For a few hours, the factory had looked like porcelain itself—a gabled ceramic lantern, with warm light seeping from the windows—but then they'd stoked the kilns and the smut from the square chimney had burned through the snow, turning it a grainy, blackish gray. Thin rain began to mist the air and in a few short hours, the swan-white down on the roof had cracked and melted. Mud churned up and the roads and pavements were soon awash with a coat of greasy slush that soaked you to the skin, then chilled you to your core.

Max's job was to help clear the main yard each morning,

along with three young local lads who'd started work the week before. It was a task so Sisyphean that they'd built a towering facade of blackened snow against the perimeter fence, which threatened to slide back and devour them like a slurry tip.

At first Max had struggled to keep up with the younger men, but his body steadily adjusted and he found a strength he hadn't thought he could possess. The cold was the worst of it; the physical effort of digging made them sweat, but they would soon lose all feeling in their feet and fingers if they stopped. The other men would shove their hands into their armpits and down their trousers to try to keep them warm. During breaks they'd smoke and joke around, jostling each other, but with Max, they kept their distance; his soft voice and Viennese accent marked him an outsider.

Max was grateful then, when word was sent that Holger wanted him to assist in loading up the next consignment. A huge order of commemorative plates needed to be packed with straw into barrels. The chance to work inside was welcome, though the younger men greeted the news with undisguised disgust. The youngest, a piggish, angry boy named Uwe, complained to the foreman that the *Österreicher*, Friedrich Marchen, had not yet paid his dues. The foreman was disinterested; he shrugged and barked at the boy to get back to it—if that's what Herr Direktor wanted, then so be it.

In the dry nest of the packing room, the old man working there explained that Ostendorff had told him he was a trained architect and so ought to be good at maximizing space. Max found he relished the new challenge, as well as the warmth. On the third day, Herr Direktor himself dropped by.

"How are you settling in?" he inquired.

"Well, thank you."

The genteel man leaned against the doorframe, polishing his glasses.

"Well don't get too comfortable; I believe we may have need of your technical drawing skills after all. We're a little shorthanded in that department. Do you think you could manage that?"

Max beamed in delight.

"I do. Thank you, Herr Direktor."

"Please, call me Holger, by all means."

And so Max found himself at the drafting table, measuring and reproducing on paper the fine details and precise dimensions of the sculptor's work. Holger was a frequent visitor to the room, overseeing every stage of the design process. He would often stop by Max's drawing desk and chat with him, asking him about life in Vienna or his experience at the Bauhaus. Holger seemed fascinated to learn that students had been trained in so many varied disciplines.

"I adore the idea that creativity is given such free rein. Music, sculpting, architecture: they're all forms of play at heart. You get the best results if you approach each with a sense of childlike possibility."

Though he had dedicated his life to porcelain, Holger's most avowed love was for opera, upon which he rhapsodized at length. He seemed delighted to have found a fellow aesthete in Max.

"Come by my office later if you like? I have a wonderful recording of Toscanini at the Salzburg Festival."

When work was done, Max had cautiously knocked on the office door and been ushered in warmly. They spent an hour

listening to Mozart as the light outside dimmed, Holger's stee-
pled fingers pressed against his chin, his eyes alight. It seemed
to Max like he had found a friend and a refuge at long last.

"Mozart makes me miss home," he admitted. "For reasons
which now seem redundant, I felt a desperate need to escape
when I was young. Weimar offered so many possibilities. Now
I feel so nostalgic for Vienna, for home, for my parents who are
still there; I hope I can go back one day."

"I recognize the sentiment. It's a journey we all take. With
the distance of a decade or two, everywhere looks different."

Behind the facade of dignified respectability, Holger had
a huge sense of fun but few friends in this small town, Max
discovered. He privately balked at the changes being wrought
around him and was ardent in his admiration of expressionism
and experimentation. "I don't understand this feting of the
classical. The Greeks were trying their damnedest to push the
whole world forward. If you want to build an empire, why
make it in the image of an earlier one? Embrace innovation,
don't try to crush it under heel."

Over the weeks, the two of them fell into the habit of staying back in the early evenings, talking or playing chess while
darkness swallowed up the world outside. They'd sit together,
Holger smoking and playing opera on the gramophone, while
Max listened and sipped a hot, sweet herbal tea. Afterward he
would walk back to his rented house sore and weary from the
day, with nothing but the stars to light his way.

Bettina came as often as she could, to sit with him and
massage the knots from his back where he'd been bent over
a drawing desk for hours on end. Together they would count
their growing pot of savings, trying to plan their passage

somewhere, anywhere, away. She excitedly told Max she hoped she might soon have something tangible to contribute.

"I've nearly finished with *The Viking* and I must say, he does look rather dashing. I've started on some smaller canvasses—sketches of farm life. The geese in the yard, the winter fields, that sort of thing. All perfectly bland and pleasant. In a few weeks I should have a decent portfolio, so I've written to an old tutor, to ask if he can make some introductions in Munich. Mother and Albrecht seem delighted by my change of heart. Albrecht's all but praising me; I've never known him be so nice. Perhaps he sees it as reflecting well on him, helping his position."

"And if he knew your intention was to raise enough money to run off with your lover?" Max asked teasingly. Bettina blanched.

"Don't joke. He's a creature of pure spite, Max. Always has been. If he found out . . ." She shuddered.

When the two of them had talked themselves out, they would fall into a fitful sleep for a few hours, cocooned together in the narrow bed, warding off the cold. Finally, knowing that to leave it any longer risked discovery, Bettina would rise and kiss him before slipping out into the black predawn.

By the end of February, the last patches of snow had melted into the gutter. Bettina felt like they were still mired in the long winter, but at least the shortest, darkest days were behind them and, better still, their pot of money continued to grow. She squirrelled away every mark that Albrecht gave her and worked from dawn until the daylight faded, stacking up her finished canvasses against the wall.

She had grown to see this new life as a test of her endurance.

Every night, Albrecht would drink and boast about the crackdowns made by the SS. He spoke of the maps they made and the ledgers kept, listing where all the Jews and Bolsheviks were living, the homosexuals, the dissidents, how they kept track of those they considered morally dubious or mentally deficient. All the casual cruelties that he'd exercised on his sister growing up were extended to the wider populace. The rancor he'd long nursed now served him well.

Marielein was in thrall to her son. She dedicated hours each day to the upkeep of his uniform. There were always new items to fetishize: caps to brush, boots to polish and brass to shine. There were huge silk flags on heavy sticks, which must be held at a precise angle, all while marching in formation on parade. There were the endless presentations and speeches all laced with invective, primed to fire them up and send them out into the town, drunk and filled with an unquestioning, unquenchable fury.

Albrecht and his friends would often roam the streets at night looking for an excuse to rough someone up, or find some other rationale for blind destruction. He'd often return home full of beer and brimstone, still spoiling for a fight, which left Bettina in his line of fire. She tried to avoid him as much as she could, spending her evenings locked in her attic room.

She focused instead on mastering this new realist, romantic style with dedication, until she finally felt she had enough good work to take with her to Munich. Her former tutor wrote and said he'd arranged for a small gallery on Lenbachplatz to take six of her paintings, to gauge the interest of their clientele. The owner, a large man with great liver-spotted hands and rheumy eyes, had sounded cautiously optimistic.

"We have a thematic show coming up on the new German pastoral. These might do well. We can but try."

After their meeting she had dashed straight back to Allach and to Max, a new lightness in her step.

"It feels like change is in the air, don't you think? Things must get better."

"You clever thing. You're right—I feel it too."

Under Holger's tutelage, Max found his own horizons expanding every bit as rapidly. The older man encouraged him to start work on his own designs and he soon had sketches for a dozen small figurines and vessels. Holger gave him the go-ahead to render a few in clay and felt more than vindicated by the results. Max was adept at both the simple, timeless staples and more intricate, sculptural forms—a rare natural ability, Holger assured him. To his surprise, Max found he truly relished the creative release, as well as the higher wages which he took home.

One evening in early spring, Max was called to Holger's office. He poured them both a large glass of Scotch, taken from a special reserve in the bottom drawer of his desk, kept for Heinrich Himmler's occasional visits.

"It's a very good bottle, as you might imagine. Himmler hates drunks but he likes a glass himself, especially when he's roused, as he was today . . ."

The *Reichsführer-SS* was an early investor in the factory and his interest had grown along with it. He had great plans to establish his vision: a new echelon of German artistic taste.

Holger raised a glass, his eyes sparkling with barely suppressed delight.

"I suppose we should drink a toast to Himmler. He wants

us to start work on a sizeable new series of porcelain soldiers, marching out. I feel quite certain we can rise to the occasion, but it does mean we have need for a new sculptor in the artist's studio to do the drudge work. What say you, Friedrich?"

Max winced internally at the reminder of his necessary subterfuge, but he gripped his hand and shook it determinedly.

"Thank you, Holger . . . I only hope it won't cause any friction. I wouldn't want people to feel I hadn't earned my good fortune."

His rapid acceleration through the Allach ranks had not gone unnoticed, especially by those he'd left behind.

"Nonsense! You clearly have a talent we'd be foolish to ignore. Can't let it go to waste on some ill-founded notion of fair play. You were born to this, Friedrich. I only wonder that you didn't realize it sooner."

Although he knew his days at Allach were numbered, Max began to enjoy honing his craft as a sculptor and to take real pride in this new medium. His future was with Bettina, as far from here as they could run, but until then he gladly dedicated himself to the work.

One morning in early spring he was crossing the yard when he caught sight of the three young men he'd first started with. They were still in their customary place, slouched behind a stack of round-bellied barrels so they might smoke and evade the attention of the yard foreman.

Max knew his various promotions had given cause for rancor. He'd caught them glaring, making comments as he passed. Uwe, with his round pink face and tight-cropped white-blond hair, appeared to be the leader. Axel and Dieter were brothers and older than Uwe, but nevertheless seemed cowed by him. It was Uwe who called out as he crossed the yard.

"Hey Österreich!"

Max raised a hand in greeting and walked a little faster, averting his eyes.

The boy repeated his shout, intent on getting his attention. He grinned at Max, his small teeth sharp and yellow.

"Good news, eh?"

Uwe was scuffing at the ground with his brown leather boots. Max looked at him, puzzled.

"Haven't you heard?" Uwe sneered. "You're one of us now."

"What are you talking about?"

The snub-nosed boy elbowed his compatriots and together they sauntered over to him.

"Your government surrendered."

Max stared, still uncomprehending. Uwe spoke slowly and deliberately.

"Austria is part of the Reich now. Keep up!"

Max tasted the metallic tang of fear.

"Nonsense. You don't know what you're talking about."

He turned and began to walk away again. The three boys broke into a trot to catch him up.

"We had to come and save you from the communists. You should be thanking us," said Axel.

Max kept walking, muttering, "Damned obnoxious . . . *Ungustl*," under his breath.

A meaty pink hand clamped hard onto his shoulder. It was Uwe.

"What did you say? Speak proper German, Österreicher; you're one of us now."

Max tried to shrug him off, but Uwe dug his stubby fingers in, pinching at the nerve.

"Axel's right; you should be thanking us. Your country needed fumigating—it's infested with Jews."

Max rounded on the boy, his hands already balled into fists, knuckles chalk white. Suddenly, Holger's voice rang out like a whipcrack across the yard.

"Friedrich! Can I see you in my office right away?"

It took a moment for Max to register the name. Holger stood at the window, his face pale with fury.

"And you boys—get back to work right now. You can collect your cards and leave if I catch you dawdling again."

Uwe glared at Max, then backed away, his neck and face a mottled pink. Max walked directly to Holger's office and knocked.

"Come in."

Holger was at the window, still watching intently as the foreman snapped out orders to Uwe and the brothers. He turned to Max and gestured for him to sit.

"I didn't hear it all, but I gathered the gist. Are you all right?"

Relieved that Holger was not angry with him, as he had feared, Max felt his own rage start to dissipate. He slumped down and Holger tentatively patted him on the shoulder.

"I take it you hadn't heard the news, then?"

Max shook his head.

"The Führer ordered the troops to cross the border into Austria. They march on Linz today."

"My parents . . ." Max croaked.

Holger looked aghast.

"Of course, I should have thought! I'm sorry, Friedrich. They're still in Vienna?"

He nodded.

"Well, I don't think you need be too concerned. It seems like there's been little resistance, so it should all pass off peaceably enough. I heard on the radio that your countrymen are greeting soldiers at the border with flowers."

Max felt his face crumple at the seemingly bland statement. Holger squatted down beside his chair, concerned.

"Dear boy, whatever's happened?"

His brow furrowed.

"Have you reason to be concerned?"

Again Max nodded, finally finding his voice.

"They've been trying to sell up and get out of Vienna for months, but my father has refused all offers. People have been . . . trying to take advantage. I told them not to wait, but it seems it's now too late . . ."

Max considered whether to say more. To his surprise, he found he no longer felt any fear.

"We are Jewish, Holger."

After months of concealment, he found the words spilled out with disconcerting ease. He waited for recriminations, though none came.

Holger simply said, quietly, "I see. Your papers?"

"A false identity." He couldn't look at him. "My real name is Max Ehrlich. I'm so sorry."

Holger exhaled deeply and went back over to his desk. He opened the bottom drawer, pulling out Himmler's Scotch and poured them both a double measure.

"You have no need to apologize. I can appreciate the need for subterfuge, perhaps more than you might think."

Holger drained his glass and poured another straightaway.

"I am . . . how does one put it delicately . . . let's just say, an unrepentant bachelor."

The idea that Holger had secrets of his own had certainly occurred to Max, but he hardly knew how to respond. He sat in silence for a moment, then gave a nod of acknowledgment.

Holger responded sardonically, "Yes, well—I was reasonably sure you might have had your suspicions."

"But aren't you at risk of discovery?"

"I don't let many people get that close. I live alone, I make it apparent that I'm married to my job. And I'm very circumspect. Suffice to say, you need not fear on my account."

"Nor you on mine."

Max slowly shook his head, still incredulous.

"How did it ever come to this?"

"By increments, dear boy. Until it was too late. I fear we're all long past the point of no return."

Max had to wait another week before a letter from his parents finally arrived, addressed to Friedrich Marchen. He tore into it like a starving man with a loaf of bread. Scanning the first page he was quickly reassured that no one had died or been injured— all were accounted for. He felt a little of the tension lift from his shoulders and started the letter again, from the beginning.

On the morning of May 11, his mother had opened their parlor curtains to discover their neighbor's boys spitting at the window. Max's parents had lived their entire married life there but now, when they looked out on the street, they saw swastikas hanging from every lamppost.

After months of hesitation, Max's father finally declared that he would wait no longer. He called his secretary and a few hours later stood on the front steps to hand over the keys to the house and the business. His parents drove away with nothing more than they could carry, abandoning their furniture, most of their clothes and all the larger paintings they owned. They even left behind a portrait of his mother painted by Gustav Klimt, which had hung above the mantel some twenty years or more. They cut the smaller paintings from their frames and rolled them up, ready to be packed into trunks along with a few clothes and photographs and the family menorah, wrapped in his mother's best fur.

Along with scores of others, they had raced straight to the station and abandoned their car in the street, carrying everything they could onto the platform. There they waited hours, having to let several trains go before they could wrestle themselves and all their luggage aboard.

At the Swiss border a patrol of German soldiers climbed on to check their papers. His parents feared they might try to send them back, but the soldiers had simply forced them to open the trunks and taken everything of value. They finally crossed the border with ten Reichsmark in their pockets.

Over the coming days, Max read and reread the letter obsessively, waking in the night to pore over the pages time and time again. They were still scented with his mother's eau de lavande. He read her anxiety inked in every line. Her thoughts moved erratically from paragraph to paragraph, barely alighting long enough to land on one cohesive narrative.

Still, Max managed to piece together much of what their last weeks in Vienna had been like and the awful realization that settled over them. Quite a few friends and colleagues had come to the house, to offer their "help": they'd heard they planned to leave and offered to buy art or certain items of furniture to help them on their way. But though they knew their true value, each had tried to bargain them down to almost nothing. His father had simply refused, laughing it all off as absurd, while his mother had argued that something, at least, was north of nothing, then cried herself to sleep at night. It stunned her to realize that, despite decades of friendship, so many thought nothing of trying to pick them over like a carcass.

Even now, safely ensconced in Switzerland, imposing on the charity of a former school friend, his father refused to accept that the world had changed. He still hoped they might return once things had settled down, so they could complete the sale of the house and the business, which had seemed to him so close.

In Allach, as the cold morning light crept over the sill and illuminated the tightly written pages, Max could see that was a futile hope. He wrote to them. *Don't wait*, he said, *keep moving. Get far away and we will join you when we can. We'll find a country that will take us in—there must be somewhere.*

Bettina came to him as soon as she could, riding her bicycle through the cold, clear night. They stood together in the dark of the kitchen, lit only by the glow of the stove, and she held him for the longest time, hardly knowing what words might offer any comfort.

"I'm sorry, my love. So terribly sorry."

She pulled back to search his face. The anxiety weighed on him still, leaving its dark bruise under his eyes. He softened a little on seeing her concern, reaching out to stroke her face. She wrapped her arms back around him.

They both remained there for a moment, content to simply hold each other, then Bettina gently broke away.

"I'll make us some tea."

She poured the contents of the kettle into a little brown glazed pot, then leaned against the stove, warming her hands around the cup.

"The photographs of Vienna in the newspaper are just heartbreaking. Swastikas and eagles appearing out of nowhere." She shook her head. "Thank goodness they got out when they did."

"I just wish to God they hadn't left it so long. We should have seen it coming. I knew it was possible, of course, I just didn't think it would happen so quickly or that they'd be met with such little resistance."

"There must be so many too frightened to speak up."

"It's the audacity that's shocking—that's how they get away with it."

Bettina's face clouded.

"Albrecht hasn't stopped crowing about it, as you might imagine. It was all I could do to stop myself from slapping the complacent grin from his face. I told him to shut up, instead."

Max frowned. "And how did he take that?"

"About as well as you might expect."

Max looked at her sharply. She turned from him.

"My father always said that any marks on me bore my own fingerprints."

With forced lightness of spirit, she changed the subject.

"Let's not choose to dwell on the things we can't change. How goes the apprenticeship? Do they let you do anything or is it all just watch and learn?"

"I've been hands-on since day one, but I'm damned grateful for it. It has given me time to think. To work out what comes next."

"And?"

"And . . . I don't think we can afford to wait any longer, do you? This has shown me, the worst can happen any time."

She had both feared and hoped for it, although the prospect of seeing it through seemed utterly unreal.

"I agree but we have no visas and nowhere to go. We'd be refugees with nothing to our name and nowhere willing to take us in."

"We've managed to put a fair amount aside these last few months. I think we should just go as far and as fast as we can, till the money runs out."

"All right then." She was pale but determined. "I didn't get a chance to tell you—I had word from the Munich gallery. They've sold some of my work. No idea how much I'll make, but it's better than nothing."

Max's brow furrowed.

"We're talking about this like it's all predetermined, but it isn't. It might be safer for you to wait here, hold out for a visa . . ."

She shook her head vehemently.

"I won't hear of it, Max, don't say another word. We've tried to do things by the book and where has it got us? There isn't a path for people like us; we have to take it into our own hands. I shan't be parted from you. All that remains is when and how we leave."

Max slumped into the kitchen chair and sank his hands in his hair.

"As to the how, I vote we just get on with it. Make our way to the border, then cross into Switzerland by foot. Then if we aren't stopped, we head to Zurich by any means necessary and try to find my parents. I don't want to risk arrest, but better there than here, surely?"

Bettina sat in silence for a moment. In the gloom of the kitchen Max found it hard to read her expression. When she finally spoke, her voice was steady.

"I'll tell Mama and Albrecht I'm going into Munich to visit the gallery, which is true to a point. You collect your pay, then come and meet me at the station. We'll get as close to the border as we can. Albrecht is out with his troop on Friday night, so Mother will go to bed early. With any luck, they won't even realize I'm gone until the following day."

"Are you quite sure?"

She stuck out her chin. "You can't stay, so we must go. I'd rather be dead in a ditch beside you than live in captivity alone."

Over the days spring unfurled, its fresh beauty bewildering in the face of all the anguish she now felt. Though she was counting down the days till they could leave, Bettina found a certain unexpected melancholy at the prospect. The thought that she might never see her home again stung more than she'd imagined. It was a small and rather shabby place, cold even on the warmest days. Her mother and Albrecht were the same: hard and often unkind, even when you hoped they might be soft. But then, Bettina reasoned, her father had brutalized them all and tried to make them over in his image.

She went across the fields every chance she got, the warmth of the sun on her face, the skylarks arcing overhead. The hares had finished their boxing, but she still looked out for them. Coming home late one afternoon, she spotted a jill and her leveret crouching under cover of a hedgerow, which frothed with flowering umbellifers. She lingered for a moment, watching as the mother crept out cautiously, the little one hesitant and dashing to the safety of her side. They nibbled on fresh green shoots until a noise disturbed them and they bounded off across the field together, kicking up their long heels.

She stayed there till long after they had disappeared, marveling at the mother–child bond and how it could be so affecting. As she turned for home, she thought about the child they'd lost while living in Berlin. She had somehow learned to fit herself around the fact of it, although the grief had never gone.

It occurred to her it had been quite a time since she'd felt the familiar quickening that heralded her cycle's end. A month? No, maybe more. The weeks had slipped by unnoticed, with every waking moment consumed by thoughts of their escape. She reached up and pressed her palms against her breasts; did they feel sore or was that just imagination?

By the time she entered the kitchen, the sky had turned to dusk. Her cheeks were flushed and she felt light headed, brain racing at the possibility. A voice from the shadows made her start.

"What have you been doing?"

Her brother was sitting by the range, smoking in the gloom.

"I might ask you the same," she retorted.

She knelt down to stoke the coals, then turned up the lamp on the scrubbed pine table. It lit his face, stubbled, tired and fractious.

"I've been out working since first light. I finally get home, and what do I find? The whole place is quiet and there's nothing on the table."

She picked up an apron and tied it loosely around her waist, smiling at Albrecht, feeling more than usually indulgent.

"I'll put on some potatoes and cabbage and I'll heat up the rest of the *Schweinshaxe*."

She took out the dish her mother had prepared the night before. Albrecht grunted in acknowledgment, the closest he could get to gratitude.

She set out a bright green head of cabbage on the cleaver-beaten chopping block. He watched her, the smoke trailing from his mouth.

"What do you do out there for hours on end?" he asked.

"The days are getting longer. It inspires me in my work."

He snorted his derision. "Do you hear yourself?"

She ignored him and continued chopping, but a little flame of malice had been sparked.

"You always sound so damned pretentious. Tell me, *meine liebe Schwester*, what kind of inspiration have you been out chasing when you come creeping home at dawn?"

It landed like a slap. Keeping her voice level, she replied coolly, "What are you talking about?"

"You think I don't hear you, going out and coming in at all hours?" He laughed. "Don't worry. Your secret's safe with me."

"There is no secret, Albrecht. I'm an artist. It's not pretension; it's just what I do. The work of observation—and it is work—can't just be done in fair conditions. I need to see the world at different times and in all weathers."

She felt suddenly emboldened.

"Wait, did you think you'd caught me?"

High, hot spots of color flamed in her cheeks.

"Maybe I have a secret lover hidden away—is that it?"

He ignored her and levered off his boots, leaning back in his chair and drawing deeply on the cigarette. He appeared lost in thought, but she knew better. She kept her eyes deliberately averted while she chopped the rest of the vegetables. She scraped everything into a pan and threw the scraps in the bucket for the pigs, before daring to steal a glance at him. He was still watching. She cursed herself for getting caught.

"Guess who I saw the other day?"

His tone was mocking.

"I've no idea, Albrecht. Why don't you enlighten me?"

She looked around the kitchen in search of further occupation. She spied a basket of clean washing and bent to pick up a sheet. She shook it out and began to fold it.

Albrecht grinned, undeterred.

"It was Peter Amsel. You remember, you *used* to be friends with his brother Richard. Very cozy, once upon a time."

She ignored the provocation.

"I thought you'd turned your back on that whole set, but Peter said to say hello to you. Now, tell me, why would he do that?"

He tilted his chair and rocked back on two legs as he stared at her, slyly gauging her expression. She pulled out the cutlery drawer and laid the contents on the table, trying to will her hands steady. She wanted to brush him off, but the right response seemed to elude her.

"I asked you a question, *Schwester* dear."

He had her pinned and they both knew it. Flustered and stuttering, she began to fumble for a response when a sudden

volley of barking started up outside. The two elderly hounds
had ceased their twilight wandering, enticed back by the scent
of cooking. She rushed to the door and flung it open.

"Do be quiet now. *Bärchen*, it's enough to wake the dead."

She breathed deeply in the cool night air and decided she
would not be cowed today. She turned back to face Albrecht.

"The Amsel boys were always so polite. Not like some."

She picked up the basket of folded washing.

"It should all be ready in five minutes. Help yourself."

She walked straight past her brother, checking the back of his
chair with her hip as she went. She heard the two front feet as
they reconnected with the stone floor, hard, and left the room
without once turning back.

The rest of the week passed slowly, with a notable frost between
Bettina and her brother. It only helped her commit to her plan
of action.

She'd resolved to travel light and take nothing that might
give away the game. She vowed to be unsentimental—all that
she truly valued would be at her side—and yet it still pained her
to say goodbye to the small mementos of her life. She allowed
herself a few photographs and precious letters, which she tucked
away at the bottom of the largest handbag she could muster.
She packed a book and the bare essentials for cleanliness and
beautifying, along with a change of light clothes, relieved that
longer days and warmer nights had come at last. When the bag
was packed, she felt the first flickers of freedom. In the final
reckoning, totems mattered little and the act of abandonment
was liberating.

Friday morning dawned bright and clear. She crept down-stairs and spent a quiet moment sitting with the two old, grizzled dogs, scratching their rough pelts and scrubbing their ears until their back legs kicked. When the rest of the house began to rouse, she retreated to her room and dressed, wearing as many layers as she could. At breakfast she lingered at the range, but-tering and devouring slice after slice from a fresh loaf of bread, causing Marielein to tut her disapproval.

"Leave some for the rest of us. Now then, are you still plan-ning to go off gallivanting to the city? I could really do with your help here."

Bettina affected an air of nonchalance. "It's not a day trip; Herr Leopold from the gallery wrote to say they've sold my work. You want me to be self-sufficient, don't you?"

Without looking up from his newspaper, Albrecht muttered churlishly.

"That would be a first. I hope you aren't expecting me to fetch you from the station. We have new recruits pledging their allegiance tonight, so you'll have to take your bicycle."

After breakfast Marielein seemed determined to keep Bettina busy out of spite. She set her to work on more eternal rounds of laundry, making her hang it all out in the billowing spring breeze. Then she asked her to help feed the pigs, collect the eggs and fetch in logs from the woodpile. The tasks were all menial and unimportant; Bettina knew instinctively, their only purpose was to delay her.

The sun crept higher in the sky and Bettina kept looking at the clock, silently lamenting how much time was passing by. In midafternoon she was gripped by a sudden fear that she might be too late to collect her earnings and decided to just slip away. She reasoned it was what she would have done anyway, had she intended to return.

She ran to her room and picked up her bag, declining to even check if she'd left anything behind. She wanted to be out and past all this, away and on the other side.

She wheeled her bicycle around behind the barn and loaded up, then set off down the lane, lingering for just a moment at the gate, looking out over the broad sweep of fields she'd known since childhood. She wondered how long it might be till she'd return, if ever. Only later did she realize that it had been far harder to take leave of the landscape than her family.

She rode to the station, a fluttering excitement powering her on. The colors of the countryside seemed brighter and sharper as the road turned into town.

When she arrived at the station, she puzzled about what to do with the bicycle. She decided just to leave it propped up against a wall. Now almost unencumbered, she waited on the platform, pacing anxiously. When the train arrived, she sank into her seat relieved: at long last, their escape was underway.

By the time she arrived in the city, the shadows were growing long. She fairly ran from the station, anxious to get to the gallery on Lenbachplatz before it closed.

When she arrived, she was astonished to see the painting in the window was her own. *The Viking* sat in pride of place, the finished work so vastly different from her first expressionistic sketch it still looked jarring to her. She'd made the whole thing over in the new romantic style, Max's dark visage transformed into a Teutonic ideal—blue eyes, blond, all overblown heroic. Himmler was keen on using neo-pagan symbolism, to prop up his fantasy of a pure European bloodstock. She rather relished the idea some Nazi hard-liner might buy the piece, little knowing it was a portrait of her handsome Jewish lover, herself beside him, drawn in her rabbit form, the pair of them eternally together, hidden only by a dab of paint.

Breathless and panting an apology, she pushed the door open.

"Herr Leopold, I'm so sorry that I'm late!"

The doughy giant was on her almost immediately.

"Not at all, not at all!"

He reached out to clutch her hands, crushing them in his two great paws.

"It is an absolute delight to see you again, Fräulein Vogel. You noticed *The Viking* on display? He draws a crowd some days!"

"But no offers yet to buy? I had rather hoped there might be."

"On the contrary, I simply felt we shouldn't let this fellow go. We've had inquiries from several prominent curators. Some expressed an interest in its provenance . . ."

Bettina frowned. "Was there ever any doubt?"

"Only the natural curiosity aroused by such an arresting piece coming from an as-yet-unknown." He whispered, conspiratorial, "And I felt the value of the painting might be increased by a little more exposure."

Under ordinary circumstances, this would have been thrilling news, but she needed something more tangible.

"Were you able to sell any of them at all?"

"Rest assured, dear lady, the other canvasses sold quickly and sold well. I simply felt *The Viking* was worth more. The true value has yet to be established and I don't like leaving money on the table." He must have seen her stricken face because he reassured her hastily. "If you are in need of funds, I would be happy to advance you."

When she left the gallery some twenty minutes later, it was with her head held high and her purse quite full. The five canvasses had earned her more in a day than she had made in the entirety of the last two years. It was a little galling that it should be a style of painting for which she felt such little affinity, but she was grateful that she could now play her own financial part in their escape. She clutched her bag to her, terrified that someone might try to snatch it all away.

In something of a daze, she started walking again, past the Great Synagogue and the columns of the Haus der Deutschen Kunst: tall and blinding white. She thought about Herr Leopold's final words to her.

"Before the next Great German Art Exhibition, I strongly recommend we put *The Viking* forward for consideration, Fräulein Vogel. It is more than worthy of a place and, if it should be chosen, it would cement your status as a rising artist of the Reich and improve the value of this painting in particular."

She thanked him for his kindness and told him she would consider his proposition, then walked away knowing she would likely never see either him or the painting again. *The Viking* was part of her, like Albrecht and Marielein, like the farm and the fields, but she could turn from it without a second glance. It was just her past; her future would be waiting for her on the Zurich train.

At 6:45 p.m. the station was still humming with commuting workers and weekend travelers alike. Tides of people pulled in one direction or another, currents passing through the crowd.

The din of voices echoed off the vast metal ribs of the building, vaulting overhead, a latticework of glass and steel. At the center of it all, the hands of the station clock marked time.

Bettina sat on a narrow bench and stared at the crowds as they bustled to and fro. Her book lay on her lap, open but unread: a weathered copy of Rilke's letters that Max had given her years before, during one of their eternal Dessau summers. She had parted with so much, but this had been too great a talisman to leave behind. The margins were crammed with notes in her younger hand, some passages barely legible, the lettering as gauche as the sentiments expressed. One in particular, underlined and annotated, came to mind: "The future is stationary," Rilke had written. "It is we who are moving in infinite space."

She felt herself approaching that liminal point now, where paths diverged and stretched ahead in all directions. She ran toward it gladly.

She moved a hand to her belly reflexively. It was still entirely flat. She had decided to keep this possibility to herself, wanting to be certain before she told him, knowing this journey was already hard enough. Her eyes flicked to the station clock, its hands like arrow shafts: it was 6:55 p.m. The train was due to leave in twenty minutes, more than enough time to get a good position on the platform when Max arrived.

On the concourse stood a group of soldiers: young thugs, looking for a thrill, rifles slung over their shoulders. They seemed bored and determined to seed chaos. Bettina had been observing their antics for the past hour, watching in disgust as they targeted anyone who looked "other." In particular, they hunted out observant Jews in the crowd and stopped them, searching their luggage and scattering the contents of their suitcases on the dirty ground. No one walking past made any comment or attempt to stop them. Most just kept their eyes averted, pretending not to see.

Bettina found her own eyes drawn to the men, in fear of what they might do next. She had hoped Max would be here by now. They wanted to secure two good seats in the last carriage, so they might have time to evade the authorities if they should board before they got to Singen.

They'd tried to think ahead, though many details still remained in flux. Peter Amsel had come up trumps again, providing them with the address of a man who might help them into Switzerland by crossing over the Rhine near Lake Bodensee. They planned to take the train as far west as they safely could, then reassess their situation. Peter had cautioned them that there were patrols on both sides of the border.

"The Swiss are the ones trying to stop the exodus," he'd said. "The SS might actually help you if they catch you. They'd rob you blind first, of course, but that's the risk you take."

The hands ticked up to seven o'clock. As Bettina searched the crowd for Max her eye was caught by a young woman, elegantly dressed, with dark, bobbed hair like her. She held a bridal bouquet in one hand and a suitcase in the other. She was accompanied by a young man—the groom, Bettina presumed—wearing a black suit and a smart hat. They crossed the busy concourse surrounded by a group of well-wishers, all in high spirits, evidently there to see them off. They were joyous and drew eyes from all around the station.

One of the soldiers standing near Bettina saw them and got the attention of his compatriots. She heard the word *"Juden"* whispered as two of them peeled off from the group and began to weave their way through the crowd.

At 7:03 p.m. the Zurich train pulled in and began disgorging all its human contents. They washed down the platform and fanned out across the station plaza, blocking Bettina's view. She stood up on tiptoe, scouring the few oncoming faces that swam against the tide, searching for Max, though he was nowhere to be seen.

When the passengers had disembarked, those waiting on the platform made to climb aboard; families loaded down with luggage and lone travelers with nothing but a briefcase. They settled in their seats, making themselves comfortable for the journey ahead. Bettina stood and moved toward the nearest carriage, pacing up and down now, ever more anxious. She looked up at the clock: 7:05 p.m.

She stared out across the crowd again. The soldiers were still there, the entire group now crowded around the couple, checking on their papers. One soldier knelt on the floor and, despite the protestations of the couple's friends, tipped the contents of their suitcase out and began to rifle through the clothing. To Bettina's disgust, he plucked up the woman's underwear and held it against his crotch, leering lewdly at his friends. The eyes of the entire station populace were drawn to them by now.

Bettina continued pacing, her eyes darting first to the entrance, then to the clock face and finally the soldiers, before starting up the cycle once again. The young bride was crying now, trying to stuff the contents of the suitcase back. Her new husband, red-faced and bellicose, fronting up to the nearest soldier, his companions trying hard to hold him back.

7:08 p.m. Now coated in a slick sheen of perspiration, Bettina trotted up and down the full length of the train, searching in the windows for Max, in case he had somehow slipped past. There was a shout from the concourse and she turned her head to see the soldiers drag the man away, his heels kicking and slipping on the tiled floor. The young woman followed, dragging the suitcase, pleading with the soldiers. Her face was streaked with tears, the battered bouquet crumpled in her hand.

The sound of running footsteps made Bettina spin, but it was just a final straggler dashing for the train. A sob began to thicken in her throat; Max was always punctual, always careful and considered. The doors slammed shut like gunshots. Passengers leaned out of the windows exchanging their goodbyes.

At 7:15 p.m. a screech of metal merged with the shrill of the whistle as the train finally ground into action. Bettina watched, feeling something inside wrench away.

A hand fell on her shoulder. Her heart fluttered blindly, beating against the bars of her ribs.

"Excuse me Fräulein. Does this belong to you?"

A young man in a brown raincoat held out the book of Rilke's letters. She stammered her thanks and took it from him, clutching it tightly to her chest.

The platform emptied out, though the concourse was still thronged with crowds. There was no sign of the newlyweds or the soldiers. There was no sign of Max.

He knew he was late. Max was always fastidious, but as the factory clock marked the final hours of the working week, he was more than usually determined to leave everything in good order. He pictured Holger coming to examine his desk at some point in the following week when it would have become apparent that Max would not return. He hoped the deliberate way he'd set things out would indicate he'd gone by choice, so his friend would not worry about him.

Many times, he toyed with the idea of knocking on Holger's office door and telling him the truth. He longed to thank him properly, to say how much he'd come to value their friendship, but decided he could not justify the risk: if anyone came after him, he wanted to give Holger the gift of plausible deniability.

Instead, he'd stayed late all week to finish every item he'd been sculpting: a tiny mouse, ears pricked for danger, and a swallow, wings fanned out, forked tail swept up. Both were delicate, finely wrought additions to the Allach catalog. Max hoped his friend might understand and see he'd taken pride in all his efforts.

At 4:45 p.m. the laborers in the yard started queuing to collect their wage packets from the foreman. Many of them would return home later that night, their pockets half empty, having drunk a good deal of the proceeds. Max could only speculate what his wages might be used for in the coming days—perhaps to buy or bribe their way out of trouble, to grease the wheels of their escape.

When he'd left his rented house that morning, he placed his small, neatly packed suitcase ready, on his bed. It contained his real passport and identity card, along with the money he and Bettina had been saving up for months on end, all sewn into a cloth belt. He planned to wear it underneath his shirt. He would keep his final wage packet at hand, ready for the immediate costs of the journey they faced. He was thankful it would be the largest one he'd earned by far.

When the clock ticked past the hour he stood and pushed the stool beneath his desk, brushing off the last few crumbs of clay. A tail end of workers snaked through the administrative offices, waiting for their wages. Max joined the back of the line and watched as the paper notes, engraved with gothic script, were counted, stacked, then slipped into an envelope and handed over.

As Max approached the front of the queue, he repeated the name on his papers over and over in his head. Despite months of living as Friedrich Marchen, he still needed to remain vigilant, in case he was called out. When his turn came, the administrator thumbed through a thick stack of notes, then placed them in a bulging envelope. Max quickly stuffed it into his jacket pocket, along with his false papers. There would be enough, he hoped, to get them close to Zurich and his parents. Perhaps even enough for a passage to England, if they got lucky and were allowed in.

He was preoccupied by these thoughts when he noticed Holger standing at his office door, beckoning him over.

"Do you have a minute, dear boy? I have something marvelous to share . . ."

Holger was in high spirits. He had managed to lay his hands on a contraband recording of an opera by Korngold, *Das Wunder der Heliane*, which he had concealed in a plain paper sleeve. The gramophone crackled as Holger whispered to Max excitedly, "It has been banned, of course, which is simply ludicrous. You need to hear it for yourself."

Max thought about Bettina waiting at the station. He had two hours before the Zurich train was due to leave.

"Just for a minute, but then I really need to go," he said.

They listened to the susurration of the needle and the opening notes, triumphal and exultant. Holger sat ramrod straight behind his desk, held aloft by the lightness of the aria, an invisible thread lifting his spine.

"It's madly tragic," he sighed, delighted. "Chaotic and yet utterly serene. Do you know the story?"

Max shook his head.

"Heliane stands on trial, accused of infidelity. She confesses to a judge that she'd stripped herself naked in front of a stranger, a young man who was destined to die, because she felt compelled to wrap herself in his grief, to bear it with him. Don't you find it all too painfully exquisite?"

As the soprano's voice rose and spread its wings, Holger closed his eyes in reverie. It filled the room with a lush crescendo that moved both men beyond words. In the gulf of silence after the final notes retreated, Max wiped his eyes.

"Thank you, Holger. I'd never heard it before, but it's quite beautiful."

"I knew you would treasure it. Why anyone would deny themselves such transformative power, I will never understand."

Holger smiled, contented. "I suppose we must slip the poor lark back in her hiding place all the same. It is a sentence which far outweighs her crimes." He lifted the needle. "Thank you for indulging me."

"Not at all, I should be thanking you. For everything you've done, not just the opera. You've been so generous to me."

Holger harrumphed. "Hush now. I have kept you long enough. Get on with you and enjoy your rest."

Max felt the weight of regret as he walked away. *I should have told him*, he thought. Should have done it days ago, but now it is too late. He resolved to write and try to explain it all once they were safe. He hoped he'd be forgiven.

As he walked out, he saw the sun was low on the horizon and his shadow stretched away. Max realized he needed to make haste; he still had to return to the house and collect his case and money belt before he could leave to catch the Munich train.

He was walking at a fair clip when he became aware of running feet behind him and started to turn toward the sound. When the first punch landed, it caught him hard and fast. He found himself face down on the pavement before it even registered. He felt no pain as yet, only confusion. Three pairs of boots surrounded him. One, scuffed and brown, pulled back slowly and then swung hard, driving into his lower ribs, forcing the breath from his lungs.

His mind could make sense of it only in fragments. Perhaps, if he stayed quite still . . . He had been going home to get his case and now . . . He should get up. He must.

He put out a hand and lifted his head. He realized his nose was bleeding; three round red coins rained down. He heard a male voice hiss, "*Hurensohn.*" Son of a bitch.

Someone grabbed his shoulder roughly and hoisted his torso up, fumbling in his jacket, ripping it. They let go and he dropped back to the ground, his temple bouncing off the road. A gob of phlegm spattered to the ground inches from his face. It merged with the drops of blood.

A shout of alarm went up from farther down the street, in the opposite direction—they had been spotted. Max tried to lift his head again, but a wave of vertigo hit, an unseen force that pinned him to the ground. Two pairs of the boots took off suddenly, the sound of their running steps receding. The third lingered briefly.

"Uwe, come on!"

The scuffed brown boots then turned and ran. Seconds passed in silence, save for Max's ragged breathing. And then yet more footsteps, pounding from the opposite direction.

Max turned himself over gingerly and put his hand beneath his chest, trying to heave himself back up to his knees. At the edge of his vision a drift of white dots floated in and merged, then slipped away. He felt strong hands grab under his arms and lift him, helping him back over to the side of the road. He was lowered gently onto the cold curbstone. A hip flask of something fortified and strong was thrust at him; he knocked it back, grateful to wash out the bitter tang of blood. As the shock started to subside, he felt pain and exhaustion begin to fill the void.

"So then, do you want to tell us what all that was about?"

Max looked up, wincing at the stabbing pain the movement induced. Three uniformed men stood over him. Max let his head drop back down between his legs, trying to quell the nausea.

"I saw them, sir." This voice was younger, deferential. "Three local lads—I know their fathers well."

The first voice spoke to Max again directly.

"So, what did these three have against you?"

Max shrugged weakly. And yet . . . he patted down his jacket and felt the ripped pocket, his papers torn, the envelope of money gone.

"They took my wages."

His temples throbbed with the rhythm of his pulse.

"Where are you from?"

Max gestured weakly to the factory behind him. "Allach Porcelain. I was on my way home."

"No, I mean where are you from?" There was a note of vexation in the older man's voice. "You're not from here, are you?"

He looked up but their faces were in shadow cast by their peaked caps.

"I'm Austrian. From Vienna."

"Where are your papers?"

Max pulled the tattered remnants from his pocket and they were taken from him. He tried to stand, but his legs were too weak. The man put a heavy hand on his shoulder.

"Stay where you are."

He called out, over his shoulder, to the third man who had moved off and was leaning against a wall, swaying as he relieved himself.

"Hey, Albrecht! Come and take a look at this."

Albrecht.

Max fought the immediate impulse to stand and try to run. He kept his head down and watched from the edge of his eye as Albrecht buttoned himself up and turned toward them. The older man handed over the tattered *Kennkarte*.

"Do these look right to you?"

"Hard to say, they're so torn up. Maybe we should take him in and check."

His voice was slightly slurred.

"Ach, let's let him go."

The older man waved him off, dismissive, his mind already somewhere else.

"I want to get back before they drink the cellar dry."

Albrecht handed back his papers and Max stuffed them in his coat, keeping his head down. He got to his feet unsteadily.

"Wait."

Albrecht peered at Max.

"What's your name?"

"Friedrich." His voice cracked; he cleared his throat. "Friedrich Marchen."

He kept his eyes cast down.

Albrecht turned to the older man, triumphant.

"That's not his name?"

He clamped a steel grip on Max's shoulder and pushed him roughly, barking at the younger officer.

"He's a lying, thieving *Juden*, and I can prove it. Help me get him in the alley. Strip him down."

When Bettina returned to the little house on Lindenstraße, just after 10 p.m. the sky was dark and starless.

She had remained on the bench at the station long after the Zurich train departed, hoping against hope that Max might yet appear, no doubt anxious and apologetic. But slowly the Friday evening rush had slowed down to a crawl and she was forced to admit it: he wasn't just late; something must have happened to him. She'd begun to feel conspicuous, having stayed in one place for several hours. With leaden feet she walked across the station to the platform where the Allach train departed, a knot of fear twisting at her core.

When the train arrived, she climbed aboard reluctantly. As they rattled back along the tracks, she stared out glassy-eyed at her reflection. Her mind skittered anxiously from doubt to optimism and back again, until the moment they pulled into

Allach station and she saw that Max was not there waiting for her and finally let real fear begin to settle in. Her legs were stiff as she walked toward the bicycle she'd abandoned earlier in the day, never thinking she'd return. She climbed on, her limbs protesting, and began to pedal through the dark.

She approached Max's rented house and saw that the door was open and there was a light on at the window. She jumped from the bike and dropped it to the ground, dashing straight up the front steps and through the door. Inside she was met by a scene of disarray. Only the sound of her own footsteps broke the silence as she tiptoed through the shards of broken china. Every drawer in the room had been ransacked, their scant contents spilled out: the kitchen dresser emptied, the chairs at the table flung onto their sides.

Slowly Bettina climbed the narrow stairway to the bedroom, where a similar scene confronted her: a tangle of sheets and torn pillows, tossed aside. On the bed lay Max's suitcase opened wide, its contents scattered, the silk lining slashed.

With trembling hands, Bettina sifted through a pile of eiderdowns and blankets, searching for any sign of Max's papers or the money belt, which she herself had so carefully sewn shut. She scrabbled under the bed, through a drift of feathers, thick as snow. Her arm stretched out, fingers reaching for a tail of cotton muslin. She pulled out the discarded remnants of the belt, torn open at the seams and now entirely empty. Everything she'd hope to find was gone and with it, hope.

BOOK TWO

A large canvas rests against the clean white wall, as tall as it is wide. Most of it is filled with the texture of a barren field, a ribbon of cloud above, rolling in coils and crossed by a phalanx of crows. Thin light pierces the gloom, but gives no warmth. It casts a baleful yellow glow across the spiked surface of the furrowed earth.

In the center stands a mother hare and her leveret, exposed to the elements. Her eyes alert, she turns her back to the coming storm, while the smaller creature huddles, sheltered by her flank. A swirling eddy of leaves surrounds them, frozen in the moment, stirred up by a sudden squall. The mother knows there is nowhere safe to hide, nothing now to do but ride it out.

CHAPTER ELEVEN

Munich

Summer 1938

In the heart of Munich, the wide lawns of the Englische Garten were thronged with visitors eager to promenade and listen to the musicians playing there. The nightingales trilled their call and response while families gathered to look out over the skyline from the temple of Monopteros, its classical columns suiting the mood. They were proud to belong to a city that vowed to reshape the rest of the world in its image.

In Neuhausen, in the north of the city, two vast windows filled Bettina's new studio with light, even on the dimmest days. The move to Munich had been traumatic for so many reasons, but finding a studio had given her some solace. Herr Leopold had helped her locate the space and lent her the deposit. Because it was in the Bauhaus style, the curves and proportions all felt familiar, a comfort when so much else in her life was anything but.

Still, she did little to make the space feel homey. In one

corner of the room stood a stack of unopened boxes containing all of Max's worldly possessions, his books and the schematics he'd been drawing of their house. She took comfort in knowing they were there, though the thought of going through them made her nauseated with fear. She could fool herself that they were waiting there for his return, ready to be picked up and completed. In truth, their very presence was a painful reminder of all she lost that dreadful day.

In the aftermath of Max's disappearance, she had stayed at his rented house for several hours, wandering from room to room in shock. Eventually, she felt the cloud of immediate panic lift enough to climb back aboard her bike. She'd cycled the dark streets to Richard's brother's home. Peter had been endlessly kind and patient, though she had arrived in such a frenzied state, she could barely remember any of it.

He persuaded her to take a sleeping draft and rest, though she felt so frantic it almost didn't take effect. He went out to make inquiries and discovered Max had been arrested and that her brother, Albrecht, was the officer responsible. When Peter told her what he'd found, she vowed to return to the farm and wreak revenge. Only the reminder that she might put Max in more danger dissuaded her. Instead, Peter helped her sift through the wreckage left behind and salvage everything she could. Within days Richard arrived from Berlin and both brothers swore that they would use whatever influence they had to find out what was going on.

A kind of catatonic fugue descended and Bettina spent days holed up in Peter's spare room. The brothers simply let her be, understanding she must process the attendant grief in her own time. When she finally began to surface, Richard tried to persuade her to flee the country or at least move back to Berlin with him, but she refused.

"I don't want to live in a country that will take me, but would not have taken him."

She was determined to stay close by and wait for Max, declaring that she could not, would not, leave without him. Staying in Allach was impossible, so they agreed on Munich as a compromise: close by, but large enough to give her anonymity. Herr Leopold offered to help and so she let him willingly, knowing work was all that she could do to save herself. He began petitioning for *The Viking* to be given a spot in a group show and lent her more money on the promise of her future earnings.

Bettina and Peter returned to the farmhouse during the summer solstice celebrations, when they were certain Marielein and Albrecht would both be absent. Peter helped her pack up the remnants of a life she'd willingly left behind. She could have taken it all, but in the end, she wanted only her art supplies, her paintings, sketchbooks and some clothes.

Life without Max, with the open, aching absence of him, was almost intolerable. And so she painted, filling the void with canvas after canvas, day and night. She found human subjects impossible, compelled to paint Max over and over, so she retreated to the safe neutrality of nature, to fields and forests, farms and landscapes. In each of them, she painted herself, an animal or bird as her avatar, to remind herself she still existed in the world, even as she felt she might disintegrate.

And through it all, she held on to her secret: the knowledge that Max's child was growing within, though not yet evident. It gave her a simple purpose in life; to preserve the three of them, whatever way she must.

Herr Leopold determined the time had come to orchestrate her introduction to the Munich art scene. For Bettina, the choice was almost entirely a pragmatic one: she needed money urgently to wait for Max and recoup their losses, so that when he was released they might finally make good their escape. She didn't know when that day might come, but she knew she must be ready for it.

She put on lipstick and her best tea dress, though it was several years old and looking rather tired. She held tight to Herr Leopold's arm and together they walked into the grandest room she had ever seen, with ice-blue walls and towering ceilings. A frieze of molded plaster cornicing ran right around the room and in the center sat a ceiling rose of fruit and flounced ribbons: extravagant, baroque.

Herr Leopold stayed by her side for the first hour introducing her to everyone he knew, but eventually he melted away and left her to her own devices. Bettina observed this new world from the fringes. The clinking of glasses merged with chatter in the room, a tinkling cacophony that rose to the height of the crystal chandelier. All the art scene parties she'd previously attended had been filled with radicals and rebels who'd talked of breaking things down and rebuilding the world as it ought to be. The conversation now was rather different; they were conquering the world and the view from here was grand.

Bettina noted that the women seemed to sip their drinks, intent on keeping their silks immaculate and themselves in check, but most of the men were three sheets to the wind before the sky was dark. Almost all were married, but they complained loudly about the state of the single women in the room: what was wrong with the modern German girl? Not enough meat to grab on to. How were they supposed to populate the Reich when all the women looked like a shop-window mannequin in a *Kaufhaus*?

For the most part, the women ignored their griping. They chattered, thrilled that Prague might soon be another jewel in the growing string of cities belonging to them, joining Vienna, Munich and Berlin. Bettina hovered at the periphery, listening to the intrigue, the choicest rumor being that Hitler had been fed a poisoned omelette and a body double passed off as him ever since.

"You'd think people might have noticed," laughed a vampish socialite. "It's not as if he doesn't have a platoon of filmmakers dogging his every step. One can hardly cross a room without making an appearance in someone's reel these days."

Bettina held on to a glass of champagne but simply washed her lips with it. Though there was much talk of abstinence, every vessel in the room was full. The guests decried the idea they should give up on their vices; that was for the common man who didn't have the wit to make decisions for himself. They were the Party faithful who embodied the spirit of the times, even when they chose to ignore its more annoying edicts.

Bettina recognized a few faces from her younger days before Bauhaus, before Max. She was greeted warmly by a group of women she'd known at seventeen. Because they had laid down their brushes and ambitions years before, Bettina thought they might envy her freedom, but instead they seemed to pity her, decrying her lack of a wedding ring. They told her she should persevere; she'd find a husband and protector soon.

Their talk turned to the state of the nation and Bettina found herself asking a question that she had never dared broach in the company of men. They'd all had Jewish friends at college; had they no qualms about the way they were being treated? Most demurred, but one, an older woman named Frieda, whom Bettina had much admired, said how sad her children had been when their little Jewish friends had stopped attending school.

"It's hardest on the *kleine Kinder*. Tragic, really, in so many ways. I took my sons down to the synagogue in the first snow, to hand out coats and shoes. I wanted them to see it for themselves."

Bettina felt relief at finding a sympathetic soul in this sea of seeming indifference. Frieda continued, "I said to my eldest, look at these clever devils. They're asking for help when you know for a fact that most have more furs and jewels at home than I. Such a vital lesson. I told them, 'Keep your eyes on them; they'll steal your watch if you shake their hand.' "

Bettina stammered an excuse and made her way out to the corridor, where she stood by an open window to catch her breath; she had rarely felt so utterly alone. The laughter from the main room seemed more like braying to her ears, so full of spite and sniping. She thought about escape, of slipping away and returning to her studio, where she might take off her shoes and stockings. It had all been too soon. She wasn't ready for this; wasn't certain if she'd ever be.

A male voice punctured her thoughts.

"Fräulein Vogel, isn't it? I expected to see you commanding the room, not loitering out here alone."

He was a tall man with a long face and deep-set eyes. He wore the uniform of an officer of the SS and stared at her intently. Bettina stuttered an acknowledgment. He smiled at her obvious discomfort.

"Don't be alarmed. Your artistic reputation is all that goes before you."

She tried to regain her composure and replied stiffly, "That's a relief. I must admit to being surprised I should be known to anyone here, let alone one of the Schutzstaffel."

He raised an eyebrow, evidently amused. "We're not a monolith, you know. The uniform gives that impression, deliberately so, but we're all individuals underneath it. Fallible men, full of foibles."

He fixed her with a frank, appraising look.

"So, you're the girl who painted *The Viking*, eh? I understand Leopold has decided to champion you."

"Herr Leopold has been very kind."

He snorted.

"He knows when someone can earn him good commission. Actually, I've been hearing your name rather a lot recently. Your fellow artist Adolf Ziegler was talking about you just last week."

"Good things, I hope?"

"Very good. So tell me: what have you been working on?"

"Rural landscapes, mostly."

"Do you know the art dealer and historian Hildebrand Gurlitt? He has been assisting the Reich Culture Chamber to identify painters that have promise. We're keen to foster new talent. Perhaps I could introduce the two of you . . ."

"But you have me at a disadvantage; you seem to know all about me, and I know nothing of you."

He held out his hand. "Karl Holz."

His dry fingers gripped hers tightly for a second and then dropped away.

"I'm actually something of a collector myself, albeit in a rather limited fashion. I even bought one of your landscapes from Leopold. You have a real command of the subject."

"That's very kind of you."

"Kindness doesn't come into it; you have talent. Fascinating to see and yet such a departure from your early work . . ."

Bettina felt the color draining from her cheeks. He cocked his head, as if intrigued by her reaction.

"Berlin isn't another country, you know. There are many who remember such a promising young upstart. I made a point of going back to see your progression as an artist. I dug up some of your earlier compositions."

He looked down at his immaculate dress uniform, his long fingers brushing away the ash he imagined having fallen on his lapel.

"They were . . . competent." The word hung in the air and stung her into silence.

"I don't mean to offend. But you could see Kandinsky's hand on your shoulder and in times like these, that really isn't prudent."

He glanced around as if they might be overheard and then smiled again.

"But don't mistake me. Not all of us are that averse to abstract expressionism; I have a fondness for it myself and still possess a few favorite items which I have no intention of parting with. I don't choose to divulge those tastes to my compatriots, but feel sure I can rely on your discretion."

She inclined her head, amazed at the steadiness of her own voice when it came.

"And I on yours?"

"Of course. You may be relieved to know that those earlier compositions of yours were burned, along with a great many other works deemed unsuitable. As far as anyone else is concerned, your career started with *The Viking*."

The corner of his mouth twitched up, almost a smile of reassurance, although she wasn't sure it reached his eyes.

"For what it's worth, I think you made the right decision," he continued. "In the current climate, romantic realism is a more pragmatic choice. It will be the defining medium of the century. Don't you agree?"

Still uncertain of his motives, she gave a little nod of acquiescence.

"To my mind, the difference between a competent artist and a great one is often just a matter of timing. In the old world you were destined to follow the men who came before you, but in this one, the page is clean. Few have made their mark as yet. Just think of the place art created in this city will have in history. The whole world will take notice."

Barely knowing how to respond, Bettina tried to laugh it off. "I have no desire to be recognized."

"Whyever not? It is an indicator of talent and it will raise your stock. You're sensible enough; you must know already that art is a marketplace, like any other. You are well placed to set out your stall, young lady." He gestured to the room, sweeping a trail of smoke. "These are the people who decide what makes great art by paying for it handsomely. If they deem you worthy, why would you deny it?"

His small eyes seemed to pin her.

"I will personally introduce you to Gurlitt; his patronage can only be of benefit to you. Together we'll facilitate your transition from someone being talked about to one who controls the conversation."

Uncertain how to respond, Bettina considered his words. She was wary of the prospect, but if she had money and influential backers, how different might the future be, for her and Max?

"Thank you." She nodded. "I would greatly appreciate it."

His manner immediately became warmer; less imposing.

"Have you been to Lake Starnberg, to the Rose Island?"

She shook her head.

"I have a summerhouse there with a little studio. Why don't you come up this weekend as my guest? I will arrange a private view for Gurlitt and some other influential people. It's as inspiring a setting as you can imagine—the light is wonderful. On a clear day you can see the Alps."

He seemed to be waiting for a response, so she gave another brief nod and a tight smile, unsure even as she did, quite what she was agreeing to. His strong hand took hold of her arm and steered her back out into the crowd.

"Come then, let's make sure Munich knows you have arrived."

Weeks passed slowly without word. Bettina tried to settle into life alone and the rhythms of the city. Finally a telegram arrived from Richard, announcing his intention to visit.

When he arrived, she ran to him and held on tight. When she finally relinquished her hold, she saw he was exhausted. She ushered him inside.

"I'll put a pot of coffee on; you look like you might need it."

While she waited for it to brew, Richard walked around the small space, surveying the sketches that were scattered over every surface. She had several easels on the go, each one a work in progress and a dozen or so completed canvasses leaned up against the walls, including some small farm scenes and several large landscapes that featured tempestuous storms. Richard went from canvas to canvas, ducking down to see each one, then standing back to look at the totality. Bettina, hovering nearby, tried to read his expression.

"Well?" she demanded finally when he had failed to speak.

"I can't believe how prolific you've become."

"'Prolific' is a weasel word, if ever I heard one, Richard Amsel." She scowled as she handed him the cup of coffee.

"I like the farm scenes well enough, but they're a little too romantic for my tastes. These, though"—he ducked back down, at a level with the sweeping landscapes—"these ones are magnificent."

"You really like them?"

"I do, I swear it solemnly. There's something of Munch about them in the proportions and the framing. But isn't any sort of abstraction rather risky if you're trying to seduce a conservative clientele?"

"Well, it would seem I've already succeeded in that aim . . . *The Viking* is going to be included in the Summer Exhibition at the Haus der Kunst."

Richard clapped his hand on her shoulder.

"That's incredible, Betti! You pulled it off, you clever thing."

Bettina allowed herself a shy smile.

"I feel a certain gleeful sense of irony knowing they're all fawning over my portrait of Max, saying what an exemplar of German masculinity he is. I just wish this wasn't what it took for me to survive."

"There's no shame in making a living." Richard glanced at her and took a deep breath. "While we're on that subject, I wanted to say how much I regret sending you back to live with Albrecht and your mother. I didn't realize at the time what a threat it posed to you."

"The decision to go back was mine."

"I hoped it might keep you and Max together."

Any mention of his name felt like a girdle tightening around her chest. Richard took hold of her hand.

"I can only imagine how hard these last few weeks have been for you, Betti. I promised you I'd find out what I could."

She felt her heart begin to race.

"There's no easy way to say this . . . I spent last evening with someone—can't tell you who, it wouldn't be safe for either of you, but suffice to say they have access to records of the district judiciary. They agreed to dig out Max's file for me."

She felt her focus narrow to his words.

"It seems that he has been charged with working under a false identity. Since the Anschluss the authorities have arrested thousands of Jews on trumped-up charges. They searched the house in Allach and found some letters from his parents, which they've used as justification to confiscate their remaining assets in Vienna."

He looked at her squarely. "Now then, I need you to be brave for me. Max has been sentenced to hard labor and sent to the dentention camp in Dachau. There is no date for his release. It seems they're intent on making an example of him."

Bettina leaned against the wall behind her and slowly slumped to the floor.

"Can you be certain?"

"I have no reason to doubt it." Richard sat down beside her. "These places aren't like prison, Bettina.

"I've heard some pretty dreadful things . . . I don't say this to upset you, but I feel you need to know."

Her stoicism abandoned her; she leaned into Richard's shoulder, a wordless, broken cry escaping her. It racked her till her voice was hoarse.

She'd heard rumors about the camps, of course. Everyone had; Dachau was close by. She had cycled past it months before and shivered, wondering what went on beyond the barbed-wire lines. The papers spoke of the internment camps quite often, though the particulars were vague. She heard people whisper about the criminals and prisoners, those identified as "subhuman" who were held there, but none of them asked questions. They did not want to know.

Richard held her for the long minutes it took her sobbing to subside. Her shuddering breaths signaled that she had no resources left. She sat, head down, breathing deeply. Eventually she stood and walked to the sink unsteadily, splashing water on her face.

"I'm so sorry. I feel awfully tired." Her voice was strained. "Would you mind terribly if I go and lie down?"

"Of course not."

Bettina took herself off to her small bed, trying to smother the sound as she cried herself into a fitful sleep.

When she woke, the sky had begun to dim toward twilight. As always, she placed a hand on her abdomen and felt the tightening hardness there, though she was certain no one else could see it. Every day she expected the telltale stain of blood that would tell her it was over, or had never been. She dreaded it, but could not bear to give oxygen to any ember of hope for fear she might extinguish it entirely. She said a prayer, a mantra to anyone and anything that might help—Gaia and Thor, Jesus, Mary, Yahweh, Krishna, Mother Nature, science— and then she dried her eyes.

Richard sat on the wide window ledge, looking out across the street.

"Why didn't you wake me?" she asked.

"I thought you needed to rest. I hope you don't mind; I opened some wine."

She sat down next to him, leaning against the cool plaster. Together they watched the sky go from deep blue to black, each lost in their own thoughts. From the studio below, a Beethoven piano sonata scaled the night sky.

"The Tempest," noted Richard. "How very apposite."

The notes rolled on with urgency. Bettina observed Richard, now lost in the music, only the streetlamp outside illuminating his features. Reflexively she picked up a sketchbook and a piece of charcoal and began to draw. The stick was delicate and had no weight; she had to hold it with the lightest touch to stop it from disintegrating into dust, like the scales from a dark-winged moth. It slid across the surface of the paper with a bite she could feel through her fingertips.

She noted again the dark circles under his eyes and the deeper creases at their corners. She wanted to ask directly what had brought on this fatigue, but began instead to chat idly of mutual friends in Berlin, of the art scene there and who she'd left behind.

"Are you still seeing Imre?"

Richard glanced at her while maintaining his position.

"Whenever I can, which isn't all that often." He paused. "She's a very sweet girl, but I don't think I can give her what she wants."

"Which is?" Bettina asked archly.

"I'm sure you can imagine."

"I suppose I can," she said. "Though I can't think for the life of me why you wouldn't want that with her."

His jaw tensed.

"Life is rather too complicated just now."

He looked as weary as she'd ever seen him. She waited for a moment before deciding the time had come.

"I know I'm hardly one to speak, but you do seem quite exhausted."

He dragged both hands down his face.

"I've been burning the candle at both ends."

"I rather thought as much . . . Care to unburden yourself?"

Richard stared down at a speckling of paint on the window-sill, picking at it with his nail.

"You remember Libertas—the woman who so infuriated your brother at your solo show? She's actually very well connected. Part of a group that want to resist this damned regime and what they're doing to our country. I've been running a few errands for her, to help out."

"Errands sound rather ominous."

"Not especially, but there are people in Munich that she wanted me to . . . cultivate. Including the person who told me about Max."

He didn't look up, his eyes and fingers still fixed on the glossy droplets of dried paint. He removed each one methodically before moving to the next.

"You remember those parties I used to take you to in Berlin: the wild ones with all those creative types? They started out in rather a benign fashion: just a forum to exchange ideas. Pleasantly drunken and debauched affairs. For some that meant freedom of speech; for others, the license to be themselves in a way that might be frowned on elsewhere. I'm sure you were conscious of it; you're not naive."

Bettina had spent many nights in the company of Richard's friends and knew there were places in Berlin that would tolerate almost any vice you'd care to mention—encourage it even. She'd always rather enjoyed being a tourist in that world, with Richard there to keep her safe—wading into darker waters knowing she could turn back.

Richard continued: "It became apparent there were powerful people in the regime who had some . . . less-than-savory appetites, shall we say, and who were keen to find an outlet."

"So, what's your part in it? Providing the fuel?"

"It started out that way. I still have my pharmaceutical connections, as you know. But now . . . it's a little more involved."

"And what does it entail, precisely?"

She made every effort to appear sanguine.

"Private parties for high-ranking people where they might indulge their peccadilloes, both chemical and carnal. We introduce them to actors, actresses, filmmakers . . . There's a lot that can be gathered from a briefcase while someone is in a stupor, or incapacitated in some other way."

Beethoven's piano continued all around them, revolving like a carousel.

"Some have appetites they wouldn't want the high command to know about. That provides us with a certain amount of leverage. They leave themselves open to persuasion. And photographic evidence can provide a measure of insurance down the line. These people I'm involved with, they're quite prepared to do whatever it requires."

He looked at her directly now. "There are a few of us—quite a few, in fact—who think we mustn't just roll over and let them have at it. We must push back. It's surprisingly simple at times, but it's not without its risks. I only tell you all this because I know you won't make a fuss."

"You can trust me."

"I do, implicitly."

Richard averted his gaze again and returned to scratching at the spattered paint drops on the sill.

"We have Berlin well covered, but we still need to make inroads into Munich. The contact who helped with Max is useful, but they're rather low-hanging fruit. I need to gain access to the upper echelons if I'm to be any real use." He rubbed his jaw, the scratch of stubble whispering. "I didn't plan to get in quite so deep, but this is where we find ourselves. My brother has been doing something similar for a time; I suppose I felt it vital that I play my part. We'll be at war soon—it seems inevitable. We must do what we can to regain our Germany, to salvage what is left."

His voice was impassioned but close to breaking. She knew the strain of living with subterfuge only too well: the fear of a knock on the door. A dual existence always takes its toll.

Richard finally looked up and gave her a weary grin.

"Sorry. I didn't mean to burden you. Only, I can't really

speak of it to anyone. I don't want to risk exposing Imre and the others in my circle have their own concerns. I hope you don't mind."

"Of course I don't. I only wish you'd talked to me before. How long has this been going on?"

"Since shortly after Max was arrested. It galvanized something in me."

Even in the softening glow of the lamplight, he had a look of grim determination. He drained his wine and dropped his head, staring into the empty glass.

"Perhaps I've had enough."

"Aren't you afraid?"

"A little. But I'll be damned if I go down without a fight. I'm surprised to find I love my country ardently. Who would have thought it of a cynic such as me?"

When Richard returned the following morning to say goodbye, he found Bettina painting.

"I couldn't sleep, so I got up early to start work."

She was sketching out another landscape—a lone swallow careening over a flooded grassland. The columns of a classical temple stood starkly white against the canvas. Richard recognized the scene from their Dessau days.

"Is that the Georgium Gartenreich?"

"Well-spotted. You should try picking up a brush again sometime. It might do you good; I feel like you need somewhere to escape."

They sat at the kitchen table, Bettina momentarily lost in thought.

"What you talked about last night had quite an impact on me."

"How so?"

"I have spent weeks worrying about Max, terrified for him and me. There have been times when I could barely function; it's eaten me up, but I've been unable to do a single thing to help him."

"It must be awful."

"It is but I'm sick of feeling sorry for myself, especially given that you have been out there, doing your bit."

"Hardly."

"I know you, Richard. I have no doubt you've underplayed the risks involved in what you're doing. I admire you for your stand and I intend to do the same."

A flicker of concern.

"And just how do you propose to do that?"

She looked him straight in the eye.

"I met someone recently and I think he's just the sort of person that should be—how did you put it?—cultivated. He's quite high up in the SS, a liaison with the Reich Culture Chamber."

Richard frowned. "I'm not sure that's a good idea."

"He's the one who introduced me to Hildebrand Gurlitt and various others. Just the sort of people you require."

"I don't want to get you involved in this, Betti. It's a messy business. Dangerous."

Bettina's jaw set with determination.

"I can't do much for Max except wait, but would you have me do nothing at all? I need to be of use. I don't propose doing anything riskier than keeping my eyes and ears open, but you said you were trying to gain access to the upper echelons in Munich; well I have that and we shouldn't let it go to waste."

Her eyes flashed.

"I need to do this, Richard. I have to—for Max and me."

CHAPTER TWELVE

Dachau

Summer 1938

In his dreams, Max heard the pounding of feet again. He could never quite tell if they were coming toward him or running away. He was paralyzed, as always, unable to move or lift his head, his limbs solid as a tree fallen in the forest, the roots still half anchored in the soil. He waited for the hand to fall, the blow to strike, the boot to land. He braced himself for contact and the blossom of agony, so fast to bloom . . .

Max awakened. The man in the bunk above him shifted mere inches from his face, a drift of dust falling, floating in the air, gritting his half-open eyes. He shut them tight again and scrambled from the wooden box, out onto the floor. There was no time to waste. The bunks in the barracks of Dachau were narrow and so crammed together that if you were the last man down you could find yourself at the end of the line for the stinking *Scheißhaus*. It was bad enough when it had been sluiced, but early in the morning the stench was so strong it would stick to your clothes and in the hairs of your nostrils for hours.

The call to rise came at 4 a.m., just before dawn. With little time to ready himself for the day, Max had learned to make every minute count. Two men carried a hulking metal pail from the kitchens to the *Stuben*, the barracks where they lived. He ate his meager rations from a metal tin, an object of great value. You were forced to use it if you needed a piss in the night and woe betide if it got lost; it meant you couldn't eat.

Roll call came as the sun rose over the yard. A chill breeze billowed through his uniform as he stood alone in a sea of men and boys, some elderly and frail, some young and terrified. All were quiet and cowed and those that weren't soon learned; they had the lessons beaten into them.

Though he was young, strong and healthy, a shiver of fatigue would often ripple through his bones. He would not allow himself to succumb to it and slump. He knew a stumble or faint could mean a brutal whipping or far worse, so he held himself up as best he could until the sun rose and warmed his face with its scornful light.

At least the morning roll call was usually finite; they had the working day ahead. The evening assembly could extend indefinitely. They might be forced to stand for hours on end as punishment, in rain and fading light, until the sky went black and the beams from the towers pinned them in their glare.

In the weeks since he'd arrived the numbers of men had risen exponentially. "Asocial" Germans, Jews and Gypsies with a criminal record, all arrested and dumped in Dachau. With thousands crammed together, sleep was near impossible, even when they weren't kept awake by the rattle and screech of the railway, now running day and night. Trains came from all across the realm, iron snakes that slithered through the suburbs, their human cargo hidden from sight.

After roll call they went to work, although often its only purpose seemed to be to break the spirit. One detail would be charged with digging in the gravel pits, another pulling carts of heavy stone, or draining nearby marshland. Some work details left the site, under the watchful eye of the *Außenkommando*, traveling to towns nearby. Max yearned to go with them; to see the world outside of Dachau, even if he was still separated from it.

His first weeks had been seen through the haze of hard labor, part of a ten-man team forced to drag a hulking roller, crushing stone to surface the surrounding roads. He knew he must escape it if he was to survive, but better details had to be earned.

With a piece of wood and a shard of glass wrapped in a scrap of cloth, he began whittling; he started with a rough comb, which he then traded up. Over time his reputation grew. He was lent a small knife in return for carving chess pieces, and though poorly formed, they led to more.

One evening Max was walking back from roll call when the sound of running feet coming up behind made him spin around, his fists already bunched. His pursuer was a young man, tall and gangly, his skin darker than any he had seen since leaving Berlin. The young man held up his hands defensively.

"I just want to talk."

He fell into step beside Max as he walked at a trot.

"Are you the one who does the whittling?"

Max looked at him out of the corner of his eye.

"Depends on what you're after. And you'll have to find the wood yourself."

The man grinned.

"I can make anything I need myself. I just wanted to see what kind of man carves a chess piece like this . . ."

From his pocket he pulled a knight that Max recognized: the legs and torso rearing up, a crude mane flowing down its back. He'd carved it for a man who worked in the kitchens and had given him a branch of winter lime. It had worked so well under his knife that Max couldn't help but add some flourishes. The kitchen man had been impressed and since then had often slopped a little extra in his tin.

"Where did you learn to make something like this?" The younger man asked, trying to keep up with Max and his fast pace.

"I was a sculptor before I was sent here."

"Have you heard of Allach Porcelain?"

Max stopped dead in his tracks. "That was where I worked . . ."

"Small world, my friend."

He put out his hand, which Max gripped in astonishment.

"Stefan."

"Max." He shook his head in disbelief. "You work at Allach; what do you do?"

"I used to be an apprentice stonemason, but the guards decided the only job I was fit for was shoveling coal."

"Do you think you can get me on your work duty?"

He shrugged. "That's not up to me."

Max seized his elbow. "There's a man there—Holger Ostendorff, the artistic director . . ."

"Tall with glasses?" asked Stefan.

Max nodded. "Can you tell him I'm here? Max Ehrlich. He'll remember me."

Stefan looked doubtful. "I don't know. I can try, but the *Außenkommando* watch over us like hawks . . ."

Max kept an eye out for Stefan from that day, but didn't see him again for several weeks. Then one morning after roll call he was directed to the gate. Stefan was there, along with half a dozen others, waiting to climb aboard a bus. He clapped him on the back in greeting.

"Thought I might see you again." He checked the guards weren't listening. "Your friend doesn't come down to the kilns often, but I saw him eventually. This one guard is the very devil; he promised me a beating, but Herr Ostendorff stood up for me and listened when I told him I'd met you."

"I wasn't sure he'd want me back."

"He must do. I suppose that's why you're here."

The journey from Dachau to Lindenstraße was short. They soon pulled up to the front yard Max had shoveled the winter before. He stood up unsteadily and looked over to where he had lain, bloodied and beaten, all those months before. Beyond, the entrance to the alleyway, where Albrecht had humiliated him. He sent up a prayer for Bettina, hoping she'd escaped her brother and his malevolence. He clung to the thought of her, holding her image in his head.

The *Außenkommando* marched Max and the rest of the work detail through the factory doors. One guard clamped a hand on Max's shoulder, making him jump, his nerves a live wire singing with tension. He steered Max toward the administration office, where he'd once stood in line as Friedrich Marchen, waiting to collect his earnings.

Holger's secretary stood up when she saw him. She asked the guard to wait and ducked her head briefly around the office door. She nodded to the guard as she sat back at her desk and he pushed Max forward at the sound of Holger's voice.

"Come in."

Max took off his cap as he entered. He twisted it in his hands, a sheen of sweat on his upper lip. The secretary closed the door.

"Dear boy."

Holger came and took him in his arms. The touch of another in kindness felt so alien to Max that he was lost for words. He hugged him back, unaware of the tears flowing from him freely.

"It's all right," Holger said. "It's all right now."

He tried his best to hide it, but Holger was shocked by Max's appearance: the roughly shorn head, his brown curls gone, replaced by stubble. And he was gaunt, his cheekbones now sharp like razors in his face. His uniform was stiff with grime and hung off him like a sailcloth.

Their conversation was necessarily brief; the guard was outside waiting for Max, but Holger promised to come and find him later. As they left the office, he told the guard to take Max to the studio, to his obvious frustration.

"But, Herr Direktor, he should be shifting coal with that black-skinned Rhineland bastard."

Holger insisted; they were hard pressed and he needed an experienced hand. Reluctantly the guard relented.

The factory was working at capacity, turning out military figures by the dozen, but Holger instinctively knew what the public wanted in turbulent times: not soldiers, but animals. The signature sentimental style of Allach was a solace in such moments.

Max was set to task modeling a doe-eyed greyhound, based

on Holger's own beloved Marthe. He was given a small work desk in a busy room of contract workers and threw himself into carving Marthe's coltish form, watching through the window as she ran in wild, looping circles on the scrubland behind the factory.

Max relished the return to working with his hands and losing himself in occupation. He worked longer hours and harder than ever before, but still, he was not pulling a ton of iron and stone and so was conscious of his fortune.

Weeks passed and the rhythm of his working day at Allach slowly settled. Max was often exhausted and found his eyesight strained, but the familiarity of these surroundings was a comfort.

Holger felt like a weight had lifted too, only realizing in retrospect how deeply his friend's sudden and inexplicable departure had affected him. The constant surveillance of the *Außenkommando* made it difficult for them to talk, but he made sure Max saw him every day. It was his annual tradition to make a pilgrimage to the summer exhibition at the Haus der Deutschen Kunst, but he put it off for weeks so he could keep his eye on Max. Eventually he realized he could delay no longer: he had to keep up with developments. Reichsführer Heinrich Himmler often became inspired by a piece of sculpture or a painting he saw hanging there, and Holger didn't want to be caught out.

He finally hopped a train to Bahnhof München and headed in through the classical columns of the portico. The three-dimensional work was his passion; he was far less enamored of the prints and paintings, which often left him cold, but on this day one piece stood out. Intensely powerful and arresting, it featured a solitary male figure, striking-looking, well-proportioned and somehow eerily familiar. It drew him in; he looked at it more closely. The uncanny resemblance to Max was undeniable, though the figure was indisputably Aryan, honey-haired and blue-eyed, where Max was dark.

Holger returned to the factory the following day and asked his secretary, Fräulein Schaffer, to have Max brought to his office.

With the guard stationed outside and the door firmly shut, Holger laid out the exhibition catalog and opened it to the image of *The Viking*. He saw Max's eyes widen in astonishment.

"I take it you know the artist?"

Max acknowledged it reluctantly.

"I do. But please, Holger, promise you won't say another word? I trust you unreservedly but I can't talk about it and no one else must know."

The summer days began to turn and Max found himself fixated. On the wooden table in front of him stood a rough clay figure of a man, one knee raised and placed firmly on a rocky outcrop underneath his feet. The body would take many days to complete, but for now his focus was entirely on the face. This was where the sculpture lived or died and his attention narrowed down to the center of his vision and the movement of the blade.

Max found he operated best between breaths. He had worked to stretch this distance, increasing his lung capacity until, like a diver, he could descend to great depths and stay there longer. When his consciousness was so submerged, he honed it further still, working almost between heartbeats. The slow thud of his blood signaled to him when to lift the pin-sharp point of the blade and when to press it in. As they emerged, the features of the face were a mirror of his own. He found it disconcerting to carve his own image in miniature.

His reference sat in front of him; a large black-and-white photograph of *The Viking* hanging in the gallery. He had propped it up against the wall beside the window, so it sat just at the edge of his vision. He referred to it frequently, wanting to capture precisely what the artist had intended, without imposing himself. It would be as if the paint had been transposed into clay. Each time he looked at it, a memory stirred in his muscles, bringing back the hours when he had stood, posed in that very same position. His thoughts turned to how the night had ended, too—the pair of them together, bound as one.

When he'd finished, he noticed that in this version of the painting, the rabbit at the Viking's heel had been obscured. Bettina had made it her avatar in the original, a self-portrait in metamorphosis. He'd often called her his little rabbit, his *kleines Kaninchen*.

He decided to lift his scalpel blade again, to reinsert the rabbit from his memory. When she saw it, she would know. It would be a signal, sent out to her the only way he safely could.

"Do me up?"

Bettina looked over her shoulder at Richard. He fastened the choker collar at the nape of her neck.

"Thank you."

Richard drifted back to the velvet chair and flopped down as she lifted a small garnet earring, fixing it in place.

"I'm most awfully glad you're coming with me."

"I'm curious to meet this Karl at last. What's he like?"

"Cultured and very wealthy. He sent this dress as a gift,

possibly fearing I'd turn up in the same ratty tea dress I've worn every other time I've seen him."

She smoothed down the skirt, which fitted her to perfection, though she noticed the slightest thickening of her waist.

The dress, boxed and wrapped in tissue, had arrived at her door a few days earlier, along with an invitation to a private soirée at the Holz residence in Munich. Opening the box, she had pulled out the long column of pale rose silk. Her first instinct had been to send it back, until she considered everything that Richard had told her about his efforts at resistance. She telegrammed him in Berlin instead, to let him know an opportunity had finally arisen.

Bettina adjusted the dress one last time; it dropped to the ground and swept the floor. She turned her shoulder to look at the lattice of thin silk straps that crossed at the back, woven into an intricate geometric design.

"Karl's a pragmatist, I think. He professed a private fondness for expressionism. He knows my own artistic history, but he doesn't seem concerned by it."

Richard looked at her with naked skepticism.

"Anyone who goes along with this for self-advancement is no less terrifying than an ideologue. At least ideologues have convictions."

Bettina sat down at her dressing table to brush her hair. Richard watched her reflection. "So, tell me, I know all about his career and contacts, but nothing of his private life. Is he married?"

"He was once; his wife died young, apparently."

Richard gave a derisive snort. "That explains why he is sending you expensive gifts and party invitations, then . . ."

"I don't get the sense that he's attracted to me, though he

is hard to get the measure of. I stayed at his lake house for a few days, before showing my paintings to Gurlitt. That's when he told me *The Viking* would be exhibited at Haus der Deutschen Kunst. He was a gentleman. In fact, he's rather cool and detached."

She applied a dark red stain to her lips as Richard leaned back on the chaise.

"Well, Libertas was suitably excited," said Richard. "It seems this Holz has a strong hand where the SS intersects with the arts. Perhaps it's no bad thing if he has taken a shine to you. But won't he mind you bringing me as your guest?"

Bettina picked up a thick sable brush and powdered her face.

"Every girl in Munich has spent the last few years trying to snag him, apparently. I'm sure he could be married if he wanted."

"Do be careful, Betti; you might think you have the measure of him, but he didn't get to wear that uniform by being a pragmatist. I've seen how they operate. They can sniff out someone who isn't ideologically driven, and they simply do not get promoted. How well do you really know him?"

She shrugged. "All I know is we both agree it's worth the risk."

"Well, stay on your toes. It's easy to be seduced by these people. I've seen it happen, felt the pull of it myself. It might seem like you're in control, but you need to keep your wits about you. It's one thing me risking my own neck; but I don't want to risk yours."

When they arrived in the lobby of the apartment building, they were ushered into an elevator by a doorman and swept up several floors. They stepped straight out into a private apartment, where a maid waited, ready to take their coats.

Nervously, Bettina glanced at her reflection in a gilded mirror. "How do I look?"

"Pale as porcelain," Richard muttered. "Pinch your cheeks and put on a smile."

When the maid returned, she ushered them into a spacious drawing room with walls the color of blue bisque. This space alone seemed vast to Bettina, but as they moved forward she found that one room swept into another. Small groups lounged or stood about talking quietly; the women were all in floor-length silk or taffeta, and most of the men were in uniform, standing with the stiff gait of the soldier.

Conscious that many eyes were on them, Bettina walked as gracefully as she could, though the carpet was so dense and deep she worried she might lose her footing, or turn an ankle. It forced her to glide in a way that felt deeply unnatural, as if she were onstage. She had always considered herself adaptable—able to adopt new mannerisms and ways of speech, to reflect whatever company she kept—but here she felt exposed, an imposter in the spotlight. She kept an eye on Richard: as ever he appeared to be entirely relaxed and self-possessed. He steered them to a pair of cocktail chairs where she sat stiffly, straightening her skirt.

"Buck up, Betti," Richard whispered. He assessed their opulent surroundings. "You weren't wrong about his wealth."

She understood that Karl Holz came from money and had accumulated more. His home on Lake Starnberg was gracious in the extreme, but this was the first time she'd been inside his

Munich residence. He had previously begged her forgiveness that he was unable to invite her.

"My sister, my nephew and my little niece are staying with me," he'd apologized. "Her husband died last year. A hunting accident. Tragic, of course, but . . . he was rather a weak man, I'm afraid. No match for my sister."

In the corner of the room there was a baby grand piano, where a rather intense young man sank over the keys playing Schubert. A maid went past carrying a tray of champagne cocktails in coupe glasses, bubbles winking through stars etched in the bowls. Richard lifted down two and handed one to Bettina. She raised it and brushed it to her lips. She found she'd developed a distaste for it in recent weeks. Along with slight sporadic nausea, it served as a reminder that time was moving on. Her life would soon be altered beyond recognition. Richard drained his glass in one and gave her rather a tight, forced smile.

"I'll go and get another. A little liquid courage never goes amiss. For you?"

She shook her head. He stood and went off in search of the maid.

Bettina gazed around. She found it dizzying that anyone really lived like this. Karl Holz chose to surround himself with nothing but the best: nothing broken, nothing out of place. It seemed incredible that someone could curate their home as one would an exhibition, each item carefully selected.

At the far end of the room, next to a marble fireplace, stood a small girl with rosebud lips and large blue eyes. She was sucking her thumb and holding a careworn velvet bunny by the ear. Next to her was a rather serious-looking boy, a few years older, with hair that refused to lie flat. He was wearing the uniform of the Hitler Youth.

Bettina felt a light touch on the skin of her bare shoulder.

"I'm so sorry I wasn't here to greet you personally."

Karl took her hand and kissed it formally. Then he raised his glass to hers, chiming them together.

"Welcome to my home. It is wonderful to have you here at last."

Bettina indicated the two children at the foot of the tree.

"Are they your niece and nephew? I'm so sorry, I've quite forgotten their names."

"Julia and Christophe. I allowed them to stay up a little later than usual so that you could meet them. Let me introduce you; Julia will be charmed by your appearance. She helped pick out your dress."

As they approached, the young girl stared, wide-eyed.

"Julia, *Liebchen*, this is my friend, Fräulein Vogel. Stand up and show her your pretty manners."

Julia lifted her taffeta skirt before dipping into a little curtsy with such a deathly serious expression, it made Bettina laugh.

"Delighted to meet you, Julia," she said, dropping a curtsy to mirror her formality.

"And this is Christophe." Karl gestured to the boy. She put out her hand to shake his, but he snapped his arm up, making her flinch.

"Heil Hitler!"

Karl responded in kind, then dropped his hand to rub his nephew's hair with affection. Bettina smiled weakly. The boy stared back at her in silence.

"Now, children . . ." Karl reached up to the mantelpiece and brought down a candle-lantern. "A very important person gave me this, a gentleman by the name of Heinrich Himmler."

The boy's eyes widened.

"I see you recognize his name, Christophe; very good. Not only is he the *Reichsführer-SS*, but he owns a wonderful porcelain factory not far from here, and the clever artists there made this. It is something very precious to me, so I know you will make sure no harm comes to it."

Bettina felt a chill pass through her at the mention of the porcelain factory. She looked around the room for Richard and saw that he was watching from a distance. He raised his glass to her surreptitiously.

Karl handed Christophe the lantern. With great care, he lit a match and held it to the wick, which glowed into life. He shook the match out in haste, lest it should burn his little fingers, and handed the lamp to Karl, who put it back in pride of place.

"Now, who is ready for some Scho-Ka-Kola? A little treat before bedtime."

He took down a metal tin and squatted at their level. Both children's eyes lit up. Karl grinned indulgently, seeming altered in their company. He signaled for the children's nanny, who was hovering nearby.

"You may take them away now, Heida."

The children so dismissed, Karl guided Bettina over to a coterie of uniformed men whose sweating faces and disheveled hair indicated a level of inebriation she hadn't been expecting. Although her brother often drank to excess while in uniform, Karl and his friends had seemed more reserved. Tonight though, they all appeared determined to shake off formality.

They teased Karl volubly, amused that he was introducing them to a woman some fifteen years his junior.

As the evening wore on, Bettina caught glimpses of Richard from across the room, charming different groups, gregarious as ever, but they barely got the chance to speak. Karl seemed intent on shepherding her around, introducing her to the other guests, most of whom she'd never met. Hildebrand Gurlitt was there and she saw the artist Ziegler passing through.

At some undetermined point, the party descending from sophistication into drunken revelry, massed voices were raised in song, bellowing out "Die Fahne Hoch," the Nazi Party anthem, which seemed to transform otherwise hard-faced old men into a sentimental mess. For a time, Bettina was cornered by one such gentleman, who pinned her to the wall with his whiskey-sodden breath.

"I'm not against Christianity, but it can be taken too far, and it starts to smack of Jewry. We should do better—German blood and German soil, eh?"

She was trying in vain to escape him when an older, angular woman appeared and begged the man's indulgence; she needed to steal Fräulein Vogel. As she steered Bettina away, she introduced herself as Liesl Braemer, Karl's sister. Like him, she seemed rather dry. Her strawberry-blond hair was waved and set hard, as if carved from cherrywood. She was pinched and thin; elbows, cheek- and collarbones protruding. The siblings shared the same long face and small, inscrutable eyes, though hers seemed rather dull. Perhaps a result of early widowhood, Bettina wondered.

"I thought we ought to meet, given the way my brother spoke of you. Now, tell me, how is it that you never married?"

Bettina was momentarily lost for words.

"I'm not sure how to answer that . . . No one ever saw fit to propose to me, I suppose."

"How disappointing. I was hoping for a little scandal to enliven things. Still, a mature, unmarried woman is a scandal in itself." She pursed her mouth in a smile and Bettina found her attention fixed on the lines around her thin lips, where the lipstick bled.

Liesl peppered her with questions, some innocuous, others seeming to be traps: Where did you go to school, do you know this family or that, who is your brother's Kommandant? Eventually, her curiosity seemingly satiated, she took hold of Bettina's fingers and squeezed.

"I'm so glad the dress fits. I told Karl that you might not have anything appropriate." She didn't wait for Bettina to respond. "Now, I must get on. You've monopolized me for far too long!"

She drifted away, signaling to the waitstaff to circulate and refill drinks. Bettina watched as she joined a clique of chic older women. Liesl's eyes occasionally drifted back to hers and she would smile and wave, her laughter shrill above the chatter.

Bettina searched through rooms on the hunt for Richard, finally locating him in a small study, playing cards with a table full of high-ranking officers. They were rather red in the face and roaring drunk. Richard raised his brows as if to ask if she needed him. She shook her head, before heading back into the fray.

She noticed that, though there were many women in attendance, they all appeared to be attached. They were the wives or girlfriends of the SS officers, the members of the Reich Chamber of Culture or Karl's friends from the art world. Karl himself appeared to be unaccompanied. In fact, as the evening wore on, he seemed more than ever to be by her side, attentive and solicitous. He took her to meet a rather rotund art collector, the buttons of his waistcoat bulging as he praised her work and offered up suggestions.

"Expand your Vikings," he said. "Paint something for the winter solstice celebrations this year: Odin with a flowing beard on his white charger and a sackful of gifts. What do you think, eh, Karl? It would be a triumph!"

"That it would. I'm certain Himmler would get behind it. The Norse gods are vitally important—they represent the Aryan ideal, the purity and longevity of our bloodline. The good burghers of this country need to be made proud of their stock again."

He turned to Bettina. "Your work does that; you take these quintessentially Germanic scenes and bring them all to life so vividly."

The collector winked at Bettina. "I'd hang on to him, young lady. He seems to like you."

Bettina could feel a blush rising on her chest.

"Will you excuse us?" Karl asked. "I need to show Fräulein Vogel something in the other room."

He indicated to her to follow, striding off down a dark corridor with the same soft carpet that seemed to swallow up the sound from the party. She hesitated, then began to follow.

At the end of the corridor was a large, walnut-veneered door. Karl opened it and ushered her in. The room was masculine, opulent and quietly luxurious. Against one wall stood a vast sleigh bed, made up with crisp white linens. Beside it stood two discreet Lalique lamps, which cast a warm glow. All was immaculate, not an item out of place. It smelled fresh and clean, of beeswax polish and expensive French pomade.

Karl strode purposely to a dressing table, where he retrieved a long black box with gold accents, tied around with an ochre bow of thick silk ribbon. He handed it to Bettina.

"Forgive me for dragging you away, but I wanted to find a quiet moment to give you this."

He gestured to a low chair, where she sat, the box heavy in her hands. She hesitated, then gently pulled the ribbon, which slipped undone and dropped across her knees. She lifted the lid, which rose slowly, sucking in the air around it.

She placed the lid to one side and peered into the box. It took a moment before she recognized what lay within—it was entirely familiar to her and yet so unexpected that she could not make sense of what her eyes were seeing.

Lying nestled in a velvet-lined sarcophagus was *The Viking*, her Viking: sword in hand, three dimensions of white, reflective porcelain.

Almost the full length of her forearm, he was cold and precise in every detail, from the rocky outcrop he stood upon to the dense fur cape that covered his broad shoulders. With trembling hands, she lifted him from the soft velvet confines and held him in front of her. She reached out a fingertip to touch the sharp point of the blade and caress the hard lines of the jaw; Max's features were mirrored in miniature. It was perfection.

She felt tears fill her eyes but couldn't formulate the words to speak. Karl hovered before her anxiously.

"I got word from a friend in Himmler's office. It was only delivered a few days ago." He laughed nervously. "I know you are the artist, so by rights it should be yours, but believe me, I had to pull a lot of favors in. They're terribly rare."

He paused, as if unsure how to proceed. A tear slipped down Bettina's cheek.

"I had no idea . . . How can I ever thank you?"

She brushed the tear away. Karl averted his gaze.

"I take no credit for the artistry; that lies entirely with you and the talented craftsmen of Allach."

Of course, it must be Allach; silly of her not to think of it—where else? Assailed by emotion, she felt for a moment as if she couldn't breathe.

"I'm sorry; did I do the wrong thing?"

"Not at all. I just . . . it wasn't something I was expecting."

She looked back at the bone-white porcelain in her hands, wanting to absorb it all at once; her eyes darted from head to toe, turning him over, side to side. And then she saw it: crouched at his heel, the faithful rabbit, her *Kaninchen* avatar. When she'd completed the transformation of *The Viking* she'd chosen to paint over it. No one else had ever known that it was there. No one, except Max.

Bettina returned to her Neuhausen studio alone long after midnight. She had searched the party for Richard, but found no sign of him. Karl insisted on waking up his driver to take her home and she'd sat on the broad leather bench, holding tight to her porcelain Viking as the silent city streets slipped past.

She fell onto the bed, her mind too occupied for sleep. Then came a tentative knock at the door. Richard was leaning against the wall, hair and dress shirt rumpled, slurring his apologies.

"Sorry, sorry . . . I saw the driver leave and thought you might not be asleep."

"I couldn't settle; come on in."

He stumbled over the threshold and apologized again.

"Where did you get to?"

"I scarcely know myself. It's been a long night."

"Coffee?"

He nodded gratefully and went to the windowsill, where he lit a cigarette. Bettina turned on a stovetop burner and filled the kettle with water.

"Last I saw, you were fleecing various Kommandants for all they were worth."

"Other way around. Nota bene: don't play cards with old soldiers, as they can rather rinse you clean."

"Oh dear."

"It proved to be rather disarming, actually—made them feel superior."

Bettina arched an eyebrow. "I take it tonight proved fruitful, then?"

"A strong start, thanks to you. Without your introduction it could have taken months."

She handed him a cup of strong black coffee and sat beside him.

"Glad to be of service."

"How was your evening? You looked like the belle of the ball."

"It was rather odd. I felt at times like I was being vetted."

"To see if you're suitable Nazi wife material?"

She frowned in consternation.

"Perhaps. He certainly quizzed me about you."

Richard's eyebrows shot up. "In what way?"

"I think he thought we were an item; I told him we weren't, but I'm not sure he believed me. In any case, he warned me off."

Richard gave a rather hollow laugh. "I bet he did."

"Do you think they might be watching you?"

Richard took a long draw on the cigarette. He picked a fleck of tobacco from his tongue.

"I think there's every likelihood."

"Then you must be more careful."

"Oh, don't worry—I can look after myself. It's you that I'm concerned about. How do you intend to keep Herr Holz at arm's length?"

Outside the dark night had begun to lift.

"I'm not sure if I should . . ."

She hesitated.

"There's something I haven't told you, Richard. Or anyone, come to that . . ." It felt unreal to say the words out loud. "I think there's every chance I might be pregnant."

She tried to force a smile but it soon wavered. The expression of shock on Richard's face softened and turned to pity. She felt she almost couldn't bear it.

"Now then, none of that. You said yourself, I've a sensible head on my shoulders, so don't make a fuss. You know it was something Max and I had hoped for, desperately."

"Dear God Betti, why didn't you tell me sooner?"

"I wasn't sure, or certain it would last. Besides, as much as I have longed for this, congratulations are hardly in order now, are they? If word got out to anyone—Albrecht, for instance . . ."

She did not have to say more. He knew the risks to unwed mothers in the current climate: the prospect of the newborn being forcibly removed and put up for adoption, or worse should there be any suspicion of Jewish paternity. They still had no idea what Albrecht might have guessed at or reported.

"And there's something else . . ."

Bettina went over to the kitchen table to retrieve the black-and-gold box, which she handed to him. He held the cigarette between his teeth and used both hands to lift the lid, revealing the porcelain Viking, lying there in state. It took him a moment to comprehend what he was looking at. Then he laughed, incredulous.

"Where on earth did you get it?"

"Karl gave it to me; they're terribly hard to come by, apparently. Which rather begs the question: why would anyone make a porcelain figurine based on a relatively obscure painting? It was made at Allach, if you hadn't guessed."

The realization slowly dawned on Richard.

"Max?"

"You never got to see the pieces he sculpted, but it certainly looks like his work to me. And you see the rabbit?" She pointed to its form, half buried in the undergrowth. "That was in my original portrait, but then I painted over it. No one else could possibly have known. It's a sign to me, I'm certain of it."

"There are factories which use prisoners from Dachau as slave labor . . . I suppose it's possible, especially given Himmler's connections. But still—you mustn't get your hopes up, Betti."

Her face was resolute. "I know. You're right, but I can't possibly ignore it . . . I think Karl Holz might be the key to get to Max."

Months passed and summer began to slip, verdant greens dying to dust. Bettina stood on a raised dais covered in plush white carpet. She wore an ivory gown with broad shoulders and cap sleeves overlapping like petals. The empire line of the dress was simple, dropping to the floor and pooling out. Behind her a young woman wearing white cotton gloves straightened out the train and stepped back to admire her handiwork.

Bettina scrutinized her own reflection in a trifold mirror. She straightened her shoulders, thankful that the cut flattered and concealed her rounding abdomen. She observed herself without emotion. Her younger self would have wept to think she'd be so cavalier when choosing her bridal gown, but as this was nothing like she had ever envisaged that day being, it mattered very little. It would do, she thought. Rows of tiny hand-sewn seed pearls descended from her neck to breast in scalloped waves, the weight of them constricting. She eased a finger in, to release their choke hold on her throat.

"Don't do that," sniped Liesl. "You'll get a turkey neck."

Reclining in a blue velvet lounge chair, Bettina's future sister-in-law cast her critical eye over the ensemble.

"I'm glad to see you're putting on some weight. You were far too thin; it doesn't flatter a more mature face. You may be younger than Karl, but you're hardly a spring bride."

Bettina swallowed hard and tried to suck her stomach in. It was at these moments when she wondered how far down this road she might dare herself to go.

After she shared her news with Richard, he had gallantly asked her to marry him. She had cried, of course, and thanked him, but told him no. She desperately wanted to protect Max's unborn child, but she could not bring herself to do that to Imre, knowing it would break her friend.

She had no further plan, beyond getting through each day,

until one bright morning out at the lake, when Karl Holz suddenly proposed to her.

He'd offered her the use of his summerhouse for a few days of escape, which she'd gratefully accepted. On the second day he turned up out of the blue and proposed to her. It was all so unexpected she was rendered speechless for a time, until she finally felt compelled to fill the silence. She found herself saying she would think about it, in the clear-eyed knowledge that she barely knew the man, and did not harbor any fond feelings for him. She was not his friend, nor yet his lover—she was merely something it seemed he wanted to possess.

Over the next few days she considered the proposition and finally concluded each was getting something they required; there was a strange sort of equity in the lack of feeling on both sides. He wanted a beautiful artist wife, and she needed protection for the baby growing inside her and a path back to Max, if she could only somehow engineer it.

But as convinced as she had been in the moment, seeing it through was quite another matter. The reality of her situation dawned on her steadily in a series of aftershocks.

Karl was offered a six-month commission in Vienna, starting almost straightaway. Liesl declared a long engagement would be indecorous at their age and so the wedding was moved up. At first, Bettina accepted the news gratefully, eager to have plausible cover for her pregnancy, which was growing harder to conceal, but as the fact of it approached she found herself sickened by the prospect of giving herself to him. She told herself it was a small price to pay for safety, that it was her own decision, but in reality she felt all sense of agency being slowly stripped away.

There was a gentle cough and she suddenly realized the young seamstress was awaiting her response. She gave a nod.

"It's fine, thank you, Gretl."

Liesl sniffed. "Now then, girl, look sharp and help my sister out of her dress. We'll have to look at going-away outfits."

"I shan't need them, Liesl," said Bettina. "Karl has to leave for Vienna straight after the wedding, so we needn't make a fuss."

"On the contrary, that's all the more reason to make it an occasion. You must insist on a honeymoon, at least."

Behind her, Gretl began the intricate task of undoing the dozens of silk buttons that ran to the base of Bettina's spine. She felt a curious detachment as one virtual stranger undressed her, while another sat and watched the process. Though she'd spent very little time with Liesl, she found herself forced into intimacy with her ever more frequently.

"You'll need a new dress for bride school at least. When do you go?"

"I don't know if I shall; I'd be at least a decade older than the other brides."

She had no desire to fight, but neither did she intend to be lectured in what it took to be a good Nazi wife.

"Oh, you simply must, Bettina. It might reflect badly on Karl if you don't."

Liesl's guiding principle was always how Bettina's actions might affect her brother's standing. Or her own.

"You're terribly lucky," Liesl continued. "We didn't have anything like it in my day. I imagine there must be such cama-raderie among the girls. There are many things one wishes one had known as a young bride. And unlike you, I wasn't fortunate enough to have a sister who could teach me."

She had taken to referring to Bettina as "sister" since the engagement, though her idea of sorority seemed to extend no further than taking charge and belittling her. Bettina had determined to hold her tongue and her temper. Liesl's inability to do the same was proving useful.

Gaining access to Karl's inner circle had proved to be more valuable to the Resistance than even she had hoped. Richard had been able to extend the operation from Berlin to Munich, using Bettina as intermediary. She kept her eyes and ears open and wrote a weekly report on all the things she overheard: the telephone calls, snippets of conversation; the jokes and rumors spread about. She dropped off her reports at the publishing house of a Catholic magazine, addressing the envelopes to Richard's brother, Peter, who'd taken charge of coordinating their efforts. Richard refused to tell her what they did with the information she gathered; he felt it safer, but assured her she was helping the cause, which was all the purpose she required.

When the dress was fully unbuttoned, the girl took her by the shoulders and turned her away, so concealing her midriff from Liesl's critical gaze.

"Stay there," she whispered.

She went to the rail and took down a long silk gown, which she wrapped around Bettina's shoulders. She knelt to tie an elaborate bow at the waist, which concealed the swell of her stomach and drew the eye. Gretl stood back again to admire the effect. Liesl shot her a dark look.

"Why must you hover so?"

Bettina flashed the girl a grateful smile and went to sit down as she hurried away. Liesl watched her go.

"That girl's a simpleton. Does she have Slavic blood?"

She turned her attention back to Bettina.

"You'll need some *Tracht*, a nice dirndl; something more traditional, more *Völkisch*, for summer days at the lake or in the Alps. You're no Magda Goebbels and you won't be given license just because you're an artist. My brother is not yet in a place where you may do as you please."

"Thank you for all your help, Liesl. I do appreciate it."

"Oh, don't thank me. Only doing my duty. As you know, I dedicated myself to the service of my brother and his career long ago." She patted Bettina on the back of her hand. "God knows, we all rely on his advancement, one way or another."

From a small side table, Liesl picked up a newspaper and shook the pages out, scanning the headlines hungrily.

"Good to see Mussolini is finally talking sense, albeit in his own rather dreadful Latin way. He's written a manifesto on race, have you seen it?"

She shook her head and Liesl sighed.

"Well, do keep up; you need to try to stay informed."

Bettina hesitated.

"Liesl, do you think we'll go to war? I have asked Karl repeatedly, but he seemed dismissive of the prospect."

Liesl dropped her voice, hissing at Bettina, "I shouldn't have to remind you. It doesn't do to speak in public about things Karl may say to you in private."

Chastened, Bettina bowed her head. She could sense that Liesl relished her contrition. Karl had warned her that his sister was intent on turning Bettina into a project.

"She's been bored, I think, with only the children for company. She's had so little to do since her husband passed away and the other SS wives in Munich don't have much time for widows. They hate to be reminded that marriage to a soldier can be a messy business in the end."

Liesl's interest in her had seemed to Bettina like a blessing at the time, but it had soon become apparent she was using her wedding to reenter Nazi high society, despite her vocal scorn for it. She had a waspish turn of phrase that Bettina liked to note in her letters to Peter, knowing that he and Richard would be amused by her vicious barbs.

At that moment, she became aware that she was being scrutinized.

"You know, I've never really noticed it before, but in daylight, I think you're more handsome than you are pretty. Not that there's anything wrong with that; it's just that you possess a . . . masculine sort of beauty."

She laid a consoling hand on Bettina's wrist.

"May I offer some advice? You don't want to go the way of Frau Himmler. How that doughy frump managed to catch her husband's eye is anyone's guess. Did you know she was married before? It defies belief."

Liesl looked around and lowered her voice. "Apparently, Heinrich now has a very young secretary whom he's rather taken with. And really, who would deny him? These are powerful men and there are plenty of other women within arm's reach, if they so desire. If a man looks elsewhere because you can't be bothered to put the work in, you only have yourself to blame."

Bettina made a mental note to add that titbit of Kaffeeklatsch to her next report.

Gretl returned, wheeling a rack of dresses and suits. Liesl tutted.

"Not before time."

She turned back to Bettina and smiled benignly. "Let's just hope there's something here which might help."

An hour later, Liesl led the way back down the marble staircase and out onto the street, where Karl's driver, Gerhard, was waiting for them. The late afternoon sun reflected on the white stucco of the buildings, making them squint as they climbed in. Liesl instructed the driver that, before returning to the apartment, he was to take them on a detour to the botanical gardens.

"We need to make the most of these last warm days; it will be winter before you know it."

The gardens were golden as Liesl linked her arm with Bettina's and they strolled past the fountain of Neptune, his gray stone mass astride a writhing horse, his trident hoisted like a spade upon his shoulder.

For a while Liesl seemed content to keep her own counsel, merely passing comment on the clemency of the weather or the prettiness of the setting, but Bettina could tell she had something more she wished to say. By the time they'd done two turns around the formal beds, she had evidently determined the time was ripe.

"Can I be candid with you, Bettina dear? I sometimes wonder if you fully comprehend quite what you've entered into."

Bettina didn't know how to respond, but Liesl continued unabated.

"My brother has a very important place in society. A place of privilege, but with that comes great responsibility. I feel for you, I really do."

Bettina suppressed a smirk, knowing Liesl only ever had her own interests at heart.

"After you're married, you will enter a new domain. A women's Reich, if you will. It's not our place to concern ourselves with what the men do out there in the world. Our realm is the domestic—the place they return to, which gives them consolation and relief."

Liesl spoke to her with the patience of a mother to a very trying child.

"In the circle you are about to enter, the women are forensic in their judgment. They influence their husbands. These men hold power and control the access others have to it, which is of vital importance to Karl. So, you can either be a help to him, or a hindrance." Bettina understood her implicit threat: if you are found wanting, it will have an impact on us all.

She felt she must push back, at least a little.

"Liesl, I have no interest in gossip or trying to climb any social ladder. I have my work."

"This is precisely what I mean. You will not work after you are married. Your sole focus will be on giving my brother a family, and soon."

Bettina had been under no illusion that this was her real agenda; she was only surprised at Liesl's being this direct.

"I intend to, though I'm not sure it's any of your business," she replied calmly.

"Of course it is. It's imperative. I won't have my future niece or nephew being raised by some kind of *Rabenmutter*, the type of woman who can't wait to push her children out of the nest if they get in her way."

Bettina wondered again how long she could survive in these waters. Everywhere she turned there were hidden dangers lurking in the depths.

"Your brother knows who I am. He has never asked me to submit myself to him, or to give up my work. In fact, he's actively encouraged my career."

Liesl gave a brief, humorless twitch of the lips.

"So sweet that even at your age, you can still be so naive. You had been left on the shelf, my dear. You were lucky that my brother deigned to pick you up. I don't deny that you have talent, but that is not your purpose in life. When the time comes, you will put your own interests to one side and you will bear him two or three exquisite children. Be under no illusion: after the wedding, there will be no more art."

She thinks she has the measure of me, thought Bettina. *That I am just an independent spirit, reluctant to be tamed.*

Liesl continued. "Our family have had the great misfortune to marry weaklings; our strength seems to attract them. In truth, Karl's first wife did us all a favor when she died without giving him a child. We saw some steel in you and we admire it, but if you do not bend, you will be broken. I'll see to it myself."

Bettina blanched at the brutality. They walked on slowly, past a low pool of marigolds and pansies—burnt orange against purple. Finally, in a measured tone, Bettina replied, "I appreciate your honesty, Liesl. It helps me understand what is expected of me. Please, let me assure you, my one and only priority is the man I love."

*

The days shortened and time gathered pace. Bettina was at a crossroads once more, sat at a dressing table in the bridal suite of an Alpine lodge hotel. It was late and her face was bare, scrubbed free of makeup. Behind her hung the white beaded wedding gown, like a flag declaring her surrender.

The haste in which the preparations were finalized had left her breathless. Though Bettina lobbied for the wedding to be a small affair in Munich or Berlin, Liesl had overruled her. She felt a wedding at Obersalzberg in the Bavarian hills would solidify Karl's status; it was beloved by the Nazi high command, and as Liesl liked to remind her, status was everything.

On their arrival, Bettina was surprised to find herself charmed by the mountains. There was a sense of calm about the place, with its dense forests and sloping meadows dotted with wildflowers in violet, orange and white. The valleys echoed with the sound of lowing bells. In other circumstances she could have been happy here, perhaps found some tranquility. But not today.

Bettina noted blue shadows of fatigue beneath her eyes; she looked as tired as she felt. The wedding guests had long since retired to their beds, lulled by the mountain air and keen to rest, but she knew she was still hours from sleep.

Since accepting Karl's proposal, she'd felt her life was sliding out from under her. In desperation she'd painted herself into a corner and was unable to change course. It seemed like hardly any time since she and Max had been planning their escape. Now she was trying to reconcile herself to the prospect of consummating marriage to a man she barely knew.

She fantasized about packing up her case and leaving. She would go on foot to the station, catch the milk train to somewhere, anywhere. She could be halfway to Switzerland before anyone discovered she was gone. But that would mean abandoning Max to his fate, which she would never do. She refused to give up hope of helping him, of seeing him again.

In the morning she intended to pledge herself to a man she did not love and who required her to give up her art, the only thing that kept her sane. She felt justified, knowing she'd do anything to protect her unborn child, and yet it weighed on her, nonetheless. The thought of years without Max or her work felt like a life half lived.

A short, hard knock at the door shocked her from her depressive trance. She wasn't expecting any last-minute well-wishers and she had no friends or family attending.

"Who is it?"

"It's me," Karl replied, his voice hoarse.

For a moment Bettina froze. She had barely seen him since they arrived. To Liesl's palpable disappointment, the wedding had not attracted the Party's upper echelons, but those that were attending all seemed busily occupied. The men had spent the day in a huddle, dissecting the upcoming talks between Hitler, Chamberlain, Daladier and Mussolini.

Bettina wrapped her old silk kimono around her and crossed the room to open up the door. She saw straightaway that Karl was drunk; his graying hair, usually combed and creamed into submission, had flopped down over one eye, which glittered with dark intention. She reached out to push him away, her palm against his chest.

"You're not supposed to be here."

"Oh, come on. Everyone else has gone to bed. I just want one last drink with you, before you are a married woman."

He lifted up a bottle of schnapps he'd been holding under his arm. It was nearly empty. He pushed back against her hand and stumbled into the room, flopping down on the bed. He thrust the bottle toward her. She closed the door quietly and fetched a porcelain cup from the dresser, holding it out and helping to steady his hand as he poured. She sat back down at the dressing table and took a small sip.

"I think you may be drunk," she observed.

"I think you may be right," he replied, kicking off his boots. She bent down to pick them up, placing them neatly side by side. When she turned back, he was pouting at her, his face almost unrecognizable in such a childish pose, his cheeks red and slightly sweaty.

"Why don't you love me?"

She was so startled she opened her mouth to reply but found that nothing came out. He watched from under hooded lids.

"I do," she stuttered finally. "Of course, you know I do."

He shook his head slowly, an expression of exaggerated sorrow on his shining face.

"I don't think so. Liesl was right. She said you don't."

Bettina's mood soured at the mention of his sister.

"Liesl can go to hell."

He waved his hand dismissively. "She says it doesn't matter, though."

"Does she now?"

He looked at her slyly, gauging her reaction.

"Can you keep a secret?"

She thought of her own, nestled in her womb. "I've been known to," she said.

"I suppose it doesn't matter now; we're almost married anyway. May as well be honest with each other."

His eyes swam a little.

"The truth is this was all Liesl's idea. She told me to propose to you."

Bettina let out a short bark of laughter in shock. Karl put up his hand to protest.

"It is because she so admires you. The first time she met you she told me, 'That's what you need. Not a milksop, but a woman with some fire in her.'"

He paused in his recollection, then added thoughtfully, "I often think she would have done better than me, risen higher, if she had been a man. She has so much more ambition."

Bettina crossed her arms.

"So, you had no say in who you married?"

He fell back on the bed and stared up at the pine-clad ceiling.

"I could see the sense of it; I want a child, so need a wife, and Liesl knows me better than I know myself."

He gave a deep sigh.

"She's so practical. She even had someone look back through your ancestry, to make sure there was no bad blood."

Bettina felt a lurching nausea, although she couldn't claim to be surprised.

"I take it I wasn't found lacking . . ."

"We wouldn't be here if you were."

He looked at her from the edge of his eye.

"So then. You do not love me."

"Under the circumstances, does it matter?"

She'd never seen him in this light, his emotions anything other than utterly controlled.

"I suppose not." He closed his eyes to stop the room from swaying. Bettina watched him thoughtfully.

"Why all the haste, if you did not want this for yourself?"

"Liesl thought we should move quickly, to make sure you didn't change your mind."

He sniffled then, self-pitying. "You mustn't tell her what I've said now, will you? She would be so terribly cross."

Bettina was utterly bewildered that this ruthless and domineering man should appear so childlike now, cowed by his widowed sister. She felt a rush of fury and embarrassment; she should tell him to get out and yet she remained stuck fast, hopelessly locked in place, pregnant and dependent on him. She must stay for Max's sake.

And then it came to her. A glimpse of hope, a way she might do more than simply wait.

"I won't breathe a word to Liesl, I promise, if you will only help me with one thing."

She tried to project an air of control and confidence, though she possessed neither one.

"I will marry you and give you the child you want, right away, if only you'll give me something in return."

She watched his expression hawkishly. He frowned, seeming to weigh her words.

"I want something tangible, Karl. In return for a family, you must give me freedom of expression. You know people at Allach—you can arrange for me to meet the sculptor who made my Viking, so they might teach me to make something of my own. My work is my life and I need it to continue."

He thought for a moment, then blinked solemnly and nodded. "Very well. It will be my wedding gift to you. But the child must come first, at least give me that. Then you can have your freedom."

"I promise," she said.

CHAPTER THIRTEEN

Dachau

November 1993

As she walked through the gates of Dachau, Clara put on the headphones of the portable CD player she'd borrowed from Lotte.

"I think I'm going to need something grounding to listen to," she'd told her daughter.

The opening notes of *Für Alina* were so familiar, they settled her and she needed that here; just twenty-four hours earlier, she and Lotte had arrived in Munich for a brief visit. The decision to come had been spontaneous—a few snatched days to mark the fact that Lotte had submitted her artist's statement.

"Now I just have to make the bloody thing," Lotte said sardonically.

In truth the trip also had some practical benefits; Lotte planned to use the opportunity to find out more about Bettina as an artist, and both longed to return to the old country. The last time they'd visited, Lotte had been a child and could scarcely remember it.

With only a few days, the pair decided it best to divide and conquer: Clara arranged to visit the archives at Dachau, while Lotte wanted to explore the Haus der Kunst, where she knew her grandmother once exhibited. They finalized their plans while sitting at the breakfast table in the little guesthouse, eating ham on rye and thick slices of a hard yellow cheese. Clara realized how rusty her German was when she asked for advice on their best means of transport. Lotte would go by foot to the House of German Art, while she went to the nearest tram stop, Der Straßenbahnhaltestelle, a lovely word she somehow dredged up from her memory.

The pair arranged to meet afterward in the old town, where they planned to compare notes and raise a sweet toast to the matriarch.

Clara finally arrived in Dachau after a journey comprising a tram, train and bus ride. Since the liberation of the camp in 1945, the town of Dachau had spread out and subsumed it. Buildings and houses now surrounded the perimeter, though she couldn't quite fathom the psychic toll of living so close to this former hell.

As she entered the gates, Clara found she kept her eyes cast down. Cracked and crumbling, the ground rolled out beneath. Her steps felt leaden, reminding her of the slow walk behind a coffin, rime running heavy in the blood.

The sky was dull with mist and bitterly cold. It was early and there were few other visitors, so Clara walked alone across the gray gravel of the roll-call square. Her brain conjured up footage she'd seen in old newsreels: sepia-toned and grainy, the negative stuttering and lurching about. She and Lotte had watched a documentary about the liberation of the camp and it sat with her still, the images seared into her brain: bodies, piled up and contorted like a pyre, the eyes of the survivors staring dully at the camera. It had all seemed so remote when they were making plans in London. Now it was altogether real.

As she walked around the site, the voice of Arvo Pärt's piano provided comfort. The negative spaces spoke as loudly as the notes themselves, something she saw reflected in the landscape. All but two of the barracks, which had held thousands, had been torn down. Nothing remained except their outlines, bordered by concrete curbs. The ground seemed almost volcanic, as if the earth had tried to scorch itself clean. All was monochromatic in this bleached-out world. Ivory buildings and black metal words embedded in an ornate gate. The phrase *"Arbeit Macht Frei"*— Work Will Set You Free—stood out in stark relief against the fogged gray sky, handcrafted by an inmate forced to reproduce the lie. A verdant avenue of poplars leading to the crematoria the only color.

Weeks before, Clara had written to register her interest in accessing the memorial library archive in order to try to establish what information, if any, they held on Professor Adler. She gave them the dates and specifics that Jacob Cohen had provided, thinking that she ought to be precise. Their response had been polite, but she soon realized she would need to be led by the evidence available and temper her expectations; she could not attempt to define the haystack she was searching for, or the nature of the needle she wished to find.

The visitor center was warmer and more populated than the

grounds. She felt a palpable relief as history was once again held at a slight distance. She walked slowly around the exhibition of photographs of the Allied forces liberating the camp. They were eyewitnesses with the foresight to make a record of what they found, understanding that future generations might come to doubt such an unfathomable truth.

When she had warmed her stiff fingers, she went to the information desk to inquire about the librarian with whom she had corresponded. Herr Albert appeared, a sweetly gentle soul, wrapped in a thick jumper and a warm scarf. In preparation for her visit, he had gathered up what he hoped might prove pertinent: among it, nineteen different microfilms containing the full names of many thousands of arrivals at the camps in the years both before and after the start of the war in 1939. For surnames beginning with B, there was a significant amount of information, but for A—Adler—less so. Albert had also readied Reel Ten—a copy of a handwritten ledger containing some 37,000 names from 1933 to 1940. Reel Thirteen was a chronological list of arrivals and departures, including deaths, from '41 to '42.

He explained that barbarity does not always beget a paper trail. The National Socialists had been efficient in finding new ways to dispatch human life and often kept methodical records of that process, but they were not naive. In one of their final acts before the liberation of the camp, the SS had destroyed vast quantities of written information.

Clara nodded. *"Ich verstehe."* I understand.

Some pages were covered in tight typewritten words and still held the perfume of the repository: of dust and faint mildew, age-old ink and cardboard casings.

Clara scanned page after page, as transparent as cigarette paper, but they told her nothing new. There was detail, clinical and clerical—of given names and the numbers they were then reduced to. Some idea of the possessions they'd been stripped of and the artifacts left behind—but there was no tangible, specific evidence of Ezra Adler the man.

Other documents pertained to the transfer of prisoners in 1941. Clara learned that as the war progressed, the porcelain factory had lost many workers to the front, and so a call went out to other camps, for able-bodied prisoners with suitable experience. As a professor of art history, Ezra was only tangentially qualified for such work, but they still shipped him off by rail to Dachau, along with several others.

There was far more about the camp after liberation, as the Allied soldiers tried to make some sense of what they'd found. Ezra's full name and age was included in a ledger, written in early May 1945, though the details were perfunctory. Clara wondered at the shock the liberating soldiers must have felt on entering the camp. The mounds of corpses so casually abandoned, the emaciated survivors, barely holding on to life. Clara marveled at the sheer force of will it must have taken for Ezra Adler to travel to the other side of the planet and start again. How great the distance from Dachau to the Play-Doh factory in Cincinnati and those austere rooms in Over-the-Rhine.

After the camp was liberated, the local citizens were brought in to bear witness to all that was done in their name. The plan was to broaden the project out, so whole swathes of the population would experience it for themselves, but practicalities got in the way. In the end, it was mostly just those who lived in close vicinity to the camps. There were photographs of a queue of men and women in their ordinary clothes waiting to pass through, handkerchiefs pressed to their faces. Clara wondered if the handkerchiefs were there to dry their tears, to hide their faces or to shield themselves from the stench of death. Perhaps, she thought, all three.

She pored over these images, looking first at the faces of the prisoners, to see if Ezra Adler might be in their midst. She didn't recognize him among the dozens who stood or sat staring at the camera, wary, hollow-cheeked, defiant or defeated. After a time, she found herself drawn to examine the witnesses waiting in line as well. She wondered if her maternal grandmother and uncle were in their number. She would be unlikely to recognize them if they were. There were no family albums and Bettina rarely mentioned them. Her mother had often spoken fondly of Berlin and Munich, of Weimar and Dessau, but she'd made no bones about her antipathy toward Allach and refused to ever countenance returning. It was only now, standing in this sacred place, that Clara realized her mother had been born and raised just twelve kilometers away. Close enough to be corralled into this queue and yet still oddly uncurious about her predecessors. Through familial osmosis, she'd gleaned enough to know her uncle was a Nazi and an alcoholic, her grandmother cold and cruel. If her mother didn't care what happened to them, neither then would she.

In English, Albert gently inquired if she had found what she was looking for. She thanked him for his kindness. A little more. Not much.

Her thoughts kept on returning to the wife and children Ezra left behind in Sachsenhausen. Would it help if she visited that site too? Albert asked her to wait. When he returned he held a printed facsimile of a ledger: Zofia Adler died in Sachsenhausen in 1942, aged twenty-seven.

But what of the daughters, Amelie and little Hanna? Clara asked. Was there a chance they might have survived, perhaps been adopted and changed their names?

"I wonder . . . could my mother have known the children, perhaps even have adopted Hanna herself? After all, she was born in 1940, so she's almost the same age as me. Perhaps I am Hanna and that is why she called my father 'the porcelain maker'?"

Albert shook his head. During the war thousands of Polish children were kidnapped and "Germanized" by being placed with German families; but those had been Aryan, deemed racially pure. It would not have been possible for the girls to have survived. The cold fact of it was that with millions dead and millions more dispossessed, the lives and deaths of two small Polish girls did not merit recording.

Lost in almost total isolation, Clara walked back out into the freezing fog. Brutalist buildings seemed to loom over her in the mist, their jagged lines and discordant simplicity entirely suited to these surroundings. The clearest impression she had was one of absence—of sound, of movement, of humanity. A large memorial was wreathed in droplets of mist, its contorted form deliberately reminiscent of those emaciated forms, skin stretched thin across the frame. The sudden toll of a nearby bell broke through the silence with its anxious, brassy peel. She realized she had rarely felt so entirely alone. She shivered, anxious to leave this place and return to the companionship of her daughter and the warm bustle of humanity.

CHAPTER FOURTEEN

Porzellanmanufaktur Allach

Autumn 1940

Max worked conscientiously, his head bent low, his shoulders rounded. He was sitting by the window of the basement room, carving an ornate candelabra. The sun warmed his back and he allowed his mind to drift. The shapes were so familiar, he could have sculpted something so simple in his sleep. His eye homed in on the fine detail; he found that he could no longer see so well at a distance, as if he'd retrained his eyes to focus on what was right in front of him. But then he rarely had cause to look to the horizon in any case—there was little here to see, save rows of barbed wire.

Increasing demand meant Porzellanmanufaktur Allach needed to expand. New premises had been found closer to Dachau, on the site of the SS training base. Holger, Max and dozens more besides had been transferred. The second factory was dedicated to fine porcelain production and was a hive of industry; since the onset of war, faithful Germans were ever more keen to make a show of fealty in some tangible form.

One morning, shortly after their move to the new building, Holger had stopped by on the pretext of inspecting a piece of work. The pair of them still struggled to communicate. Max was under constant scrutiny from the *Außenkommando* and any brief words they could exchange seemed unequal to the gulf they had to cross. Instead, Holger brought his greyhound, Marthe, with him, knowing she was Max's favorite. There was safety in any conversation that revolved around her. After receiving her fill of his affection, she had slumped down at Max's feet, her wet nose sucking at the cold air coming through the ventilation holes in the wall. It had been cold that day and Max was shivering in the draft, which pricked his skin like needles. Holger had remarked on it loudly.

"Terrible blast coming through. You ought to stop that brick right up."

After he left, Max had stooped down to check the wall. He realized the brick could be removed and that behind it was a deep, dry recess. At the very back, rolled up in waxed cloth, were a pair of woolen fingerless gloves, a bar of soap and a slab of chocolate. Max had felt his heart lift at the sight of them, but he'd shut them away in haste, scared that they might be some sort of trap. He watched the space for days to see if it was disturbed, but the brick remained untouched. Eventually, he dared summon up the courage to retrieve the gloves and the soap and squirrel them back to the barracks. He left the chocolate where it was, allowing himself a square every few days, the taste like nothing he'd experienced before.

Max had pulled out one of a growing number of white

hairs from his temple and placed it between the brick and the wall. It remained there, untouched, for quite a time, until one day when he checked he saw the hair had fallen. He levered out the brick and found two apples wrapped in paper. A few days later, there was a strip of cured meat and, later still, a box of matches. So it went on. Sometimes the items were useful— things Max might trade: such as tobacco or even a penknife. Sometimes they were sweet: a paper wrap of dried apricots or sour cherries. The items were sporadic, but often seemed to coincide with times when the weather was bad for days on end, or illness broke out in the camp and tore through the prisoners, malnourished as they were.

Max was only too aware of what might happen if this hiding place was discovered. Possession of a prohibited item, such as a tool or knife, was deemed particularly egregious and was listed in the *Lagerordnung*, a catalog detailing what punishments might be meted out by guards. Being caught with contraband could mean forty-two days of solitary confinement in a cell with a hard bed, on bread and water rations with one warm meal a week. If you happened to cross the wrong man on a bad day, it could mean far worse.

Now, all these months on, Max thought about the paper bag of sweet, dried dates that he knew lay waiting in the recess for him. When the ever-watchful guard went outside to relieve himself, he intended to retrieve them. Until then, the detail of the candelabra required softening and finishing, so he picked up a hunk of ragged sponge, which had all but disintegrated, and dipped it into a pot of water. He used it to smooth the edges where the candle would be placed. He longed to make something wild—something natural, less uniform—but that was rare these days. More often he was left to work on plates and medals, candlesticks and trinket bowls.

He heard the sound of guards approaching and stopped his work to stand at the side of the bench, head down, eyes on the ground. He looked at his rough boots torn and dusty, the soles on them worn paper-thin. Still, he was glad of them. They'd kept his feet relatively dry through winter and now that the sun had burned off the mud, they protected him far more than the clogs and sandals that were all so many others had. The barbed-wire corridors that led in and out of the camp were paved with small, sharp stones. Even with his boots, he could still feel their keen edges biting.

From the corner of his eye, he could see the boots of the two guards from the camp. They were polished, the soles heavy and relatively clean, given the dust within and without. The men were talking to the young guard left on duty. They'd found him lolling in an open doorway, throwing pebbles at a stray dog scavenging for scraps of food. Faint hope here, thought Max.

He listened to their conversation, hoping the guard would be reprimanded, though it seemed the men from the camp were too busy to be bothered. They had forms to fill in and paperwork to be stamped and signed. They wanted the young guard to take receipt of a new worker for the porcelain factory, as requested. He'd come by train to Dachau main camp, then been sent on down here.

"Who sent him?" the young guard demanded.

"The letter says you need workers to replace the men who've been called up; they put out a call to the other camps."

"Well, what am I supposed to do with him?"

The others shrugged. "We just have orders to transfer him to this *Außenkommando*. He's the subcamp's problem now."

Max tilted his head slightly so he could see the prisoner without getting caught looking. An older man stood by with nothing but the clothes on his back and a few belongings, rolled in cloth. The guard barked questions at him. He answered that he'd come from Sachsenhausen, he was a Jew from Krakow, an art historian.

The men from the camp handed over the paperwork and left, happy to pass the problem on. The factory guard turned to Max. "Find him something to do." He shouldered his rifle and rolled up the papers, stamping from the room. Max lifted his head to the visitor and put out his hand.

"Max Ehrlich."

"Ezra Adler."

His hand was large as a paddle, his grip firm.

"Welcome to Porzellanmanufaktur Allach, Ezra. You were at another camp, before?"

Ezra nodded, looking around the room, taking in the ornate candelabra, the clay-covered surfaces, the drying sculptures on the sill. Apart from Max's station, the other tables were unoccupied. It was still too early in the day for the factory workers from the town. Apart from the ever-present churl of a guard, Max was left alone with his work and thoughts at this hour of the day.

"You're a sculptor?" Ezra asked, his tone betraying disbelief.

"I worked at the old factory in Allach town before I was arrested," Max explained. "Then they opened a new factory, closer to the camp and moved us here. Did anyone tell you about Allach Porcelain?"

The older man shook his head.

"I was just told I was going to work in a manufacturing plant. I must confess, I know very little about porcelain production. I was a professor of art history before, in Krakow."

"Do you draw?" asked Max.

"Always."

"Well, that should stand you in good stead."

Max fetched a bucket with relatively fresh water and a rag for Ezra to wash his hands. He cleaned himself up as best as he could, scrubbing off the grime and soot from his long journey.

"How is it here?" he asked.

"We're better off than some, depending on your detail. I feel fortunate in many ways. Factory work is mostly warm and dry."

Not only that, but he had a guardian angel in Holger, though he didn't dare to mention it.

"Keeping the kiln stoked is backbreaking, but you get to sleep by the fire, which is a godsend in the winter."

He thought of the furnace with its red sulfuric maw and of his friend Stefan who toiled there, sweating and stained with coal dust.

"Too damned hot right now but rail duty is the worst: pulling up the carts of stone from the depot. They put a couple of men on it and work them till they drop."

The two men exchanged glances, hoping Ezra wouldn't draw that straw.

"What about food? We've had almost nothing at Sachsenhausen, not since winter."

Ezra was a big man, but his skin was gray and his collarbones protruded from his uniform. Max felt another pang of guilt at his own good fortune; he was often hungry, but he received a ration of bread and soup every day, meager as it was.

"If we're lucky there's sometimes a bit of fish in the soup on Sunday."

He lowered his voice.

"My advice: gather up any little bits of clay that you can get your hands on. You can make things to trade: a comb, perhaps a little spoon. There's a farmer near here who gives me a potato for a clay pipe whenever he needs a new one. Watch yourself, though—God help you if the guards find you with stolen goods."

He clammed up at the sound of the guard's sullen steps returning. He spoke to Ezra, his face dark with vexation. "Seems like you're to stay here and help prepare his clay." He turned and snarled at Max, "Well don't just stand there. Show him what to do."

He returned to the doorway, lighting up a cigarette.

"We better get started."

Max took Ezra over to a workbench, observing him indirectly. He wasn't that much older than him, he thought, though he had a few more gray hairs peppered through his stubble.

Under the bench was a sack of wet clay, wrapped to keep from drying out. Max pulled off a large hunk of the malleable material and pushed it to form a ball in his hands.

"Do you know how to wedge clay?"

The bearded man looked at Max with seriousness. His voice was resonant and deep.

"I can tell you a great deal about the origins of sgraffito in Byzantine pottery, should you so desire, but I don't think I've ever actually laid my hands on a ball of clay in my life."

Max laughed out loud.

"Then let me be your guide."

He slapped the clay down onto the tabletop.

"You're really just trying to get all the air out and ensure that it's ready to shape."

He stepped back to let Ezra get his hands on it. They were broad with thick, strong fingers, which he sank into the densely supple clay.

"My grandfather was a baker; perhaps I will have a natural affinity for this."

Ezra took to the task with gusto. Over time the room slowly filled with the workers from the town, though few of them spoke to Max in the ordinary run of things. The two men in striped uniforms talked quietly when they could, slowly sharing their histories. Max talked about his life as an architect and sculptor before his arrest. Professor Adler spoke of the university in Krakow. Both were reluctant to broach the personal, though in the course of talking about his transfer from Sachsenhausen, Ezra mentioned the family he'd been forced to leave behind.

"I can only assume they are still there. I haven't seen them since the day we all arrived."

Ezra worked the clay as he remembered. "We'd been crammed in the train like animals for hours on end. We were so relieved to be out in the fresh air. Then they separated the men and the women. It was so fast, we couldn't say goodbye. I looked back and all I could see was Amelie, either waving to me or reaching out, I couldn't tell. I thought perhaps they would process us separately, then bring us back together but . . . I haven't seen them since. That was eight months ago. I got word from a rabbi who heard that Zofia and the girls were still together, but there was no warning when they moved me here. I asked the men to get a message to my wife, but it's in God's hands now."

His fists punched deep into the heavy sediment. There was no more to say.

When they returned to the camp that night, Ezra was given a bunk in a different barrack from Max, though both were housed in the Jewish section, separated from the political prisoners; the Russians and the Roma; and the homosexuals, also known as the 175ers, with their pink triangles. Everyone here was categorized—by sex, race, nationality, number, age, working status, well or ill.

Max and Ezra were reunited the following morning, when they left the camp to travel to the factory, passing from camp guards to work detail guards, who snapped and snarled their orders like Alsatians on the end of a chain-link choke. At least the prisoners had a purpose here and it served the authorities to keep them working, though it wouldn't do to test the limits of that need. The factory workers were, by and large, thankful for their good fortune, though their usefulness could save them from only so much. If one less slave returned to the camp at night for whatever reason, no tears were shed by those that did the counting.

At Porzellanmanufaktur Allach, prisoners from Dachau were scattered around the building, some in the studios, others in the yard. Max's friend Stefan worked on the great kilns, which fired up day and night. He helped tend them and carried the long wooden trays filled with heavy molds of plates and bowls and urns around the building.

Until Ezra's arrival, Max had been the only prisoner working as a sculptor. By and large the other workers from the town ignored him, so he would sit alone. They arrived later than the prisoners, filling out the benches where they produced lanterns for the next solstice, along with candelabras and statuary. Above every station, a small enamel lamp hung to light their work. Girls and women worked in one room, their nimble fingers worming into tiny spaces as they smoothed down every piece, readying it for the oven. The churn of the manufacturing process was such that at every stage and every station, there were dozens of items being worked on, one after another. Progress was relentless, something always passing through.

As the day got underway, Max returned to his candelabra and Ezra started on the morning drudge; he had clay to haul in and ready, the slip to press into canvas. There were tasks that he needed to start again as soon as one was finished, the ceaseless cleaning and clearing of clay, of lifting in sacks loaded with raw ingredients, and taking out the planks weighed down with the finished pieces.

Both men quickly found a sense of kinship in the other's company. Art was a shared passion and it helped transcend the high walls and barbed wire. Ezra told Max that in Sachsenhausen, he'd kept his sanity by remembering galleries and temples he'd visited in the past. He would visualize walking through the entrance, retracing a path he might have taken decades earlier, and would picture himself standing in front of a favorite painting or window, trying to recapture every detail.

"There's something about that quiet act of contemplation—it brings you closer to God. You should try it."

"I haven't been observant for years," Max said, "but the idea of escape, even just in my imagination? I like the sound of that."

The factory was abuzz. For the first time in several months Reichsführer-SS Heinrich Himmler himself was due to visit the site and the entire workforce was occupied in preparing for it: prisoners and workers alike had cleaned, tidied and polished, spending hours sweeping up the all-pervasive white clay dust that seemed to drift into every corner of the building.

For Himmler, Allach was not merely a factory that produced trinkets for the home. It was a vital resource in building the idea of the Reich; new traditions could be introduced and old ideas cemented. It was a tool of propaganda, selling an ideal, of both art and family life.

At 10 a.m. precisely on the morning of the inspection, a large group of middle-aged men began their scuttle through the gates. They all appeared to be wearing different shades of brown, from pale tobacco to loamy peat, in tweed and mackintosh, wool and waxed cotton. All were well-fed and comfortable, full of bonhomie and backslapping, like schoolboys let out for the day.

Among these crumpled brown creatures, Reichsführer Himmler stood out. His slate-gray uniform immaculate, the starched white collar of his shirt pristine, his knee-high boots polished to a shine. When he returned to his office later that day, his aide would find white clay dust penetrating every fiber, which needed to be beaten from the cloth and buffed from the leather.

Once they entered the factory, Himmler led the way. As they moved from room to room, his attendants scurried along beside him, an army of invading soldier ants. Himmler's small eyes darted behind a pair of frameless, pince-nez glasses perched on the bridge of his nose. When he spoke the other men listened. When he joked, they laughed—a little too loudly, a little too forced. Himmler clearly delighted in surveying the premises this way, a feudal king with Allach as his fiefdom, his solace in an otherwise dirty, dangerous and complicated world. By necessity, most of his working life was occupied with war. This was his reward. He came for art and pleasure, not for pain.

The men around him massed and moved together, hands clasped behind their backs, heads inclined forward so they might observe, but never touch. Almost every flat surface was filled with fragile porcelain, ready to be inspected and judged, before the colony moved on in unspoken accord. The men in brown were jovial and attentive, smiling and chatting to the supervisors and each other, though all the while they kept their ears cocked to the figure in their center. They inspected the worktables where the girls sat, their plaits neat, their aprons clean, their stations swept. On shelves beside them stood a multitude of unfinished *Julleuchters*: the lanterns lit at the solstice. Although it was still months till then, the men in brown knew that dutiful Germans would soon be scurrying to the shops, lest the lack of one in their home cast a shadow on their reputation.

Occasionally the *Reichsführer* stopped to speak to one of the workers, inquiring about some minor detail. He would lean in to hear their whispered reply and, as he did, the leather straps that bound his chest would creak. Although no one ever dared to meet his eye, he would assure them that the objects they made here would play an important part in German life; they would be treasured and preserved for years to come. Before he took leave of each room, he informed the occupants that they were not merely artisans bent to a noble craft, they were also playing a vital part in restoring the spirit of the nation and the dignity of the German people.

Throughout the tour, a tall man hovered at his elbow. Dressed in an immaculate horsehair suit, Holger Ostendorff laughed less frequently than the jocular brown ants, his expression often tense. But who could blame him? As *Reichsführer* of the Schutzstaffel, Himmler controlled Holger's destiny, along with that of every man, woman and child in the building.

Himmler was a son of Munich, born in the city at the start of the century. A soldier and a lover of porcelain. He had his passions, chief among them soldiering, porcelain and fencing.

"In many ways, it is the ultimate sport. It is a duel in its purist form: two fighters pitted one against the other, both stripped bare of everything except their skill and strength. These are traits we should be celebrating. I want a figurine which does justice to the subject. Holger, you will see to it."

It wasn't a question; it never was. It was presumption of compliance. Himmler had long held a stake in Allach Porcelain but now the SS had taken de facto control of the factory and the entire manufacturing process. He was God inside these walls and so held sway over creation. His attaché, who never strayed far from his side, took out a small leather-bound book and made a note.

As the tour continued, Holger's eyes rarely left the face of the bespectacled man, as if trying to read his mood or predict his next request. Holger found himself staring at the smaller man's chin and jaw: it slid back into his neck, while his hairline rose above his spectacles. Had he not been so aggressively dogged, it was the kind of face that might be associated with weakness, but no one dared to joke about it, even behind his back. He was anything but weak, full of capricious cruelty. His men knew to fear the shadow of his Messerschmitt temper and wait for it to pass.

The gravity of the group centered around him. When they went outside to inspect the perimeter at the end of the tour, they all drew close, but he walked as if alone. He stopped at the precipice of a ditch to admire the groundwork. A dark watchtower loomed and layers of fencing were laid out in ascending and descending heights, each topped with barbed wire, razor-sharp talons on rolling coils. He held forth once again, explaining that, since so many workers had been called up, the factory would need to make more use of the prisoners. He would not call them men, as he declined to think of them as fully human, but they were a necessary part of the machinery, made for heavy work: for shifting sacks of minerals or hefting vats of slip. Wouldn't it be more expedient to combine these elements in the same place—the manufacturing and the moving parts? The brown men all agreed. It was admirable in its efficiency— like cogs in the clockwork, they must be maintained, but they were still expendable. And, unlike metal, humans could be easily replenished.

As the agreeable murmuring died down, Holger gave a gentle cough, which Himmler eventually acknowledged. They had reached the end of the tour; would he care to retire indoors? Perhaps a little beer to revitalize? Himmler moved and so they followed, orbiting planets continuing their cycle around the sun.

The room they returned to had wide, curved walls lined with wooden cabinets displaying examples of the factory's most recent work. Under the dimly lit domed ceiling, it looked like a chapel devoted to the cult of porcelain, the relics of the Reich.

The room was thick with cigar smoke and Holger's secretary circulated with bottles of beer and a chilled Moselle, opened especially for the occasion. It was a good bottle, but most of the assembled company restricted their consumption, familiar with the *Reichsführer*'s intolerance of those that lost their wits to drink.

"It is a deficiency, albeit one which can be overcome. There's little one can't achieve through self-discipline and willpower. I, for example, am right-handed, so I make sure to practice shooting with my left, to compensate for any weakness on that side."

Himmler peered into the cabinets as he pontificated, examining the items on display. He picked up a catalog for the coming year. On its cover were a drummer boy and a handsome geometric vase filled with spring blooms. As he thumbed through the pages he remarked to Holger on the work of different artists, both praise and criticism. His chin sank into his wattle when he came across a piece he didn't like and he shook his head in disappointment.

He was pleased to note the catalog reflected a country now at war, military figures outnumbered only by dogs. A small figure of a flag-bearer caused Himmler to exclaim in delight and he was equally fulsome in his praise of a helmeted soldier, looking pensive.

"I like this; you've really captured his humanity. Soldiers feel what they do so deeply. That's why the art of Allach is of vital importance—to find a way to express nobility so our nation can see and understand."

Holger was relieved that the work met with his approval. He

chanced to be at his shoulder when Himmler came across an image of the Viking and paused to examine it. Holger could recall his own instructions to the photographer: it was to be shot on a low black velvet plinth, against a plain black backdrop, in order to highlight the shining detail Max had wrought.

"Ah, the ever-elusive Viking!"

Himmler's fascination with Nordic mythology was well-known, but still, Holger was surprised to find he was aware of it, they produced so many such artifacts each year.

"Do you have the piece on hand, Holger?"

Holger indicated to his secretary, who went to the curved wall of wooden cabinets and retrieved the figurine. She handed it to Himmler, who laid it on his forearm as if it were a baby, smiling down.

"Fine detail. Who was it, Holger; was it Debitsch?"

Holger paused for a moment as he considered his answer. The fact of Max's arrest and return to Allach as a prisoner suddenly appeared like a trap he should have managed to avoid.

"No sir, I believe not . . . I'd need to consult my records, we have so many great artists working with us these days."

Himmler's small eyes scrutinized him.

"My office was inundated with people trying to get hold of this last year; it seemed they were in short supply, though I cannot for the life of me think why. We furnish you with everything you need."

Holger tried to steer the conversation onto safer ground; there had been a slight delay, he acknowledged, but the piece did moderately well. Perhaps the *Reichsführer* might care to look ahead at some examples of new work yet to come?

But Himmler wouldn't be derailed. He turned the figure over and examined it.

"Bringing the Nordic nations back into the fold is key to our war effort. A piece like this speaks volumes." He fixed Holger with a stare. "I have yet to receive a satisfying answer to my question. I ask again, who made it?"

The chattering men in brown, ears ever cocked toward their leader, noted the change in his tone and let their own conversations drop. Holger felt a cold sweat come over him.

"Have you lost your memory or your wits?"

Himmler turned to the young secretary and snapped, "You; go and find out who it was."

Holger placed a reassuring hand on the terrified girl's shoulder.

"That won't be necessary."

He turned back to the *Reichsführer*, trying to regain his composure.

"I remember now. The sculptor in question is a gifted former architect. Quite an astonishing natural talent, as you see . . ."

He had nowhere left to turn.

"He is one of the prisoners—the only one who sculpts. He actually worked for us prior to his arrest last year. His name is Max Ehrlich."

Himmler's lip curled. "I take it he's a Jew?"

Holger gave a small, curt nod, holding himself still. Once again Himmler turned to the secretary, who stood close by, whey-faced and wide-eyed.

"Fetch him for me. At once."

The woman skittered from the room and Himmler sat down at the dining table. He took out a cigar and pressed it between his fingers, placing the tip into a cutter and guillotining the blade so the stump of it dropped onto the damask cloth. He addressed Holger without looking at him.

"I am a busy man and yet you would make me busier still. In future I must insist on having veto over all commissions. I won't have *Untermensch* sculpting these heroic forms. Do I make myself clear, Herr Ostendorff?"

He rolled his Rs like the low patter of a military drum. A timid knock signaled the secretary's return.

"Enter."

She led Max into the room. His striped uniform was covered in dried clay and he ran a gray hand over the stubble on his head. His eyes skipped around the room, finally meeting Holger's and finding a look of apprehension there.

Himmler snapped his fingers and Max flinched, turning to him. Gesturing to the figure of the Viking, Himmler asked, "You made this?"

Max gave a nod, his eyes now dark with fear.

Himmler looked at the figurine in front of him.

"It's not bad. But then, you had good source material."

He turned to the closest man in tweed and gestured at the figurine.

"Incredible to think a woman could have painted the original, isn't it? Such a study in masculinity. Old Karl Holz was rather taken with her, from what I understand. Married the girl and got her pregnant straightaway—who would have thought the old dog had it in him?"

He turned back to Max, who was listening to his every word, his features as white and inscrutable as the Viking.

"As I was explaining to Herr Ostendorff, we can't have

Jews sculpting such heroic figures. It wouldn't do, but I see no reason why you can't continue here. Just keep to animals and inanimate objects from now on. You understand?"

Max looked to Holger, who gave a curt nod and jumped in on Max's behalf.

"Thank you, Reichsführer."

Himmler turned from Max and waved him away. So dismissed, Holger's secretary led him from the room.

Himmler rolled the glowing end of his cigar in the bowl of a porcelain ashtray. The fine gray ash dropped away, leaving only a rounded, smoldering tip.

"We need more beer, a little liquid bread for my *Kameraden*, before we return to Munich."

Holger nodded and dipped into a bow.

"And Holger?"

Himmler picked up the Viking and looked at it for a moment before tossing it back on the thick cloth. It landed hard and heavy, but did not break.

"I never want to see this again. Destroy the molds."

CHAPTER FIFTEEN

Munich

November 1993

Somewhere between Dachau and Munich, the rain began. Clara caught the tram to Marienplatz, guiding herself with a paper tourist map. She took a seat and tried to manage its damp origami folds as best as she could, following along the route to her final destination.

As she stepped off the tram she found herself swept along with the crowd, heads down, umbrellas up, past the grand opera house. They barely seemed to notice the graceful columns and opulent friezes. She pushed against the tide and broke free from the current, coming out alone in a narrow side street lined with tall, gray stone townhouses. Ornate windows and gables gave them the appearance of children's book illustrations, as if the architect could not resist embellishment. She peered through the windows as she passed until she finally saw Lotte at a table, her nose pink from the cold, a steaming drink in front of her.

Lotte looked up at the sound of the tinkling doorbell and waved to Clara as she weaved her way between the tables.

"Goodness, you did get drenched," her daughter admonished. "I ordered you a coffee with brandy. That should warm you up."

A waitress brought a second cup to the table, topped with a whorl of cream and grated chocolate. Clara took a sip and felt the fire of the brandy slip down with the sweetness.

"That is quite the concoction."

"A real kick up the *Auspuff*! So, how was Dachau—did you find anything?"

Clara shook her head, disconsolate.

"It was terribly moving, but I feel as if I've run out of road. How about you?"

Lotte had made her own pilgrimage to the Haus der Kunst, where her *Oma* had been exhibited before the war. As a consequence, *The Viking* had become her most famous painting.

"I couldn't have timed it better, Mum. There was this brilliant exhibition on—work by contemporary artists expressing their feelings about the institution's Nazi past. Really inspirational for my finals. Anyway, I got talking to someone—she was about your age."

"Rare, to see us in the wild." Clara grinned and Lotte rolled her eyes.

"She knew all about *The Viking*—she said there were so few female artists chosen to exhibit in those days. Oma was really quite a rarity."

"And?"

"I asked her what happened to the original painting. She

thought it had sold at auction a few years ago—she got on the phone to a friend of hers, an art critic, and he remembered it well. Apparently there was quite a furor in the papers at the time; there was a whole catalog of what they termed 'Nazi art,' though the critic said it was rather more nuanced than that. It became quite a cause célèbre."

"Is there any way we can find out who bought *The Viking*?"

"Well, that's the thing. The man who bought it offered to donate it to the city, but it seems they turned it down. It hasn't come up for sale again since, so they think it's probably still in his possession. Get this, Mum—they phoned him up . . ."

"So? Don't leave me in suspense!"

Lotte beamed.

"His name is Holger Ostendorff and he's agreed to see us this afternoon. Turns out he lives in the old town, just a few streets away."

She clapped her hands together in delight.

"Come on, drink up—we don't want to be late."

CHAPTER SIXTEEN

Munich

Autumn 1940

"Heida, can you get Clara ready to go out for her walk, please?"

Bettina herself was wearing a gray silk peignoir and showed no signs of getting dressed. She watched as the young woman pulled ruffled bloomers over baby Clara's dimpled knees. She was not really a baby anymore. No longer an infant, she was unable to sit still and unwilling to surrender to her nanny's ministrations. Clara stood and tried to run away, though Heida held fast to the straps. Bettina felt so grateful to the good-humored girl who took on her indomitable daughter. By contrast, she sometimes found herself exhausted at the very sight of Clara straining at her bonds, determination written into every feature. Her face, symmetrical but sharp: all edges and doleful, dark gray eyes.

In the first months after her daughter's birth, Bettina had sunk into a deep depression, barely able to rouse herself each day. She would wake determined to be on good form, to wrest back control, until the life force that radiated from her daughter drained her of all energy. Eventually it was only Liesl's determination "to come and help" that seemed to do the trick. The threat stirred something in her; Bettina declared she would sooner die than submit to Liesl's tender mercies.

Instead, Heida, the nanny, had been dispatched to care for Clara. Christophe and Julia no longer required her full-time ministrations and she was relieved to report to someone other than Liesl. Her help gave Bettina the space she needed to beat back through the black clouds. Week after week, little by little, she returned to herself and, belatedly, to motherhood.

The doctor told them it was likely because Clara had come so early, though she was a notably sturdy soul at birth and her cries were never less than lusty. Bettina, knowing all too well the child was born full-term, understood her own mood stemmed entirely from the loss of Max. Richard came to visit her a few times and she found he lifted her spirits more than almost anything.

Karl hadn't been much affected by these domestic dramas. He was now stationed in Paris with Hildebrand Gurlitt, as they worked their way through Western Europe's greatest art collections. The chilly atmosphere of the apartment seldom drew him back—only the child could do that. He seemed to relish little Clara's spirited nature; he bounced her between his knees, her dark waves springing, energy coiled within her stocky form. He would toss her up in the air until she squealed so with excitement that Bettina had to threaten to get Heida to remove her to the nursery.

When Karl did come home, his wife would soon start on her usual refrain: when would he arrange for her to visit

Allach? Heida could look after Clara, she needed to occupy her mind again. Karl procrastinated; he swore he'd contacted Himmler's secretary and was awaiting her response. You couldn't hurry these people, he reminded her. They were terribly important and had other, more urgent priorities—the war, for one.

Bettina responded with increasing vehemence that he had promised, and she had kept to her end of the bargain. Be patient, he replied; enjoy motherhood. Relax.

Imre's letter arrived along with the first snow. Light flurries began as soon as the nights started to draw in, failing to settle at first, but returning again and again, until they built to an impenetrable layer that seemed like it would never melt.

Bettina woke one morning to the reflected brightness of the snow, which bathed the room in light. She determined to make the most of it and sprang from the bed with uncharacteristic vigor. She discovered the envelope on the dining room table and turned it over, curious that she did not recognize the hand. She opened it and saw a single page of script, a scant few paragraphs, and beneath them, Imre's pretty signature, the cursive letters neatly formed.

Dearest Betti.

It's been an age since we last spoke—I hope you will forgive me. Honestly, I hesitate to write, lest you think me quite hysterical, only I must ask if you know of Richard's whereabouts. No one in Berlin has seen him in these several weeks and both Libertas and I have grown concerned for his well-being. The last we knew he was planning to go

*to Frankfurt and then intended to visit you and Clara
in Munich.*

*If he has met someone and decided not to return to Berlin,
please tell me, as a friend. Let him know that I shan't quarrel
with him, only I must know that he is safe. I find I am beside
myself, worrying where he is.*

Yours.

Imre

Bettina sat down at the table, consumed by a powerful sense
of déjà vu.

How long had it been, she wondered, since she'd last spoken
to him? He'd called her on the telephone, though he usually
avoided it for fear that "some SS goons were likely listening,"
so she'd been surprised to answer it and hear his chipper voice.

"How are you fixed next weekend?" he'd asked.

"Free as always; the life of a new mother is nothing if not
repetitive."

"I'm going to try to visit my two girls, but let's see how I get
on. Are you well, old lady?"

She'd laughed. "All things considered, I suppose I am. Are you?"

"As I can be. Listen, I must go. I hope you don't mind me
calling, but I wanted to hear your voice . . ."

"Not at all, it's lovely to hear yours too. I miss you."

"Miss you too, Betti. Sorry to dash—I'll be in touch."

"Of course."

That had been four weeks ago, by her calculations. Not
unusual, but if neither she nor Imre nor Libertas knew where
he was, who would?

*

Bettina stepped off the train at Allach station the following afternoon. She shivered to be back there, vividly recalling the night that Max had gone missing, when she'd scanned the empty platform for him, desperately hoping she might find him waiting there. It had changed little in the intervening time, though she barely recognized herself.

After reading Imre's letter she had spent hours fretting, before deciding the only person she could turn to was Peter Amsel, Richard's older brother. She'd scarcely seen him since he helped her in her hour of need, but she'd felt a kinship with him, writing her occasional reports on Karl and Liesl and addressing them to him. She knew she risked exposing them both by visiting him, but felt she had nowhere else to turn.

She walked through the wet streets quickly, turning up the thick velvet collar of her coat, her shoes crunching through the frozen powder of a recent flurry. The terra-cotta roofs were barely visible under the snow, their shutters closed tight against the cold. At a crossroads, black tire tracks stood out in stark relief, their swooping arcs lit by the low winter sun sinking on the horizon. She waited for a military motorbike and sidecar to pass, shielding her face in case by some bad luck the driver recognized her. The last thing she wanted was a confrontation with her brother. When it passed, she dashed across the street and opened the gate in a tall hedge dusted with snow.

The house behind was three stories high with a carved wooden balustrade, the shutters a weathered shade of Prussian blue. She knew both Richard and Peter had been born under this roof. Their parents had died when Richard was still at school, leaving Peter to raise his younger brother, the two of them living there together until Richard had moved into the city to study art.

Bettina took off her thick woolen gloves to knock. The door opened and Peter stood before her—thinner and less arresting than his brother, blond hair close-cropped, blue eyes half hidden by glasses. Behind him the house was gathered in gloom.

"Peter. I'm so sorry to turn up unannounced. Would you mind if I come in?"

A frown of concern crossed his brow.

"Of course, of course, it's freezing out. I've got a fire going in the kitchen—come through."

He led her down a dark passage to a small cluttered room that looked as if it hadn't changed in twenty years or more. The walls were painted a pale and peeling buttercream. A small table sat in the center, covered in piles of newspapers and stacks of pamphlets. It smelled of woodsmoke and the sulfuric ghosts of cabbages.

"Can I get you a glass of water?" he asked.

"No, thank you." She saw the anxiety written in his eyes and addressed it straightaway.

"It's Richard, I'm afraid. I wanted to ask when you last heard from him?"

"Not for a few weeks. Perhaps a month."

Bettina felt the hope she'd harbored drain away.

"Why, what's happened?" Peter could sense her disappointment.

"I had a letter from Imre. It seems like no one in Berlin has heard from him in four or five weeks. He traveled to Frankfurt and then spoke about coming on to Munich, but as far as I know, he never did. I was hoping you might have an idea where he could be . . ."

Peter took off his glasses and ran both his hands down his face, a habit of his brother's so familiar it hit her like a sucker punch. She reached out to steady herself and took several deep breaths in.

"Let's try not to panic." Peter pinched the bridge of his nose. "My little brother can take care of himself, you know that. He might have felt he had to go to ground."

"It's just not like him to go without a word."

"I know people in Frankfurt; we have some friends in common—they might know where he was staying. Let me see what I can find out. In the meantime, you go home and sit tight."

She started to protest, but he wouldn't hear it.

"I appreciate you coming, but honestly, you mustn't do anything so rash again. If Richard has been arrested, then we're all in danger. He would sooner die than point the finger at any of us, but he wouldn't be the first person forced to talk. God only knows what they might do to him."

She had promised herself she would stay strong, but she could feel her resolve crumbling. She simply nodded, too afraid to speak.

"If you hear anything, don't risk coming back here. Drop me a letter at the Catholic publishing house; you remember?" She did. She still took an occasional report there, though she had less to share, with Karl and Liesl rarely home.

"I'll write to you when I have news. Do you think your post is intercepted?"

It had never occurred to her.

"I shouldn't think so; there's just me and the staff there most of the time."

Bettina picked up her gloves and Peter gripped her hand. He hesitated briefly, then wrapped his arms around her tightly. He held her for a moment, then backed away, embarrassed.

A sudden thought occurred to her as she made to leave.

"Perhaps I should see if my husband can help; ask him to look into it, see if he can pull some strings?"

"No." Peter shook his head. "That's a danger to you, and to Richard. What if he turns up tomorrow, right as rain?"

"Oh, Peter, I hope to God he does."

Peter tried to give her a reassuring smile, though it looked more like a tortured, rictus grin.

"If anyone can talk his way out of trouble, it's my little brother. He has done so many times before, believe you me."

A few days later, Bettina found another letter on the dining room table. It was brief; the friends in Frankfurt said Richard had checked out of his hotel four weeks earlier. No one knew where he was headed or where he might be now. There had been raids and arrests across Frankfurt around that time; he may have been swept up. It was quite possible he'd gone into hiding. There was no reason to assume the worst.

But Bettina knew if Richard had been able, he would have moved heaven and earth to let someone know that he was safe. That he had not only compounded her darkest fears.

Bettina checked the table every morning and asked Heida and Gerhard, the driver, to let her know as soon as any post arrived, but still the weeks went by without word.

Karl telegrammed to say he was returning for a few days over the winter solstice. Bettina, now desperate, determined that any risk engendered by asking for his help would be far outweighed by the reward. She dressed with great consideration, picking out a new carmine crêpe de Chine—elegant but conservative. She waved the hair she had started to grow out and that curled beyond her shoulders. She carefully applied a little rouge and lipstick; not too much. She wanted to look the very essence of a dutiful wife, to give Karl no reason for reproach when she asked him for his help.

She had hoped for an intimate dinner in a quiet corner, but the Osteria Bavaria, which he took her to, was noisy and crowded. Ruddy-faced officers bellowed at one another as they smashed their glasses down. The scrape of their chairs and the timbre of their voices bounced off the hard tiled surfaces, giving her a headache that pressed in on her temples. She tried her best to hide it.

Karl ordered steak and she listened patiently to every detail of his trip. He listed the onerous tasks involved in reshaping a culture, the endless bureaucracy required to force the conquered to comply. He peppered her with questions about Clara: how was she doing, could she write her numbers yet, what new words had she learned?

She feigned jollity, though it soon grated on her nerves; she felt her laugh too loud, her grin too broad. Could he tell? He often appeared to have a sixth sense, but he seemed comfortable enough. She tried to remain attentive while she rehearsed her lines. If only she could get the words out in the right way, then all would be well. When he called for a second bottle of wine, she felt her moment had come.

"I wonder if I might ask you for a favor . . ."

"I can't debase myself by going back to Himmler's office yet again, Bettina. They will tell me when they have news."

"No, it's not that." Although it stung her that he fobbed her off so quickly. "I know you're most awfully busy, but it seems a friend of mine has gone missing. I haven't seen him in an age, but his fiancée is concerned and she wrote to me, to see if

I could help. Not much I can do, of course, but as you are so terribly well connected . . ."

She trailed off and laughed, a brittle artificial trill.

"What is the name of this friend?" he asked dryly.

"You met him once. He came to your summer party. Richard Amsel?"

Although Karl's expression didn't change, Bettina could sense his body stiffening. He remembered, all right, but made no reply. The noise of carousing men swam all around them, but they sat in silence, a chasm that seemed to take an eternity to cross. She felt an overwhelming need to fill the space.

"As I say, I have barely seen him in months and months, but Imre is beside herself with worry."

Karl looked at her unsmiling, though his voice was genial enough.

"And what is it you think I can do to help?"

Could he see the alarm written on her face? She regretted saying anything; Peter had been right, it had only put them all at risk, though she couldn't back down now.

"He was last seen in Frankfurt. I thought perhaps you might speak to your contacts there, see if they know anything. Find out if he got himself into some trouble."

"And you think he's been arrested." It was a statement.

"Mistaken identity, perhaps? One hears of such things."

She took a large swig of the wine and swallowed hard. It stung as it hit the back of her throat. Karl stared at her like a curious bird.

"Does one? In my experience, people are usually arrested if they're guilty of something."

She flushed. He looked down at his plate and recommenced cutting his bloodied steak with sharp precision.

She reached out a hand to him. "He's a good man, Karl. A good German."

Karl did not look up from his meat.

"I have a few friends in Frankfurt, in the Gestapo. It puts me at a disadvantage, but I will ask them for their help."

She felt relief flood her system.

"But I warn you now, if he has brought trouble on himself, there will be nothing you or I can do for him."

"Thank you, Karl; you are most awfully kind. I can't tell you what it means . . . to Imre. She's such a sweet girl and she's been terribly anxious."

"As are you, it would appear."

She forced a tight smile. "He's an old friend. Nothing more."

He inclined his head.

"I should certainly hope not."

After the meal at the osteria, Karl returned to Paris and the weeks of winter stretched on endlessly into the new year, cold and dull and dark. Bettina's mood reflected it, until even Liesl grew concerned about her listlessness and lobbied Karl to lighten her spirits.

He asked her to join him in Berlin for a few days, while he traveled out to Carinhall, Reichsmarschall Göring's country home. Karl had spent months "encouraging" a museum in Paris to part with a few choice pieces, which were to be given to the Carinhall collection. The *Reichsmarschall* wanted them hung in time for his birthday celebrations and so a trip to the capital had been arranged in haste. Bettina had seen little of Berlin since she and Max had left it.

As the day drew near she felt invigorated by the prospect of travel, knowing there was a good chance that she might pick up interesting intelligence in such high-ranking company. She thought about writing a report, which served only to further remind her of Richard's absence from the city.

Karl came back to Munich to collect her. Always immaculate, he appeared uncomfortable at the sight of all her clothes and chaos. He stood stiffly by and watched her from the doorway as she folded items into a small suitcase. She turned to look at him over her shoulder.

"I never know what to pack for these things."

He shrugged. "Do as you normally do, you always look fine. There will be dinners, of course; some riding, I imagine."

The prospect of having to maintain a facade for so long almost made her fade.

"There will be plenty of people there whose company you'll enjoy, don't worry. Walter is an art dealer and his wife Bertha restores paintings; they'll put you at your ease."

He looked at his watch. "I really don't want to keep the *Reichsmarschall* waiting . . ."

"Sorry. Why don't you go and say good night to Clara? She's feeling sad she has to stay behind with Heida."

She lifted down a few last dresses, among them the crêpe de Chine one that she'd worn to the osteria on the night she'd lobbied him for help. Her eyes flickered to Karl and she saw he recognized it too. Wordlessly, she returned it to the hanger and took down a gray velvet dress in its stead.

"I heard back about your friend, by the way."

His tone was casual but cool. Bettina felt a stillness steal over her, as if a false move might scare him off.

"I'm afraid it's not good news. There's a warrant out for his arrest, but his whereabouts is unknown. They suspect he's left the country. Gone to ground, in order to evade it."

"But he would never . . ." Bettina stuttered.

"A guilty man will do an awful lot of things to save his skin."

She fought to conceal her rising panic.

"What has he been accused of?"

"I can't get into the specifics, but suffice to say he's been mixing in bad company. That's treason, at a time of war."

She felt his hard eyes on her.

"I warned you off him long ago."

"I remember." She knew penitence was expected. "I should have listened."

She turned back to the bed to hide her face, blood pounding in her ears. She visualized grabbing Karl by the shoulders and trying to shake the truth from him. She picked up a silk blouse and laid it down, folding the sleeves carefully.

"In any case, let that be an end to it. I do not wish to hear his name again."

He relishes chastising me, she thought. *Just like his sister.*

Not trusting herself to speak, she simply nodded. She continued to fold, feeling as if she were floating above the scene, watching herself. Tears rose in her eyes. With her back still turned to him, she felt one drop, staining the silk. She rubbed at it surreptitiously; she knew she could not let him see her cry.

"Goodness," she murmured, "I nearly forgot my stockings."

She walked quickly to the bathroom and shut the door, biting into the soft flesh at the heel of her hand to keep the sobs from spilling out.

*

When they arrived in Berlin, Bettina wrote to Peter at the Catholic publishing house and dropped the envelope into the hotel postbox. She chose her words as kindly as she could, imagining the journey the letter would take and its effect on the recipient; she wished she could travel with it, to be there for Peter when he read her words, though she knew that would risk exposing them both to even greater danger.

She passed the week in ill-concealed misery, though Karl was either oblivious or willfully blind to it. She supposed he was keen to draw a line under events. Besides, the two of them had scarcely any time alone together, caught up as they were in the social requirements of the trip. Bettina had never spent so much time with the upper echelons; while Karl stayed late carousing, she lulled herself to sleep each night repeating the information she would share with Peter on her return, too terrified to commit it to paper far from home.

On the last day, Karl was unexpectedly called back to Carinhall. He was apologetic, but she brushed him off. She was fine, she maintained; she would go to a gallery.

Instead she boarded a tram and crossed the city to the kindergarten where she knew Imre worked. She stood at the window, peering through the crosshatch of paper glued there to stop the glass from falling in, should British bombs let fly. She spied Imre kneeling on the floor, speaking to a child, and rapped her knuckles on the glass. The younger woman looked up at the sound and, seeing her, turned pale. She jumped to her feet and spoke to her colleague: a hasty, muttered conversation. Moments later she came outside, pulling on a cardigan against the cold.

"Is he dead?"

"I don't know."

Fearful of being overheard, they simply walked together aimlessly through the wide, wet streets. Bettina shared the precise words that Karl had said to her, though there was little comfort in them.

"He knows more than he has told me, I'm certain of it. I don't think Richard would ever leave the country. He knew the risks but was determined to stay."

Imre shivered as she listened, the cardigan wrapped tightly around her. She tucked her hands into the sleeves to keep them warm.

"His luck ran out. We always knew it would."

She stated it flatly, almost without emotion. When they returned to the school, they hugged each other wordlessly, as if they were holding on to Richard one last time, each unwilling to let go.

On their return to Munich, Bettina found the cloud of her depression had returned. She couldn't sleep and Clara's boisterous demands were almost more than she could bear. She retreated to the master bedroom and sat drawing sketch after sketch of Richard and Max, trying to preserve them in her memory, though she fed each one into the fire, afraid of what might happen should they be discovered.

Karl decided to stay on in Munich, so he might attend the Nazi Party's birthday celebrations at the Hofbräuhaus. It was a prestigious invitation and, as her sister-in-law constantly reminded her, might even mean an introduction to the Führer.

When the day arrived, Bettina felt so sickened by the prospect that she claimed a migraine and begged Liesl to take her place. She joyfully accepted and Bettina, weak with relief, went to bed early.

On their return, the siblings seemed to have been transformed by the experience. Liesl came into her room triumphant, fairly beaming in the afterglow.

"Everyone was there, simply everyone. You missed the most stirring speeches I ever heard."

"And you were missed, Bettina," Karl said, more warmly than he'd spoken to her in many months. "I would have liked to have had you on my arm."

Liesl listed the names of those in attendance: Hitler, of course, Hess and Bormann. And Heinrich Himmler, who spoke to Karl himself.

"Evidently he remembers you, or at least he knows your work. He spoke about *The Viking*, didn't he, Karl?"

"He did indeed." Karl smiled at her proudly. "He said he'd be delighted if you wanted to collaborate with Allach. For the good of the Party, of course."

He still sounded gruff and paternal, but a thaw was evident.

"And now that Clara is a little older, I see no reason to object." He looked to Liesl, who nodded vigorously, clearly giving him her blessing. "I suppose Heida can look after her well enough."

Grateful to her benefactors, Bettina leaped up and kissed them both excitedly. She could not fully comprehend that she might see Max again, at last. She felt she might burst and hugged the knowledge to herself, sensing the black dog snapping at her heels retreating.

CHAPTER SEVENTEEN

Munich

November 1993

The building they were searching for turned out to be four stories high and terribly narrow—no more than one room wide. Clara scanned the brass panel by the door and found the name she sought at the very top: Ostendorff, written in a neat print on a cream card. She pressed the doorbell and waited. The intercom crackled and a young woman asked if they were dropping off a package. If so, they might just leave it in the lobby.

Clara tried to explain they weren't there to deliver something, but she hoped they were expected. She blushed as she struggled with her mother tongue. Somehow she'd forgotten what she once knew well.

"Ich habe Deutsch verlernt."

The intercom cut off and she listened to the empty silence, wondering if she should ring again. Eventually there came another burst of static.

"Wie heißen Sie?"

"*Mein Name ist Clara Vogel und meine Tochter ist Lotte Woolf.*"

Thankfully, her nursery German was still intact. The line went dead again. Clara stood back and stared up at the windows. Thin rods of rain dropped on her face; there was no sign of movement up above. Lotte pulled a face at her; had they been forgotten? Clara shrugged. Finally the woman on the intercom spoke again: they were to push the door hard and come to the top floor.

The electronic lock clattered into life and Clara and Lotte stumbled forward, into the dark cool of a marble lobby. Old money spoke in hushed tones here; the building looked as it might have done a century before, handsome and well maintained.

Beyond a bank of ornate letterboxes and pigeonholes, Clara had expected to see a lift: perhaps some prewar relic with a cage and sliding doors. Instead, there were simply dark-veined marble steps and ironmongery, starting wide then narrowing and ascending steeply in a spiral. Up and up and up; by the time they had climbed four flights of stairs, Clara's thighs ached with a stiff fire and she felt almost out of breath. Even Lotte slowed down for the final flight.

Clara sucked in a lungful of air and knocked on the door. A young woman opened it and beckoned them both in. She had her hair scraped back in a ponytail and was wearing a pale blue tabard over jeans—the uniform of domestic service. She clearly wasn't the daughter, or granddaughter, Clara had supposed her to be when she first heard the voice.

The woman led them down a long corridor. The apartment was narrow but deep. Each wall they passed was covered in framed pictures: etchings of exotic birds and rows of botanical watercolors. There were clusters of oils in pairs and singles, some set symmetrically, others more haphazardly. There were ornate occasional tables, one with a collection of coral, another with an old French wedding dome, its once plush red velvet cushion now fading pink. Every surface displayed a beautiful object paired with a maidenhair fern or a vase of dahlias in boudoir shades of café au lait and cream. The effect of it all was one of elegance, a collection of items curated over a lifetime, of taste and money and self-knowledge.

The young woman opened a door into a study that smelled of woodsmoke and heady, perfumed candles, rich with incense. Deep mahogany shelves were lined with books, from floor to ceiling. Two worn leather sofas sat before a fire. Small side tables on spindle legs were loaded down with yet more books, many of which had been left open, with notes between their leaves. This was a room of occupation.

"*Warten Sie hier, bitte.*" Wait here.

The young woman closed the door gently behind her. Moments later, they heard a vacuum cleaner start up in a distant room. From the hearth a crack of burning wood caught Clara's attention. As she turned to take in its warmth, her gaze was drawn above the mantel: there, surrounded by a heavy ornate frame, was *The Viking*, Bettina's famous painting. Clara reached for her daughter's arm to steady herself. Lotte let out a gasp of recognition.

Having only ever seen it in reproduction, Clara was immediately struck by the size of it. Most of her mother's earlier works had been smaller, more constrained. This was large and unapologetic; it filled the wall above the mantel, dominating the space.

For Clara, there was a powerful dissonance between the

reality in front of her and the painting she had carried in her head for many years. Her idea of it was purely based on photographs and cheaply printed poster reproductions. She'd bought one herself as a student, but never hung it, feeling somehow embarrassed by the drama of the scene. It had reminded her of the cover of a romantic novel, far too windswept and overblown to suit her simple, youthful tastes.

The color palette was darker and more extreme than she'd expected. The versions she'd seen must have been desaturated and toned down, because the painting in front of her was vivid, its colors almost garish in places. It lent the scene a sickly sense of foreboding. The paint was more textured than she'd imagined, too; this was the scratched surface of an uneasy sea. The thick, rolling clouds were dense and full of dark energy.

In the center stood the Viking himself, buffeted by a wind that whipped at his hair and stirred the pelt of fur that lay across his shoulders. He was handsome enough, but too real to be entirely heroic. His features were angular and his jaw was set hard, but he did not seem defiant to her. He seemed resigned to his fate, not fighting it.

Lotte muttered dryly, "I think my artist's statement might need some revision now, don't you?"

They were both so focused on the painting that they didn't realize they had company until a cough came from behind. Clara and Lotte spun around simultaneously, half expecting the Viking himself to have appeared, but there was just a frail old man; rather tall and rail-thin, with a neat white beard and wire-framed spectacles. He wore a camel blazer with a silk handkerchief and leaned his weight on a slender cane. When he spoke, it was directly to Clara and in perfect idiomatic English.

"Clara, my dear. How wonderful to see you again. You cannot know how I have longed for this day. I thought I might not live to see it."

CHAPTER EIGHTEEN

Dachau

Spring 1941

The girl loved the giant rabbits at Dachau best of all. Their fur was the softest she had ever felt, the little tufts at the tips of their ears making them so comical. They were fine, stout fellows, so big it took all her strength to lift them. She named her favorite Fluffig. He was a grand chap; he filled her lap and overflowed it, his downy fur pillowing across her narrow thighs.

Whenever Püppi accompanied her father to work, she would ask to visit the rabbit cages. She loved them all, but Fluffig held a special place in her heart, and she always spent the longest time with him, for he was the prize. She would bend her head over him, her blond plaits swinging, and whisper endearments as she stroked his ears, holding them tight in her tiny fists and letting their warm lengths slip like silk through her grasp.

On this occasion, before she was allowed to visit the rabbits, she had been taken to the orchard to inspect the pear trees. She'd enjoyed an hour wandering there, swinging on their low boughs, making the blossoms rain down. Afterward they'd gone on a tour of the vegetable patch, just like the one they had at home. She'd picked baby peppers and pea shoots and hid them in her pocket to feed to Fluffig later.

When people asked her for her name, she'd tell them it was Gudrun, but her father called her Püppi because she would forever be his doll. While they toured the site he slipped her candied almonds, their pastel carapace almost too pretty to consume. He made a shushing gesture; it was to be their little secret. He would squirrel them out from deep within his pocket and hold them behind his back, palm up, while he spoke to one of many gentlemen who seemed to hang upon his every word.

Days such as these were her favorite because she could be with Papa while he worked. He was so often called away and then she missed him terribly, though he would telephone each night and write to her quite often. His work was vital, Mother had explained, and the Boss kept him at it, harder than anyone else, which seemed terribly unfair to her.

Despite that, she understood that she must share him; there were so many people who relied on his wise counsel—half of Europe, truth be told. And there were consolations: very occasionally, if work kept him from home too long, he might have them fly her out to meet him. She'd run to him across some far-flung airfield and he would catch her up and throw her to the sky.

Today they hadn't had to travel far. Dachau, where her beloved Fluffig lived, was close to home. After lunch Püppi had finally been allowed to visit the rabbit cages, stacked like neat apartment buildings, row upon row, one above the other, many higher than her head. The hutches were heated, so every snuffling bundle came out toasty warm. Her little velvet jacket with its puffed sleeves was very smart, but it didn't keep out the cold, so she was glad of their cozy, soft little bodies. She lifted the rabbits from their clean hay and held them tight to her chest, pressing their cheeks against her own.

By and large, the rabbits were quite tame and gentle. Only a few had a vicious or depressive streak, which might lead them to scratch or bite. A very small number were so distressed by their incarceration that they consumed their own young, but facts of that nature were kept from Püppi, who wouldn't hear ill of them in any way.

She was busy selecting which animal to cosset first when she noticed the prisoner. A poorly clothed, unshaven fellow on the far side of the yard, who was cleaning out the hutches and laying in fresh hay. She watched as he reached into the cage and knew at once he had the misfortune to choose one of the few that nipped. He said a rude word and almost dropped the rabbit as he tried to loosen the grip of its sharp teeth and bundle it back into its cage. Püppi had watched the drama unfold, solemn and silent, fascinated by the blood. Later on she sidled up to her father and whispered to him, pointing out the culprit, then watched as the man was taken hurriedly away, his arms locked tight behind his back, his feet hardly touching the ground. Good, she thought. Good riddance to bad rubbish.

But when the man did not return, she had begun to worry. When she inquired as to his whereabouts, she was hastily assured she would never have to see the man again. She began to cry, afraid he might have been punished on her account. Even at eleven she'd heard and seen enough to know that, in this place at least, all men were not created equal.

Her tears could not easily be staunched. Her father had been sent for with whispered urgency. The secretary tasked with looking after her knew to keep the little doll content, fearing for her own safety should she not.

When Father returned, Püppi had Fluffig in her lap and was brushing his fur with a fine-toothed comb. The rabbit snuffled contentedly through his baby-pink nose. The tears that had run down her bone-china cheeks had dried to streaks, a few lingering hiccups the only sign of her earlier anxiety. Her father sat down by her side and stroked the back of her blond head as he bent over the giant rabbit. She looked up, her lower lip plump in a pout of discontentment. He mimicked her, his weak chin receding.

"Come now, Püppi, don't be sad. If that creature hurt the rabbit, then he deserves to be punished. These little animals are very precious, and their fur will keep our brave pilots warm."

He reached down to scratch between Fluffig's tufted ears.

"We treat animals with decency, perhaps the only people in the world who truly do. Let it be a comfort to know that, when it comes to these human animals, we are not heartless, but really, you must not worry yourself about them. It would be a crime to waste your tears. Now then, cheer yourself. What would you say if Papa was to have a special porcelain rabbit made just for you—would that be good?"

She nodded, though her face remained grave. He signaled for his secretary to bring over the rabbit kits. Püppi squealed with delight as their tiny, trembling bodies were tipped into her arms. There were so very many of them here at her disposal, to play with on a whim. Row upon row upon row.

*

Grim-faced, the guard marched up to Max, his rifle slung over his shoulder. He gripped a torn and dirty burlap sack, its heavy cargo swinging underneath, and dumped it on the table.

"Ostendorff sent you a present."

Max blinked. The guard shoved the dirty sack toward him.

"Go on, then. Take a look. I warn you, though—you're not allowed to cook it."

Max slowly pulled the sack toward him and peeled it open, recoiling in shock at the sight of a large and very dead white-furred rabbit. The guard laughed at his expression of disgust.

"Best work quickly. They want the fur and skin before it decomposes. I'll come back for it in a day or two."

After the guard left, Max lifted the rabbit out of the sack and laid it on the table. Its mouth and eyes were open, the color of them deep and shocking pink, as if they'd been flooded with watery blood. Max thought the rabbit must be newly dead; the body was limp and its long ears, with their ostentatious furry flourish, lay flat along its back. Max propped it up, trying to re-create a lifelike pose. He had no doubt that he could capture the creature's scale and detail, but it would be a challenge to bring it back to living, breathing flesh upon the page. Still, it was a welcome change from the plates and urns. He took out his sketchbook and set his hand and eye to the task ahead.

A run of balmy days descended on Dachau like an early precursor of summer and it didn't take long for the stench of rot from the rabbit to become almost unendurable. Gases bloated its stomach and a thin, red fluid leaked from the eyes, leaving pale bloodied tear tracks that stained the fur. Max became hardened to it, intent on capturing the detail while it sat in front of him. The dead rabbit soon stiffened, so he laid it flat on its side, but on the page he had it hunched and crouching on all fours, as if braced to run.

One of the youngest guards was so enraged by the foul smell he had taken to sitting on the ground outside the door. He threatened Max with a beating if he didn't finish sketching soon, swearing he'd throw the reeking corpse into the kiln. Max knew he wouldn't follow through; the guard who'd given him the rabbit would wring his neck. It wouldn't do to damage such a precious commodity. Since the move on Russia, the need for warm, angora-wool-lined clothing had increased.

The effects of this push east could be felt throughout the camp. Day and night, Soviet prisoners of war poured in through the gates of Dachau, some on foot, others spilling from a convoy of lorries or the steel belly of a cargo train. They brought with them lice and typhus and filled up every bunk in their barracks, three or four men to a bed, taking it in shifts to sleep. Max watched them arrive, their worn-down faces weather-beaten, their greatcoats still caked in thick Russian mud. The guards seemed to see them as entirely expendable; scores were shot or starved to death in weeks, diminishing their numbers visibly. The brutality of it all seeped into Max's dreams and he found he couldn't find rest, no matter how tired he felt. After several sleepless nights he discovered a package waiting for him in the recess behind the brick: carbolic soap, an apple and a twist of barley sugar. Holger's kind gestures—however small—made life more bearable.

As the last frosts thawed and turned the ground to mud, more and more factory workers were called up to serve. The influx of Russians meant there was never any shortage of human parts for the machine, but skilled craftsmen were harder to replace.

Reinforcements from other camps arrived; from Flossenbürg, Mauthausen and Neuengamme. Max, Ezra and Stefan made patient teachers. They welcomed the men into their ranks and helped them to bed in, until there were a dozen or so prisoners working on every stage of the production.

On one cold but cloudless day, the guard told Max he was required in the artist's studio upstairs, instead of his own smaller quarters in the basement. Max followed the man through the building, assuming that he was going to be given a new team of novices to train. The studio was an airy room where the contract artists and modelers worked, their creative space usually unsullied by the presence of prisoners. This was the public face of Allach, closer to an artist's workshop than a factory. It was filled with large-scale pieces, from urns to busts and figurines. Even on the shortest day, the room was washed with light. After a winter spent in the basement, Max felt like he was ascending to the heavens.

When the guard opened the door, he was dazzled by the brightness and surprised to find no weary recruits waiting for him there. Instead at the center of the room stood a solitary figure: a woman facing away from him, bending to examine a sculpture of a trophy stag. She wore a tailored velvet jacket with heavy folds of fabric in peacock green.

She turned at the sound of their approach and spoke curtly to the guard.

"Thank you; you may go now."

The guard hesitated.

"I assure you, I'll be quite all right. Fetch Herr Ostendorff and tell him we are ready."

He turned sharply on his heel and they both listened until his footsteps on the metal stair receded in the distance.

Max braced his weight against the nearest table, leaning into its solidity. He looked down at the hand gripping the edge: his skin was cracked and caked in clay, which he could never truly clean. For a moment he felt afraid she was a vision. He lifted his eyes again in disbelief.

"I'm so sorry," said Bettina. "I didn't mean to frighten you."

He realized he had entirely forgotten how her voice sounded. The timbre of it low and sweet. How was that even possible?

"We only have a moment, but I didn't want us to meet in the office, with other people milling around, so I'm afraid that I insisted."

Stood before him, she was the same and yet entirely different. Polished and poised in a way that his Bettina never was.

She came toward him, tentative, although he still doubted she was real until she reached out a hand to touch his own.

"Say something," she beseeched him softly. "Are you angry?"

He opened his mouth to speak, but found he couldn't make a sound. He shook his head and took a step away, conscious of the smell of the rabbit, which still clung to him. He knew how he must look: dusty and disheveled, gaunt and undernourished.

She wrapped her arms around herself.

"They cut your beautiful hair."

He lifted a hand to the close-cropped stubble that rasped beneath his fingers.

Bettina turned from him then, fumbling in her sleeve for a handkerchief.

"I'm so sorry. Please forgive me."

He smiled weakly. "I actually think you might be a mirage."

"Pinch me. I promise, I'm just the same as ever."

She held out her hand, the gold band glinting dully on her finger. She saw his eyes alight on it and snatched it back, as quickly as if scalded. She pushed it deep into her pocket.

So Himmler had been right; she was married.

He looked away, trying to steady his racing heart. He stared out across the vast horizon, to the rows of single-story buildings that stretched away for miles. When she spoke, he heard a tremor in her voice.

"I waited for you. At the station."

Anxious, she continued: "I tried to find you. I never stopped. I did everything I could . . ." She trailed off weakly.

"I tried to send a message to you too," he said.

"The Viking? I knew that it was you! You remembered the rabbit."

"*Mein kleines Kaninchen.* As if I could forget."

He wanted to reach out, to hold her, but filled the gulf between them with words instead.

"Reichsführer Himmler has me making a rabbit for his daughter."

"Herr Ostendorff told me. He said he thought that it might help your cause."

"He's a good man; he looks out for me."

"I'm glad there's someone here that does."

She tried to brave a smile, but he saw it waver.

"Max, I need to tell you something." She was earnest and intent. "It's not the way I'd ever choose to break this news to you, but we have so very little time . . ."

From her pocket she drew out a photograph that she handed

to him. It was a picture of a smiling child, sitting doll-like, legs held stiffly out in front. The picture was hand-tinted; the artist had picked out several different tones—soft, brown wavy hair, pink Cupid's bow lips and in the background, a lake painted an impossibly bright, azure blue.

"Her name is Clara and she's nearly two years old. She is your daughter, Max."

He heard the words and understood their meaning, but felt a curious detachment. A daughter? It was too much to comprehend.

Bettina's hands were shaking; she clasped them together to still the trembling. His gaze locked back onto the tinted dark gray eyes in the photograph.

"I wish I could tell you all about her; she has so much spirit and such capacity for joy. I will tell you everything, but not today. There's no more time."

She glanced nervously at the door, as if expecting it to open at any moment.

"I've made a deal with your Herr Ostendorff. An arrangement, so I can keep on coming here to see you. Everything I've done, *everything*, is so that we can be together."

A sound came from the stairwell; it was Holger's voice, echoing upward, bouncing off the tiled walls. Normally soft-spoken, he seemed to be approaching with uncharacteristic vigor.

Bettina thrust the photograph into his grasp.

"Keep it safe."

Then she stepped back and walked stiffly to the window. He stuffed the picture into his pocket, then bowed his head, his hands held tight in front of him.

Holger entered the room first, a few steps ahead of the rest.

"Gentlemen, allow me to introduce Frau Holz. I trust that everything's in order?"

Max could not help but glance up at Bettina when he heard the name. He could sense that she was acutely aware of his eyes on her.

"Absolutely. I cannot wait to begin. This is a project long in the making and very dear to me."

Holger turned and fixed Max with a look.

"Thank you, Max. You may return to your work."

Max gave a sharp nod and put his head back down, walking quickly from the room. He turned back when he reached the door. Bettina was holding out a gracious hand as Holger made introductions to the group. She looked the very picture of refinement. Their eyes met and she held his gaze until the door swung shut and she was lost to him once more.

Pictured, the celebrated painter Frau Holz, formerly Fräulein Vogel, as seen at Porzellanmanufaktur Allach. The artist is wearing a bottle-green tailored skirt and a fitted jacket with wide shoulders and a modish, nipped-in waist. The lapels are embellished with jet-black beads and she is wearing an exquisitely sculpted hat of crushed black velvet.

The photographer staged Bettina in the center of the room with smaller, detailed works in the foreground and the larger, more dramatic pieces creating height behind. He placed a few of the artist's naturalistic, rural paintings strategically in view.

Later, the copy editor would add enthusiastic captions to accompany the photographs, applauding the beauty of the blushing woman pictured at the heart of the Allach empire, ready to bring her artistry to life with the help of their talented craftsmen.

The new collection would feature a porcelain menagerie, each based on an animal from one of her paintings. The traveling exhibition of Great German Art had taken her work out to the provinces, where their pastoral themes and spectacular realism had won her many devotees. They had bought reproductions of her gentle lamb, the spring hare running in the field and the songbird trilling on the branch. Soon they would be available for purchase as hand-painted porcelain figurines.

Representing Allach was Herr Holger Ostendorff, one of their creative leaders, responsible for bringing this new work to a grateful German public.

"We are honored to have Frau Holz collaborating on this collection and look forward to working with her closely in the coming months."

When asked if there were plans to reproduce Frau Holz's most famous work, *The Viking*, the writer was surprised to learn of the existence of an earlier figurine. It formed the origin of this collection, but was sadly no longer available. These new pieces, however, would be hand-painted by Frau Vogel herself, giving them a unique place in the annals of Allach's already impressive history.

Reichsführer Himmler had given his blessing to this collaboration and was looking forward to seeing the new work in the near future. Although none of the hand-painted pieces were yet available to view, Herr Ostendorff was delighted to present a preview in the form of a porcelain rabbit, personally commissioned by the *Reichsführer* himself. This exquisite item could be seen in the current catalog and was available for purchase in Allach stores.

Frau Holz posed for more photographs while the reporter

peppered her with questions the readers of *Frauen Warte* would appreciate. This was the Nazi Party's women's magazine, after all, and art was of limited interest to their readership.

How was motherhood finding her? Delightful, she assured him, though it was a little lonely; her husband was occupied with the war and would be stationed in Paris for the next three months. Undoubtedly many German women would understand. What did her husband think of her collection? He was very pleased for her and looked forward to seeing them on his return. How did she find time to work and maintain a loving home at the Holz residence in central Munich? It was such a gift to be able to combine those efforts and make items with which she would decorate their home. She had already amassed quite a collection of Allach porcelain by her favorite artist; she would be so proud to add her own to them.

When the journalist asked what recipes she cooked, she'd laughed uproariously. Like any mother, she was dedicated to finding new and frugal ways to feed her family. She enjoyed making *Eintopf*, a one-pot dish that she cooked with chicken and potatoes. It served her especially well in a time of rationing.

"Besides, it's the only thing I know how to make, and even that I can't cook well," she said, though the copy editor chose to omit that quote from the finished article.

Before the *Frauen Warte* team took their leave, Herr Ostendorff requested one more photograph.

"I wonder, would you mind if we took a group shot very quickly? For marketing, you understand."

Throughout the interview, two men had stood nearby, sketchbooks and preliminary models in hand. These were the workers who would shape and glaze the clay, Herr Ostendorff explained. Frau Holz would attend the factory once a week, to hand-paint the finished pieces.

He beckoned the two men closer in, to stand on Frau Holz's right side as he took his place on her left. The pair had rubbed their dusty hands down their smock coats, then across their shaven heads, trying to make themselves presentable. Frau Holz had beamed at them, a picture of beauty and sophistication.

"Send me a few copies, if you wouldn't mind?" Herr Ostendorff requested.

Later, in the dark room, when the photographer showed the copy editor the proofs they had to choose from, they'd both exclaimed over this shot.

"She's really very pretty here. All lit up," he said.

"She is. Shame about these two." He gestured to Max and Ezra. "You can clearly see the uniform, underneath their coats. That wouldn't do. Give me one of her alone, instead."

Every Tuesday thereafter, Gerhard took Bettina from the broad streets of Munich to Porzellanmanufaktur Allach. She would gaze from the windows as they slipped through rain-washed streets, reflected in the swooping wings of the black sedan. The journey gave her time to mentally prepare herself and shut emotion down, so by the time she was ready to descend the steps to the little workroom, she knew her fear and sorrow would not be on display.

When they drove onto the grounds of the SS training base, the driver would start to slow. He would cruise past the watchtowers and brambles of barbed wire that littered the barren landscape. Bettina searched the faces of all the officers she saw, wondering if her brother might be in their number. Without his intervention on that fateful day, she and Max could have escaped, might now be living as a family in the house that Max imagined. She sometimes lulled herself to sleep with fantasies of revenge on Albrecht, a lullaby of wrath.

Besides numerous officers in SS uniform, pockets of prisoners could be seen working in small groups, digging up the road, or dragging heavy carts filled with stone or coal. Their faces haunted her, their eyes sunk in hollow sockets. It would be easy to look away, to ignore their humanity. It was only by reminding herself that Max was one of them that she felt she truly saw them. She wondered what Max was eating, how he was treated by the guards of the *Außenkommando*; she felt the heavyweight guilt of her own good fortune.

The factory itself was pale and squat, the basement jutting out from it like a platform at a station. There was a flight of steps at either end, but little thought had gone into the aesthetics. The need for daylight and illumination far outweighed any other consideration. Dozens of giant, metal-framed windows ran in rows around the building, which made the rooms bitterly cold in the winter and incendiary on a summer's day. There was little shade to be found; just a handful of cedar trees stood nearby, their dark boughs sagged and weeping.

When they reached the front of the building Gerhard pulled up and parked. He always escorted Bettina to the front door, handing her over to Fräulein Schaffer, Holger's secretary, who would be waiting for her there. Gerhard would drive back to town and then return for her late in the afternoon.

Once inside the factory, Fräulein Schaffer led the way along a central corridor that ran like an artery through the body of the building. Bettina followed, shedding her outer layers as she went and putting on a mask of smiling positivity.

The journey took them through the heart of Porzellan-manufaktur Allach, the entire process exposed for her to see. The building's lifeblood flowed in shades of white, from dove-gray slip to the ice-blue of the finished, burnished figurines. There were suites of rooms entirely dedicated to these: open-slatted pine shelves, filled floor to ceiling with urns and vases, a library of specters.

At the far end of the corridor came a swift descent to the basement, where the windows were small and the work a little dirtier. This was the factory's engine house; black soot mixed with white clay dust, like the ashy residue of a crematorium. This was where Max worked, floors below the spacious studio where her photo shoot took place. His room had low ceilings and square windows, small enamel light shades swinging over-head. Next door was a small team of craftsmen too old to be called up. Skilled in the most delicate tasks, each had decades of experience but were seen as artisans at best.

Fräulein Schaffer had encouraged Bettina to use the upstairs studio, to work alongside other artists and simply send the pieces back and forth to Max and Ezra in the basement. She was shocked when Bettina had insisted on going down to work with them directly and equally surprised when Holger readily agreed.

The *Außenkommandoführer*, responsible for the prisoners on work duty, had been put out. He took personal responsibility for Frau Holz's safety and, as a consequence, Bettina, Max and Ezra found they were rarely interrupted but never quite alone. A guard was always present, either in the room itself or in the corridor outside and two or three times a day, the solicitous Fräulein Schaffer would "pop down" to check in on Frau Holz.

The presence of so many people meant few conversations were ever truly private. In the brief moments they were left alone, Bettina would talk about their daughter and Max would listen rapt, with full attention. She tried to ask about his life in the camp and the circumstances of his arrest, but he seemed unwilling and would often shy away. She understood; she had her own raw wounds. She told Max about Richard's disappearance early on, confessing to him she was now certain he was dead.

"I want to stay hopeful, but my heart knows; I can't deny it."

The subject of Karl was almost entirely off-limits; she told Max the barest bones of her decision, the path she'd chosen to protect Clara and to wait for him. She made sure he knew that Karl was largely absent from their lives but beyond that, he didn't need to hear the details—her dread at the prospect of Karl's eventual return, her misery at his touch and worst of all, the painful fact that little Clara thought he was her father.

Bettina tried to focus on their blessings instead: that Max survived, that she was here, that their daughter was alive and thriving.

When Bettina left the basement at the end of the day, she would often walk in a daze to Holger's office and knock on his door. Max told her he trusted him implicitly and he clearly understood the true nature of their relationship, though neither of them ever spoke of it directly. Better not to state the facts out loud, leaving them all the cover of deniability.

Holger's friendship brought a comfort that had been missing from her life since Richard's disappearance. Just to know that she and Max had one ally in this otherwise friendless world made such a difference.

"I cannot bear to see him here," she said.

"You're doing everything you can. Your presence gives him strength."

Over time their little basement backwater began to come to life. At Holger's instruction, Ezra was elevated to support their work: to help Bettina prepare her paints, to glaze and fire all their experiments. He was meticulous, but it was his deep and abiding love of art that really made her warm to him. In his quiet voice he would muse about the symbolism and layers of meaning. It took her back to her Bauhaus days, of making art for its own sake.

Bettina's collection was to be made up of porcelain animals lifted from her paintings. The plan was for Max to sculpt them, then she would follow up and paint them all by hand, re-creating the brushstrokes of her originals.

The planning and execution sustained them all in unexpected ways. For the two men, it gave their days a purpose and meaning. For fifteen hours at a stretch their brains were fully occupied with the effort of sketching, sculpting and shaping each animal. From Wednesday to Monday they would work on a figurine, readying it for Tuesday, when Bettina would return.

After many trials, she decided to decorate the pieces' underglaze with the same level of detail as she rendered on the canvas. It took many hours to replicate the results she required for each piece. The depth and tone of the colors changed during firing and Bettina's own technique developed as she found her way around unfamiliar textures, unused to working in three dimensions, or on such a porous surface.

With great patience Ezra attempted to match the tones and textures of the creatures she'd painted years before, such as a hare leaping through a plowed and foggy field.

"Max tells me that these animals are your self-portraits?"

"They are in a way, although it sounds silly in the abstract."

"Not at all. The shape-shifter has a long and noble tradition in art—you might call this therianthropy. Some see cave paintings from that perspective: each animal symbolizes something for and of the artist, depending how you read it."

As he talked to her, he loaded the day's work onto a long, thick plank, ready to take to the kiln for first firing.

"Your rabbit, for instance; the Dutch were always very fond of painting them, dead ones at least: Voluptas Carnis. They stand in for the sins of the flesh. And you are familiar with *Der Feldhase* by Dürer, of course? You know, if you look closely, there is the reflection of a window in its eye. He wants to warn us that a wild thing can be captured." He put up his hands. "Not a lesson we require here."

He gestured to the rabbit Max was sculpting. "The Torah tells me these creatures are unclean, but I've known scholars who say they represent the Diaspora and survival. What do you think, Max?"

Max had simply smiled in response, lost in the satisfaction of company while he worked. The three of them often spent long periods in comfortable quiet, broken only by the sounds of the factory above and all around them, or the barking of the ever-present guards outside their door.

As well as a rabbit and a hare, Bettina planned to make a field mouse, a song thrush, a raven and a mole. Each was at a different stage, though the rabbit, based as it was on the one that Max had made for Gudrun Himmler, was now all but complete. Bettina would soon begin to paint, once they had the color palette down.

She found these new processes harder than expected and was glad of the rabbit's simplicity to help her find her feet. She struggled to replicate the right shade of deep pink for the eyes. Each test resulted in what looked like glossy pools of blood after firing. Sample after sample had been sent to the kilns, but each returned a disappointment.

"Don't worry. We will persevere," Ezra reassured Bettina, though she found herself secretly delighting in delays. She could not bear to face the thought of what would happen when the work was done.

The following Tuesday, Bettina woke with renewed determination. They might all be in mourning for a life they couldn't have, but she could at least bring a little brightness to the dank basement. She went to her wardrobe and picked out a cream wool jacket, with a warm gray woolen scarf to protect her from the sleet.

She descended the basement stairs early that morning, before the artisans were at their desks next door. She found Ezra waiting for her, his eyes dancing with excitement. In the days since her last visit, he had been working on further color samples that had fired well. He handed them to her for approval.

"These are wonderful, Ezra, thank you," said Bettina.

"Don't praise me—it's thanks to Stefan."

Max, Ezra and Stefan had formed a brotherhood of sorts. Stoking the kilns was heavy, dirty work, but like Max, Stefan had an innate sense of the spatial, the ability to think and plan in three dimensions. He grew so skilled in stacking the kiln that he found himself charged with firing the most delicate and precious pieces. Max insisted Frau Holz's work would be fired by no one else.

Together, Stefan and Ezra had prepared and fired dozens of different test pieces across the week. Finally, they both agreed they'd landed on just the right shade of pinky red for the rabbit's eye: a liquid raspberry that glistened with life.

"We can begin at last," said Ezra. Bettina smiled with gratitude, though inwardly she felt a pang at being one step closer to completion.

Over the chalk-white base, she started to paint solid blocks of color; first the soft gray-brown down of fur along the rabbit's nose, then a putty-colored flesh tone between the toes, the blush pink of the inner ears and finally, the rabbit's eyes. When she'd finished painting those, she moved on to a more translucent technique. Here she built in layers to re-create the texture of tiny filaments, like the feather-soft fur on the rabbit's cheeks and chest.

When her first figure was complete, she sat back to admire it. They all agreed it was a work of great precision—romantic realism but with an edge of the wild that lent it authenticity. Bettina asked Ezra if he could rush it to the kiln. She wanted to know if the colors worked as soon as possible. There would be further glazings and firings to come, all of which would alter the tones, making them deepen gradually and become enriched, but this first would be the proving point where she felt she would sense if they were heading in the right direction.

The young *Außenkommando* on guard that day was standing

bored and listless by the door. At Bettina's request he stirred himself and reluctantly agreed to open the doors so Ezra carrying his plank could gain access to the firing room. He'd slumped out after the older man, shouldering his rifle.

When they had gone, Bettina sat back at the desk and drew the next piece toward her, anxious to keep improving her technique. She was determined to find the right balance between opacity and texture. A calm clarity descended on her as she began to paint and everything around her dropped away.

Suddenly, from nowhere, she felt a drop of something liquid spatter on her cheek. She touched her fingers to it and stared at their tips, uncomprehending. They were smeared with what looked like wet blood. She saw drops of the same soaking into the breast of her jacket and a wine-red tear on the face of the rabbit.

She looked up at Max and a moment of absolute silence descended: he was sitting across the desk from her, claret-colored paint dripping from a brush held in his hand. They both burst out laughing in the shock of recognition, though Max immediately clamped a hand over his mouth.

"What on earth did you do that for?" she asked, still laughing.

Max drew his hand down his face, his jaw pulled slack with shock.

"I am so, so sorry. I . . . I have no idea what came over me! You just looked so intensely occupied and I wanted to make you laugh . . ."

"Well, it worked."

"It looks like you've been shot. Oh God, your jacket . . ."

The look of horror on his face made her dissolve into laughter once again. Max jumped to his feet, grabbing a relatively clean rag and dipping it in water. He dabbed at the wool, though it made no difference.

"Please don't worry. It doesn't matter in the slightest. I don't know what I was even thinking when I put this on. I'm such a fool—I'd never normally wear a getup like this when I'm working, I just wanted to look bright and sunny. I thought it would make you happy."

"Your presence does that anyway, no matter what you're wearing."

"Still, I must look awfully silly, coming in here all dressed up."

"I fell in love with you when you were wearing a sackcloth smock, sitting on top of a ladder, in case you don't remember."

She blushed to think of the naive, prickly girl she'd been when they'd first met—haughty and hot tempered.

"Of course I do, but I was ever so much younger then. In almost every way."

She took the cloth from him and rubbed at the splash of red on her cheek.

"Did I get it all?"

Max reached out to wipe the last smear of pink. He lingered, relishing the feel of her flesh.

"You know, the next time I saw you, you weren't wearing anything at all."

He brushed his thumb across her lips. They parted with a sigh. She reached toward him, the tips of her fingers brushing his. They laced together and entwined.

"Max . . ."

From high above came the sudden sound of bootsteps on the stairs.

They sprang apart, Bettina flushed, a flare of high color on her pale skin. Max searched around him, his panicked glance skipping from the door to the paint-spattered rabbit on the table.

Bettina whispered urgently, "What is it? Have you lost something?"

He shook his head. "Only my mind."

The nervous anxiety sent Bettina into a fit of giggles that brought tears to her eyes. She tried to constrain them, which only turned them to a coughing fit.

The guard entered the room with Ezra close behind him, evidently concerned.

"Is everything all right, Frau Holz?"

"Fine, thank you," she said, wiping at the tears. "I'm afraid I've just made rather a mess of myself in your absence."

She indicated the drops of red paint that still spattered the table, the rabbit and her coat.

"I clearly can't be trusted on my own."

Ezra and Max helped Bettina clean up as best they could, though both the rabbit and her coat were impervious to their efforts. The guard took a walk outside, to smoke and stretch his legs.

When they returned to their desks and Ezra was occupied with clearing up, Max whispered an apology. "I honestly don't know what came over me; some mischief just took hold."

She shook her head, smiling. "I thought I knew you, Max Ehrlich, but you clearly still have some surprises left for me."

"Evidently."

She shivered at the memory of his touch.

"We must be more careful, though; what if we'd been caught?"

"You're right, I'm sorry. I know you're right."

As the hours passed they talked on in whispered snatches and coded language, though they would stop as soon as anyone came near and, minutes later, pick back up where they'd left off. Subjects that had once seemed too raw to touch were now like newly healed scars. Tender, but allowing exploration.

"I'm not sure how much longer I could have borne this if you hadn't come."

"Once I found out where you were, nothing could keep me from you."

Despite returning to their tasks, both found it hard to concentrate. When Bettina looked up she found Max watching her. She held the rabbit up for his inspection; although she had applied several layers of paint, the bloody teardrop remained stubbornly visible.

"I suppose it will disappear eventually," she sighed. "But I quite liked the bloody tear."

Max craned across the desk to see. "Oddly enough, it looked just like that when I was sketching it."

He took out the drawings he'd made for Gudrun Himmler's rabbit.

"They brought me a real angora rabbit to work from. Dead, of course. It had this thin, red liquid seeping from its eyes, as if it were crying blood."

Max spread them out on the table. "They breed them for their fur at the main camp; hundreds of them. Rumor is they're treated better than the prisoners."

"The perfect metaphor for this godforsaken place," Bettina whispered, eyeing the guard's shadow outside the door. Max snorted derisively.

"If only they were half as merciful with humans. Locked up,

starved and beaten. Kept in overcrowded, freezing barracks in the pit of winter, while the rabbits have their heated hutches."

"Truly?" she asked. The inhumanity never failed to shock her.

He fairly spat his words out in reply. "I can't describe it adequately. They tear families apart, deny our liberty and crush our spirits. They kill without a second thought; shoot the weak or ship them off to God knows what worse fate."

In all the weeks since they'd been reunited, she'd never heard him talk this way. His voice rose as his anger caught flame.

"It's a human farm, this place. A slaughterhouse."

She checked the shadow of the guard again, anxious in case he should hear. She put a finger to her lips in warning and he lowered his voice back down to an angry whisper.

"Instead of carving pets, we should be making work which shows this hell for what it truly is."

He turned the pages of his sketchbook, containing image after image of the rabbit decomposing, rotting right in front of her, sunken eyes weeping blood. His fury was contagious.

She nodded, vehemently.

"You're right—a rat in a trap or a fox ripped to death by dogs. We should use this damned anemic medium as a way of showing every form of torture which goes on: how humans are starved, poisoned, shot at, beaten, trapped, ensnared."

"I can see it. A butchery but the cattle are taken to their death on two legs."

Bettina's eyes were flashing, lit by the visions that passed before them.

"What if we could take the sculptures we've been working on and turn them into true art, to show the world what's happening? A subversion of this supposedly 'pure' form which is anything but. Never mind a kiln, we should fire them in the crematorium."

She was talking so fast, her thoughts outpaced her.

"I could smuggle them out, though God knows if they would ever see the light of day. We could, Max, even if we did it just for us. Like *The Viking*; simply knowing that it was you made it so meaningful to me. That gave me strength."

She was breathless now. "Can't you just imagine it? We would have jumped at something like this when we were younger. We must do something, or we may as well be dead."

"But what's the use? You know it wouldn't change a thing."

"It would for us. We have to put this pain and anger somewhere, give it form," she insisted. "Richard fought back, but I was too scared to. Now he is gone and you are locked in here. If I don't fight it now, then when?"

She pressed on, beseeching. "We both need a purpose, something more to live for, to get us through. If this all ends, when it ends, as it most surely must, then our souls will be intact. I need Clara to know that I fought for her, for us. Promise me you'll think about it?"

He shook his head.

"I don't need to think. I *know* you're right. I've never been more sure."

"Truly?"

She was almost breathless with excitement.

"We'll sign them as The Porcelain Maker of Dachau. A real collaboration: you and I, working as one at last. As it was always meant to be."

CHAPTER NINETEEN

Munich

November 1993

The elderly gentleman responded anxiously to Clara's stunned expression.

"I do apologize. I didn't mean to startle you. *Die Putzfrau*, Paulina—the young woman who cleans for me—when she told me your name, I couldn't quite believe it. But as soon as I saw you, I knew it right away. Please, both of you, come and sit down."

He walked stiffly to the pair of couches by the fire and lowered his narrow frame down.

"So here you are at last—Clara Vogel, all grown up! And this is . . . ?"

"My daughter, Lotte."

He wagged a finger at her. "Lotte Woolf, yes! Now you, I was expecting. So, let us begin again."

He leaned forward on the cane between his knees, his hands a knot of veins.

"How did you come to find me—Bettina sent you, I suppose?"

Clara and Lotte exchanged an anxious glance.

"I'm afraid my mother died three years ago."

"Ah." He dropped his head, a slight nod of resignation.

"*Meine liebe* Bettina. I rather hoped you'd tell me she was alive and well. I should have liked to see her one more time. I cared for your mother very much."

"I'm so sorry. We only learned of your existence very recently."

Lotte chimed in, "I spoke to someone at Haus der Kunst who told me about *The Viking*."

Clara opened the clasp on her bag and retrieved the photograph of her mother from its depths.

"And I believe this might be you, in a photograph that recently came into my possession."

She handed over the grainy black-and-white image, which he peered at closely.

"It's from 1941," she explained. "Am I right—this is you standing alongside my mother?"

"You are correct. But tell me, *bitte*—you gave your name as Clara Vogel. You never married?"

"Married and divorced. I reverted to my maiden name."

"Just like your mother."

"Did you know her husband, Karl?"

He grimaced.

"Not really, I only met him once or twice. I didn't like him. He wasn't worthy of her, which I rather believe that he suspected."

Clara couldn't quite comprehend that she was finally with someone who might hold answers to the myriad questions crowding her head.

"Forgive me, Herr Ostendorff—I don't quite know where to begin. We came to Munich to try to find out who my father was. You might be the only person living who can help. My mother refused to ever speak about him, but she did once refer to him as 'the porcelain maker of Dachau.' Does that mean anything to you at all?"

He gave a short guffaw.

"But of course!"

He gestured to the fourth figure in the photograph: the crop-haired stranger, standing between her mother and Ezra Adler.

"Here he is—this is your father, Max Ehrlich, my dear friend."

He handed the photograph back to her, grinning broadly now, his face transformed.

"I still remember that day vividly."

Clara scrutinized the photograph, seeing it from a completely new perspective. The muscular man with the dolorous dark eyes was her father.

"You both look so much like him. I think I would have known who you were, even if you hadn't said your name."

He pointed up at the painting over the mantelpiece.

"Surely you must see the resemblance?"

Both Lotte and Clara turned back to look at *The Viking* once more. Clara felt her daughter's hand grip onto her own—they had only ever seen Bettina's features reflected in their faces: the bowed lips and arching brows. Now they both took in other details from the painting: the strong jawline, the long straight nose, the serious eyes that looked out.

"*The Viking* was based on a portrait of your father, Max. Beneath that painting, another one is hidden—an expressionist sketch your mother made of your father. I never saw it, of course, but she told me it was there. Bettina was never able to fully realize her talent, but all the layers of that painting tell her story nonetheless."

Again, he gestured to it with a shaking finger.

"For decades I longed to share it with the world. Now it is your inheritance and you must both decide to do with it what you will."

CHAPTER TWENTY

Porzellanmanufaktur Allach

Spring 1942

In Munich the parks were carpeted with blossoms blown down by the gusts of a turbulent spring. Seventeen kilometers north, the scoured earth of Dachau showed few such signs, for nothing much was growing on that ground.

Along a muddy track a rough cortege of carts came by, dragged by men in harness. The wagons were usually filled with soil or gravel, but on this day contained the bodies of men too ruined to carry on. Their pale limbs looked hollow, like the bones of birds, almost light enough to blow away. This was a sacred cargo treated as profane.

Death often went unobserved in Dachau. There was no rite of passage, no dignity afforded to the final days. No funeral, no time to mourn or grieve. Cruelty was commonplace; a life could be snuffed out in front of you at any time. The end came suddenly and in so many guises that the inmates became almost inured. It came at morning roll call or on the road to work and when it did it was seldom heroic; for some it might seem like a blessing, after what had gone before.

Alone in the early morning, Max had watched as the carts passed by. The sight was only too familiar, but still he stopped to bear it witness. He prayed for the dead, in the hope that someone might do the same for him. He knew if he fell ill, he would likely be taken off to Hartheim near Linz, where the sick of Dachau were removed to die. There was some comfort in knowing he might be buried in Austrian soil, but he knew that no one there would pray for him at all.

He still feared death, but no longer found it shocking, surrounded by it as he was. Greater terrors dogged his thoughts; he felt their breath on him when he imagined his world without Bettina. All hope lived and died with her.

In the factory, the day began with shouts and clangs and banging. No time for reverence. For the able, life was work.

Sometime later, Max was bent over his desk when he heard Bettina's voice echo in the distance. He felt his spirits lift a little; these were the moments that gave him purpose. On the days when she was absent he felt a stillness creeping over him, only feeling himself revive when she returned.

As she entered the basement room, the guard stood to attention. She greeted Ezra and inquired after his health, asking if he'd heard anything from Sachsenhausen yet. He'd been given permission to write to Zofia, so Bettina supplied him with paper and postage, but he had no idea if his wife ever received the letter. He chose to keep on hoping, awaiting a reply. Bettina understood; it was the way she felt about Richard. When she and Imre exchanged letters they spoke of him in the present tense, neither willing to entirely give up hope.

Max watched as Bettina took off her coat and pulled on her old tobacco-brown painting smock. The bright tailored outfits she had worn in the early weeks were now consigned to the wardrobe. They belonged to Frau Holz; this was his Bettina.

She smiled and bobbed a curtsy.

"Good morning, Max."

"Good morning, Frau Holz."

Though the formality felt peculiar, he almost relished it. A signal that their day together had begun. After this moment, time sped by. She would be gone again before he knew it.

"Are you well?"

"Very well, thank you."

Ezra took himself off to the far end of the room where he began to wedge new clay with noisy vigor. They all kept up appearances, though Max was certain Ezra understood the true nature of their feelings. Bettina glanced around, then reached across the work desk for a pencil, briefly brushing her fingertips against his hand. Opportunities for any kind of intimacy were few and far between. Though they knew it could be their undoing, they were drawn together nonetheless. In the moment the reward of a fleeting touch or glance seemed to outweigh the risk, but afterward they'd both be consumed by guilt and fearful of the consequences if they were discovered.

In her last few visits, they had begun work in earnest on their secret menagerie, which gave them something more to focus on. They knew their time together was finite—the main collection was close to being finished. The whole factory was gearing up for the *Reichsführer*'s next inspection when Bettina would present the pieces to him personally. Beyond that lay the unknown: an end to weekly visits and the stories she told him of their daughter; an end to everything that gave meaning to existence. It meant these remaining hours must be savored and sharing this endeavor meant the world to both of them. Bettina spoke in a low tone, though the guard was on the far side of the door and Ezra was singing loudly as he worked.

"I've been thinking about the songbird."

Their assembly of subversive animals had started small enough; a simple porcelain mouse caught in a real trap, its neck snapped, a smear of blood staining the whiskers and teeth. They had passed it between them surreptitiously, working on it till they judged it complete. Max had concealed it in the recess behind the ventilation brick.

Next came a rabbit laid out on a marble slab. Afraid that Holger might stumble across the pieces behind the ventilation brick, Bettina had taken to keeping the pieces in a large carpet bag she carried with her, wrapped in a damp towel and waxed cloth. It was only a temporary solution; she lived in fear she'd be discovered.

Then, one bright morning a fat wood pigeon flew into the room and took up residence in the rafters overhead. They could hear it cooing for hours, but it remained hidden from sight until the guard had climbed up with a broom to sweep it out. The following day, Bettina brought the mouse and rabbit back in and transferred them to their hiding place above. All they had to do was fetch them down any moment they could snatch alone. A third figurine—a raven—soon joined the other two, each at different stages of completion.

They worked steadily, but the subject of the next piece

became the source of some discussion. For expediency, they needed it to be a variation on one of the creatures from the official collection, but Bettina was determined to imbue it with real meaning.

"I want this piece to talk about propaganda. This factory churns out art which tells a story—about the war, about a partial version of the German way of life, but we know that story is a lie. For one thing, it's made on the back of forced labor, which the public doesn't see."

"Or so it seems. They choose not to ask too many questions," Max replied.

"That feature in *Frauen Warte* magazine was propaganda, pure and simple. Our main collection is the same. I've no regrets—it allows us to be together, but working for them in any way just feels like collusion, whatever my intent. That's what makes this secret collection so important; I need to do something to counteract this siren song."

"So what should it be—a warning, perhaps; some sort of statement?"

"This feeling of being complicit, it's been churning around inside my head. It sickens me and reminds me of a feeling from my childhood. I couldn't quite put my finger on it. Then last night it came to me: this thing Albrecht did when we were growing up. It's haunted me for years."

Max's expression darkened at the mention of her brother.

"I must have been ten or eleven; he was a good bit older. A young man. One day, he went into the woods behind our farm and caught a little bird. I think it was a song thrush, perhaps a nightingale. Anyway, he gave it to me in a little cage, saying it was to be our secret. I knew Mama and Papa would have made me let it go, so I followed his advice and kept it under cover in the cellar, to make sure it didn't sing.

"I loved it so much. I would dig up worms and find caterpillars to feed to it. I'd let it out to hop on to my finger, but over time it seemed to fade down there. Eventually I told Albrecht I thought we ought to let it go, but he refused. Not long after, I went down there and it was gone. I knew he must have taken it, so I ran to find him in the woods."

Her eyes were awash with long-remembered shame.

"I couldn't find him anywhere at first, and then I heard it. A bird began to sing and it was so beautiful I somehow knew that it was mine."

Max could almost envisage the scene and the song.

"By the time I got there, I was too late. The cage was hanging from a branch and there were other birds around, five or six, all dying. One was gone already, hanging from its little feet, although it somehow held on to the bough. I couldn't understand what I was seeing, but he told me. He relished it, in fact."

Her pale lips pressed together.

"It's a poacher's trick. He'd painted all the branches with strong glue; thick like a varnish. He hung the birdcage in the tree, then took the cover off. My little bird had been so happy to finally see the sky, it sang its little heart out. The other birds were drawn to it; they landed nearby to just listen to its song. When they tried to fly off again, it was too late— they were stuck fast. They'd panic and flutter and thrash until everything—feathers, wings and beaks—was caught. They almost tied themselves in knots just trying to escape, but the more they fought, the worse it got."

"He didn't try to hide it from you?"

"He laughed; he stood and watched them while they struggled. Eventually they all gave up and died. He even killed my little bird. He wrung its neck and threatened to beat me if I told my mother what he'd done."

She flinched from the memory. "He was a sadist. Still is, as we know all too well. I'm sorrier than I can ever say that I brought him into your life."

"It wasn't your fault. Any of it."

She turned her face from him, waiting for the shame to ebb away. Max was sketching when she looked back up. When he finished, he pushed the picture toward her.

"We can use the song thrush from the main collection as the starting point; is that what you were thinking?"

In his sketch, the wings were arced in flight, but one was stuck to the branch. The bird's head was twisted, the neck contorted as it tried to free itself.

Bettina nodded gratefully.

"That's just it. Could you make the branch it sits on a little bigger? I want to use the *Frauen Warte* article to cover it. And the glue needs to be transparent, something that can harden like molten glass."

"I'll see what I can do."

She placed her hand flat near his. "I have been thinking . . . Perhaps these are our golem, Max. Remember?"

"Of course."

"We shape them together from clay, then send them out into the world for our protection."

"With any luck they will preserve us," he said.

"I hope so. We have every need."

*

The following morning Bettina insisted on returning to Porzellanmanufaktur Allach. She told Karl's driver she would be going to the factory every day from now on. With Himmler's inspection just over a week away, time was of the essence.

When she arrived, the basement room was filled with industry. Max and Ezra were inspecting newly fired pieces and discussing how the final work might be displayed. Himmler would choose some items for mass production and Max was convinced the collection would prove popular.

"Perhaps that way you could keep coming here and painting?"

Bettina smiled and nodded but seemed distracted. Ezra exchanged a look with Max and announced that it was time to take the next few pieces to the kiln. The guard opened the door for him and helped him to ascend the stairs.

"Tell Stefan to take care of them!" Max shouted after him.

When they'd gone, he spoke to Bettina with quiet urgency. "Is everything all right?"

She shook her head, a tremor in her lower lip.

"I had a telegram from Karl last night. He's coming back far sooner than expected: a few days after the inspection. Even if Himmler does commission another collection, Karl only ever agreed to me making one."

She could no longer hide her agitation.

"We have to do something, Max; I cannot walk away and leave you here," she whispered. "Week after week, I have allowed myself to sleepwalk to this place. After so long apart it felt like enough to ask. But I can't go back to my life before. I've seen what happens here, what they have done to you and might yet do . . ."

Her voice flailed on wings of anxiety, a panicked moth flying at the light.

"Oh, why didn't I just agree to leave all those years ago, when you asked me?"

"We didn't know; we couldn't see the future."

"I've made the wrong choice at every turn. I still don't know what to do, except . . . I know that I can't leave you here and I can't stay with Karl a moment longer."

"You're sure he wouldn't let you go?"

She shook her head. "No more than the *Außenkommando* would let you. We're both trapped, but I'm in a prison of my own making. I keep hoping something will come to me—that a solution will present itself, but there's no way out. It's hopeless."

They heard voices outside and fell silent, Bettina's fingers twisting in her lap. The guard opened the door and Fräulein Schaffer entered.

"Sorry to disturb you, Frau Holz, but Herr Ostendorff asks if you would care to join him later, for some lunch?"

Bettina straightened her shoulders and tried to look enthusiastic.

"Thank you, Fräulein. Kindly tell him I accept."

"I'll ask the guard to bring you in an hour."

She exited the room and they heard the low murmur of their exchange. Max whispered to her urgently.

"Listen to me, Bet, we can't wait any longer—you and Clara must just leave. Her safety and yours are all that matter. Go to Switzerland, find my parents. If I know both of you are safe, then I'm sure that I can persevere. Talk to Holger," he entreated. "He'll help, I'm sure of it."

"You're certain you trust him?" she asked.

"Implicitly—as much as I trust you."

Bettina shook her head, denying his assertion. "I'll talk to him, but I won't leave you—I won't ever leave you. We have to find a different way."

The heavy door swung open once more; the young guard put his head around the frame.

"Apologies, Frau Holz, I've been summoned to the *Außenkommandoführer*, I'll take you to Herr Ostendorff's office on my return."

"Thank you."

Max waited until he'd safely gone, then stood.

"I have been working on something for you. If nothing else, it might provide you with distraction."

He reached above him, into the beams that arched overhead. A shower of dust and debris fell and pattered to the table. He lifted down a small clay sculpture of a song thrush, still wrapped in a damp cloth. He'd turned the wing, just as Bettina had described, and made a new branch, slightly larger than its official twin.

Pasting on the newsprint propaganda would be easy enough; the real challenge came in finding time and a safe place to do it undisturbed. Although she had occasionally smuggled the pieces home to work on overnight, she dared not risk exposure by keeping them there too long. The staff had access to every room in the apartment and little Clara was of an age when she'd begun to investigate the contents of everything she came across. Bettina looked at Max's detailed work; she longed to share it with the world, though the hope of that seemed faint.

She often found herself dreaming of another life, where they could work freely. What effect might it have if their art could live beyond these walls? She pictured the factory surrounding them, filled with shelves of statuary, barrel after barrel, packed with straw to send art out around the realm. Each week hundreds of pieces were shipped from here to Berlin and all across the Reich. If only they could do the same. It would be simple enough; one barrel would contain their whole collection.

Slowly, a realization crept over her: what if subterfuge was not required, but bravery instead? After all, figurines were sent from here all the time, with hardly anyone sparing them a second glance. All she need do was ensure she had the right packaging and the courage of her convictions.

She wondered now why she had been cautious for so long; if she just wrapped them all up and took them out in a fine Allach box, tied with a ribbon, then who would even care? She laughed aloud, astonished that she hadn't seen it clearly before now.

Holger was sitting at his desk, a recording of the opera *Dalibor* playing quietly in the background. He was working through a preliminary draft of the new catalog when he heard the guard's knock on the door.

"Frau Holz, what a pleasure! Come, come. Fräulein Schaffer has arranged for a cold lunch to be laid out in the dining room, but I thought you might enjoy a brief moment of respite here first."

He dismissed the guard with a nod and closed the door behind him.

"Can I get you something; a hot chocolate, perhaps?" He knew her predilection.

"Thank you, no." She smiled. "But I will take something

stronger, if you have it in your bottom drawer? I heard you might keep a drop or two in there, for emergencies."

Holger's eyes sparkled at the opportunity for such mischief. He took out the bottle and two small glasses. Bettina knocked back the Scotch in one, feeling the fire of it. She hung her head for a moment, waiting for the warmth to give her courage. If Max really trusted this man, then so must she.

"I need to talk to you on a matter of some delicacy. It's about Max . . ."

Holger felt a dart of concern. "Is everything all right?"

She took a deep breath. "In truth, I come to you in desperation. This will come as no surprise to you, but Max means a very great deal to me. He means everything, in fact."

"I hold our friendship very dearly, too."

"You've kept him safe, so far, but that safety cannot be relied upon." She cleared her throat. "We have always danced around this subject, but time is short and so I must be frank. I've learned that my husband will be returning to Munich in just over a week's time."

She looked down at her hands, fingers knotted in her lap. "Our marriage was always a matter of expediency on his part and necessity on mine, but circumstances have changed and I realize I can no longer remain with him. I must take my daughter and get her right away, but . . . we can't leave without her father."

She did not dare say more, but watched Holger's eyes grow wide as the implication of her words settled on him.

"I see . . ."

"There is great risk in all directions, but I have seen for myself what Max endures and that far outweighs any other consideration. I believe I have a plan, but I require someone now to help me execute it . . ."

"My dear lady; what can I do? You only have to ask."

Her face almost crumpled with relief but she determined to stay strong. She set her shoulders, as if daring Holger to question her conviction.

"I believe that Max can walk out of this building and escape. It sounds absurd, but I'm certain there's a way and I need your help to convince him."

They spoke for an hour and then again the next day. Holger tried to argue with her, setting out the reasons why her plan was folly, but she faced each of them down. When he finally assented, he said it was against his better judgment: they'd survived so far and ought to carry on as they were, but Bettina wouldn't be deterred.

"You know as well as I do, human life is worthless here. Not just the men, but women and even children, too," she persevered. "Children, Holger! The stories of barbarity I've heard, the things I've seen. I know you've seen the same . . ."

Finally Holger couldn't argue, though he still declared it madness. She didn't disagree. "I know it is, but still . . . I cannot just abandon him to fate."

Now Max was the only one she needed to convince and time was of the essence: Himmler's inspection was mere days away, her husband's return soon after. She knew in her heart they must move now.

In small snatched moments, while they worked, she laid out the whole scheme for him.

Under the cover of the *Reichsführer*'s inspection, the pair of them, along with Clara, would escape. The crux of it, she explained, was that Max would be hiding in plain sight, disguised as her erstwhile husband. Karl's spare uniform was hanging in their wardrobe, clean and pressed. She planned to smuggle it in for Max to wear. She would bring Clara with her to the factory, ostensibly to meet Herr Himmler. Instead Holger would smuggle the three of them out and drive them to the station where they'd make good their escape. She reasoned that few would have the nerve or cause to ask to see the papers of an SS officer, but still, she would take a fine paintbrush and a magnifying glass to an old passport of Karl's, just in case. At a glance she knew she could make it look enough like Max.

On first hearing, Max was horrified and refused to even countenance her plan; it was madness to leave the safety of her marriage to Karl and the protection that he offered her and Clara, but Bettina would not be derailed.

"We can't go back to how it was. I did what I had to do, to wait for you, but now I have seen it for myself. I cannot leave you here a day longer than is necessary. Believe me, I would rather die."

He pushed back, but she met every reason with logic and determination.

"We held on to hope for a long time, but we must now face reality. How many lives have you seen taken in these few years? How much have you seen that you haven't told me; what horrors? I know it, Max. I see how it haunts you."

He couldn't deny it.

"This is only what we planned to do before you were arrested. We can do it now; I know we can. We will be a family, as we were always meant to be."

Bettina had squirrelled away warm clothes for Clara in the carpet bag that now lay hidden at the back of her wardrobe under several old blankets. She would go in the outfit she stood up in. She would take nothing more. Max argued against it until he could fight no longer. He wanted it too; he felt alternately elated and terrified. Finally, he felt resigned.

Three days before the inspection, Bettina found herself so full of nervous energy she could barely suppress it. She would jump at every noise and gabble her thoughts when they weren't overheard, trying to make plans for an as-yet-uncertain future.

"You can start work on designing the house again. We'll buy some woodland somewhere safe, just as soon as ever we can, and build it right there: our forest haven. And when it's done, we'll work together and show the world what's going on in here."

"A haven in the forest—it sounds like a very heaven."

Max's own thoughts were fixated on their daughter. To the doll he'd still only ever seen in a photograph. That remained his most treasured possession, hidden away under the blankets in his bunk, among the straw and dust. But that was not all that lay in hiding. Above his work desk, in the dark, their golem did the same. Max hesitantly suggested they destroy them, concerned they risked discovery, but Bettina wouldn't hear of it.

"They're too important—they are our voice. We could tell a thousand stories about what goes on here, but who would listen? These speak in a way that surpasses language. We have to take them with us   we simply must."

She planned to smuggle the pieces up to the studio when they were setting out the official collection for inspection. There she could transfer them to the carpet bag, in the space once occupied by the uniform, wrapping them in Clara's clothes.

"And when we get to Switzerland we'll make a dozen more. I had an idea for a porcelain mole; we could hang it from barbed wire."

Max looked confused, so she explained, "I always forget you were a city boy. The land stewards do it, to prove how many pests they've killed. I'd see them all the time when I was growing up; rows of moles hanging from the wire, left to rot. They thought their corpses would stand as a warning and deter others."

Max's eyes grew clouded. A memory he'd consigned to the depths rose up and he shuddered.

"Yes. That would work."

When Bettina took her leave of them that evening, Ezra and Stefan were present, along with the guard at the door. She had to content herself with a brief exchange of glances with Max.

"I'll see you all tomorrow."

She smiled at Max and he returned it. There were still vestiges of sunlight in the sky as she left the building. *The days are getting longer*, she thought. The certainty of spring buoyed her up and carried her back to Munich.

When she stepped out of the lift into the apartment, she was surprised to find Liesl snapping orders at servants running to and fro. There were trunks and boxes in the hall and piles of fresh linen. Bettina looked around, bemused by the activity.

"What on earth is going on?" she asked.

Liesl shot her a sharp look.

"I might ask the same of you. Where have you been?"

"I was at the factory. Working."

"I'm not your secretary, Bettina. You normally go once a week on Tuesdays. How was I to know where you were when Karl telephoned and asked to speak to you? I had no idea what to say."

"Did he say when he would call again?"

"Your husband will be home shortly, Bettina, no doubt wondering where his wife has been gallivanting off to."

"But he's not due back for days," Bettina protested.

Liesl narrowed her eyes.

"I think what you meant to say is: how wonderful, my husband is coming home to me at last."

Liesl looked her up and down, taking in the dusty work smock and her scraped-back hair. She pinched the arm of a passing maid, laden down with clean laundry.

"Ursi, go and draw a bath for Frau Holz."

She turned back to Bettina, her thin lips pursed.

"You might at least try to make yourself presentable."

Bettina stood in front of the open wardrobe, staring at Karl's uniform still hanging there. Beneath it, under the pile of blankets, was the carpet bag. Had it been moved? She thought not. She knelt down to check inside; Clara's clothes and toys were there, just as she'd left them. She became aware of her own breathing: fast and shallow. She slumped back against the bed. Her legs were telling her to run, although her mind would not comply. Logic was smothered by confusion and fogged in fear.

From what seemed like a vast distance, she heard Karl's voice reverberate through the wall. Then came Liesl's shrill reply and the sound of Clara racing along the thick carpet of the corridor. Bettina got up on her feet, walking to the door. She placed a hand on the cold brass handle, waiting and listening. She could make out her own name in the soup of voices. She closed her eyes and pressed her forehead against the doorframe; it was too late now, there was no way out. Seeming to float, she opened the door, forcing a smile.

In the vestibule Clara swung from Karl's neck, his starchy, uniformed arms wrapped around her, lifting her up.

"You've got so heavy, *Liebchen*!" he laughed.

Bettina moved toward him. He swung Clara onto his hip and lurched forward to kiss his wife, laughing when she flinched away.

"Sorry," he said. "Clumsy of me."

"Not at all."

She duly offered up her cheek and he leaned forward to kiss her again. Clara grabbed a fistful of her hair and pulled; Bettina winced and loosened the grip of her tiny fingers.

"How was your journey?"

"Tiresome. I'm glad to be home."

With a tinkle of laughter, Liesl reinserted herself. "And we are glad to have you here, aren't we, Bettina?"

She urged the corners of her mouth up further still. "Of course we are."

Liesl lifted Clara down from her brother's arms.

"I thought perhaps we might all have supper together. Will you want to change first?"

Karl kept his eyes on Bettina.

"Actually, Liesl, I would prefer it if my wife and I could dine alone."

A whine of protest went up from Clara, but Liesl shushed her.

"Of course! I will take supper with the children, to give you two a chance to catch up. Come along now, Clara dear."

The maid reset the table for two while the housekeeper brought out a porcelain tureen filled with a creamy, wine-soaked hasenpfeffer stew with steaming bowls of minted new potatoes and asparagus. Karl opened a bottle of champagne.

"*Zum Wohl.* Drink up! There's plenty more where that came from."

Bettina assented, taking a sizeable gulp before pushing it away, conscious of Karl's gaze. He delicately speared his meat and chewed a mouthful in meditative silence. She had been expecting animated conversation; he usually returned with endless tales of his exploits with Gurlitt and the vicissitudes of the Vichy government, but tonight he seemed uncommonly distracted. After a few minutes he finally spoke up.

"So tell me, what have you been doing in my absence? Liesl says she could barely keep track of you."

"I've been at the porcelain factory most of the time, finishing the collection."

He nodded thoughtfully. "And are you pleased with the results?"

"As much as one can be at this stage. Himmler is coming to inspect the pieces himself in three days' time."

"Well then, let us hope it has been worth the effort."

Another tortured silence, then finally he spoke again.

"I suppose I might as well share my news, although I note you didn't ask."

"All good, I hope?"

"I dare venture that it's cause for celebration—Hildebrand

Gurlitt has officially invited me to join him in acquiring art for the new Führermuseum."

She raised her glass to him. "Congratulations, Karl, that's wonderful! And so very well deserved; I know how hard you've worked for this."

He allowed himself a slight self-deprecating smile of acknowledgment. She took another large gulp of champagne.

"So tell me, where will you be based?"

"Paris, as you might suppose. And I'm afraid I'm needed right away. I will have to head straight back."

She suppressed a sigh of relief; she hadn't dared to hope his visit might be so short.

"That's such a shame—Clara will be disappointed; she had all sorts of plans for you."

He smiled indulgently. "As have I for her."

He set down his knife and fork and paused for a moment, appearing to consider his next words.

"I feel it only fair to inform you, I intend to stay on in Paris indefinitely."

"Oh?"

"And given that . . . I have decided that I must have Clara with me. I find I miss her dreadfully when I'm away."

"But we can't go with you, Karl. For one thing, there's this inspection . . ."

He shook his head determinedly. "You won't be returning to the factory. There is no need."

Bettina felt a pale terror creep over her. He held up a hand.

"Neither do I have any intention of taking you with me to Paris. Only Clara."

"For what possible reason?"

She frowned at him, aghast. His smile was acidic.

"I have long hoped a little leniency on my part might help you settle. But I see now, it has rather spoiled you. Made you think you could neglect your duties, both as a wife and mother."

An expression of benevolent patience was etched on his face, despite the implication of his words. Determined to stay calm, Bettina placed her cutlery down quietly on her plate.

"Kindly explain yourself."

"I would have thought it obvious. You have abused my generosity long enough."

She felt the desire to nip at him. "I see. And what am I supposed to beg forgiveness for this time?"

"Perhaps we might dispense with these pretenses." He sighed.

"The staff, *my* staff, have kept me well informed of all your movements these last several years. All the clandestine meetings with unsavory friends, gentleman callers at your studio. More recently, the almost daily visits to the factory when we had agreed, one day a week. Secret letters and phone calls. And now, I'm given to understand, a packed bag sits hidden in your wardrobe. Did you really think you went so unobserved?"

"You have been spying on me . . ."

"With good reason, it would seem."

She blanched at the prospect. He threw his napkin down, determined to chastise.

"The very idea that I would ever let you leave with Clara! You must know I won't allow it and yet you insist on taking this charade to such absurd lengths. I can turn a blind eye to your dramatics, but I will not sit idly by as you scheme to rob me of my child."

He shook his head, apparently wounded.

"What saddens me most is that I truly thought you'd learned your lesson last time. The disrespect you show me now is galling."

"What are you talking about? What last time?"

"I don't appreciate having to clean up your mess, Bettina."

She stared at him, now utterly bewildered.

"Come, must I spell it out? That unfortunate episode with the gentleman in Frankfurt."

She felt a dawning realization.

"Are you talking about Richard?"

"I have told you before, I don't care to hear his name in your mouth." His jaw set hard. "Suffice to say, that . . . gentleman will not trouble either one of us again."

She searched his face and saw he meant to silence her, but she refused.

"What are you saying?"

There was a moment of absolute quiet.

"I warned you, but you wouldn't listen. Then you had the temerity to come to me with your sorry tale."

"What did you do, Karl? Talk to me!"

He seemed incredulous that she should even ask.

"What would you have me say: that your missing 'friend' won't see the light of day again, unless they decide to dredge the Rhine?"

Her missing friend.

"You only have yourself to blame, Bettina. You brought him to my attention. You damn near rubbed my nose in it."

Bettina's hands fluttered to her face like birds, panic rising, a look of abject horror in the moment of comprehension.

Karl looked at her with ill-disguised contempt. "We're at war and I am fighting for my daughter's future. There are bound to be casualties. It would serve you well to remember that, for your own sake."

She felt the vomit rising in her throat and ran from the room. She barely made it to the basin before the pink rabbit meat spilled out, curdled with the cream. She felt like a child on the *Teufelsrad* at the fair, the devil's wheel that spun and spun, then spat you out against the wall and left you broken on the ground.

She stood for minutes, looking at her own face in the mirror, losing track of time. Trembling, she wiped her mouth with the back of her hand; she was all eyes and waxen skin, a smear of lipstick like dried blood. An expressionist painting, not a real woman at all. Unsteadily, she returned to the dining room where Karl was smoking, his composure seemingly regained.

"I've called the doctor. I told him you are overwrought and need to get some rest. I thought it likely that my news would precipitate these . . . vapors. It seems a decent treatment is now available in Italy. You may pack lightly; you shan't have need of many clothes."

"Please, Karl—don't do this."

"It's out of my hands. You are utterly hysterical and when they lock you up, as they most surely will, it shall be for your own good."

"Don't send me away, I beg of you," she pleaded with him. "Clara needs her mother—you must see that!"

"Clara can live with me in Paris until you come to your senses. What use to her are you, the state you're in? Heida will look after her perfectly well—you said as much yourself when you begged to be allowed to work."

Karl was staring at her coldly. She could not understand how she had got here, how she had ever let it come to this.

"For pity's sake, why punish me this way?"

"You left me with no choice. This isn't punishment, it's rehabilitation and you should thank me for it. Others would not be so forgiving, but that is the kind of man I am."

"Oh, I know precisely what kind of man you are."

An image of Richard swam before her.

"You are a murderer. A monster. You're all your own worst fears realized and I'll make certain Clara knows it too."

In that moment she didn't care what more he did to her. Without Max, she was already nothing. In utter desperation the words spilled out of her and slipped in like a knife.

"I never loved you and nor will she. I shall make sure of that."

Karl moved to stand, gait rigid, as if the blood in his veins had crystallized. She saw his mouth work, chewing up the words to spit at her, though none of them could taste quite right, for he made no sound. He lunged at her briefly, as if he might skitter across the table to her throat. She recoiled, then watched as he regained control, his knuckles now like polished ivory.

"It doesn't matter," he hissed between his teeth. He poured himself another glass of champagne, though she saw his hand was shaking.

"You are my wife. Clara is my daughter, and I will do whatever I deem best for this family. Now go and lie down. The doctor will be here soon."

In Dachau, the early morning came and went with roll call. Every hand was set to cleaning out the barracks until they were scrubbed and orderly. Himmler might decide to inspect while he was at the factory and the Kommandant knew all too well his passion for cleanliness. Disease must not be allowed to run free, as it had done here several times. There was no vestige of humanity in the edict, he simply took it as a point of pride.

At the factory, preparations continued. Today, the final pieces would be chosen. In the basement, the copies of each figurine had been laid out. Bettina would choose which were best and add a few finishing flourishes: a little extra luster to the eye, to bring each one to life. They would then be displayed, nestled in a bed of straw, each in its own perfect Allach box made for the occasion.

But first came all the normal morning labors: preparing clay for the day ahead and readying Bettina's station. Max felt anticipation in his every move, electrifying him. The more mundane the task, the more momentous it became. He felt the echo of all the days he'd spent since his arrest, performing these same rotes and rituals, each one ordered and unchanging. Only now could he lift his head and look back across the years that had elapsed. They felt to him like a lifetime.

The sun crept through the window, briefly filling the room with light. Max glanced at the ceiling, worried in case something there might catch the guard's attention, but the golem remained safely shrouded in shadow. Only the very brightest days could penetrate the deep gloom of the basement.

Whenever someone walked into the room, he looked up, searching their faces for her familiarity. Ezra, Stefan, even Holger came and went, but still her seat stayed empty. Max forced himself to work, starting on a simple vase to keep his conscious brain distracted. He ran through the first stage of their planned escape repeatedly. Together she and Holger had finessed the scheme further still. Though he hadn't had an opportunity to speak to his friend about it, Bettina had traced it out the day before in hurried whispers.

On the morning of the inspection, Holger would call Max to his office, where they would wait and keep watch for Bettina and Clara. Max had been relieved that he would see his daughter from a distance first; he hoped it might prepare him for their meeting face-to-face. He didn't want her earliest memory to be of him breaking down in tears.

Holger's secretary, Fräulein Schaffer, would escort Bettina and little Clara to the studio, before fetching Holger and Max to join them. On their arrival, Bettina would feign illness and Holger would offer to take her home in the absence of her driver.

Fräulein Schaffer could see them out, leaving Max in the studio alone, where he would change into Karl's SS uniform, which Bettina would have concealed, along with their porcelain golem. He would leave by the fire escape, making his way outside. The factory stood at the heart of the SS training campus, so one more man in uniform would draw no real attention. Holger would be waiting on the drive to pick him up. He would take them to the station, where he would deposit them, before returning to the factory, in time to be seen by dozens of others making the final preparations, providing him with an alibi. In the chaos of the day it might be hours before anyone was missed.

Max, Bettina and Clara would make their way to the Zurich train—the family Holz, complete with all the necessary paperwork. Max was concerned that Clara might protest at his company, or disavow him if they should be questioned, but Bettina assured him she loved playing elaborate make-believe.

"If I tell her you're her father in a game, she'll go along with absolute ferocity. She has a powerful imagination."

"Just like her mother," Max had replied.

He had only the vaguest notion about the next stage of the journey to the border: a faint hope it might pass uneventfully and a more likely fallback where they might abandon the train entirely and cross by foot, under cover of night. It was a tremendous risk, whatever way you looked at it, but better than any alternative.

Max heard a noise outside and came back to awareness. The sun was now at the height of its trajectory and the task in front of him remained untouched, the blade in his hand held loosely. The door swung open but, to his obvious disappointment, it was only Holger.

"Everything all right in here?"

The young guard standing at the door was scuffing his heels. Max nodded, his eyes turning pointedly to Bettina's empty chair. Holger caught his look and asked the guard, "No sign of Frau Holz today?"

The guard shrugged and shook his head.

"I wonder where she's got to . . ." Holger ruminated, turning his eyes back to Max.

"No doubt she'll be back first thing tomorrow morning. We must just wait and see."

By the time Holger descended the echoing staircase the following morning, Max was gray with worry. His eyes were already shadowed from malnourishment, but Holger could now see his veins through the tissue-thin skin, his pupils dark as a flooded pit.

The guard informed him what he knew already—for a second day, Bettina was absent. Holger nodded, grimly reassuring, and said out loud, "I will look into it myself, right now."

He returned to his office and asked Fräulein Schaffer to telephone Frau Holz's apartment directly, but there was no response. He sat at his desk for a full five minutes, head in hands, trying to decide, then sprang to his feet and informed the office he was going out. He walked to his car and drove straight into the city, parking on the wide street opposite the Holz apartment. For a moment he considered what to do next. He watched the building's flow of traffic, the people coming in and going out, then crossed the street. He entered the lobby at a clip, marching directly to the elevator. With an air of assured confidence, he stated his destination: the Holz residence. Were they expecting him? Of course. The operator had little option other than to convey him upward. The elevator opened out into the soft silence of the top floor, where a solitary maid could be seen. Holger stepped out and hailed the girl.

"Could you kindly tell your mistress that Holger Ostendorff is here to see her?"

He waited, standing alone in the plush, expansive vestibule. There was no sign that a child lived here, no toys, no trace of the familial. Elevated views of the city stretched out from every window. Bettina undoubtedly existed in some comfort here, but even a gilded cage could make a wild bird long for its escape.

The maid returned with a pinch-faced woman in a long silk housecoat, clenched tight at the collarbone by a gaunt hand.

"Am I supposed to be expecting you?"

Her face was somehow both incredulous and bored.

"I do apologize for the disturbance; I was hoping to see Frau Holz."

He took a neat letter-pressed card from his pocket and handed it to her. "Holger Ostendorff. Artistic director of Allach Porcelain."

A single eyebrow rose. "And?"

He continued, "And I am a friend of Frau Holz. We have been working together for several months."

Her face soured. "I didn't know my sister-in-law had any friends. But given the extensive porcelain collection she's bought in recent months, I'm not surprised. My brother's wallet must be keeping you afloat!"

She gestured to the nearby mantelpiece where Holger saw displayed many of the pieces Max had made over the past four years.

"We were expecting to see her at the factory this morning. I grew concerned; is she well?"

"I'm afraid not. She was taken ill, quite suddenly. Overwork, the doctors think."

She glared at him pointedly, as if he might be personally to blame.

"I only ask because she was due to meet with the *Reichsführer-SS* tomorrow and I am certain he will inquire about her absence."

Mention of Himmler, at least, garnered her attention. She

sighed, clearly frustrated that he seemed determined to get a more substantive answer.

"Not that it is anybody's business outside the family, but she evidently had some sort of latent nervous condition. She has been sent away to Italy for treatment. Please send our apologies to the *Reichsführer*."

"And when might I tell him we expect her to return?"

"I'm sorry, Herr Ostendorff, have I not made myself clear? Bettina isn't coming back. You shan't be seeing her again."

She called for the maid.

"And now, I really must insist you leave. This is a very difficult time for all her family, as well you might imagine."

Holger sent for Max and broke the news as gently as he could, but there was no way to soften such a blow. He half expected him to break down, but he simply listened, his expression unreadable. Eventually Holger felt his efforts to console were having the opposite effect, so he trailed off into silence and Max spoke at last.

"There was no sign of Clara?"

"No sign of either one."

Max was picking at his nails unconsciously. Holger stared at the ragged cuticles, deep trenches of raw pink flesh exposed.

"You think the worst."

"Don't you?"

He stopped picking when he noticed the direction of Holger's gaze.

"It's the clay. It's hardened the skin, however much I pick away. I sometimes dream that I'm turning into a golem."

Max tucked his hands out of sight and turned to end the conversation.

"Max?"

He looked back.

"Please don't lose hope, you found each other once before."

"I wish I could believe you. I think they somehow realized she intended to escape. They nearly lost their little pet. They won't make that mistake again."

When he'd gone, Holger felt too restless to settle to his work. Instead, he meandered slowly through the building, observing the preparations for Himmler's visit, now fully underway. He headed first toward the kiln, where Ezra and Stefan were busy preparing a few seasonal trinkets for firing—a last-minute request from the *Reichsführer*'s office. Now Bettina's collection was complete, Ezra was required to help out in other departments. The fact that Max would spend his day almost entirely alone only served to make Holger worry even more. He shared his fears with the older man and told him what he'd said to Max.

"And how did he respond?"

"He said very little, but what he did was fairly fatalistic."

"He needs to grieve, Herr Ostendorff. We have to let that take its course."

Holger took off his glasses and rubbed his eyes; he couldn't seem to focus.

"I'm worried for him."

"Then keep him busy; let him prepare for Himmler's visit and work all the hours that God sends. He needs something to occupy his mind. That is why all cultures have some version of a *levoya*, a funeral."

"She isn't dead; she might yet return at some point in the future."

"Whatever has happened, they've been taken from him— both of them. Believe me: we still mourn them, even if they live."

Fräulein Schaffer made arrangements with the *Außenkommandoführer*, who oversaw all the prisoners on work details: Max was to be put on special duty, required to prepare the studio, ready for the *Reichsführer*'s inspection.

The major works took priority. Of primary importance were the human figurines and busts, which included a drummer boy, a fencer and even Der Führer himself; each one was a model of glacial perfection. They would take the center of the room, exhibited on separate plinths. Then there were the urns and chalices with oak leaves, runic signs and symbols, all looking like they'd been conjured up from a Viking banquet. They would be staged on a series of square columns, set along the right side of the room. On the left, a long table would display the collection of animals made in collaboration with Frau Holz. Each creature would be presented in an Allach box bearing the dual lightning sigils of the SS and nesting in a bed of straw.

As a piece of theater, it needed careful planning, construction and choreography. As a method of distraction, it required Max's full attention.

The night before Himmler's visit, Holger came to look over the studio himself. The echoing space was pooled in darkness, save for the moonlight shining through the vast windows. Max looked exhausted, like a wraith, but the room was immaculate, the presentation of each item flawless. He showed Holger the tables, plinths and shelves, all ready for inspection. As they went around, he made further small adjustments to each piece, to show them at their best advantage.

Finally Max led Holger to the long table where his own work stood. The six boxes sat perfectly aligned. Holger lifted the lid of the first and saw Bettina's handiwork, the delicately painted rabbit, lying cushioned in a bed of real, sweet-smelling straw. In the low light it appeared so lifelike, Holger could almost imagine its pink nose twitch.

"I'm so sorry that she couldn't see this, Max. But you must know, you've done her proud."

Max shuffled his feet and shook his head.

"I only ever wanted to protect her. I should have done so much more."

Hours later, Max woke in the predawn darkness. He had barely slept, his fitful dreams a torment of paralysis. Each time he surfaced from sleep, the knowledge that Clara and Bettina had been taken from him would return and roll across him, crushing the breath from his lungs.

The last time he'd woken from a vision that all three of them were drowning, a scream had risen to his lips and almost escaped him as he felt his lungs begin to fill with water. After that, he decided it would be better to stay awake and wait for morning. Roll call would come soon enough, followed by the *Reichsführer*'s inspection. He could not envisage any future after that; it stretched ahead of him, a barren landscape, a vast bank of fog on the horizon.

A little distance from him in the barracks, a rabbi woke and uttered a short prayer of thanks for another day of life. He was grateful that his soul had returned to his body from the small death of sleep, though he did not dare invoke God's name, for he had yet to wash his hands. Max wondered how the rabbi maintained such gratitude. He'd seen the bald patches on his chin where the hairs had been pulled out individually, the guards intent on punishing him for his continued faith in the face of their barbarity.

Slowly the light turned from black to inky indigo and Max felt beneath his straw-filled mattress for the photograph of Clara hidden there. He would have only a few moments in which to gaze at the precious image of his daughter before the call went up to rise.

The photograph was a window on another world. The child sat on the gray-green grass, which rolled down to the water's edge. Behind her a lake, like the one where her mother and father last felt the sun on their shoulders. Both had been separately nursing the pain of loss, but had found each other when they'd returned, shivering, from the blackest depths. They had been happy again after that, but never so carefree.

Max listened to the sounds of men in their dozens rousing from sleep. The hard boards they slept on creaked in protest.

Several bunks held men who did not welcome a return from sleep. Daybreak was hardest for the sad-eyed skeletons, jaundiced and feverish, who knew their time was short. For the sick and dying there was no chance of treatment; the only medics at Dachau were those determined to learn what a human body could endure. The rising blade of the sun simply pared down their chances of survival. If they stumbled or fainted, then a guard might choose to beat the last of life from them. Those spared that fate would soon be sent away to Hartheim.

Second after them, in Max's eyes, were those who'd lost all hope. They lived, although life's purpose had abandoned them. Their only desire now, a swift end of their own choosing. In the early days of his incarceration Max had felt that level of despair loom over him, but he'd felt it lift a little when he was reunited with Holger and further still with the arrival of Bettina. The thought of her, of Clara, had sustained him ever since. Now he felt its cold encroaching shadow lumber into view again; he shivered at its touch.

Max tucked the photograph back in its hiding place. He did not need to see it to recall each crease and fold and every freckle on his daughter's sunny face. He offered up a silent prayer for both of them, wherever they may be. He did not invoke God's name, for he dared not hope that anyone was listening.

All the workers returned to the factory early. There was still much to prepare and the *Reichsführer-SS* was a stickler. Woe betide any man caught slacking when Himmler was in the building. Even the *Außenkommando* stood a little stiffer at their posts.

The day dawned brighter than any had for months on end. Spring was finally here and with it the fierce radiance of the sun, which brightened the world but exposed all flaws. Holger had requested that the studio be swept first thing, so the clouds of powder would have time to settle, and then be swept once more, but small drifts of white particles still formed like sand dunes against the edges of the room and filled the cracks between the floorboards. They flew up again as crisp white table linens were snapped like whips and then laid down. Bone-dry bisque and milk-gloss figurines received a final brush and polish before being set back on their plaster columns to bask in shafts of clean spring light. Finally, everything was set.

The artist modelers of Allach took their places and stood beside their work. Not all the pieces were guaranteed to pass muster, but those that did could soon be reproduced in multitudes and sold across the Reich. Each sculptor wore their long white smock coat, immaculately clean, given the occasion. Only Max bore the yellow Star of David on his arm.

At 10 a.m., an entourage of cars pulled in along the gravel road. Holger had left Fräulein Schaffer to greet them at the door and guide Himmler and his men through the building. He knew better than to compete: Himmler enjoyed leading a procession through the tiled streets of his porcelain domain. On this day he traveled with a group of other senior officials, five in total. Clad in almost identical uniforms, only the coded language of their pips and stripes and buttons, their medals and ribbons, dictated who could stand close to the *Reichsführer* and who should hover on the edges, who might pass comment and who was merely there to nod and listen in rapt attention. Though Himmler was the smallest man by far, he exerted a force far outweighing his stature. His slight shoulders might be rounded under the weight of his stiff leather coat, but the men still flocked around him like carrion crows, jostling for place.

Their footsteps echoed around the stairwell, ricocheting off the hard ceramic walls as they climbed toward the studio. At the sound of their approach Holger closed his eyes momentarily. Then they swept into the room, Himmler at the front, nodding serenely at all he surveyed. Everyone present thrust out their chests and stood a little taller, snapping their arms up in brisk salute. Holger stepped forward.

"So, my dear Ostendorff, what have you got in store for me today?"

"Some very fine work, Reichsführer. Very fine indeed."

He led him first to the trio of plaster plinths, each topped with a human figurine, the apex of Allach art. There was a decorated soldier riding on a rearing horse, a gentle shepherdess cradling a lamb, and a drummer boy, shirtsleeves rolled up and hair slicked back. The five men surrounding Himmler made tentative noises of approval, their eyes flitting from the figurines to his face and back. No one wanted to give offense by praising too much, or not sufficiently enough. Himmler took his time. He stooped to look at each in detail, running a cautious finger over the finish before he made his judgment. Finally, all three were deemed ideal and a murmur of delight bubbled up from his companions. Now they knew which way the wind was blowing they could afford to be effusive in their admiration.

Holger deemed it a good moment to show the bust of Hitler. It was an excellent rendition, but still had the potential to provoke: his clay lips were pursed, his jaw clenched and jutting, the very picture of pugnacity. Himmler crouched down, coming face-to-face with his dear leader. His small eyes narrowed for a moment.

"It is good," he declared.

Holger sucked in a great lungful of relief.

"But you must ensure it stays exactly so—it mustn't be ruined by a glaze, that is most important." He glanced at the secretary and snapped, "Well, write it down then, Fräulein!"

Holger led the way to a side table laid with various seasonal plates: a palate cleanser, pure in their simplicity. Himmler examined each in turn, passing them on to the officer, who exclaimed over the different mottos. Eventually Himmler addressed Holger, handing him a plate with a sun wheel at the center and a motto running around it: "*Meine Ehre heißt Treue*," Loyalty Is My Honor.

"Let's use the wheel, it is more appropriate for winter and I like its elegance. But still, there is something about the torch . . . I have a large recess on either side of the doors to my office. I'll take that motif on a pair of urns."

Holger nodded. "Of course, Reichsführer; it will be our pleasure."

Finally, he directed the men's attention to the row of six boxes.

"These pieces were part of an alliance between Allach and the artist, Frau Holz. A collection of hand-painted animals, inspired by her paintings."

He stole a brief sideways glance at Max, who stood with his eyes cast down.

Himmler looked around. "Is she here?"

Holger addressed the man directly, lowering his voice, "I'm sorry to say that I have been informed that the lady is not well. She's had to go away for treatment."

Himmler raised an eyebrow, disinterested.

"Poor old Holz, doesn't have much luck with wives."

Holger took a step back, inviting the six gentlemen to open one box each. His eyes flicked again to Max, who stood by, still as a statue.

The uniformed men were excited to be called on to participate; they took hold of the lids and lifted, eager to see what lay within. There was a gasp from first one, and then another. Then began the exclamations, not qualified this time, but given freely. Each bent to examine the piece in front of them more closely. Max had excelled himself and the exquisite detail of Bettina's brushwork elevated them higher still. Though he was familiar with them already, Holger saw each one anew. These were not docile pets; they had somehow captured something wild about their nature. After the blank white parade of plates and busts and bowls, these creatures were alive with color that glowed beneath the glaze.

Himmler lifted the rabbit from its bed and turned it over, tracing Bettina's signature, which sat beside the SS sigil. Then he walked along the table, lifting each piece up and holding it to the light: the songbird on the branch, beak wide, as if at any moment it might begin to sing. Every filament of feather was delicate and distinct. The mouse, braced to dash away on nimble feet, its rose-pink ears so petal-thin the light shone through.

Himmler was nodding to himself, clearly pleased by what he saw. He turned to Holger and clapped him on the back.

"A triumph, Herr Ostendorff. We must ensure the Führer sees them for himself."

He beamed around at the men, who seemed delighted their dear leader might learn of their part in such a coup; in the midst of war it made sense to attach oneself to good news, wherever possible. A ripple of applause broke out, which Himmler seemed to accept for himself, bowing modestly.

At that moment, Holger became aware of a disturbance just outside the door. The guards who had escorted them to the studio were gathered in a huddle with the *Außenkommandoführer*, conferring in low whispers. The exchange became heated, causing heads to turn. At the loss of their attention, Himmler rounded on the offender.

"What is the reason for this interruption?"

"Apologies, Reichsführer."

The *Außenkommandoführer* crossed the room toward him. Holger saw he was holding something, a small porcelain rabbit, laid out on a slab of marble. Even from a distance, Holger recognized the style.

The porcelain rabbit was anatomically perfect and alabaster white, which made the long slash of red at the rabbit's core even more arresting. It appeared as if it had been slit from throat to crotch, leaving a wound so dark it was almost black. Bloody viscera and a churned knot of blue-gray entrails spilled out onto the slab and glistened wetly.

Himmler frowned. "What is the meaning of this?"

The *Außenkommandoführer* turned and gestured to the guards, beckoning them to join.

"The guards discovered a cache of these . . ."

The two men stepped forward, each holding a porcelain creation, their bright colors and contorted forms at first utterly confounding. Here was a songbird sitting on a bloodied branch, the bark bound in newsprint. It was similar to the bird perched on the table, save for the shocking raw pink skin exposed beneath the wing where it had ripped at its own flesh, trying in desperation to escape the crystalline glue that held it fast.

The second guard was holding a pine box, reminiscent of a simple wooden coffin. Lying in it was a porcelain raven, petrol-blue and black and resting on a bed of rocks. A jagged crimson-colored wound crowned its skull, where a stone had staved it in.

Holger did not know how to reconcile this vision with the

other figurines: he stared at the rabbit on the marble slab, the glassy, blood-rimmed eyes and the tracks of rusty tears traced into the fur. The four paws of the creature were pinned down like a crucifixion.

The grizzled guard muttered to his commander.

"There are more of them downstairs, Reichsführer . . ."

Although Himmler was turned away from him, Holger could feel the smaller man draw himself up, his spine now ramrod straight, his very essence bridling. His companions were all staring at the porcelain pieces, repulsed and uncomprehending, but Himmler seemed to fully understand the threat they implied. His face was ashen with fury and his gaze was fixed on Holger.

"Can you explain this, Ostendorff?"

"I can't, Reichsführer. I've never seen any of these before; they're not in any way the kind of work which we'd commission."

"And yet, they are here, in a factory under your artistic direction . . ."

His voice glistened with menace. He turned to the guard. "Where did you find them?"

"In the basement, Herr Director."

"And so, the culprit will be revealed. Who works there, Holger? Give me names."

Out of the corner of his eye, Holger caught the movement of one man stepping forward. Cold panic flooded through him; he tried to shake his head imperceptibly, but Max took another, more determined, stride.

Himmler turned to him, a flicker of recognition.

"I know you."

His tone was ominous; it did not do to be known.

"My name is Max Ehrlich."

Holger's legs almost buckled underneath him; a feeling of weightlessness, of separation from his form.

"This is my work—no one else's." Max seemed to waver for a moment, then gained more strength. "I made them and hid them in the rafters—ask the guards, they'll confirm that's where they found them. I stole Frau Holz's work and then repurposed it, to show the world what happens to us in this charnel house. I am the porcelain maker of Dachau and this is my collection."

He drew a breath, but before he could speak again the bespectacled man had crossed the ground between them and raised up his firearm, knocking him to the floor in an instant. Himmler stood over Max, breathing hard, fingers wrapped in a fist around the barrel of the pistol, his knuckles white, his slicked-back hair swinging across his face in a great, greased curtain.

Max got back to his knees and lifted up his face. He opened his mouth to speak again, a smear of scarlet on his teeth, but he was silenced by the harsh retort of the pistol. The first bullet pierced his chest and left a small red bloom on the white of his coat, like a splash of paint or a buttonhole rose. It slowly blossomed there before a second joined it, both their edges ragged black. A third bullet lashed into the core of him and left him doubled over. A fourth tore through his cheekbone, just below the black pool of his eye, fathoms deep and shining. That one spun him sideways and took him down. He didn't put out a hand to save himself, for there was nothing left to save. He lay there, his eyes open but unseeing. And still a fifth bullet and then a sixth pummeled into him, though no spark of life remained.

Consumed by a savagery which even six shots couldn't satiate, the bespectacled man rounded on the guard holding the porcelain rabbit. He snatched it from him and dashed it to the floor. He brought the handle of his pistol down, over and over, a jackhammer of rage smashing it to splinters. The hard clay exploded upward, glassy shrapnel piercing the air. With wordless grunts of effort, he raised his arm up time and time again, the anger never dissipating; an endlessly renewing source of fury that refused to stop until there was simply nothing left.

In the screaming stillness that followed, the air filled with powder—motes of dust, falling through a beam of light. They settled slowly on Max's broken body, like pollen falling on a summer's day.

CHAPTER TWENTY-ONE

Munich

November 1993

By the time Holger had finished his story, the rain had stopped and the apartment had grown dim. The setting sun reflected a rose glow on the roofs and stuccoed buildings of the old town. Lotte sat with her arm around her mother and they stared into the dying embers of the fire. Minutes passed. From somewhere in the apartment, a clock chimed.

Clara, her head clouded with images so vivid they seemed more like memories, was the first to break the silence.

"I always believed I didn't feel the absence of a father growing up—how can you miss something you never had? But now I know how much I lost; I would give anything to have known him."

Holger's voice was thick with emotion. "In that moment I believe he thought he would not get that opportunity. He did it for your mother and for Ezra, and for me. He took the blame and the bullets to save us all. Had he had faith, it might have given him the strength to fight and carry on. You would have been his sun and moon and stars—both of you."

"May I ask what happened to you, Herr Ostendorff . . . afterward?"

Because he was sitting in silhouette, Lotte could not make out his expression.

"I was guilty by association; arrested and sent to Dachau myself, though only for a few months. Himmler pardoned me himself, on the proviso that I came back to run the factory. My punishment was only necessary as long as it served his purpose."

"I don't know how you survived it. Any of you." Lotte's voice was barely above a whisper.

"To my eternal shame, I was angry with Max for a time: furious that he sacrificed himself so willingly. But then my time in the *Lager*—the camp at Dachau—gave me some greater understanding of what he had endured. I never had to suffer his losses. If I had, I feel certain I would have done the same."

Holger stretched over and switched on the table lamp. The white glass dome glowed with warm light and illuminated his face, carved in sorrow and regret. He stood up and gathered his strength, crossing over to a large armoire that dominated the space between the windows. He opened a pair of inlaid oak doors. They could make out the dull gleam of the contents: a single shelf, covered in broken shards of porcelain.

"Ezra swept up the remnants of Max and Bettina's collections—both the official and the subversive. He kept them safe and gave them to me before leaving for America. In return, I gave him one of the last surviving Viking figurines. It seems entirely fitting that he led you back to me."

"So Oma's porcelain collection and the architectural drawings—they were Max's work?"

Holger nodded. "In the end, art and love are all we leave behind."

Clara felt her tears begin to flow, overwhelmed by loss, by love and anger at all that had been stolen from her. She covered her face and Lotte bent to her, concerned.

"Are you all right, Mama?"

Clara shook her head vehemently. "I don't understand. Why did she keep all this from me—why hide my father's existence when it's clear that he meant everything to her?"

Holger came and sat down beside her.

"I had the same question. I went looking for you both, after the war. I tracked down the sanatorium where they'd sent her and wrote, but she never replied. Then a few months later a telegram arrived, inviting me to visit you both at the lake house. You lived there for a time, before you moved to London."

A phantom memory floated to the surface—of sunlight dappling a tree bent over, the branches weeping on bright water.

Holger continued: "I remember sitting on a lawn that sloped down to the water's edge. Your mother and I watched you swimming in the lake. You looked so like him, even then."

He reached out and clasped her hand in his.

"Your mother thought she could spare you the torment of losing your father by bearing it all herself. Max had sacrificed himself for all of us and she believed, rightly or wrongly, that she should do the same for you. At the time I questioned her decision, but I think I understand it now—

she couldn't bear to move beyond her grief. She didn't want to let him go."

His pale blue eyes sought out her own, beseeching.

"You must understand, Clara—you were the only thing that kept her anchored to the world. She chose to live for you, but she died with him that day."

CHAPTER TWENTY-TWO

Lake Starnberg

Summer 1946

Holger watched Bettina as she stirred a spoon of ice into a glass of lemonade, which rattled against the glass. She handed it to him and sat back down. He felt her eyes on him as he watched Clara playing in the water, diving like an otter, a ring of water rippling out around her.

"You see the resemblance?"

He nodded.

"It's not the comfort you might think."

The sun cut sharp shadows under the umbrella, the atmosphere heavy in the heat of the afternoon. Barely a breeze stirred the surface of the water; only Clara's splashing and the lapping waves intruded on the stillness. Bettina fanned herself; she wore a yellow cotton sundress over a white swimsuit, her eyes shielded by sunglasses, a style she'd taken up in Italy. Holger remained squinting, watching the light dance on the water, reflecting on the branches of the trees.

"It's very peaceful here," he said.

"Do you think so? We can take a dip in a while, if you like. Cool off. I must say, I've always found it rather stiff and formal, but if you're in the market, I'm selling it. We need a fresh start, far away. For both our sakes."

"Where will you go?"

"Wherever we can—it doesn't much matter as far as I'm concerned. None of these places offered us safe haven when we needed it. The irony is that, thanks to Karl, I now have all the money I need to make it happen."

"He left you everything?"

"He did. After they discharged me from the hospital, I came back here—I had nowhere else to go. He refused to give me a divorce, but he did send Clara back at least. I only heard about the will after he took his own life. The tide of the war had turned by then and he saw what was coming. He changed his will for Clara's sake. I certainly wasn't expecting it. Nor was Liesl, come to that."

Holger snorted. "I met her, you know. I went to see her in Munich, when you disappeared. It was she who told me you'd been sent away."

"I imagine she rather relished that. Much as I relished telling her that Karl had left her nothing."

"And what of your own family; what happened to them?"

She glanced at him over her glasses.

"Mother died in '44 but sad to say *liebe* Albrecht is still with us. He was arrested and is awaiting trial, which I can't imagine will go well for him, given all the people that he harmed over the years. Can you guess where they sent him?"

He shook his head. The corners of her mouth turned up, though it would not be described as a smile.

"Dachau. They've turned it into a confinement camp for war criminals and the SS. Finding out he'd been arrested and imprisoned there gave me the greatest measure of satisfaction I've felt in years."

"I can imagine," he replied dryly.

He sensed she was observing him, though her glasses were too dark to tell. He tried to keep his tone as light as hers.

"So, how did they convince the doctors you were mad?"

Though the question had been weighing on him heavily, he kept his eyes averted, not wanting to witness its effect on her.

"They didn't have to; it became a simple fact. After Max was murdered, I was interrogated by my brother's *Kameraden*. They wanted to find out if I had known about his plan. I was forced to disavow him. If I hadn't, they would have killed me, leaving Clara to be raised by Karl."

She took a sip of her lemonade, her hand trembling.

"If I could have willed us both out of existence, we wouldn't be here now."

He looked across the water, feeling cold despite the heat. *This is a wake*, he thought. *For Max and everything we've lost.*

"It took me months to even begin to regain my senses after that. I can't remember much of it now, if I'm honest. Probably no bad thing. Karl paid for the best treatment—electroconvulsive therapy. It's all the rage in Italy. It brought me back, after a fashion."

"I'm very glad it did."

"Yes. I suppose I am."

She held out her hand and looked at it. "I can still feel the current running through me. I haven't been able to paint a stroke since then. I don't suppose I ever will again."

She scowled at the anguish she saw on Holger's face.

"Don't fret; it's part of my penance. The least that I deserve."

"You have nothing to atone for. We all feel our share of guilt."

"Ah, but do we all have the blood of the two men we loved most on our hands? Perhaps not."

"That simply isn't true."

"Isn't it? Max gave his life in order to protect me and was gunned down like an animal. Richard, my dearest friend, was murdered by my jealous husband. All because of me."

She seemed remote and far removed from what she was describing.

"There was always bad blood in my family. I tried to outrun it, but how can you when you carry the poison inside? We are a product of that which flows through us."

"If that's the case, then Max is still here, in Clara."

"Which is the only thing that keeps me on this earth. She's all that's left of him and as long as she needs me, she will have me, much good may it do her. I must say, I rather pity anyone who has the misfortune to be loved by me."

Bettina took a long breath in and exhaled it slowly as Clara's laughter floated over the water, like a seed borne on the breeze.

"What will you tell her, when she's older?" he asked.

"I don't yet know. I want to protect her from the awful truth and let her have her chance at happiness. The damage it could do if she understood what had been stolen from her, the evil that people are capable of . . . How any of us continue in that knowledge is beyond my comprehension."

"But man is also capable of great good, of sacrifice."

She frowned determinedly. "And Max was the finest example of that, but Clara never even got to meet him. It is too cruel. Unspeakable and inhumane."

"You can't protect her from it entirely—she will need to hear the truth one day."

"Who decided that truth was somehow this moral absolute? It isn't neutral—it is callous and sadistic and I won't inflict it on her. She's untarnished, the one good thing in all the world; the last of him, with only me left for protection."

Holger blanched. "That's quite a burden to carry."

"And it should be mine to bear alone. To have something so precious taken from her . . . Perhaps it's kinder if she never knows."

Shimmering heat hung heavy in the air, the drone of insects intruding on the quiet. Bettina inhaled again deeply and put both hands on her knees.

"Enough. You can't listen to me maunder on like this all day."

She stood and waved to the girl splashing in the water. "Clara darling, I'm coming in."

She turned to Holger and smiled, full-faced this time.

"Wait for me? I don't think I trust myself to come back unless I know you're here. I just feel the need to immerse myself, to wash it all away."

As she spoke, she pulled the cotton sundress over her head and threw it on the grass. She looked across the moving water of the lake. The light reflected off the water, blinding her, shining in waves on her face. She walked down to the water's edge and started to wade out. The lake was cold as death; she put her head down and dove in.

EPILOGUE

Munich

Summer 1994

Pinakothek der Moderne München
(Museum of Modern Art, Munich)

You are invited to a Private View of "The Porcelain Maker of Dachau: An Exhibition of Degenerate Art."

Among the works on loan is *The Viking*, a painting by Bettina Vogel, once admired by the Nazi Party and considered emblematic of German romantic realism, seen here as disguising an expressionist portrait belonging to the artist's little-known avant-garde phase.

The upper surface depicts the Viking as an Aryan ideal. Beneath it lies her earlier portrait of Max Ehrlich, a visceral chromatic rendition of a Jewish man. Artist and subject had a lifelong relationship, cut short by his murder at the hands of Heinrich Himmler in 1942, while a prisoner working at Porzellanmanufaktur Allach, a subcamp of the Dachau concentration camp.

The dual portraits are revealed in all their dramatic complexity as their daughter, Clara Vogel-Ehrlich, has authorized the museum's restoration department to dissolve part of the outer layer of *The Viking*, in order to bring the original portrait back to life.

The painting is shown alongside a retrospective of the artist's other work and selected pieces by Max Ehrlich and Lotte Woolf:

Gudrun's Rabbit and Other Works—Porcelain figurines sculpted by Max Ehrlich between the years of 1938 and 1942, on loan from the private collections of Clara Vogel-Ehrlich and Holger Ostendorff.

Schematics of Forest Haven—Max Ehrlich 1936–1938 Working architectural drawings in pencil, black ink and colored washes on paper.

Golem—Mixed Media by Lotte Woolf, 1994 An imagined reconstruction of the subversive works of the artist collective "The Porcelain Maker of Dachau": Max Ehrlich and Bettina Vogel.

Acknowledgments

Easton, May 2023

Though set in a time and place which writers and readers return to again and again, *The Porcelain Maker* is a work of fiction. It feels like familiar territory, and yet there is much we do not know about the specific details of this time. I have tried my best to be accurate, but I am no scholar and I'm certain the detail will be found wanting. Some historical figures, institutions and places are based in reality, while others are works of pure imagination. Gudrun and Heinrich Himmler were real enough, but I make no claims to understand their inner workings. Gudrun did visit the concentration camps with her father and traveled to Dachau in the spring of 1941, but I chose to send her to the rabbit hutches. The rabbits themselves, and their heated barracks, were well-documented—Himmler bred 65,000 of them at the different camps across the Reich and kept angora-wool-bound photograph albums of his favorites. Allach Porcelain and the Dachau subcamp Porzellanmanufaktur Allach certainly existed, and the latter used slave labor from the camps. However,

Bettina, Max, Richard, Holger et al. never breathed outside of these pages.

In the course of my research, many people and resources proved invaluable.

My particular thanks go to Dmitri Abrahams and Richard Freedman of the Cape Town Holocaust & Genocide Centre, who were so helpful.

To the Wiener Holocaust Library, David Irwin and Ben Barkow, who were incredibly generous, sharing their recollections of the library in times past.

To Albert Knoll and the Comité International de Dachau, who work tirelessly to ensure that the crimes committed at Dachau Concentration Camp and the subcamps are not forgotten.

The United States Holocaust Memorial Museum, an invaluable resource which brought so much to life for me, from artifacts to survivor testimonies. And most crucially, to the survivors of the Holocaust who shared their stories with the world, so that we would never forget what they endured.

I would like to acknowledge the artists of Ukraine for their powerful example of the vital role art plays in communicating the effects of war. I hope this novel serves as a reminder of the humanity of all refugees. Had the nations of the world welcomed them in more readily in the late 1930s, who knows how many millions might have survived?

Writing *The Porcelain Maker* would not have been possible without an incredibly brilliant team of kind and clever people guiding me, whose sage advice has made this book far more readable than it might otherwise have been.

First and foremost, this story would simply not exist without the inestimable Walter Iuzzolino, my mentor and friend. If I'm the mother of this story, he is the father, and his DNA is in every page. Walter gave me the confidence to try to write in the first place and his constant support and advice has kept me going through the good and the bad. A force of nature and an extraordinary human—I can't thank him enough for all he has done. So glad I had the good sense to glom onto you all those years ago, dear heart.

Jo McGrath has been a friend of many decades, a champion and an incredibly generous and thoughtful reader—an absolute inspiration and hugely gracious counselor. None of this would be possible without Jo. I can't express the thanks I owe for all the time you've given me and the faith you've had in me.

Clare Hey and Louise Davies at Simon & Schuster, thank you both so much for helping me take the rough clay of the first draft and shape it; your wisdom and experience made it all so much better. You have been incredibly patient and understanding and I am truly thankful for this opportunity.

Charles Spicer at St. Martin's Press—your enthusiasm and energy have been so gratefully received. Kind words and great insights made such a difference in honing this, and I can't thank you enough for all your efforts to bring it to a wider audience.

Cari Rosen, not only a fantastic copy editor but an old friend; synchronicity meant our paths crossed again at this time, to my great good fortune. You went above and beyond to help me in my efforts to tell this story. It has been a privilege to write, vastly improved by your thoughtful and generous contributions at such a vital stage.

I'm also very grateful to all the creative teams supporting the novel, from the beautiful cover designs to press and marketing, and production and sales—huge thanks for your wonderful work.

To all my friends and family, thank you for being so supportive and encouraging me in this madcap scheme.

Philip Nockles, my love. You let me have the time and space to do this and it would never have been possible without your support, in every way imaginable. You have been endlessly patient, taken on so much and sacrificed a lot to make room for me, for which I am truly thankful. Thank you, Thing, my quiet champion throughout. Thank you for your forbearance, your support and all the funny; I wouldn't have started and couldn't have finished without you.

To my daughter, Esme, my darling mouse. Thank you for all the inspiration you have given me. I hope that one day you will read this and all the little pockets of time I squirrelled away to write will be forgiven. You are my sun, my moon and stars.

To my mama, to whom I owe everything, including a love of reading and writing and art and so much more—you are an inspiration and my greatest cheerleader and I love you so very much. And to my wonderful sister, who completes the coven—I couldn't ask for a better Sissy; you've always, always had my back and I adore you. I do love us.

To my brilliant brother—so grateful that you came into my life. Love you ever so. And to Liz for being the best possible Milly, so kind and eternally supportive. I got so lucky with you and Merv.

So many friends deserve thanks for reading and cheering me on: my bestie forever, Shaheen, and my goddaughter Rania; the Village ladies: Heather, Charlie, Dionne, Natalie, Fi, Leila and Sophie.

Special thanks to Rebecca for spending hours listening to me bang on about Bettina, Max and Richard, helping me to bring them to life, and to Catherine, who so generously gave me her experience, advice and considerable German language skills.

To Edmund de Waal, whose writing was such a source of inspiration. And Dan Snow, whose writing and broadcasting provided a window into so many seldom-told stories from this time. Thanks to Elizabeth Haynes, Rebecca Horsfall and Claire Fuller for their wisdom and generosity to an ingenue.